HOT FOR TEACHER

THE SINGLE MOMS OF SEATTLE, BOOK 1

WHITLEY COX

ISBN: 978-1-989081-36-5

For my sister in-law, Elyse.
I'm so glad my husband has an awesome sister.
Love you.
xoxo

1

_____

"BUT I LIKE THESE BETTER, MOM," Sabrina whinged, holding up a pair of ugly-ass heavily ripped light gray jeans.

Blech.

Celeste fought the urge to roll her eyes at her hopeful, clearly fashion-inept teenage daughter. "I can find you a pair of jeans _without_ the rips for half the price and then put the tears in myself. Why is it the _in_ thing right now to wear clothes that look like you've been mauled by a small bear? What next, blood stains?

Sabrina growled like a small bear and put the jeans back on the rack. "I'm going to be the only kid at school _without_ these then."

Celeste gave up the fight and rolled her eyes this time. "Listen, kid, I'm all for following the trends and looking good, but those jeans are butt-fucking-ugly." She'd never been one to mince words or filter herself around her kid. "And as your mom, I have an obligation to tell you when something is as hideous as those things are. I mean, look ..." She grabbed the jeans back off the rack and shoved her hand into one of the pockets. Her fingers poked out of a giant hole right beneath it and she wiggled them. "Who the hell puts pockets in pants and then deliberately puts a hole *in* the pockets? I mean come on. Women all over the world are fighting for pockets in dresses, pockets in pants, and they go and set us back fifty-odd years with this nonsense? Please."

It was Sabrina's turn to roll her eyes.

The older Sabrina got, the more she was looking like Celeste: dark red, wavy hair down past their shoulders, green eyes, fair complexions, freckles across their noses. If it wasn't for how much Sabrina acted like her father, Celeste would have wondered if there was any of Declan in there. And the fact that her kid was only about three inches shorter meant she would either be the same height as Celeste when she reached adulthood or taller.

They could already share a lot of the same clothes, but if Sabrina's taste continued on the path it was headed with ugly jeans and the like, Celeste wouldn't be shopping in her daughter's closet anytime soon.

Celeste shrugged. "You've got all that money from working at the bistro for Paige, as well as babysitting. Buy them yourself, but I will not fork over my hard-earned cash for a fashion—and function—abomination like that. I cannot, and I will not. Your father would haunt me in my sleep until I took those pants and either returned them or burned them."

"You're such a drama queen, Mom," Sabrina said with a huff, heading off in the direction of the T-shirt dresses.

"You say drama queen; I say practical," she called after her doppelganger, snorting a laugh at the way Sabrina ducked her head when eyes around the clothing store flitted back and forth between the two of them.

"They are an absolute fashion atrocity," came a deep, sexy rumble from behind a tall shelf of neatly stacked men's jeans.

"I agree. But who am I agreeing with?"

The sexy rumble continued, morphing into a chuckle that grew louder and deeper, like he had a cavern in his chest. The man drew nearer, finally turning the corner to reveal himself. "I didn't mean to eavesdrop, but the mother-daughter banter was rather entertaining."

Celeste squinted. She knew this man. Tall, handsome, with dark, thick brows and a slightly too big nose. But he pulled it off. He owned it. His beard was close-shaved, and the rest of his dark brown hair was trimmed shorter on the sides, leaving the top a little longer. He hadn't had a haircut like that last time she saw him though, when it'd been longer, more unkempt.

He mirrored her narrowed brows and curious expression, each of them having gone quiet, wracking their brains to place the face.

She was the first to make the connection. "Mr. Travis!"

His expressive silver-gray eyes went wide. "Celeste Marchand?"

Smiling, she nodded. "It's Celeste Howard, but yes. How are you? I hardly recognized you."

Max Travis. Celeste's high school math teacher. He'd been a baby-faced twentysomething when he started teaching. Barely out of college and thrown into the snake pit that was high school math. He'd been scrawnier then, too. Nerdier, but even with the dorky haircut, the glasses, wrinkled pants and crappy plaid shirts, within a month he'd still be labeled as the hottest teacher at school. Oodles of Celeste's friends had thrown themselves at him.

As far as she knew, not a one had caught him. He rebuffed their advances as gently as he could. Then the gay rumors started.

Poor guy.

He still hadn't answered her. Hadn't said a word.

Clearly the last fifteen years had served him well. Exceptionally well. He put on bulk in all the right places, figured out what to do with his hair and ironed his pants. Yes, Mr. Travis had aged well. Like a fine wine or a juicy hunk of meat.

Back when all her high school friends were fawning over geeky Mr. Travis, she'd been madly in love with Declan and secretly pregnant with his baby. She had eyes only for the love of her life. Sure, she knew Mr. Travis was a decent-looking man. She *had* eyes. But those eyes were only for Declan. Now, however, those eyes were wide open, and they were staring into the equally wide eyes of a man not too much older than her but whom she'd been forced to call Mister.

Finally, after what seemed like a painfully long silence, he chuckled. "Sorry, I just ... Wow, Celeste. I'm ... I'm doing well. How are you?" Red stained his cheeks as his eyes unapologetically climbed her body from toe to top and back.

She felt her own cheeks grow hot. "I'm all right. Thank you. Out school-clothes and -supply shopping with my daughter, Sabrina. She's around here somewhere, probably pretending she doesn't know me."

His laughter was forced, but his smile was as natural and handsome as ever, showing off the deep dimples on either side of his very delicious-looking lips.

"Mom!"

Celeste swore she jumped high enough to hit her head on the vaulted ceiling of the clothing store.

She spun around to find Sabrina standing right behind her, a glare as intense as the sun cruising down her nose.

"Honey, jeez, you scared me nearly out of my skin."

Sabrina lifted one brow. "I'm ready to go if you are?"

Swallowing, she nodded. "Be right there." She dug her wallet out of her purse, handed her kid her credit card and gave her a warning glare of her own. "Don't make me wish I wasn't doing this. Only what's in your arms. I don't want to find those jeans on my receipt."

Sabrina's gaze flicked over Celeste's shoulder toward Mr. Travis, then back to Celeste. Her lips twisted, and a sparkle emerged in her eyes. A small, wary but also amused smile curled one half of her mouth. "All right. Don't be long."

Celeste waited until Sabrina walked a decent enough of a distance before she turned back around to face Mr. Travis.

"Sorry about that, Mr. Travis." Well, now it just felt dirty calling him that at her age.

A glint of something roguish and not quite pure—but certainly exhilarating—flickered in his eyes when she addressed him formally. "You can call me Max. I'm no longer your teacher. And I'm pretty sure I'm only like six or seven years older than you. Makes me feel a hell of a lot older when you call me *Mr. Travis*."

Her cheeks were now on absolute fire. "Right. Max."

His eyes lifted from her face to where Sabrina was standing at the checkout. "*She's* your daughter?" He didn't even bother to hide the surprise in his voice or his face.

Celeste nodded without glancing backward. "She is. She's fifteen."

His mouth opened. Closed. Opened again. "Fif ... teen?"

"I was pregnant when I graduated, yes."

Understanding dawned in his eyes, followed by sincere curiosity. "You were with Declan Howard, right? How's he?"

Celeste cleared her throat and averted her gaze for a moment in search of strength before she glanced back at him. "He passed away almost eight years ago, I'm afraid. Construction accident."

His face fell, eyes turned sad. "I'm so sorry."

Well, this little reunion with the hottie teacher had taken a depressing turn. Maybe she shouldn't have brought up her dead husband. That was always a mood-killer no matter who she was speaking with. But then she also wanted Mr. Travis—Max—to know that she wasn't married.

Why did she want him to know that?

"Mom!" Sabrina called from the checkout.

Right, her kid.

Flustered like she couldn't remember being in quite some time, she gave Max (it still felt weird thinking of him as Max and not Mr. Travis) an odd little one-directional wave. "It was nice to see you. Still teaching at—"

"Mom!"

Oh, for Christ's sake.

She turned to face Sabrina, who was staring at her with mounting impatience. The line behind her daughter was pretty severe, and Sabrina's cheeks were the color of a candy apple.

"Nice to see you," she repeated, taking off toward the checkout. "Take care."

His amused expression wasn't lost on her, however. Neither was his keen look of interest or the disappointment in his eyes as she created more distance between them.

His wave was bigger and grander than hers, as was his smile. "Nice to see you too, Celeste, and no, I'm not teaching at Rainier Beach anymore, I'm—"

"Mom, seriously. This is so embarrassing."

Finally, reluctantly, she turned around and gave her daughter and the heavily pierced and tattooed girl behind the checkout her full attention. "Sorry. What's going on?"

Sabrina let out an impatient huff. "It says your card is declined."

"I tried it like five times, ma'am," the shop girl said. "I think I'm supposed to cut it up now."

Panic filled her gut, and Celeste reached for the card from her daughter, shoving it into the abyss of her purse. She yanked out her wallet and handed the girl her debit card.

"Not sure what's going on, but I've got the money. I'll call the credit card company when we get home."

Sabrina gritted her teeth and glanced awkwardly behind her. "This is so embarrassing."

Celeste rolled her eyes at her daughter. "Get over it, honey. This shit happens. I have the money. I'm not destitute. *We're* not destitute. There's just something going on with my card."

Sabrina appeared to shrink where she stood. "Yeah, but did it *have* to happen when Eleanor Shelby was in line behind me?" She dipped her head low until her hair hung over her face.

Who the fuck was Eleanor Shelby, and why did we care about her?

She finished paying for the clothes, waited for the cashier to bag them, then handed the bag to her daughter. "Ignore *Eleanor.* I'm sure even queens get their cards declined once in a while. It happens." Her hand fell to Sabrina's back, and she ushered her daughter out of the store. The line behind them had grown even longer, and the glares being thrown at them were hot enough to boil potatoes.

Once outside of the strip mall, in the shade of a big gingko tree, she led her daughter over to a bench, where they sat down. She turned to Sabrina, who was still attempting to retreat within herself.

"Honey, what happened in there?"

"Ugh," Sabrina scoffed, turning away from Celeste. "You were too busy *flirting* and embarrassed me in front of one of the most popular girls at school. First, because I had to call you like *ten* times. Who was that guy, anyway? He seemed like really old. And second, because it looks like we're poor, because your card was declined. I haven't even started school, and already they're going to be talking about me. I just know it." She crossed her arms in front of her chest and hunched over, her hair hanging down in her face again. "And did you happen to see how many girls my age had those exact jeans in their hands? I'm going to be the laughingstock of the school without them ... if I'm not already."

Celeste gnashed her molars together, exhaled through her nose and dug down deep for some patience. She had to get into the mindset of a fifteen-year-old girl. Sure, to her as a thirty-three-year-old woman, this made absolutely no sense. What Eleanor Shelby thought didn't matter a fucking bit. If jeans were ugly—which those ones definitely were—you just didn't buy them. But the adolescent world was a whole different kettle of fish. High school, cliques and being accepted by your peers were the only things that mattered at the tender age of fifteen. Oh, and boys. We can't forget boys.

Did boys ever stop mattering?

Maybe when they turned into sexy men. Then they mattered, but they mattered in a different kind of way.

Mr. Travis had certainly grown up in the last fifteen years. He was definitely not a *boy* anymore. This teacher was all man.

She was getting off topic.

She needed to think like a teenager. Think with her hormones. Think with her feelings. Think with her head up her ass.

With a hand on Sabrina's shoulder, she bent her head, tucked a strand of dark red hair behind her daughter's ear and dropped her voice. "What can I do to help? I'm at a loss right now. The grown-up in me just thinks you should shake it all off, and to hell with *Eleanor Shelby*, but I know that as a kid, it's not as simple as that. School is hard. Cliques are hard. I want to help you get through the next four years as easily as I can. What can I do?"

Please don't say buy you the jeans. Please don't say buy you the jeans.

Sabrina lifted her head just slightly. "You could buy me the jeans."

Oh, for fuck's sake.

Deep breaths. Deep, deep breaths.

"How much were they?"

"Two hundred dollars," Sabrina managed to say sheepishly. "I only have a hundred left of my money after you made me pitch in for my new phone. The rest goes straight into that savings account for my car."

Well, no shit. Of course she was going to make her kid pitch in for her new phone. That thing was nearly a mortgage payment.

Realizing that she needed to help her daughter and not put her in more social peril, she nodded. "Let's go halvsies on them then." She grabbed her wallet again and reached for the two fifty-dollar bills she kept in a separate compartment. It was her emergency money, and apparently those jeans were an emergency. She handed the money to her kid. "You cover the rest and the tax. Can you do that?"

Sabrina nodded and took the money, standing up from the bench and wiping the back of her hand beneath her eyes. "Thanks, Mom."

Celeste smiled grimly. "Why don't I stay out here and you go in and buy them on your own? God forbid I embarrass you any further in front of *the* Eleanor Shelby. I might see if she'll sign my bra when she comes out. I had no idea she was *the* Eleanor Shelby of Lakewood High."

Sabrina's lips twitched into a half smile, and she rolled her eyes.

Swatting her cheeky spawn on the thigh, Celeste wrinkled her nose and smiled. "Go. We still have shoes and supplies to buy." She flicked her wrist toward the storefront.

Smiling that thousand-watt smile, Sabrina nodded and headed for the door. Celeste had already grabbed her phone from her purse and was checking the time when a heavy force collided into her where she sat. "Thanks, Mom. I'm sorry I'm such a pain in the butt sometimes. Thank you for loving me anyway. You really are like the best and coolest mom ever." Sabrina squeezed her tight, her body hunching over Celeste's in an awkward way as she hugged her, but that didn't make the embrace any less significant or wonderful.

Celeste squeezed her daughter back. "I'll love you no matter how big of a jerk you are, kiddo. Just don't let it last past eighteen, okay?"

Sabrina chuckled. "I'll try."

"That's all I can hope for. Now go buy those *beautiful* jeans. I can't *wait* to borrow them."

Sabrina pulled away with another laugh and an even bigger smile than before. She headed toward the store, and Celeste glanced back down at her phone, the smile on her face making her cheeks ache.

Ah, September. Was there a better time of year in the Pacific Northwest? The afternoons are warm, the nights are cool, the scent of fall hangs crisp on the ruffling breeze, and yet summer still holds her fist tight around each day, even as the leaves begin to drift to the ground and the sun sets earlier and earlier each evening.

It was Celeste's favorite time of year. Though it had nothing to do with the frost on the windshield in the morning or the leaves on the maples turning vibrant shades of fire. She loved September because that was when school started again. That was when she got her life, her house and her sanity back.

And when you're a single mother to a fifteen-year-old girl with rampant hormones, mood swings and enough attitude for quintuplets, you wanted that child out of your house and their ass back in school long before the Labor Day weekend rolled around.

The countdown was on.

T-minus twelve days to the start of school, and Celeste could finally see the light at the end of the invariably long tunnel that had been the summer.

Not that she didn't love her kid and all. She'd take a bullet for Sabrina and all that jazz, but even though they both worked and Sabrina was more concerned with her friends than her mother, the lack of routine and constant mood swings were killers.

She glanced at the shopping list on her phone and ticked off the things they'd already purchased for the new school year. They still needed to go and get Sabrina new shoes for gym class, along with a few binders and all the other paraphernalia that accompanied a teenager to high school.

She blew out a slow breath and shook her head.

She had a teenager.

She was thirty-three, and she had a fifteen-year-old.

Where did the time go?

If she blinked, would she be fifty-three and a grandmother?

With a lump in her throat and a single tear in her eye, she jumped when she realized she wasn't alone.

"You're a good mom." Now she'd recognize that sexy, raspy rumble anywhere. Her nipples peaked beneath her turquoise tank top, and her pussy clenched in her white denim capris as she was pulled from her thoughts.

"Mr. Travis, I don't remember you being such an eavesdropper." She stowed her phone and glanced around to find where he was lurking. "The things you must have heard in class with that bionic hearing of yours ..."

"You mean that I was the *hot* teacher, or that because I refused to sleep with any of my students, I had to be gay?"

So he had heard the rumors. Yikes.

The chuckle grew even deeper, even grittier. Her panties

became damp, and she crossed and uncrossed her legs, squeezing. "I was sitting here long before you two came over. You just didn't see me behind the tree." He shuffled on his own bench to reveal himself. She hadn't even been aware of another bench on the other side of the tree, but now she was all too aware of how close they were and how good he smelled. Fresh and manly. Woodsy and delicious. Like a frosty forest. He grinned at her, those dimples back in full-on attack mode. "Long enough to hear that your daughter thinks I'm *really* old and that you were flirting with me."

"M-Mr. Trav—"

He held up his hand to stop her. "I'm not. You were, I was too, and you really need to call me Max."

2

MAX STUDIED the woman in front of him. Because one thing was for certain. Celeste Marchand—or Celeste Howard, as she'd corrected him—was all woman. Fifteen years ago, he'd been wet behind the ears, green as they come and eager to make his mark on the impressionable young minds of tomorrow. Only, he must have either not been that kind of student or forgot in his seven years out of school what high school was really like.

It was a viper pit. It was a dragon's den. But the snakes, dragons and beasts that congregated in the pit were hormonal, poorly parented and determined to be the next YouTube sensation even if it literally killed them.

Teaching high school math for the first five years of his career had been an absolute fucking nightmare. Toss in the fact that several junior and senior girls decided that they were going to try to seduce him because no matter how dowdily he dressed, they still called him the *hot teacher*. And when he rebuffed their advances, they made up the rumor that he was gay and had crazy-hot monkey sex with the history teacher, Mr. Bishop—who, although decent-enough-looking, was old enough to be Max's father.

Yeah, those first five years had been rough. And then suddenly, he hit thirty. Not only did the kids seem to become more tolerable, he was also shown more respect by the students and his fellow teachers, and he allowed his sister to give him a much-needed makeover. Bridget overhauled his image, bought him a whole new wardrobe, made him cut and style his hair, and told him to get better glasses and grow a beard. He also got engaged, then married and subsequently divorced between the ages of thirty and thirty-five. In that time, though, his sister and wife convinced him to start working out. So he did.

Since getting back to Seattle, he'd caught up with Zak at Club Z Fitness again. Zak had prodded him in the stomach but then grinned when he realized Max hadn't let himself go in his four years overseas. Nonetheless, he put Max on another insane muscle-building regiment just like before. Max wasn't interested in getting as jacked as Zak, because the man was massive, but since Zak got ahold of him six years ago, he did like the new cut to his body and the way his biceps popped when he flexed them. He'd also started doing jujitsu and continued to do so while in Vietnam. He returned to his former haunt in Seattle and was sweating it out with his trainer, Ryan, on Mondays, which helped with toning, balance and cardio.

Deep down, though, no matter how much he changed his hair or developed a six-pack, he was a nerd to his core. Math, numbers, trivia, and books, that's what he loved.

"If you're not teaching at Rainier Beach any longer, where are you teaching?" Celeste's voice drew him from his stroll down memory lane. The stunning woman in front of him had lifted one brow and was staring at him quizzically. Had she asked that question a few times and he hadn't heard her?

Shaking the cobwebs from his brain, he smiled, stood and moved around to sit next to her on the bench, careful to leave an appropriate, platonic-size gap between them. "I'm actually waiting for a placement."

Her brilliant green eyes grew wide, and he had to push down the groan in his chest at the thought of her looking at him like that while on her knees. "You? You don't have a permanent contract by now?"

"I did and then I left." With a slight shrug, he allowed his gaze to drift toward the door of the storefront. Hopefully, the line to the checkout was long and her daughter was still toward the back—he was enjoying talking to Celeste. Earlier when they'd bumped into each other the first time, he'd taken one glance at the long checkout line, ditched his new jeans and shirts and walked out. No way was he standing there with a bunch of teenyboppers to buy clothes he could get online. Particularly since he spent his days dealing with teenyboppers, and the chance that some of those boppers in line might be his future students was awfully high.

Her nose scrunched. "What do you mean?"

"I worked at Rainier Beach for a while, moved over to Roosevelt, then Nova. Then I got divorced and decided Nova wasn't big enough for me and my ex. Hell, Seattle wasn't big enough for me and my ex, so I applied to go teach in Vietnam for a while. Was over there for four years, just got back in July. Now I'm waiting for a placement."

"So Seattle's no longer too big?" The expression on her face was that of challenge and amusement, complete with a raised brow once again and a lip lift. All it did was make her that much more appealing. He liked his woman with a healthy dose of sass. And he could already tell Celeste had sass in spades.

"It still is, but she moved down to Santa Barbara in May. That's where her new husband lives. So I took that as a sign to come back to home to Seattle. How about you? What do you do for work?"

"I'm a freelance copywriter and book editor. I also do a bit of ghostwriting when I have time, but I haven't done that in a few years." Her eyes really were unlike anything he'd ever seen, the color of hanging moss in the setting sun, and they sparkled as her lips drew up into a coy smile. "Been meaning to try my hand at writing my own book, but alas, I need to pay the bills, and all the other stuff does that. Not sure a writing career could."

"I never knew you were so ..."

"Into *words?*" she finished for him.

Sheepishly, he nodded. "Yeah. You never seemed to struggle in math. I always thought you'd go the science or business route. You just seemed to have a knack for it." He wasn't trying to offend her; he just didn't expect her to be so well-rounded. She had always been on the quieter side, her boyfriend, Declan, the popular, louder one of the two. But she'd always been good at math, and as a math and science guy himself, he wasn't the most wordy person—despite his love of books—so to meet someone who not only understood numbers but was also a word whiz was rare.

Her gaze turned wistful as she tore it away from him and focused on the doors to the store. "I actually planned to become a forensic investigator. Had my *whole* future planned out. All my college classes decided, the works. Then I got pregnant at eighteen, and those plans were astronomically derailed. Declan went into construction because we needed money. He'd planned to go to law school."

She shook her head, and a small, sad smile drifted across her mouth. But it was gone just as fast as it was there.

Turning back to him, she pulled at a loose thread on the hem of her shirt, not looking at him but still giving him her attention. "I'd always enjoyed English and creative writing, got good grades in those classes too. Once we graduated, got married and became settled, Declan started on with a construction company, and I looked into some distance and online courses. I needed to do something, but I had to be able to do it from home with a squalling baby on my hip. I got the necessary certification, and by the time Sabrina was one, I was working like twenty-five hours a week. I just kind of *fell* into copywriting and editing gigs, same as the ghostwriting. Right writers' forum, right time."

"What genre do you ghostwrite for?" He'd never met a ghostwriter before. Could she tell him who she wrote for? Was there some nondisclosure agreement where she had to keep it on the DL whose voice she was pretending to have?

That sexy little coy smile was back. "I mainly write women's fiction, some western historicals, and I've done a few regencies. And before you ask, I can't say who I write for. It's classified."

"That's really cool. And I wasn't going to ask."

Liar.

The door to the store opened, and out stepped Sabrina, smiling nervously next to a girl her age who could only be *the* Eleanor Shelby, followed by two other girls. They all stopped abruptly, eyes focused forward on Max and Celeste. All of their mouths opened like pre-teen codfish.

Should he take that as his cue to leave?

Celeste cleared her throat beside him and stood up. "Nice catching up with you again, Mr. Tr—I mean, *Max*. I hope you end up at a great school this year. Whoever gets you as a math teacher should consider themselves very lucky."

"Ew, he's a math teacher?" Eleanor asked, her tone dripping with contempt as she finished off her head-to-toe, disapproving once-over of him with a sneer. The girl didn't even bother to whisper. Who the hell was raising children today? Wolves?

"And that's my cue to leave," he said, standing up next to Celeste and stretching. "Nice to see you again, Celeste. Let's not wait another fifteen years to catch up."

He glanced at Sabrina. "Nice to meet you, Sabrina. I hope you have a great school year." He fixed the rest of the girls with a look that he hoped conveyed his complete lack of interest in them, but he'd never really been one to understand or know how to handle teenage girls. They'd either been after him to sleep with him or spreading rumors about him. There was only a brief window where he seemed to know how to reach them and teach them math. The rest of the time they beguiled the fuck out of him.

Sabrina didn't say anything, but she did watch him as he stepped around their group and out of the smothering, judgmental air of adolescence. He took a deep, gulping breath. "Take care, Celeste. And I hope you *do* write that book someday. Let me know when you do, and I'll be the first to buy it … so long as you promise me a signed copy." He flashed her a smile he thought made the ladies swoon, but judging by the way the teenagers grimaced, he was no longer sure of its potency. Not that teenage girls were his target audience. Gah, gross.

Celeste smiled though. She even laughed.

Bingo. It worked.

"I'll send you the first copy for free. How's that?" she asked with a chuckle, inconspicuously edging herself between her daughter and her cabal of mean girls.

He laughed as well, gave a final wave and reluctantly turned to leave.

"Is that your mom's *boyfriend?*" he heard Eleanor ask. "He's so not hot. And he's like really old. Did you see his boots?"

Max glanced down at his footwear. What the fuck was

wrong with his boots? They were practical for what he drove. They were also crazy-expensive and still in mint condition.

"No. I've never seen him before until today," Sabrina replied. "Mom, he's not your boyfriend, is he?"

"He's my old high school math teacher, you guys," Celeste replied with a classic mom tone to her voice. "I haven't seen him since I graduated. It was just nice to catch up with a friendly face. And who knows, he might be *your* math teacher this year. So maybe you should have been a bit nicer to him, *Eleanor*."

Yeah, Eleanor.

A part of him did hope he was Eleanor's teacher. Maybe then he could teach her more than just logarithms. Like manners, respect and kindness.

Parents today were seriously failing their children. They were raising little shitheads because rather than be their parent, they were more concerned about being their friend.

If you added to the already overpopulated earth because you were desperate for friends, then you were not fit to be a parent.

He wasn't a parent himself—so perhaps he was speaking entirely out of his ass—but he didn't think he was. A big part of him was glad that he hadn't had children—at least not with Sharmaine. He and his ex would have butted heads constantly on how to raise children. He was strict; she was not. She let her chemistry classes run roughshod over her. He ruled his math classrooms with a fair but iron fist. She had absolutely no authority and commanded zero respect from the children she taught. He liked to believe that now, at the ripe old age of forty, he'd figure out how to get through to kids while also earning their respect.

He'd spent the last fifteen years teaching shitheads trigonometry and fractions, and he'd used his skills with probability and odds as a way to help him figure out just how hard to bring down the hammer in order to apply enough pressure to get the kids to focus and listen to him, but not too hard that it caved in their skulls. It'd certainly taken some finesse and over a decade to perfect, but he'd like to think that his students now viewed him as a respectable, fair but authoritative educator.

There was always one rotten apple in the bushel though, no matter how many wonderful pies he created out of the moldable minds of his pupils. And something told him Eleanor Shelby was as rotten as they came. Maybe he was better off *not* teaching her anything, because he was seriously too old for high school mean girl bullshit, and he could tell a mile away that she came with it by the bucketload. That girl would cause him nothing but grief.

It would also mean that he would be working at the same school as Celeste's daughter and could possibly be *her* teacher. Awkward.

But was it?

He had no relationship with Celeste. He was her former teacher, she his former pupil, and yet, seeing her today, speaking with her, he didn't see her as the eighteen-year-old fresh-faced youth she'd been in his class. Today he saw her as a beautiful, vibrant, strong, smart woman. And she was single.

And he was single.

Would asking her for her number have been too weird? Did she still see him as her teacher? That was certainly how she'd referred to him to her daughter and the mean girls.

He approached his Triumph Bonneville Bobber, shrugged back into his leather jacket and pulled his shades out of his pocket. His helmet was still locked to his bike and in one piece. That wasn't always the case, but he'd specifically chosen a strip mall in a richer part of town to do his shopping, in the hopes that his bike and helmet would be there when he returned.

Unlocking his helmet, he swung his leg over the bike and plunked the brain bucket on his head. The helmet was a sauna inside and immediately started to bake his scalp and make him sweat. His bike was now parked directly in the sun. He'd parked it in the shade of a tree when he arrived but didn't account for the sun moving. Which he should have. He knew better. He also hadn't planned to be gone that long, but seeing Celeste changed all of that.

He released the kickstand, put the key in the ignition, pulled the choke all the way out, set it to neutral, squeezed the clutch and hit the start button. Was there anything sexier than the throaty purr and the vibration of pure power between your legs?

Fuck no.

Well, maybe if there was a gorgeous redhead behind him on the bike, with her thighs squeezing his, her hands on his chest, and her tits pressed up against his back.

Now *that* would be the sexiest thing ever.

He'd always been a motorcycle buff, had always had a bike, even as a teenager in high school and a broke college kid. They hadn't always been *nice* bikes. But they ran and he babied them. The Triumph Bonneville was a gift to himself when he returned to the States. He'd lived like a bit of a pauper in Vietnam for four years, not that it was difficult to live well for cheap there, but he'd lived mediocre for even less. And in doing so, he saved up so that once he returned to Seattle, he could afford to buy a condo, buy a truck, buy a motorcycle and still have a bit left over in his retirement savings. He returned in July in order to give himself some time to transition back to the western style of living.

With his Bobber rumbling like a kitten desperate for

another pet, he crab-walked the bike back into the lane of the complex.

As necessary as the dark jeans, leather jacket, biker boots, shades and helmet were, he was hot as fuck. He needed to get home so he could throw on a pair of shorts. No need for a shirt. The summer was still brutal, and the sun was still ruthless.

He was about to gun it and drive off when the glimpse of several teenagers standing directly in front of where he'd been parked caught his eyes. He turned his head.

Sure enough, Sabrina and the mean girls, along with Celeste, were all standing there watching him.

Eleanor looked like she'd just smelled her own fart, but the rest of them seemed to be in awe. Particularly Celeste.

Smiling, he waved at *her*. Not them. *Her*. Then he took off out of the complex, careful not to give the bike too much throttle because he wasn't a dick, but he also didn't dog along like a seventy-five-year-old on a trike with his Pekingese and old lady in a side car.

Celeste Howard.

Would it be weird to Google her? Would it be weird to find her on Facebook and friend her? He hadn't been on Facebook in over a year, but that didn't mean he didn't have an account. He just hated social media.

Maybe you should wait to see if you're her kid's math teacher first.

Right. Good point. Because then he wouldn't have to resort to social media stalker behavior. Something he loathed the thought of and had never actually done before.

But then she'd also be your pupil's mother.

Right. Another good point. He made a lot of good points. Shit.

Maybe he should have asked for her number.

He had no idea how things worked these days. How

dating worked. Did people even talk on the phone anymore to people besides their parents? Social media was probably easiest. He was good on the computer but barely went on social media except to update his photo every year or so. He probably wouldn't even know *how* to find her. It'd been a brief, platonic, friendly run-in with a former student. Nothing more. Nothing less.

Only, he really wanted it to be more.

3

"I'M JUST HEADING over to Bianca's," Celeste called up the stairs to Sabrina on Saturday night. "Just text me if you need anything, or walk down the path and knock on the door."

She waited for her hatchling to reply. No answer.

Of course not.

"Sabrina, did you hear me?"

An irritated growl preceded her holler, its tone less than stellar or respectful. "I heard you. Go. I'll be fine."

Oh no, she didn't.

Kicking her shoes off, Celeste set the bottle of wine and the fruit kebab platter down on the kitchen counter and stalked up the stairs. "Young lady, lose the tone or I will stay home from wine night and cramp the crap out of your style. Don't think I won't." She arrived at her daughter's door. It wasn't entirely closed, so she wedged it open a bit more with her foot. "What's with the attitude? I thought we had a nice day and dinner yesterday. We went to bed liking each other. Today was good. Where's the snot-nosed vibe coming from?"

Sabrina was lying facedown on her bed, her head at the

foot, legs kicked up in the air. "It's nothing. I'm sorry for the attitude. I didn't mean it. Just go."

Celeste sat down on the bed and glanced down at her kid's phone. "How's the new phone?"

"It's fine." Sabrina slammed it screen-down onto the mattress. "Aren't you going to be late for you *single moms club* or whatever?"

"We're *The Single Moms of Seattle,* thank you very much, and seeing as there are only three of us and we all live in this same townhouse complex, I think they'll be okay if I'm a little late." She patted her daughter's butt affectionately. "Talk to me, kiddo. Come on."

She could see the eye roll even through the back of her kid's head. It was just that strong. "Eleanor is making really nasty comments about you." She glanced up at Celeste. "Like that you're an unfit mother and stuff."

She was going to wring this little Eleanor bitch's neck if it was the last thing she did.

Tamping down the rage, which only escalated her desperate need for wine, she took a couple of deep breaths, shut her eyes, counted to ten and then opened them again. "Honey, what are you talking about?"

"She thinks you're a crappy mom and has joked online about calling child protective services. Because your card was declined and you made me buy my own jeans and phone. She says a parent should be able to provide for their child entirely and not force their kid to pay for their own things. Don't have kids if you can't afford them."

Holy mother of fucking fuck!

She what?

She WHAT!

Oh hell no.

Now Celeste needed all the wine.

"I think I need to call this Eleanor Shelby's parents and

have a word with them. This has all gotten way out of hand, and school hasn't even started yet—"

"No!" Sabrina was up from her prone position and shaking her head emphatically. "No, Mom, you can't. If Eleanor found out you called her parents, she would make my life a living hell for the entire year—for the next *four* years. You can't."

"Is that how she gets away with shit? She bullies even harder those she already bullies if they report her? How do you end that kind of tyranny? What is she, North Korea?"

Sabrina seemed to be in physical if not mental anguish as she pleaded with her mother. "Please, Mom. Please don't go to Eleanor's parents. I'm sure this will all go away. Just ... don't do anything else to give her cause. Just stay away, okay?"

"I'm sorry, young lady, but I am your mother. I will not *stay away.*"

Sabrina exhaled a sigh that seemed to make her whole body crumple. "You know what I mean."

Determined to keep her fury in check until she could let it loose over at Bianca's, Celeste took her daughter's soft, pale hand in hers. "You cannot let Eleanor Shelby or any of her *followers* dictate how you or anybody else lives their life. I am not a bad mom, and you know that. Sure, I'm not the world's best mom, but I'm not the world's worst either. There are clothes on your back, food in your belly and a roof over your head. I provide for you as best as I possibly can.

"But Mom—"

Celeste held up her hand to stop her child's protest. "As your mother, it is my job to do everything in my power to protect you. I'm going to sleep on this Eleanor Shelby issue, and then we'll tackle more of it in the morning. Maybe you should get off your phone for a bit, go outside, read a book. Social media is great and all—but it can also seriously mess with your mind." She stood up from Sabrina's bed. Her limbs were hot, her pulse racing. Who the fuck was Eleanor Shelby, and why did she think she could control, ruin and torture people the way she did?

Sabrina picked up her phone, and the screen illuminated. She glanced at it.

"I mean it, kiddo. Put the phone down."

She made to leave the room, but a hand on her arm stopped her. "You like him, don't you?"

"Who?"

"That Mr. Travis guy."

Yeah, I think I do.

But she couldn't tell her kid that. Not yet. She needed to meet Max for coffee or something to see if there was more than just a spark there.

Softening her gaze, she faced Sabrina again. "I had a thirty-second conversation with him, followed by a five-minute conversation with him. The rest of my memories about Max Travis involve him standing in front of the class with chalk-dust handprints on his butt, a wrinkly plaid shirt, dorky glasses and messy hair. He was my teacher, and I was madly in love with your father and pregnant with you. Yesterday was no more than two grownups chatting and catching up."

Methinks the lady doth protest too much.

Yeah, methinks so too.

She leaned forward and pressed a kiss to Sabrina's forehead. "Stay off social media. I mean it."

She was only halfway down the stairs when her kid called after her. "You never answered my question."

Yeah, she knew she hadn't. Because she knew her kid would not like the answer.

"WHO THE FUCK IS ELEANOR SHELBY?" Lauren blurted out, a bowl of salsa and another bowl of chips resting precariously on her plump belly.

"That's what I keep asking myself. That's what I keep asking Sabrina, the universe, and anybody else who might know. Who the fuck is Eleanor Shelby?" Celeste leaned forward toward the coffee table in Bianca's living room and upended the rest of her merlot into her glass.

"This all just sounds so fucked up," Bianca added. "Makes me glad my kids aren't there yet. I have my hands full enough with Charlie and the terrible twos—which by the way have started early, because he's only sixteen-months—and my mouthy six-year-olds."

The women all sat back, sipped their wine and stared down into their wineglasses contemplatively.

Since Celeste found out her sister's boyfriend was part of a single dads' club that played poker every Saturday night, Celeste was determined to find her own tribe. She loved the idea of a single mom club, particularly one full of sarcastic, cynical, wine-loving women like herself.

It'd taken her a while to find women she connected with on a level beyond the superficial. Women who could be as brash, crass and emotional as her, as well as women who liked their vino beyond the point of a little buzz. Eventually, after sifting through a heap of duds, she found Bianca and Lauren, and now she was determined to keep them, holding on to them with both hands. They also happened to be her neighbors.

Bianca, mother of three, was Celeste's brother-in-law's little sister. In July, she moved up to her hometown of Seattle from Palm Springs with her three kids, after her lying, cheating bastard husband got his secretary pregnant. She moved into a townhouse owned by the wife of her other brother, Liam. It happened to be a few doors down from Celeste.

Kismet? Fate? Or just perfect timing?

And Lauren, who also lived in the complex, had been one of Celeste's friends since she moved in eight months ago. She revealed on their second ladies' night out for wine and nachos that she was pregnant with a booty call's baby. He ghosted her the moment she told him he was going be a father.

A *thunk* sound upstairs had them all staring at the ceiling.

"Did one of them roll out of bed?" Lauren asked, her cornflower-blue eyes shifting back and forth between Bianca and Celeste. "Should you go up there?"

Bianca was still staring up at the ceiling, the brown of her eyes barely visible, they were tipped up so much. "Wait for it. If there's no crying, then it was either a book that fell to the floor, or the kid didn't wake up, *or* they didn't get hurt and just put themselves back to bed."

No crying radiated down the stairs or through the vents.

All quiet on the western front?

"You're not worried one of them bashed their head on something and isn't crying because they're unconscious?" Lauren asked, genuine panic now in her eyes.

Bianca and Celeste exchanged amused glances.

"You're cute," Celeste said, sipping her wine. "You'll make a great mom. Just don't helicopter around BCB too much."

"You have to stop calling my baby that! When it finally arrives, I need to *not* have that nickname in my head."

BCB, or *Booty Call Baby*, was a nickname Bianca had coined a few weeks ago when she and Celeste were drunk and signing Lauren's AWOL baby daddy up for male enhancement product coupons using his email address and phone number.

"What about TBD?" Bianca suggested with a giggle. She

tucked her thick, wavy, chestnut hair behind her ear and sipped her wine. "That's not mean, is it?"

Lauren rolled her eyes and dipped a chip into her salsa. "Let's get back to Mr. Max Travis, shall we. Do we have a picture of him?"

In addition to seeking advice from her friends on how to help Sabrina navigate this Eleanor Shelby problem, Celeste also let it slip that she'd run into her old math teacher and the man had gotten hot over the years.

Bianca had her phone in her hand, and her fingers were flying across the screen. Within a minute, she was grinning and turning her phone around to show the others. "We have one now. And he is *fine*."

Lauren's mouth made an *O* shape. "Oooh, Celeste, are you hot for teacher? He is fine. I'd let him put a baby in my belly and then never call me again."

Bianca and Celeste turned to look at her with stunned expressions.

"Just kidding," Lauren sang before she rolled her eyes. "Sorry, I'm just really horny lately. It's the hormones. But I can probably kiss getting laid goodbye for the next ... eighteen years?"

Celeste frowned. "God, let's hope not." She took Bianca's phone from her and enlarged the photo of Max. He was tanned, smiling and shirtless. Well, hello. Those were some abs. Yes, they were. He was also holding up a fish on a line. The boat was narrow and wooden with chipping paint and the water behind him was the same color as her turquoise pendant. He must have been fishing while abroad and posted that.

"That is *quite* the nice tummy." Bianca raked her top teeth over her bottom lip and waggled her brows. "A nice tummy indeed."

"Mmm-hmm. I could do my laundry on that," Lauren added.

"So what ended up happening with your credit card?" Bianca asked, taking back her phone and ogling Mr. Travis again. Gah! Max! She really needed to start referring to him as Max.

Max Travis, her former math teacher, now an incredibly sexy, motorcycle-riding, tanned, six-packed Adonis.

Was she drooling? Discreetly, she wiped the back of her hand beneath her bottom lip to check. No, she wasn't. Thank goodness.

"Credit card?" Lauren reminded.

Celeste rolled her eyes at the ridiculousness of the entire credit card situation and reached for one of the fruit skewers she'd brought over. "I handed her the wrong card. It was expired. I forgot to remove my expired card from my wallet when I got the new one. So the dumb girl at the checkout wasn't interpreting it right. Because after all my years working retail in high school, I know that if a card is expired, a little *expired* notification pops up. And if it's declined it says *declined.*"

"What, was she like twenty?" Bianca asked.

Celeste nodded. "Yeah."

"Way to embarrass the hell out of Celeste and her kid by announcing it to the entire store that Celeste's card had been declined," Lauren said, defending her.

"It was a mistake," Celeste said, feeling bad for calling the cashier dumb, even though she did have an awfully vacant expression on her face. Retail would do that to a person, though. It killed the soul.

"So now this *Eleanor Shelby* witch thinks you're a shitty mom and is going to call child protection services?" Lauren winced and rubbed the side of her belly, the bowls of chips and salsa jostling when her little ninja-baby kicked. "Calm down." She jammed the heel of her palm into the side of her stomach. "Get your foot out of my ribs."

"Don't miss that," Bianca said with a laugh, eyes twinkling at the same time she drank more wine. "Three is more than enough for me. Plus, I like wine too much to do the whole pregnancy thing again. Tubes are gone. I am closed for business. Not that I'm getting any *to* get pregnant, even on a fluke. I'm pretty sure there are cobwebs growing up there. Hasn't been a dick up yonder in way too long."

"Yeah, well, at least you can see the door to your *yonder*. I haven't seen my door or the once tastefully trimmed hedging around it in what feels like forever. I think I need some serious pruning." Lauren's pout would have been cute if she hadn't followed it up with a growl and another heel palm to her side. "I mean it, child. I will come in there myself and remove your foot."

"I'd pay money to see that," Bianca teased. She turned back to Celeste. "What are you going to do about Sabrina and this Eleanor witch?"

Celeste shook her head and glanced out the window into Bianca's small backyard. It was about the size of a postage stamp, but there was enough grass for her kids to run through a sprinkler and for a small potted garden. Low maintenance, which was exactly what Bianca needed because her life was nuts. With three kids and a busy job as a property manager for a bunch of rentals, the woman rarely sat still for long.

"I don't want to make Sabrina's life any harder. I remember high school, and although I wasn't unpopular, I wasn't Eleanor Shelby, and I certainly wasn't friends with girls *like* her. But she also shouldn't be allowed to get away with how she treats people."

"Agreed," her friends both said.

"Maybe just wait and see what happens in the next

couple of weeks when school starts. This could all blow over. Sabrina is a smart girl. You've raised her well. She may surprise us all in how she chooses to handle this little Eleanor snot. Right now, it's all still raw." Bianca glanced at Lauren. "Move the salsa bowl. Otherwise, it's going to dump."

Lauren gave her a sophomoric sneer. "I know what I'm—" And as predicted, she moved—or maybe the baby kicked— but either way, the salsa bowl on her belly fell over and sent chips and dip all over the floor. "Oh shit."

Bianca was up and out of her seat. "I'll get the towel. Though I really should just drape the living room in towels when Lauren comes over."

"I was a klutz before I became with child. It's who I am, and you love me for me," Lauren called into the kitchen, but her confident smile faded and she looked about ready to cry. "But I am sorry, B. I'll pay to get the carpets cleaned."

"It's fine," Bianca called back.

"Became with child?" Celeste repeated with an eyebrow lift and smirk.

Lauren grinned again, grabbed a chip off the couch and scooped salsa off her shirt with it, popping it into her mouth. "I think it sounds more refined than *knocked up*. Don't you?"

"I have three children," Bianca said, beginning to clean up. "I can spot an impending mess a mile away."

Lauren nodded and pretended to bow. "I still have so much to learn from you, oh wise one."

Bianca rolled her eyes before dipping her head and scrubbing the salsa from her carpet. "I want to know if Celeste is going to say *yes* when Professor Washboard calls her for a date."

"She better." Lauren was eating the fallen chips rather than putting them back in the bowl.

Celeste bit into a juicy strawberry from her fruit skewer. "He doesn't even have my number. He's not going to call me."

"You can find people other ways than the white pages these days," Lauren said. "Social media, for example. That's how we found him and those abs of his."

Celeste snorted a laugh. "It was just a chance meeting. Am I attracted to him? Sure. Definitely. Did I think we had a spark?" She nodded. "Yeah, I did. But that may have all been in my desperate-for-love, lonely-vagina head."

"Doubt it," Bianca and Lauren said in unison.

"You should send him a friend request on Facebook," Lauren suggested.

"No."

"Does the fact that he is your former teacher weird you out at all to the idea of dating him?" Bianca asked.

Celeste thought about it for a moment, but the longer she thought, the less weird it seemed. She kind of liked that Max wasn't a complete stranger. She saw him at least five times a day for ten months of her life. Even if he'd had thousands of students since then, and she a husband and a child, they weren't strangers.

"It makes it hot," Lauren said before Celeste had a chance. "Professor Washboard is fine. Forget that he was your teacher. He's not anymore, and that's what matters."

Celeste chewed her strawberry. Lauren certainly had a point. "He's not a professor. He's a high school math teacher. I mean, he's really smart, could probably become a professor, but don't you need like a PhD or something to do that?"

"You're changing the subject. The subject we're focusing on right now is whether or not you *want* to sleep with, date or hook up with *Teacher* Washboard. *Mr.* Washboard? *Daddy* Washboard?" Lauren made a disgusted face. "Ew. No. Not Daddy. Never Daddy. Professor Washboard works for me until we come up with something better."

Rolling her eyes, Celeste popped a chunk of pineapple into her mouth so she didn't have to immediately answer.

Did she want to sleep with Max? Her shower fantasy this morning would indicate that yes, she most certainly did. But was it because it was Max, or because she was thirty-three, in the sexual prime of her life and hadn't been with a man in a very long time? Was it just because Max was attractive, she kind of knew him and he showed interest in her? Or was it because she actually wanted to jump the man's bones and grind them into dust?

"She's been quiet too long for her answer to be anything but *all of the above*," Bianca teased, standing up and taking the towel back to the kitchen. "She wants him."

Lauren's grin was diabolical as she rubbed her hands together, her eyes wide and eager to begin scheming. "Yeah, she does. Now let's figure out how to get her some of that."

"Down, girl," Bianca said to Lauren, returning from the kitchen. She pivoted her gaze to Celeste. "Do you want to pursue something with him? If he does contact you—"

"He will!" Lauren practically shouted. "Look at her. She's hot. Red hair, curves. Green eyes. She's like the girl—nay, the *woman* next door every guy wants to bang."

Celeste gave her thin-filtered friend the side-eye. "Thanks?"

Lauren nodded with a big smile.

Bianca curled her leg up under herself on the couch. "Okay, so let's say he calls you. You go out, then ..."

Then she jumped his bones and ground them into dust.

Nibbling on her lip, she glanced out into the backyard. The sun was beginning to set, lending the entire sky a rich orange glow. "We're getting a bit ahead of ourselves here. I bumped into him after fifteen years. We chatted. He left." He did, however, confirm that he was flirting with her, so there *was* that. She raked her fingers through her hair and shook her head, laughing, turning her gaze back to her friends. "I mean, what if he does get a job at Sabrina's school? Isn't that like a conflict of interest or something?"

"I don't know if it is. Didn't Gilmore Girls do something like that?" Lauren wrinkled her nose. "Yeah, I think they did. Lorelai dated Max—" Her eyes went even wider than before. "Max! How crazy is that. Lorelai dated Rory's teacher named Max, and you're dating Sabrina's teacher named Max."

"I'm not dating him."

"Yet!" Bianca and Lauren said in unison.

Celeste snorted and rolled her eyes. "Before I even think another thought about my love life or lack thereof, I need you guys to help me figure out what to do about this Eleanor plague."

Bianca sipped her wine. "If it were me, and my child was having an issue with a kid at school, I would go to the school and talk to them about it. Go to a teacher. But since they're all starting high school this year, migrating from the same junior high, I would go to the guidance counselor at the school and ask for advice. This would also make them aware of the situation. Speak with the principal. Ask for his or her advice and then go from there. Rally your troops. Gather yours and Sabrina's allies. People who are on your side and will have your back if something does go down because you made them aware of the situation before it escalated."

"Damn, you're smart," Lauren said, staring at Bianca in awe. "I'm going to send BCB over to you when he or she has problem. You're bound to give them better advice than me."

Bianca grinned. "You just called it *BCB*."

"Ah, fuck!" Lauren growled. "See what you've done?"

"That is good advice, though," Celeste said, mulling over what Bianca suggested. "Go to the school, which is most likely already open, and speak with the principal and a guidance counselor. Maybe we could even make some kind of suggestion that Eleanor and Sabrina not be placed in any classes together, mitigate how much time they're around each other."

"That's an idea." Bianca nodded. "Though if they take any specialty classes that are only offered once, that could be tough. But do your due diligence the best you can."

"I would also find out *who* Eleanor's parents are," Lauren added. "That way if some kind of teenage drama shit does hit the fan, you know where to find them."

That wasn't a bad idea either. School started a week from Tuesday. So she only had next week to get her butt into the school and her concerns heard.

"So, have we solved the mindfuck of a problem that is Eleanor Bitchface Shelby?" Lauren asked, grabbing a fruit skewer and popping a big piece of honeydew melon into her mouth.

"It's a definite start." Celeste patted her friend's belly. "Thanks, you guys."

Lauren nodded. "No problem. Now let's work on the next issue, getting you into Professor Washboard's swim shorts." She made a *gimme* motion with her fingers to Bianca. "Let me see that picture again."

4

FOR THE FIRST two weeks of school, Celeste listened to her daughter and she did not intervene. She did not get involved. She was going to go to the school before it started to speak with the principal and a guidance counselor but Sabrina pleaded with her not to. So she did as requested with the caveat that if things got worse she would step in.

And of course, things got worse. Way worse.

Celeste's daughter came home from school bawling because of something Eleanor Shelby had scrawled on the bathroom wall about her.

Now the fight was on.

Now the claws were out, and Celeste was putting on her mama bear suit and harnessing the rage.

Nobody messed with her cub. Nobody.

And especially not a little trust-fund brat like Eleanor Shelby, who thought spreading rumors and slandering someone else's name on school property was a fun way to pass the time.

It'd taken a lot for Celeste to get what happened out of her daughter, but when she finally did, all she was able to see after that was a deep, dark shade of red. The same shade as her daughter's eyes after she'd cried all the way home from school.

Which was why she was currently headed to the school to go and meet the guidance counselor and principal. They didn't know she was coming, but it was an in-service day for teachers, so she knew they would be there. And she wasn't leaving until they saw her.

She felt like such a failure as a parent. She had no idea how to help Sabrina navigate this bully that seemed hell-bent on making her life miserable.

Fury fueled her and she gripped the steering wheel until her knuckles were white and achy as she drove toward the school, which was only a couple of blocks away from her house. She told Sabrina she was going grocery shopping, because she was sure if her kid knew the plan, she'd fight Celeste not to go.

Too bad. Celeste had zero clue how to help her kid, so she needed advice from the professionals.

Sabrina Howard likes it in the ass.

A buck a suck. Call Sabrina Howard. It's the only way she can afford her clothes.

Two hand-jobs for two bucks under the bleachers. Call Sabrina Howard.

Like seriously, who the fuck was this Eleanor witch and what kind of a beef did she have with Sabrina? Thank God, Sabrina had the smarts to take pictures of the Sharpie-covered walls before she used a Magic Eraser (herself) and removed the heinous lies from the bathroom walls.

The question that remained unanswered in Celeste's mind, and the minds of both Bianca and Lauren when she texted them the pictures, was: How low was Eleanor willing to stoop, and were these things also on the walls in the boys' bathroom?

Celeste was going to go with a *yes*, because when it came to Eleanor, it seemed better not to underestimate her. Think the worst, rather than the best.

She pulled into the school parking lot, which was only a quarter full because no student vehicles were around. She parked, took ten deep breaths, counted to ten and then stepped out of her SUV.

Even though she was still enraged, it would do nobody any good—particularly Sabrina—if she went into the school prepared to rip out jugulars. She came by her temper honestly, but right now she needed to go into the school with a level head and purpose and not let the emotions and feelings of parental failure cloud her judgment.

Max closed the back passenger door of his truck and adjusted the box in his arms as he made his way toward the school door. It was a Friday afternoon and the first in-service day of the year. Boy, they were scheduling these things sooner and sooner. Was it because they figured by the first week of school, teachers already needed a break from the students, along with extra prep time?

They—whoever they were—weren't wrong.

He had to be at the school for a workshop at one, but until then, he was free to work in his classroom to get some shit done. There were no students around to bug him. They all got to be little latchkey hoodlums and hang out at home, raid their parents' fridges and watch *The Price Is Right* until their eyes bled.

He'd loved those days when he was a kid. When his parents were at work but he got the whole day off to do dick all.

But now, as the teacher, the wise one, the overlord, he had

to get his ass into work and be a productive member of the academic team.

At least it would give him time to get his classroom a little more organized.

The first week of school was always pure chaos anyway. Nobody knew where they were going, kids got shuffled around like cards in a deck and even teachers got moved around to different classrooms.

But it looked like he finally had a classroom he could call his own. And he intended to make the most of this student-free Friday to clean the room and make it his new home away from home for the next ten months.

He was teaching freshman, sophomore and senior math, as well as AP calculus—his favorite.

It'd been a while since he stood in a classroom like this one, but if felt good to be back. Teaching in Vietnam had been rewarding on an entirely different level, and he'd enjoyed it immensely, but now he was eager to get back to teaching students from his own country. Contribute to the future of his own nation.

He was on his second load, bringing boxes in from his truck, when he called out to a woman in front of him to hold the door. He didn't want to make the woman holding it for him wait too long, so he hustled as best he could, despite the load he carried. He reached the door. "Ah, thanks."

"Mr. Travis!"

He nearly dropped his boxes.

She'd had her head down and was staring at her phone, which was why he hadn't recognized her right away. But now he could definitely see her. How had he not recognized her immediately?

"Celeste! What are you doing here?"

Anger curled her lips down into a deep frown. "I need to find the principal's office and the guidance counselor's office."

"Why?"

She shook her head. "I tried to let Sabrina handle it *her* way, but Eleanor is bullying her—*still*." With her hand shaking, she glanced at her phone again and brought up images. She showed them to him.

"What the fuck?" Lava filled his veins as his eyes flew back and forth between her phone screen and her. "What the hell? Where is that? Here?" He pointed at the ground to indicate he meant the school.

She nodded. "Bathroom walls."

"I can go find a janitor right now and have them removed." He made to move, but she grabbed his arm.

"No, it's okay. Sabrina went across the street to the hardware store on her lunch break and bought a Magic Eraser, and she cleaned off the walls herself." Her eyes shifted around the hallway nervously. "Though I think there might be things on the walls in the boys' bathrooms too. Just a hunch, though."

"I can check. I can go do that right now."

Her lips pursed. "Thank you. I appreciate that."

"What else can I do?" Even though he'd only bumped into Celeste that one time two weeks ago, he had not been able to stop thinking about her. It also didn't help that Sabrina was in fact his student, and she looked an awful lot like her mother. Not in a creepy old man lusting after a young girl kind of way. Gah, no! But more that, because Sabrina was in his class and he saw her every day, he saw Sabrina and thought of Celeste.

"She asked me not to come here, not to talk to Eleanor's parents, but I can't sit by and do nothing."

They began to walk through the hallway.

"Ah, shit. This really sucks. I'm sorry." He pointed down toward the south wing. "The principal's office is that way." Then he pointed toward the east wing. "Counselors are down there."

She nodded and thanked him, though she seemed awfully distracted.

Understandably so.

Setting his box down on a bench, he turned to her. "Hey."

Her pain and helplessness hit him hard when she lifted her gaze to his. Deep, mossy green eyes stared back at him, seeming lost and almost scared.

"Come find me downstairs in my new classroom once you've talked to the counselor and principal, okay? Let me know what the counselor and Principal Pelton have to say."

She nodded but just barely.

He reached for her hand, and thankfully, she didn't pull away. He squeezed it. "You're a good mom. Coming to talk to the right people at the school is the right thing to do. It's happening on their watch, on their property, and she's vandalizing school property as well. Pelton needs to know."

Her deep inhale and long exhale had her whole body slumping, and at that moment, he ached to take her in his arms and let her collapse against him. To take away some of her pain. Let her know she didn't have to shoulder this alone. He wasn't Sabrina's father, but he could be Celeste's friend.

"I don't feel like a good mom. I feel like a failure. It's such a helpless feeling. Your kid is hurting, and there is so little you can do to help them."

He took her other hand and squeezed it as well, his eyes watching as her gaze fell to their linked fingers. She didn't pull away though.

"We'll figure this out. Don't worry."

He knew his words were probably hollow, but he had no idea what else to say.

She nodded and pulled her hands free from his.

He'd overstepped.

Shit.

"Thanks. I'm going to go speak to the guidance counselor first. Have you met him or her yet?"

He shook his head. "They're doing a mixer next week at Prime on Friday for all the teachers. Up until now, it's just been a hectic mess."

She pressed her lips together until they formed a thin, flat line. "All right, I'll come find you in a bit."

He reached for her hand once more and squeezed it before she pulled free from his grasp and disappeared down the hallway toward the east wing.

CELESTE KNOCKED on the guidance counselor's door and held her breath as she waited for a reply.

"Come in," a female voice called from the other side.

With her hand on the knob and only a few butterflies in her belly, she opened the door.

A woman roughly forty or so with pale blue eyes and dark brown hair greeted her with a stiff smile. "Hello, how can I help you?"

"I'm, uh ... I'm looking for a guidance counselor."

The woman's eyes narrowed. "You're a bit old to be a student." Was that her attempt at a joke? Because the delivery was all wrong.

Celeste shook her head. "No, sorry. I'm the mother of a student. My daughter is a freshman."

"Ah, okay. How can I help you?" She put down the pen in her hand, and her facial muscles relaxed slightly. Why did she seem familiar? Celeste knew she'd never met this woman before—she had a very good recollection of names and faces —and yet something about this woman struck a familiar and not altogether pleasant chord inside her.

"My daughter, Sabrina, has been experiencing some

online and in-school bullying from a classmate of hers. They went to junior high together, and both moved over to Lakewood. It started before school began, but my daughter asked me not to intervene. We both hoped it would die down once school started."

"But it hasn't?"

Celeste shook her head. "No, it hasn't. It's escalated."

She picked up her pen and tapped it against the desk while make a humming noise and pressing raspberry lips into a flat line. "Can you elaborate on what's happening online?"

"We were shopping before school started and one of my credit cards was declined, which it wasn't. It was expired. I'd just accidentally handed over an old card. Anyway, this *girl* starts harassing my daughter online, saying she's going to call child protective services on me for being unable to provide for my child. Sabrina wanted a pair of jeans that were well over our new clothes budget—and which in my opinion are ugly as hell—so I made her pitch in for half. Apparently, this is a parent no-no to this student. She says that if you can't afford to provide for your kids, then you shouldn't have them."

The woman hummed again. "Yes, I'm *well* aware of the new jean phenomenon. Hideous, if you ask me."

Celeste nodded. "Right! Anyway, I asked my daughter if I should talk to this child's parents, but she said that would only make things worse. That if the other girls found out I went to her parents, she would make my daughter's life a living hell."

"I see."

"So I didn't do anything. But now, things have gotten worse. She's calling my daughter names, teasing her. Trying to turn her friends against her by spreading rumors. She wrote some nasty things about her in the bathroom stalls. It's gotten bad, and school has only just started. I'm getting really worried."

"I see."

Celeste tossed her hands up and let them fall against her sides. She hadn't been offered a seat and was feeling really awkward standing there staring down at the woman sitting behind the desk.

"I'm just here for some *guidance*. I don't know where to go from here or how to help my daughter. I'm a single mom, so I don't have Sabrina's dad to bounce this off of."

"Divorce?" she asked, almost eagerly.

Celeste palate turned sour. "No. He passed away eight years ago."

Sad eyes met hers. "Oh, I'm so sorry."

They needed to get back on topic. "Anyway, I figured coming to the school and speaking with a counselor and the principal before the year started was a good start. If all the right people were made aware of the situation, we might be able nip it in the bud before it becomes even more of an issue." Even though she still hadn't been offered a chair, she took it anyway. But then her knee began to bounce. A nervous twitch she'd had all her life. Her fingers tightened around the kneecap to stop it, to little success.

"Have you spoken with Mr. Pelton, the principal?"

Celeste shook her head. "I came to you first."

The woman nodded again. "I see."

Did she though? Because she'd said diddly-squat.

But then, in all her years of grief counseling and seeing various therapists to work through various issues, Celeste had always been the chatty one. The counselor sat there and listened—as was their job. Maybe this woman was just really good at her job, and what Celeste perceived as judgmental bitchiness was actually just a really good listener with an unfortunate resting bitch face.

"I appreciate you coming to me with this," the guidance counselor finally said, after having sat there in silence for a painful minute.

Celeste nodded. "I'm just looking out for my kid, you know? I don't remember high school being like this, but maybe it was. I was just fortunate enough to not be caught up in such drama."

"I agree. I don't remember my high school years being quite so challenging either."

Celeste blew out a breath, smiled and nodded. "Thank you. So you see, it's just me raising my daughter. And even though I was a teenage girl once and we had the internet while I was at school, we didn't have the access to it like they do now. I didn't have a phone; I didn't have all the social media platforms. It's a different world, and although I'm doing my very best to keep her safe, there are keyboard bullies out there determined to hurt her even while she sits at home on my couch right beside me. And those keyboard bullies are also haunting her at school. Being real bullies."

"I understand."

Okay, the counselor speak was getting to be a bit much. Celeste had come here for help, not to spill her guts and then be shown the door. She ran her eyes over the counselor's desk, taking in the neatness of it, the perfectly arranged office supplies all at a ninety-degree angle to each other. All except the nameplate. That was oddly askew. Enough so that she wouldn't have been able to read it from where she'd been standing.

Mindy Sh

Laughing, Celeste reached out to adjust the plaque. "Sorry, this is bugging me." She straightened it and gasped.

Mindy Shelby.

"Is something wrong?"

Celeste stood up and nearly tripped over the back of the

chair and her own feet as she made her way to the door. "I—um ... Are you Eleanor Shelby's mother?"

She nodded. "I am, yes, why?"

No wonder she looked so damn familiar. She was the spitting image of her daughter, just twenty-some-odd years older, much the same way Sabrina was a younger doppelganger of Celeste's. She should have connected the chromosomal dots sooner.

"I, um ... I've just heard my daughter mention your daughter's name before, that's all."

Suspicion filled Mindy's eyes. "Is Eleanor the one who has been bullying Sabrina?"

Oh shit.

Swallowing, she managed a single, barely-there nod.

Mindy's nostrils flared. "I see."

Oh, for crying out loud, she needed to stop saying that.

"I had no idea. Your name isn't on the door. I would have gone to another counselor, it's just the receptionist lady at the front pointed me toward your office. I—I can't ..." She raked her fingers through her hair. "I don't know what to do now." Dread swirled inside her gut like grocery store sushi eaten right before a traveling carnival ride. "Please, I ..."

Mindy stood up from her spot behind the desk. "I just got transferred to Lakewood from Albert Talley, which is why there isn't a nameplate on the door yet." She wandered around her desk to stand in front of Celeste. She easily had a good ten years on Celeste, though it was evident she took care of herself. Her clothes were expensive, her makeup perfection. It even looked like she dabbled in Botox and fillers. She could easily pass for late thirties. "I will speak with Eleanor—"

"No!"

Mindy held up her hand to stop Celeste. "I will speak

with Eleanor and make it clear that this type of behavior is unacceptable."

"But—"

"Let me finish ... please."

Celeste nodded.

"I will say to her that I found, through the grapevine, evidence of her bullying another student and that she's been spreading rumors and writing things on the bathroom walls. I won't say you spoke to me. Because, in fact, you didn't come to Eleanor's parents, you came to the school guidance counselor. It just so happens that now, I am one and the same. I will keep an eye on the situation."

Celeste exhaled the breath that had been caught like a sinister hiccup at the back of her throat. "Thank you."

Mindy nodded. "I am sorry that my daughter has been treating your daughter this way. She is acting out a lot right now, considering that her father and I recently split up. It's a cry for attention, but it's the wrong way to go about it."

No shit.

"You're welcome to go speak to Principal Pelton if you wish."

"Thank you. I might, if he's here."

"Let him know you spoke with me so that we're all on the same page."

Celeste stood again and took three long strides to the door. Her insides were heating up and beginning to churn. There was something not quite right with the way Mindy Shelby was looking at her, but she couldn't put her finger on what. With her hand on the doorknob again, she opened it and stepped halfway over the threshold. "I appreciate you taking the time to speak with me, and I also appreciate your discretion."

Mindy nodded, but her mind already seemed to be elsewhere. "Thank you for coming to see me, and once again, I am sorry for my daughter's behavior, as well as for the loss of your husband. I'm new to this single mom thing, and I already find it daunting."

Ah, too bad your daughter is a conniving little witch, otherwise, I'd consider inviting you to the single mom wine night.

But then she abolished that thought as fast as it emerged. There was still something slightly off about Mindy. And Celeste hadn't vetted her club members as hard as she had only to let her guard down now and invite a dud or demon into the mix.

So rather than an invitation, she decided to leave with words of wisdom. "Love her as hard as you can. That's all that matters in the end. She'll remember the love and time you spent with her more than the arguments and the purchases. As hard as the hard days are, love her even harder and it will make those hard days just a bit easier." Then she took her leave of Mindy Shelby and booked it down the hallway toward the principal's office.

5

MAX STOOD in his classroom with his hands on his hips like Superman, taking in his new surroundings for the next ten months. It wasn't the best classroom—a little dark and had an odd smell in one corner, but it would do just fine to mold the minds of tomorrow. He grabbed the box off the table again and headed for the supply closet door when hurried footsteps outside in the hallway and an *"oh, thank God"* in a breathy voice had him turning around.

"There you are," Celeste said, looking in almost a panic.

He set the bin back down on the table. "What happened?"

Her eyes were wide, her cheeks rosy. "The guidance counselor is Eleanor Shelby's *mother!*"

No.

Did he know that already and he just didn't put two and two together? Shelby wasn't a super common last name, but it also wasn't overly uncommon either. He'd gone to high school with a guy name Dwight Travis who was a year older than him, and they were of no relation as far as they knew.

"So what did she say then when you told her about Eleanor?"

Celeste's face fell. "She said she'd talk to her daughter but say she found out about the bathroom graffiti and bullying from other sources. I'm still worried this is going to blow back on Sabrina though. I think I might have made a terrible mistake speaking to her at all."

He hadn't met any of the guidance counselors yet, but now he was worried to meet this one.

"What did Principal Pelton say?"

"He seemed deeply concerned but also said he wasn't prepared to point fingers as nobody *saw* Eleanor write on the walls and it was now gone."

"What the fuck?"

"My thoughts too. Did you find anything on any of the walls in the boys' room?"

He shook his head. He'd come up fruitless in that regard, thankfully, and he made sure to check every bathroom and every stall, which was why it'd taken him so long to finally get into his classroom.

Her shoulders relaxed slightly. "That's good at least."

"So Pelton's not going to do *anything?*"

"He said he'll keep an eye on things and that if there is more graffiti, Sabrina is to come to him instead of removing it herself. I just think she was trying to get it off the walls more than she was trying to place blame."

"But she was smart enough to take pictures first," he added.

"Yeah, she was. "

"So now what are you going to do?"

Celeste shook her head. "No clue. Worry. Homeschool?"

He smiled. "My mom told me that the day before you become a parent is the last worry-free day of your life."

She dipped her head. "She's not wrong there."

"Sabrina's in my class. I'll try to keep an eye on her. Eleanor's in one of my other freshman math classes. I'll keep an eye on her too, and I'll check the boys' bathrooms frequently to see if there is any new slander."

Her eyes closed. "Thank you."

"Sabrina's a good kid. Reminds me a lot of you and—"

"Her father?"

He nodded. "Looks like she got the best parts of you both. She's shy like you were but—"

"Brilliant like her father."

"You're no dunce. Never were."

Her cheeks turned an even darker pink. "She's a lot like him. Flies by the seat of her pants. Is messy as hell"—her eyes adopted a wistful glimmer—"but so incredibly kind. I spend far too much time worrying that she's going to be taken advantage of and that kindness will be killed by manipulation and greed from others."

"You can only arm them and protect them so much, but eventually she's going to have to figure out how the world works and how to fortify her heart on her own."

She glanced up at him. "You have kids?"

He shook his head. "No. But I've worked with them for over fifteen years, and I've picked up a few things along the way."

Twisting her lips to hold back a smile, she peeled away from where they stood, her nose wrinkling just as his had when he went to that part of the room. She glanced back at him while pointing to the supply closet door. "What's in here? Secret passageway to the long-lost treasure of Lakeview High?"

He shrugged and followed her. "I think it's just a closet. Let's open it and find out."

He unlocked the door with one of the keys Pelton had issued him for that room and turned the knob. The scent of the small room hit them hard like a bag of mothballs.

"Oh my." Celeste coughed.

Well, that would explain where the smell was coming from.

He'd need to air the place out. Get some Febreze, maybe one of those essential oil diffuser things his sister constantly had going in her house.

He stepped inside and flicked on a light.

The room was narrow but surprisingly long. Whoever his predecessor had been, the person had managed to get a wooden desk and chair into the room to act like an office.

Shelves lined all the walls on either side. Stacks of dusty, old, early edition textbooks sat next to boxes of graphing calculators. He pushed the door open wider and skirted around the desk to the worn wooden chair on wheels.

He fell into the old chair, and a puff of dust wafted up around him, along with a musty, old-man, body-odor and mothball smell. Who had taught here before him? A dinosaur with questionable personal hygiene? Seemed about right.

It groaned and squeaked beneath his weight when he swiveled to continue checking out his new "office." How many other teachers at the school had such a thing? Or was this a secret from everyone but those who taught in this very room?

Celeste stepped into the supply closet slash office as well and took a seat in the chair across from him. "This place is cool. Smells bad and has no windows, but it's neat that whoever it was turned this supply closet into an office of sorts."

Cool indeed.

Glancing around his new space, he took in the strings of cobwebs in each corner, the constant flickering of the light overhead, and the way one panel of the wooden wall seemed to be offset.

He reached forward and pulled on the panel. It gave way with no resistance, only to reveal a secret cubby hole.

"Even cooler," Celeste said, standing up and hinging forward over his desk. "What's in there? A treasure map to the lost gold of Lakewood High?"

Snorting, he shoved his hand into the hole and hoped nothing inside was alive and decided to bite him. Rabid and foaming at the mouth would not be a good look for him. His fingers wrapped around the neck of a glass bottle. "Not a map, but it's definitely treasure," he said, pulling out an unopened bottle of some nice-looking whiskey.

"I'm in the wrong profession," Celeste muttered. "Teachers leave each other gifts of booze. What do I get?"

"To work from home in your pajamas?" He reached back inside the cubbyhole and pulled out three more bottles—these were opened and half-full, but all coated in a thick layer of dust. Whiskey, scotch and gin. All nice choices too. None of that cheap shit they serve in the well at a local dive bar.

Raking his fingers through his hair, he studied the woman in front of him. Even though she seemed to have calmed down from when he saw her earlier, or when she'd come barreling into his classroom just now, she still looked frazzled, which, he hated to admit, made her look all the more gorgeous. Color filled her cheeks, her hair was a bit wild, and an alertness filled her eyes. He knew she was upset, worried and unsure what to do next. Like a doe caught in a thicket surrounded by cocked guns and hounds.

He stashed the booze back in its hidey-hole and stood up, maneuvering around his desk to perch one ass cheek on it. He was now directly in front of her, his crotch at eye level.

Fuck, he hadn't thought that move through. Could he move back behind his desk without it appearing awkward?

His eyes followed her gaze, which skimmed his body, down to the V of his legs. Her expression changed, too. She was no longer a doe caught in a thicket surrounded by hunters; she was a doe in oestrous. Heat radiated off her. Her nostrils flared, and the way her green eyes unabashedly stared for a fraction of a second too long at his crotch said she had a lot of dirty thoughts parading through that head of hers.

Clearing her throat, she stood up, but the space between where he sat perched on the desk and she was in the chair was so tight, they were face-to-face with barely enough room for a basketball between them.

Fire flickered in her eyes. They were close enough he could feel the warm puffs of her breath on his lips, the scent of her skin swirling around him like some intoxicating vortex of feminine musk and subtle hints of spice.

"It's not a terrible idea," he said on a shallow breath, the act of being so close to her without touching making his chest grow tight and his body ache.

"What's not?" she whispered, her eyes landing on his lips. Her pink tongue darted and slid across the seam of her mouth.

He barely contained the groan that fought its way up his chest. "Us."

She lifted a brow. "Us?"

"Yeah, *us*. We're both adults. Consenting. Single. It's not a bad idea at all. In fact, I think it's a tremendously *good* idea."

It was the best fucking idea he'd had all damn year.

Was it him, or were her breasts now straining against her top? Maybe it was just the way she was standing, with her back arched so as to give them a bit of distance even when there wasn't any to give. She was also breathing quite heavily.

"Max ..."

"I like the way you say my name."

Her eyes closed. He could see her resolve beginning to

crumble. She wanted this just as much as he did. Maybe more.

"We can't ..."

"Can't we?"

"Max ..."

He hadn't touched her, but fuck did he ever want to. He wanted to do more than just touch her. He wanted to pull her against him, take her lips with his and have his way with her right on the desk. But again, Celeste was worth so much more than a hot, quick fuck in a dank old office. She deserved to be wooed and courted. Seduced and treated to dinner and nights out. She deserved to be dated and shown that she was worth a man's time beyond fifteen minutes or so of hot, sweaty, naked fun.

Though with him, it'd be a hell of a lot longer than fifteen minutes.

Smiling, he pushed off from the desk and invaded her space just slightly. The heat and determination from the beguiling woman in front of him exuded from her in waves he felt through every cell of his body. But he engaged in some well-practiced biofeedback and tamped down the lust. He backed up next to his desk. "I'll let you go."

Her sigh of relief hit his bottom lip, making his cock twitch in his jeans. Her shoulders slumped slightly, and her breathing evened out. She skirted around the chair, putting as much distance between them as she could in the small, stuffy space. Blinking, her hand fell to the doorknob. "Is it hot in here?" She pulled the collar of her tank top away from her chest a few times and breathed out as if just having finished a run.

It was really hot in there.

He lifted one shoulder, leaned against his desk and crossed his arms. "I'm fine. Perhaps even a tad chilly." He glanced down at his nipples. They weren't hard. It would've been poetic if they had been.

Her eyes rolled, and an amused smirk curled her lips. "You're funny."

"You're beautiful."

The sharp inhale from her nose had him digging his nails into his arm to keep himself from launching forward, grabbing her and locking them both in there until she agreed that they weren't such a ridiculous idea. That they were a fan-fucking-tastic idea.

"Mr. Travis," she whispered.

"Max. Give me your number. I want to take you for dinner or coffee or something."

He'd always hated head games, but he did believe in fate —kind of. And the universe had put Celeste Howard into his path two weeks ago for a reason. It'd also put her into his path today for a reason, and he wasn't about to mess up their second encounter by not asking for her number.

She was back to having that sexy deer-in-a-thicket look to her, but the continuous flare of her nostrils and the sudden dilation of her pupils said she wasn't against the idea.

"Your number?" he probed.

The smile that spread across her face made his dick lurch, his heart pick up tempo and his whole temperature go up a couple of degrees. The smile went from elated to coy, just adding to her appeal. "You don't think it's a problem that you're my kid's teacher?"

"I think it'd be a problem if I were *your* teacher, but I'm not. Not anymore."

"So no problem?"

She grabbed her phone from her back pocket, fiddled on it for a moment and handed it to him. Her number was on the screen. "So no problem."

IT WAS SATURDAY AFTERNOON, Sabrina was at work at the bistro, and Celeste was busy working on a manuscript for one of her favorite authors. The woman was seriously a genius with words and constantly left Celeste in awe. It was always a joy to get her work and help it sparkle more brightly than it already did when it popped into her inbox.

With a cup of tea beside her, a half-eaten turkey sandwich and tired eyes from staring at a screen all day, she cracked her neck side to side and rubbed at her forehead. Her work day wasn't over yet, but she needed a break.

Taking the rest of her tea, she wandered out to her back deck, which was still in a fair bit of sun. It was warm on her bare shoulders and almost instantly chased away the tendrils of afternoon fatigue that had been coiling through her.

How powerful a little bit of Vitamin D could be.

With her eyes shut and her brain blank, she leaned over the rail and sipped her oolong.

It was days like today, when the sun was shining and the air was warm, that she really missed Declan. Even though he'd been gone for eight years, and it had gotten easier to be without him, she still missed him every single day.

He'd been the best father, the best husband and the best friend in the entire world, and in the blink of an eye, he was gone.

A soon-to-be father, Declan put his aspirations of college and law school on hold when they graduated high school, and he got a job immediately in construction. Over the years, he worked his way up in the company, and they even paid for him to get his journeyman ticket—which he did. Then, he had the opportunity to start his own company. It hadn't been easy or cheap, but he'd never steered Celeste wrong before, and when he came to her with his plan, she backed him up one hundred percent.

Of course, Declan's company succeeded. It did amazingly well in its first year, and Declan was already talking about expanding into other ventures and not just building houses for other people but building them for his own profit—for *their* profit, for their future.

But one rainy November day while on the job site for a new apartment complex, he slipped and fell out of window that didn't have the glass installed yet, and he landed on exposed rebar.

She was both grateful and furious that he'd died instantly. Relieved that he hadn't suffered or been in any pain but angry that she'd never had the chance to say goodbye. To kiss him one last time. To tell him how much she loved him and always would.

They'd had the discussion several times during their marriage, particularly after Sabrina was born, about what they would want if something happened to either of them. She wouldn't want him to raise Sabrina alone or live his life alone. She knew how much he loved her, but she also wanted him to be happy. And he had felt the same for her.

Easier said than done when you lived life in the hypothetical, though.

But now that she lived the reality of it, it was still tough to imagine any man coming close to replacing Declan in her heart, her bed or her home.

But she was lonely.

She had Sabrina, but Sabrina was getting older and wasn't home as often. And soon she would leave the nest, be off to college, and Celeste would be on her own.

Then what?

Did she really want to wait another three years before she started looking for a man? That would put her at thirty-six, and although that wasn't *old*, it did limit the dating pool more than it was now.

Opening her eyes, she glanced out into the parking lot of her townhouse complex. Children raced their bikes, scribbled with chalk on the sidewalk and played jump rope and hopscotch. It was amazing how games of her own youth never lost their popularity. Would Sabrina's children and Sabrina's children's children still play the same games years from now? She hoped so.

As she was about to head back inside and tackle the remaining three chapters of the manuscript, her phone warbled in the back pocket of her jeans.

Thank you, caller ID.

Max Travis.

Finishing her tea to dampen her palate and stall for a moment, she hit the green button, shut her eyes and put the phone to her ear. "Hello?"

"Celeste, it's Max ... *Mr. Travis?*" The unease in his tone was charming. Like she might have forgotten who he was since yesterday.

That could not be further from the truth. She hadn't been able to stop thinking about him, particularly the way his jeans left very little to the imagination when he sat on the corner of his desk the way he did. That image alone had made her Friday night with Henry Cavill—aka her battery-operated boyfriend—one hell of a memorable one.

She pushed the memory of Max's lap out of her head, cleared her throat and finally responded. "Max, hi. How are you?" *I was hoping you'd call.*

More like praying, wishing and willing it. But she wasn't about to say that.

She could hear his sigh of relief over the phone, and it made her smile. "Good. What are you up to?"

"Like right *now?*"

"Yeah." The man was obviously not a fan of small talk or prolonged pleasantries.

"It's a work day. Sabrina's working at the bistro, and I'm trying to finish up a manuscript. But as much as I love this author and her work, my eyes are glazing over every time I look at the screen. And it has nothing to do with *her* or the content. I think I'm just burnt out. I stare at screens all day long. My eyes hurt."

"What time is Sabrina off work?"

She glanced at her phone to check the time. It was only one o'clock.

"Five, why?"

"Play hooky from work and come meet me for a coffee."

"Now?"

"Yeah, why not?"

Yeah, why not?

She failed to come up with a reason, besides the fact that she wasn't wearing any makeup, had her red hair up in a messy topknot and couldn't remember if she'd put on deodorant that day. The perks of working from home were the same as the downside. You didn't have to dress to impress, but you never knew when the UPS guy was going to look like a Chippendales dancer or you were going to be invited out for an impromptu date.

"You still there?" he asked.

"Uh, yeah. Sorry. Sure, I can do coffee. Want to give me like half an hour?"

"Totally. Do you want me to come and get you, or should we meet somewhere?"

Heat and anticipation spiraled through her at the thought of going on a date with Mr. Travis. Even something as innocuous as a midday coffee.

"How about we meet at See You Latte Café in the university district? It shouldn't be too busy yet, as classes have only *just* started."

"I think I know where you're talking. Sounds good. So like, forty-five minutes?"

She smelled under her arms. She should shower, just in case.

In case of what?

In case of anything.

"How about an hour?"

"See you in an hour." He hung up.

Celeste wandered back into her house and set her phone down on the kitchen counter, unable to blink, her body full of pins and needles. She sent a group text to Bianca and Lauren. *I have a date with my math teacher.*

She was just pulling up to the café when the sexy purr of a motorcycle turning the corner had her pausing mid-park. A car behind her honked, making her jump, apologize, even though they couldn't hear her, and pull the rest of the way into the parking stall.

She double-checked her lipstick in the rearview mirror before unbuckling her belt and exiting her Volvo SUV. Max was just parking his motorcycle and pulling off his full-face helmet.

"Nice set of wheels you've got there," she said, allowing her eyes to travel the length of him. Like the other day, he wore biker boots, dark jeans, a black T-shirt, a leather jacket and aviator sunglasses. He was what orgasms were made of.

With a grin that made her fresh panties instantly damp, he locked his helmet to his bike, pushed his shades up into his hair and gave her a chin lift. "I'd love to take you for a ride sometime."

Was that an innuendo?

Had he intended it to be?

The pink that flooded his cheeks beneath his scruff said

he hadn't meant it to be the double entendre it came across as. That only made her want him more.

He cleared his throat. "What I mean is, if you ever want to hop on the back, I'd be more than happy to take you for a ride *on ... my ... motorcycle.*"

Smiling like a buffoon, she giggled. "Either-or is fine by me."

Damn, where had that come from?

He was obviously wondering the same thing, because the sexy smile and new smolder in his eyes said she'd shocked him with her response too.

"Shall we?" she asked, tilting her head toward the front door of the café.

He nodded. "You find a seat out here under one of the umbrellas, and I'll go grab our drinks. What's your poison?"

"Chai latte with extra cinnamon on top, please."

"You got it." He winked, and then he was gone.

She had to keep herself from swooning.

She was, after all, a thirty-three-year-old woman. Her swooning days were over. Weren't they?

She found them an empty two-top bistro table tucked off in the corner with an umbrella guarding them from the intense glare of the sun. The café was a popular study destination for students but also a hotspot for many Seattle coffee lovers who wanted to step outside of the Starbucks box. Once a month, they hosted a poetry slam and usually had an acoustic guitarist playing on Friday and Saturday nights.

Celeste just liked the place because they made the best lattes and chai cinnamon buns in town.

She glanced at her phone but didn't unlock it. Instead she checked her hair and makeup in the black of her screen. She'd showered, but she knew she wouldn't have time to wash *and* blow-dry her long, red tresses, so she'd just hit the crown of her head with some dry shampoo, did a bit of a fluff and hoped for the best.

The door to the café opened, and out walked Max, two to-go cups in his hands along with a brown paper bag. He spotted her and made his way over, giving her another view of his whole body and a chance to do a little swoon from that sexy swagger.

"Your latte, m'lady," he said, plunking the cup down in front of her. "And I grabbed us a chai cinnamon bun to share as well. They're massive, and they looked really good."

Oh, he was already scoring bonus points.

She thanked him for his drink and took a sip. Damn, that was good.

He took a seat across from her. "So, how have you been?"

"You mean, since you last saw me, yesterday? Or in the last fifteen years?"

He smiled over the lid of his drink. "Both."

She glanced at the paper bag with the cinnamon bun in it. "Well, first thing you should know about me: I'm a terrible sharer. I usually eat one of those things myself."

Those smiles of his were going to dehydrate her. She just knew it. And the matching dimples? Those were lethal.

"Say no more. I'll be right back." He made to get up, but she grabbed his arm, his skin warm and soft beneath her fingers. But when she tightened her grip, all she felt was muscle.

"I'm just kidding," she said. Which was only *half* true.

He slid his arm out from her grasp but then squeezed her hand. "What the lady wants, the lady gets." He let go of her hand and was gone again before she could say another word, leaving her with a tingly sensation on her hand where he'd touched her.

It'd been so long since she'd felt any kind of a spark or a true connection with a man that she forgot what it was like.

And back then, as a horny teenager in love for the first time, it was like rainbows, unicorns and fireworks all the damn time. Now she was older, more mature, and the way she reacted to a man's touch was different.

Though no less exhilarating.

He was back in a flash, the smile on his face rivaling the sun in its brilliance.

He took his seat and placed another brown paper bag in front of her. "Grabbed you two, *just* in case."

She opened the bag and peered inside, where lo and behold, two decadent chai cinnamon buns sat oozing caramelized sugar and dripping with frosting She dipped her finger into the thick frosting of one and popped it into her mouth.

The heat from his eyes scorched her.

"Careful," Max said slowly.

She lifted her eyebrows but smiled coyly. "So, *Mr.—Max,* tell me all about Vietnam and your travels. It looks like you did some fishing?"

His head reared back, and his eyes narrowed. "How did you know that?"

Oh shit.

She took another sip of her latte and averted her eyes. "My friends may have Googled you and found you on social media." She glanced back to see his reaction.

Oh, thank God, he was smiling.

"They did, did they? Does that mean you've been talking about me?"

She shrugged. "I may have mentioned *in passing* that I'd bumped into my *old* math teacher and that the years have not been kind to him. Hardly recognized the guy, what for all the gray nose and ear hair."

He tossed his head back and laughed. "I had an orthodontist like that. Dr. Gallagher. It was torture having to stare into his face when he tightened my braces. I thought mice were trying to escape through his nostrils."

Celeste jolted in her chair and slammed her hand on the table. "Oh my God, I had him as an orthodontist, too!" She put her hand in front of her nose and wiggled her fingers. "Eva and I used to run around the house and chase each other like this, taking turns who was the *Dr. Gallagher Monster.*"

Max laughed. "It was the worst." He flashed her a big, cheesy smile. "Guy knew his way around teeth and hardware, though."

She smiled big as well. "That he did."

He opened up his paper bag and pulled off a piece of cinnamon bun. "So, what other photos of mine did you and your friends ogle?"

6

THEY WERE four weeks into the school year now, and Max and Celeste had been on a total of one date.

One.

It'd been two weeks since they'd had coffee, and Max was already going through some serious Celeste withdrawals.

And it wasn't like he didn't want to take her out again. The woman was just incredibly busy and didn't have the time.

But she said she would make the time Saturday afternoon, which incidentally was tomorrow, so he needed to start planning.

They texted a lot, which was fun, but it wasn't the same as seeing her. She hadn't told Sabrina she was seeing him, since they'd only been on one date and she wasn't ready to cross that bridge with her child.

But one thing was for sure. Max was definitely interested in pursuing the relationship with Celeste, even if she wanted to take it slow.

Since he was Sabrina's teacher, Celeste didn't want to rush into things and complicate the first month of school for Sabrina even more than it already was.

Celeste's words, not his. But he understood.

It was torture for him, of course, because all he wanted to do was take Celeste home with him and *teach* her a few things, but he understood her hesitations.

In his opinion, Celeste wasn't giving her daughter enough credit and was blowing the whole thing a bit out of proportion, but he wasn't a parent, so he had no clue how these things worked.

It was Friday afternoon, and he was sitting in his makeshift office eating his lunch and catching up on the news on his phone.

This was normally the time of day he and Celeste caught up with each other. She would take her lunch break at home, usually with a turkey sandwich and sparkling water while she sat on her deck, and he ate his leftover burrito from last night's dinner in his dusty, *slightly* mothball-scented closet. The essential oil diffuser he bought and the oil blend his sister suggested were doing wonders to mask the mothball stench.

He waited for Celeste's text.

Like clockwork, because the woman was nothing if not organized, predictable and scheduled to the minute, she texted him at 12:05 on the dot.

Hey, how's your day?

He didn't bother responding and just called her.

"Hey," she answered on the second ring, her mouth full of food. "How goes the day?"

He chewed his burrito, swallowed. "Day's been all right. Thought my head was going to explode earlier, given the way Eleanor was glaring at me. That kid has some serious issues."

Celeste grumbled. "Yeah, Sabrina messaged me earlier. Apparently, Eleanor is up to her old tricks from last week. There was a new message on the bathroom wall."

Fuck. He'd go check the boys' bathrooms before he left

for the day. Last week, he'd only been able to find one message about Sabrina in the boys' room, and he'd removed it immediately. "What did it say?"

"Sabrina Howard is a slutty little snitch who'll give head for a stick of gum."

"What the fuck?"

"I know. I'm livid. I think I need to come back to the school. Talk to Pelton and Mindy again. Sabrina said she left it on the wall and went and told the principal, but I don't know if anything has been done about it. She just wants it *off* the wall, but I told her to wait and show Pelton."

"I'll follow up on that. But you should wait until Monday before you talk to Pelton. I'll make sure all the bathroom walls in the school are slander-free, but I think it's best to tackle this Monday with a clear head. When you've had time to calm down."

Was that a growl? "Did you just tell me to calm down?"

Yep, it'd been a growl. Shit.

"No. I didn't. I just know that last week you came in here on a rampage, and I don't know how well it was received. I will go talk to Pelton and make sure *he* speaks to Mindy and Eleanor's father. The girl needs to be stopped."

She made another noise in her throat. "Fine, but I'm not going to sit by and let my daughter be humiliated by some little high school bitch with an ax to grind. I will protect my baby."

"That's fine, but let me help you."

He practically felt her sigh on the other end, it was so deep and dramatic. But he also felt her frustration, her helplessness and her pain. His mother had once told him that you are only as happy as your unhappiest child, and since Celeste only had the one kid and Sabrina wasn't having the greatest time at school, he could only imagine she wasn't doing too well either.

"Fine," she finally said. "Can we change the subject? My sandwich is really good, but this is making me lose my appetite."

Chuckling, he checked the time on his phone. Lunch at the school ran from eleven forty-five until twelve thirty. They had a little over fifteen minutes left to talk.

"What are you doing tonight?" she asked. "Any big plans? A hot date perhaps?"

"Hot date is tomorrow," he quipped. "Tonight is the staff mixer at Prime."

"Ohhh, that's right. Teachers gone wild."

"Something like that." He laughed. "What about you?"

"No plans."

Damn, now he wished he didn't have the stupid mixer to go to and they could move their date up.

"Well, get some rest. We have a *big* day tomorrow."

He could hear her smile in her response. "Do we now. Like what?"

"What time do you have to drop Sabrina off at work?"

She groaned. "Eight."

"Yikes. Okay, we'll grab breakfast then. I'll be by to get you at nine."

"Do I get to ride"—*you*—"on the back of the motorcycle?"

"Unless you'd prefer if I came and grabbed you in my pickup?"

"I'd like to ride on the back of your motorcycle." That made his dick stand up. He'd wanted nothing more—well, besides Celeste in every way shape and form—than having her on the back of his bike. Her thighs squeezing his, her tits up against his back, hands on his stomach. He'd love to fuck her on his bike too. Find a secluded place somewhere near a lake or something.

"I'd like that too."

Did she just purr? His dick jumped again.

"So I'll come get you. We'll go for a drive, maybe to Mukilteo. I know a cute little breakfast place right on the water."

"Sounds wonderful."

"Not sure how keen you are on old books, but they have an awesome used book store there too. Lots of first-edition stuff that is hard to find anywhere else."

"Did you steal my diary from when I was thirteen?" she asked, her voice almost a whisper.

He chuckled and took another bite of his lunch. "No. Why?"

"That's like my *ideal* first date."

Gold stars and bonus points for him. Woot woot!

Still laughing, he tucked his food into his cheek. "I'm not big on reading teenagers' diaries, I have to admit. But I am glad I'm not proposing a date that is going to bore you."

"It honestly sounds like the best date, Max. I can't wait."

He swallowed his lunch and stored the empty container in his backpack below his desk. He had five minutes to hit the bathroom before class started. "I can't either. Next time don't make me wait two weeks to take you on another date, okay?"

Her giggle was deep and throaty and stirred all kinds of things inside him. "I promise."

"See you tomorrow, Celeste."

"Not if I see you first," she said.

He was about to ask what she meant by that, but she'd ended the call.

Was she going to show up on his doorstep at midnight tonight wearing nothing but a trench coat and heels? Did she even know where he lived?

How deep did her friends dig when they Googled him?

FRIDAY NIGHT, Celeste gripped the brass handle of the big wooden door and heaved it toward herself. "If anybody asks, it was *your* idea to come here," she said to her sister, allowing Eva to walk ahead of her and into Prime Sports Bar and Grill.

Eva gave her a weird look. "What do you mean? We come here all the time. Mason owns the place."

Celeste dipped her head and let her hair fall down around her face so when they entered the bar, she wouldn't be immediately recognizable. "I know that, but ..."

"Hey, they're already here. Snagged the good booth. Come on." Eva grabbed Celeste's arm and hauled her off into the corner where Lauren, Bianca and Richelle were already sitting, glasses of sangria in front of them while a big, beautiful pitcher dripping with condensation was smack-dab in the center of their table.

Eva scooted in next to Richelle, and Celeste took up the last spot next to Lauren.

"Uh-uh," Lauren said, shaking her head. "Switch spots with me. I have to pee like every twenty minutes, so I need to be on the end."

Rolling her eyes, but understanding better than anything, Celeste stood back up and waited for Lauren to stand. Her friend slid her slender frame with the basketball under her dress out of the booth so Celeste could slide in.

"Thanks," Lauren said with a heavy exhale, plopping back down into the booth. She reached for her drink. "Mason made me a virgin sangria. Though it's pretty much just sparkling grape juice with chunks of fruit in it." She sighed and sipped her drink. "I miss booze."

"Only a few more months to go," Eva said with an understanding smile.

There were empty glasses next to the pitcher, so Richelle began to pour Celeste and Eva their own drinks.

"I'm glad we're doing this," Richelle said, pushing

Celeste's drink toward her. "I mean, I know I have another wine night tomorrow when the guys play poker, but this is great too. I missed having girlfriends." She bumped shoulders with Bianca and then Eva. "And now I also have sisters."

Bianca grinned. So did Eva.

"It's too bad Paige and Zara couldn't make it," Eva said.

"Where are they?" Lauren asked, making a slurping sound with her straw as she drained her drink.

"Zara's visiting with an out-of-town friend, I think. And Paige had a catering gig." Eva thanked Richelle for her drink.

Commotion at the front door drew their attention away from one another. At least ten people between the ages of thirty and seventy wandered into the bar, chatting and laughing. They paused, checked with Mason behind the bar and made their way toward a series of tables on the other side, all pushed together to form a long line.

"Party?" Bianca asked, glancing at her phone.

"Must be," Richelle said. She shook her head and rolled her amber eyes. "Stop looking at your phone. The kids are fine."

Bianca glanced at her phone again before turning it screen-side down on the table. "It's not my kids I'm worried about. It's the girls. My kids are crazy."

"Sabrina and Mallory know how to babysit, and Hannah, Hayley and Charlie love them. Mallory hasn't come home once saying the kids were too difficult. And with both girls there, I'm sure they'll have those little ones in bed, no problem." Richelle nodded at Mason, who was already on his way over, his big frame and tattoos an intimidating presence unless you knew him for the teddy bear that he was.

"Good evening, ladies," he said, flashing that big, panty-dropping grin. "How are we doing?"

"Would be better if we could get some of those killer

nachos on our table," Richelle said sassily. "Extra jalapenos, please."

Mason's smile grew, which only made him that much more handsome. "You got it. Extra guac?"

"Need you ask?" Eva teased.

He laughed and nodded. "And how are we for drinks? Another pitcher?"

"Keep 'em coming," Richelle said. "I cabbed, so I'm free to get blottoed."

Eyes around the table widened, curious glances exchanged.

"Tough day in the salt mines, Richelle?" Mason asked.

Richelle's smile faltered a bit. "It was a little, yeah. New client, sad story. Need to get my mind off her predicament for the weekend before I go in ready to kick ass and take names on Monday."

Like her husband, Richelle was a divorce attorney. She was known as *the* woman to go to in town if you wanted to nail your cheating-ass husband's taint to the wall. She had a soft spot for women who were victims of domestic abuse and often took their cases pro bono or offered a reduced fee. The only problem was, she tended to get a bit emotionally involved in those cases and brought those emotions home with her. Which was why when she got together with her friends, with the people she trusted, she let loose.

"I'll send a round of shots then." Mason's perma-grin dipped, and his expression became somber and understanding. "Just let me know if you guys need anything else." He jerked his head toward the long table. "It's going to get loud in here. Teachers' mixer is starting up over there. They're expecting like forty or so people. "

Celeste watched Lauren and Bianca's postures change. They had a wordless conversation with their eyes.

Shit.

"I'll go order your nachos." Mason took his leave of them just as the doors at the front opened again and in walked Max.

"Oh my God," Lauren whispered, well, more like purred.

"Did you know?" Bianca asked, her eyes glued to Max as he stood by the doors and surveyed the room. He spoke a few words to Mason, who pointed in the direction of the ten teachers already at the long table. Max nodded, smiled and headed off to the table, the farthest away from Celeste he could possibly get. Thank God.

"Did she know what?" Richelle asked. To look at her, you'd never expect her to be the fierce woman she was. Not quite five feet tall, with a slim build, pixie-short blonde hair and fine features, she looked more like a wood nymph than she did a ferocious attorney. But you'd be an idiot to assume she didn't have sharp claws and teeth that were no stranger to a man's jugular.

"That Max was going to be at the bar tonight," Lauren finished, the woman's blue eyes following Max across the bar. "Well, hello, Professor."

"He's not a professor," Celeste said, grimacing and sinking down into the booth to hide herself.

Lauren licked her lips. "I don't care. I'd let him find my square root."

Jesus.

Richelle snorted. "Horny much?"

Lauren made a pained face and rubbed her belly. "So much."

"Can someone please tell me what the hell is going on?" Eva asked. She and Richelle exchanged confused looks. Eva and Celeste looked a lot alike. Both had long, dark red hair, green eyes and fair skin. Only Eva was taller and had curves Celeste would kill for. She'd always been envious of her older sister's beauty, feeling ordinary and bland in comparison.

"The man candy that just walked in the door, who Lauren is currently eye-fucking like he's made out of silicone and has ten speeds, is Celeste's old math teacher," Bianca said, catching everyone up.

"Mr. Travis!" Eva blurted out loud enough for people three booths down to hear her.

"Shhhh," Lauren, Bianca and Celeste all scolded.

"Mr. Travis?" Eva whispered. She craned her neck around the booth to look, then spun back to face them all. "That hottie that just walked in, the one with the dimples, *that's* Mr. Travis?"

Celeste nodded and sank deeper into the booth. What had she been thinking coming here when she knew he was going to be there too? They were going out on a date tomorrow. Couldn't she wait?

Obviously not. She wanted to see him. She also wanted her friends to see him.

She wasn't entirely sure what came over her when she got off the phone with Max earlier, but as soon as he reminded her it was his staff mixer at Prime that night, she was texting her friends for a last-minute ladies' night at Prime.

"He and Celeste bumped into each other a few weeks ago," Lauren started to explain. "Sparks flew, nearly caught the mall on fire, as well as their underwear. And they have a date tomorrow." She bobbed her eyebrows up and down. "Though it looks like she's not interested in waiting to find Professor Washboard's square root tomorrow. She wants it tonight."

Celeste groaned.

Bianca grinned.

"So you knew he was going to be here?" Eva asked. Her eyes went wide, and she slammed her hands on the table, leaning forward. "Is that why you told me that if anyone asked, it was my idea to come here?" Her mouth opened in shock. "Are you stalking—"

"Professor Washboard," Lauren cut in. "That's the nickname we have for him at the moment. But we're open to suggestions."

Eva's head shook. "What are you getting into, Celeste? Is he Sabrina's teacher?"

Celeste shrugged, sinking even deeper into the booth. "We've only been on one date so far. And it was just coffee. We're spending the day together tomorrow, though. Breakfast in Mukilteo and then ..." She shrugged. "Who knows?"

"I know," Lauren said with a sassy smile and nod.

Celeste leaned over in the booth to see if she could see him.

Her insides quivered when she finally caught a glimpse of his profile. He looked so damn good. Dark jeans, black biker boots, a leather jacket and a dark black button-down shirt. It also looked like he'd skipped a shave, and thick, dark stubble coated his chiseled jaw.

"Shots!" A young waitress with a hooped nose ring and a half-sleeve of black and white floral tattoos came over with a tray. Eight shot glasses sat full on the tray. The waitress's eyes fell to Lauren. "Mason wants to know if you want more sparkling grape juice."

Lauren made a pouty face, slurped back the rest of her drink and nodded. "Yes, please."

Celeste sat up and reached for a shot. She slammed it back. It was good. It was potent. She had no idea what it was, but the tang and sweetness, not to mention all the alcohol in it, zipped right down to her toes.

"So you've been on one date, and you're going on another," Eva said, concern in her eyes. They were almost the same shade of green as Celeste's but perhaps a touch darker.

Celeste nodded. "Yes."

"Have you kissed yet?"

She shook her head. "I need to take this slow. I haven't really played the field much since Declan, and since he's Sabrina's teacher, I don't want to jump in with both feet in case it doesn't work out and then Sabrina is left with an awkward year in math."

"Does she know yet?"

Another head shake. "I'll tell her when there is something to tell. Right now, we're just spending time together. She's having a rough enough time as it is at school right now. I don't want to add this to her plate. You know how much of a worrywart my kid can be."

"What's going on at school?" Richelle asked, sipping her sangria.

Celeste squeezed her eyes shut for a moment before she opened them, reached into the center of the table and took another shot. "Ah, let's start from the beginning."

"And this little Eleanor Shelby bitch is still walking the halls of that school?" Richelle asked, her tiny fists glowing with white knuckles and her face red and pinched with fury. "How the fuck has she not been expelled already?"

"Nobody *saw* her do it," Celeste said blandly. "At least nobody that is willing to come forward and admit that she did it. But we all know she did. Nobody at school has an ax to grind against Sabrina. She's well-liked."

"And her mother has done dick all?" Eva asked.

"Dick. All," Celeste repeated.

The slight squeak of the heavy wooden front doors echoed through the large space to reveal none other than the demoness herself.

"Speak of the devil," Celeste murmured.

Mindy Shelby stood just in front of the wooden doors, every bit the cougar. She'd even worn a bit of leopard print to fit the bill. Not that Celeste didn't love a good animal-print top or shoes, but Mindy's bold leopard-print cropped jacket was paired with tight black pants—think Sandy from *Grease* at the end of the movie—and a white top with frills along the low cut, drawing attention to her cleavage. And if that outfit didn't say she was hunting, the strappy five-inch gold stilettos on her feet would have said as much. Her dark hair fell in thick curls around her shoulders, and her makeup looked professionally done. She was stunning. She really was.

"Pretty woman," Eva said with a sneer.

"She is lovely," Celeste agreed. "I'm not one to cut a woman down, and Mindy Shelby is gorgeous. But she's on the prowl."

"You here to stop her from coming on to Max?" Bianca asked. "Is that why you're here?"

Celeste wasn't going to lie and say that the thought hadn't crossed her mind when she figured out that the gorgeous Mindy Shelby and Max were going to be at a party together where there was alcohol. She had no plans to infiltrate their soiree, but she didn't mind playing the fly on the wall, at least for a little while.

They all watched as Mindy spied the table of teachers and clickety-clacked her way over. Her eyes—along with everyone else's—fell on Max, and she elbowed her way through the standing, chatty mass of educators until she was at his elbow. He glanced at her, smiled and said hello.

Celeste's gut did a gigantic flip-flop, and a little green-eyed monster murmured something mean from her perch atop Celeste's shoulder.

She told the monster to shut up.

Mason arrived with another pitcher of sangria, the same waitress as earlier in his wake with a giant tray of nachos and all the condiments to go with it.

Lauren dove into the nachos like she hadn't eaten in a week. "I'm so glad this kid hasn't given me any major food aversions. Just the appetite of a wrestler." She heaped salsa onto a big stack of chips and gracelessly shoveled it into her mouth.

Everyone tucked into the nachos.

Try as she might to keep herself focused on her friends, Celeste's gaze kept veering back to the teacher's party. In a sea of over forty people, Max was easy to pick out. He was taller than most, and his carefree smile and the way his lips parted and curled up when he laughed made her insides tighten and her nipples bead into painful points.

She must have been looking too hard at him, or too long, because he broke his eye contact with the man he was speaking to and glanced up, his gaze hitting her square between the eyes. His expression changed instantly. Gray eyes widened, smile wobbled.

Oh shit.

She averted her gaze, but it was too late.

He took his leave of the man beside him, and with purposeful strides he made his way toward their table.

Oh shit.

Oh shit!

OH SHIT!

"Ladies," he said, his voice smooth, his smile cocky. But despite that cockiness, Celeste's body did rebellious things. Heat flooded her face, her heart pounded in her ears, and what was going on in her lower belly and between her legs was something she usually read in one of her dirty romance novels.

"Professor," Lauren cooed.

His brows narrowed in confusion. "I'm not a—"

"Just ignore her," Richelle said.

Lauren sat upright in her seat and fixed Richelle with a glare. "Hey!"

Celeste squeezed her eyes shut and shrank behind Bianca. This was not happening. This was not happening.

"Fancy seeing you here, Celeste. Ladies' night on the town?" He leaned one shoulder on the wooden panel above their booth seats.

"Just a bunch of single moms having some drinks and chilling out after another week with our children," Bianca said. "I mean, Richelle and Eva have men, but they were single moms once, so we let them hang with us."

Richelle and Eva snorted.

"Thanks," Eva said sarcastically.

Bianca shot her a big grin. "Love you, sister."

Eva rolled her eyes and smiled back. "Love you too."

"We also know Mason, the owner," Richelle added. "He's a good friend. So we come here to support him."

"And get the freebies," Lauren added, scooping another enormous pile of guac-covered nacho chips into her mouth.

Max's eyes landed on Celeste. "Oh, well, here I thought I had a stalker. After all, I *did* tell you that the teachers' mixer was happening tonight at Prime, right?"

Flames licked up her cheeks, and heat swirled in her gut.

To say she was embarrassed was an understatement.

She couldn't explain why she felt the necessity to be where he was going to be, but then sometimes things were so primal, so *need*-driven, they were beyond rationality. She was going to chalk this up to one of those times.

She was irrationally driven to sort of stalk him because he made her feel things she hadn't felt in a long time and looked at her in a way that made parts of her body tingle in a very pleasant way.

She also wanted to see his interaction with Mindy.

"Celeste?"

Lauren nudged her.

Oh shit!

She'd been staring at the cords in his forearms and the way they bulged and rippled when he clenched his fist. She swallowed and shook her head to clear the sexy cobwebs. "Huh?"

Snickers drifted around the table. Max's mouth lifted into an even bigger, even cockier smile—if that was possible. And there were those damn dimples again. "I said you look nice tonight."

Now her whole body was engulfed in a white-hot blaze.

She swallowed, sipped her drink and looked up at him beneath her lashes. "Thank you. So do you."

His grin was huge, his dimples now in full-on attack mode. "So it was pure coincidence you being here tonight then?"

He was goading her now, enjoying the way she squirmed in her seat.

She cleared her throat and tossed her shoulders back. Two could play this game. "Oh, was that tonight? Here? I don't remember. I mean, like Richelle said, we come here all the time. Do these ladies' nights often. Pure coincidence." She smiled, but it was fake. Anybody could see that.

Lauren snorted next to her. "About as much of a coincidence as this baby is the product of immaculate conception."

"Filter," Bianca hissed, glaring at Lauren.

Lauren shrugged and ate more nachos.

"I'm going to assume your friends are in the know," Max said, his gray gaze hitting each woman equally before he leveled it back on Celeste.

"They are," she said with a swallow.

Max nodded. Celeste swore she heard each one of her friends sigh.

His lips pressed together to form a flat line, but even that didn't detract from how good-looking he was. "Well, I suppose I should return to my party, though yours looks a hell of a lot more fun." He glanced back toward his group and their tables before swinging his gaze to Celeste again. "Don't drink too much. I don't think you want to ride on the bike with a hangover tomorrow. It's not much fun." He winked and was about to turn and leave when Lauren reached out and snagged his arm.

"We're watching you, bub. She's our friend, and I might be pregnant and able to wash my socks on your stomach, but that doesn't mean I still won't kick your ass if you hurt her."

"Filter," Bianca hissed again.

"The filter broke when the condom did," Lauren snapped back. "It was never very thick to begin with." She finished her sparkling grape juice and glared at Bianca before pinning her gaze back on Max.

"Neither was the condom, apparently," Eva said under her breath.

Max's lip twitched, and his eyes sparkled. "Friends who have your back are the best." He hit each woman with his gaze once again before focusing it back on Celeste. "My *intentions* with your friend are pretty clear. I like her, and I want to date her. I have no intention of hurting her. If anybody gets their heart broken here, it'll definitely be me."

"Hot and respectful," Bianca whispered. "I bet he never got his secretary pregnant with twins."

Max glanced at her with confusion. "I haven't and I wouldn't ... I don't have a secretary. I mean the *school* has a secretary, but I just met her, and I think she's old enough to be my mom." He focused back on Celeste, which only made her whole body feel like someone had thrown her into the mouth of a volcano. Was her upper lip sweating? She certainly felt like the back of her neck was damp. The look Max was giving her was as if no other person were at the table, as if no other person were in the entire building. The place could have been engulfed in flames—no doubt from her burning loins—and he probably wouldn't have noticed. His eyes were only for her.

"That's hot," Lauren whispered, biting into a chip but staring at Max.

He removed his elbow from the wooden partition of the booth and nodded at all of them, his eyes still on Celeste. "Enjoy your evening, ladies." He turned to see their waitress behind him. "Next round is on me, please. Add it to my tab." Then he took his leave of them, but not before hitting Celeste one more time with a look that liquefied her insides.

"Another pitcher?" the waitress asked, taking away the tray of empty shot glasses.

"You know it," Eva said. "After what just went down, the night's just getting started."

7

BECAUSE HE RODE his bike to Prime, Max only had a couple of beers in his three and a half hours at the pub, so he was A-OK to ride home. He'd excused himself to use the bathroom after paying his tab, only to emerge and find Celeste and her table of friends gone.

It'd made him happy to see her sitting over there in the booth. Had she shown up because she knew he was going to be there? The reactions of her friends and the way she was cowering in her seat said that she had. He liked that.

He'd done everything he possibly could all night to avoid Mindy—the woman was looking for a new man to call *hers*. She kept finding ways to get herself next to him. Whether they were sitting or standing, within five minutes she had pulled up a chair, switched seats with someone or simply sidled up to him, taking up residence next to his elbow, which was at the exact same height as her breasts.

She'd also ordered herself an entire bottle of white wine and had polished it off in an impressive amount of time. He worried about her on those ridiculously high shoes. The woman was going to break her neck or at the very least roll an ankle based on the way she was walking.

"Max!" Speak of the devil. "I thought I saw you head to the bathroom. Are you leaving?" There was a mild slur to her speech, and it was a lot higher-pitched than earlier in the evening. Whinier too. She was behind him but not for long. Her arm looped beneath his, and she pressed her body against his side, holding on to his arm with her free hand. "Want to share a cab?" she asked. "I'm done here. But I'm still up for a party." The way she said *party* made his mouth dip into a frown. He was quick to stow it, though, before she glanced up at him all hopeful and flirty.

"Ah, maybe another time, Mindy," he said, gently prying her fingers from his arm and sliding out from her grasp. "I rode my bike, and I only have one helmet." That was a lie, but no way was he letting her drunk ass on the back of his bike. She'd probably slide her hand down his pants and cause an accident.

He normally wore a full-face helmet, but he kept a small, bucket-style helmet clipped on the sissy bar at the back just in case. Since he'd had a motorcycle of some kind his entire life, he'd learned early on it was a good idea to carry a spare. It was a pain in the ass, but he would never be able to live with himself if he could have helped somebody get home or out of a dangerous situation but didn't because he didn't have an extra helmet with him. And his mother had made him swear on a freaking Bible that he'd never ride his bike without a helmet, so giving someone his and riding without one himself wasn't an option.

"Oh, poo." She pouted.

He made sure they were a respectable and unassuming distance apart before they came into view of the people at their table. The last thing he needed was a rumor about him and a colleague hooking up within the first month of school.

"Your cab is outside for you, miss," their waitress said to Mindy when she spotted her.

Mindy made a deeper pout. "I guess this is goodbye."

Max forced a smile. "I guess it is. I will see you on Monday. Enjoy your weekend."

With a drunk, glazed-over expression, Mindy nodded. "You too." Wobbling on those ridiculous heels and causing a few people in the restaurant to hold their breath, she nearly fell over completely as she made her way to the door. But she must have been an expert in those contraptions because she caught her balance, tittered, teetered, swung the door open and left.

He said his final goodbyes to the table and made his own exit, taking care to leave more than enough time for Mindy to catch her cab and leave. The last thing he needed was to head outside only to find her waiting there for him. She'd probably think he did it on purpose and interpret it as a come-on, pushing him into an alley and ravishing him.

More like ravage.

The air outside had grown a touch chilly, which spoke of impending fall. The days were still hot—they did, after all, have four days left of summer, officially—but tell that to the evenings. The wind off the water held a bite that could chap your cheeks if you faced it directly and a kind of crispness you only felt when the leaves were preparing to change.

Shivering, he slouched into his leather jacket, zipped it up and headed toward his bike.

What he saw next was the second surprise of the night.

The second *good* surprise of the night, he should say.

Leaning against his bike like she belonged there was a slightly drunk, gorgeously grinning Celeste.

"You suck!" she called out to him as he approached, her bottom lip snagging between her teeth.

His grin hurt his cheeks. "I *suck*? Why do I suck?"

She shrugged. "I dunno. I just couldn't think of anything witty to say. But you don't suck. You're actually pretty darn wonderful. I'm sorry. Do you forgive me?" She closed her eyes and flashed him a cheesy grin.

He slowed his roll and approached her cautiously. "How much sangria did you have to drink?"

She opened her eyes. Even in the dark, the green was piercing beneath the streetlight. The intensity of it hit him hard in the solar plexus. "I had a fair bit, but I'm not that drunk. I drink *a lot* of wine, so my tolerance is impressive for my size."

He had to chuckle. For a *drunk,* she was still awfully articulate. There was no slur to her speech, unlike Mindy.

"I also had a few shots too," she went on. "I mean it's not like I have anybody to go home to. Sabrina is having a sleepover with Mallory—Richelle's daughter—at Richelle and Liam's. I'm going home to an empty house. Who's gonna care if I'm stumbling drunk?"

Was that why she was leaning against his bike? Because she had nowhere to go, no one to get home to. Did she want to take him home?

"Do you have an extra helmet?" she asked, glancing around his bike.

"What's going on, Celeste?"

Her lips formed a pout he wanted to kiss—as well as do other things to. "I told you what. I have no one waiting for me at home. Do I have to spell it out?"

"Uh, yeah."

She rolled her eyes again and made a sassy, impatient face. "I hope you're a better math teacher than you are a detective or clue cracker or whatever."

"Celeste ..."

"Take me home, Max! Have your way with me." She bobbed her eyebrows, but because of her level of intoxication, they wiggled and waved more than bobbed in the salacious way he was sure she intended.

"Ah, Celeste, you're a charmer when you're drunk. There's no doubt about that. And I'll take you home, but I'm not *having my way with you,* as you say. You're drunker than you say you are, and I am not that kind of guy." His dick protested his proclamation as he walked around to the other side of his bike. He adjusted himself in his jeans before turning to unlock his helmet and then the spare. Handing the helmet to her, he asked, "You gonna be able to hold on?"

Her smile was close-mouthed and adorable. "You just worry about driving. I'll worry about hanging on. Giddyup."

"Giddyup?" He plopped the helmet on his head, clipped it, then checked to see that hers was on properly and snug.

She hadn't put it on yet. She was watching him, her eyes roaming his body, hungry and not too shy about showing it.

"Why'd you come here tonight, really?" They were face-to-face now, less than a foot apart.

Her goofy, drunk smile had faded, and she was looking at him with a sincerity, an openness that he felt deep in his chest.

She shook her head and made to look away, but he gripped her chin in his fingers. "Don't look away. Look at me."

"I was worried you might take one look at Mindy Shelby and cancel our date." Her eyelids dropped, and her chin quivered in his hand. "It was stupid."

He couldn't make up his mind whether to laugh, kiss her or search for a tissue because she looked like she was about to cry.

She opened her eyes. "Maybe I'm drunker than I thought."

His mouth twitched. "You think?"

She rolled those green eyes and sighed, her shoulders dropping nearly an inch.

"I want *you*, Celeste. Not Mindy. You and only you, got it?"

"I want you, too," she whispered.

"But you also want to take it slow. For Sabrina's sake and ..."

For her own sake, right? Because that's what she'd said. She was dipping her toe in the dating pool with him and wasn't ready to jump in with both feet. Or at least that was how she'd put it during one of their many phone conversations.

Was she having second thoughts, though, and rather than riding the brake through their dating, she wanted to put the pedal to the metal? Dive in headfirst?

He was mixing metaphors, but in his head, they still made sense.

She glanced away from him again. "I did, yeah ..."

"But ..."

"But I dunno ..."

Not saying anything, he took the full-face helmet from her, plopped it on her head, secured it and snapped down the visor. Straddling his bike, he encouraged her to do the same. He didn't have to give her any directions. She knew where her feet went and where to put her hands. It felt so good having her on the back, and he hadn't even started it up yet.

He squeezed the clutch and hit the start button. His baby began to rumble and purr beneath him. Celeste's grip around his waist tightened. The pressure of his dick against his inseam tightened too.

"Ready?" he asked.

She gripped him tighter and squeezed her thighs against the back of his. "Ready."

He gave it some gas, kicked it out of neutral and peeled out into traffic.

Just like he'd imagined it, Celeste on the back of his bike with him was the sexiest thing in the goddamn world. He'd caught himself a few times as they waited at a red light, checking out their reflection in a storefront window. You couldn't tell by the full-face helmet that it was her, but he knew it was her, and that was all that mattered. Her thighs squeezing his, her ass on the seat, her chest tight against his back, her hands on his abdomen, red hair flying behind her from beneath the helmet. His cock had been rock-hard before he even let out the throttle. Uncomfortable as hell for sure, but if it meant a little discomfort to have her behind him, he'd take it—willingly.

She gave him directions as needed, usually with a gentle tap of either her left or right hand on his stomach to indicate which way to turn. It worked well, and before he knew it, they were pulling up to her townhouse on a quiet street not too far from the school.

He killed the engine and waited for her to climb off before he did. He unbuckled the helmet from beneath his chin just as she unfastened her helmet and handed it to him.

A new sparkle filled her eyes, and color clung to her cheeks, making them extra rosy, competing with the dark red of her hair. She was gorgeous. Beyond gorgeous. The woman was fucking stunning.

"Thank you for the ride," she said quietly. "It really sobered me up."

"Yeah?"

She nodded, unable to hold his gaze for long. "I'm sorry about earlier, surprising you on your bike like that and demanding what I demanded." She shut her eyes and turned her head way.

He removed his helmet, set it on the bike seat and stepped into her space. "Don't be embarrassed. I happen to like a woman who knows what she wants."

"Yeah?" she asked, pinning her eyes on him again and lifting a brow.

"Yeah." He took her mouth, holding her face between his hands and wedging his tongue between her lips.

She didn't fight him. She grappled at him, tugged him harder against her, and opened her mouth for his exploration.

He rode for twenty minutes with an iron bar in his pants, and he knew she knew he had one because at one point they went over some speed bumps and her hands jostled, hitting his thigh. His erection also hadn't deflated completely as they stood there. And it sure as hell wasn't going anywhere now.

The night had grown chillier in their time standing on the sidewalk, darker too. Stars filled the sky, and a cool breeze lifted a strand of hair across her cheek. He tucked it behind her ear and cupped her neck. "You hold the cards here, Celeste. Every damn one of them."

"I wish I didn't," she whispered. "I wish you held the cards and I could just play along."

He fought down a groan, but it snuck up from the back of his throat anyway. "Don't invite me inside," he murmured, pulling her tight against him once more and pressing his lips to the side of her head. "I'm a good guy. I respect women. I respect boundaries. We have a date tomorrow. I want to do this properly with you."

Her whimper and the shiver that accompanied it had his cock throbbing.

"It shouldn't be like this, should it?" she said, her words coming out in an almost ragged pant.

His lips made a trail down from her temple to her jaw and beneath to her neck. "Like what?" She smelled incredible. He laved at an extra soft spot on her neck and enjoyed the way she relaxed against him and her entire body seemed to sigh.

"This insane attraction. I haven't seen you in fifteen years. I didn't even have a crush on you back then."

"Ouch."

She giggled. But it wasn't a high-pitched bird-like twitter. It was more of a throaty, raspy chuckle, and it did nothing but stir the embers of arousal in his belly into licking flames.

"I was eighteen. You were ..."

"Twenty-five."

"Yeah, so ancient."

"Watch it." He nipped her jaw.

She inhaled quickly and whispered, "And I was with Declan."

Right. Her dead husband, who had also been one of Max's students. Declan had been a good kid. He was smart, he was funny, and he was kind. Popular for all the right reasons.

"I haven't felt like this since ..."

Did she mean she hadn't been with a man since her husband died?

Suddenly it didn't seem like the right moment to be kissing her neck. He pulled away but didn't let go.

"I've only slept with two men since Declan died. One of those was a one-night stand I had at a wedding in Olympia." She made a face of contradiction. "Well, more like a forty-eight-hour stand, but you know what I mean. And the other was a guy I dated for a few weeks, but after we slept together, I just wasn't feeling it. He also didn't understand why he couldn't just come over at any time of the day or night."

"Because you have a life and a child." His gender could be really stupid sometimes. Gave the rest of them a bad rap.

"Yeah, he didn't get that."

"I feel something real with you," he said, staring down at her. "It's strange and wonderful, and I don't want to *not* explore this connection, this attraction."

"Me too," she said with a frown he wanted to kiss away until it was no more than a distant memory. Until her mouth forgot how to dip down like that when he was around. "But I also want to take it slow. It's not just my heart involved anymore. And the fact that you're Sabrina's teacher does complicate things."

"But it doesn't make them impossible," he said cautiously. Was she getting ready to cancel their date and put a freeze on everything?

"No, it doesn't. I mean teachers have their own children in their classroom sometimes, for goodness' sake. I remember my junior high math teacher taught his daughter math for sixth and seventh grade. There was no weirdness, at least not that I could tell. And we wouldn't be the first teacher and parent to date. *Gilmore Girls* did a whole season on it. Lorelai dated Rory's teacher, and the guy was even named Max."

"Can't say I've ever watched *Gilmore Girls,*" he said dryly.

"You should. It's really good. Except for the four-episode recap years later; that was garbage."

Okay ...

She stepped farther away from him and turned toward her front door. "I'm sorry. I ramble when I'm drunk. I also ramble when I'm flustered. And when I'm confused. And right now, I'm all of those things." She fished her keys out of her purse and opened her door.

He wasn't sure if he should follow her inside or not. He had told her not to invite him in. A man only had *so* much willpower. He knew he shouldn't. The angel on his shoulder was telling him to hit the bricks. But the horny devil on his other shoulder already had a box of condoms out and was doing some calf stretches in case things got acrobatic.

Stepping inside, she kicked off her shoes immediately and slid her feet into a pair of very comfortable-looking slippers. He still wasn't sure if he should go inside with her.

"It surprised me how jealous I felt tonight seeing you chat it up with Mindy." She wandered through her townhouse, talking.

Max figured she was probably talking to him, so therefore she expected him to follow her. He entered the house and shut the door behind him.

Her house was just as he would imagine it to be. Clean, contemporary but also incredibly homey.

Greens and tans made up the living room, aside from dark brown leather furniture. The color palate continued on through the rest of the house. He found her in the kitchen chugging a tall glass of water. Her kitchen, although still sticking with the same hues as the house, was big and bright with white cabinetry and white appliances. An enormous desk with a laptop sat in one corner of the dining area, while a small booth-style nook with an oval table took up the other corner.

"Every conversation I had with Mindy tonight was initiated by her," he said. "She was like a ghost, the way she just sidled up beside me without making a sound. Half the time I wouldn't even know she was there until she would make that horrible bird-like laugh."

Celeste's head bobbled as she mimicked Mindy's laugh. "Like that?"

He grimaced before smiling. "Yeah."

"I don't trust Mindy as far as I can throw her," Celeste continued. She paused, tilted her head in thought and twisted her lips. "Though to be fair, I could probably toss her farther than I think. She's not very big, and I'm like crazy-strong."

"Are you now?"

She spun to face him. "Sure am. Feel." She flexed her free arm and offered up her bicep. He squeezed it, and it was remarkably hard. She had some muscle on her for sure.

"Very nice," he said with a smile. "So what do you want to do?"

She turned the faucet on again and filled up her glass. "Want something?"

"I'm good," he said, watching as she chugged another full glass. A small tributary of water trickled down the side of her face, and he itched to wipe—or better yet kiss—it away.

"*Ah*." She wiped her mouth with the back of her wrist. "I don't know what to do, Max. I honestly don't. I mean a part of me—a *big* part of me—thinks we should just say fuck it and head upstairs now."

A big part of him wanted that too. A big, throbbing, impatient part of him.

"But then the logical, responsible, selfless part of me—the *mom* part of me—knows that my kid is going through something right now, and I don't want to make her life more challenging by hooking up with her teacher." Her green eyes held a sadness that he felt deep in his heart.

Their connection and attraction to each other were beguiling. He hadn't been so instantly, so deeply attracted to a woman like this since his ex-wife. And even though his and Celeste's history was that of a teacher-pupil nature, it wasn't as if they were meeting for the first time. They *did* have a history.

She took a step back from him, which only ended up cornering herself in the wraparound style kitchen. "I need to get to the bottom of why Eleanor wants to hurt Sabrina. My kid isn't telling me everything—unless she doesn't even know the whole story. And Mindy is shady as shit and wants to haul you off to her lair—the cougar."

"She is that," he agreed. "Say what you will about me and my self-serving ways as I try to convince you *not* to end us before we even start, but I think your daughter is stronger and more resilient than you give her credit for, because she was raised by a warrior of a mother. You can have both. You can have a life, a relationship and the things—and people"—

he bobbed his brows, which made her laugh—"that you want, as well as take care of your kid. I will never make you choose between me and Sabrina. I will never give you a hard time if you have to cancel because she came home from school in tears over a boy. You're all the other person has had for a long time now, and I would be a deluded moron with an enormous ego if I thought for a second that I could come between that."

Wide, sparkling eyes blinked back at him, and her bottom lip slowly separated from her top lip until her mouth form a surprised and sexy little *O*.

"All I'm asking for, Celeste, is a chance."

Her throat bobbed, and her hands reached out and grabbed the sides of his leather jacket, her fingers holding on. The smell of sweet sangria and Celeste hit him hard as warm puffs of air from her lips drifted across his face. "You actually get it. How have you not been snapped up and made a husband and father already? You're like ..."

"High-maintenance and terrible in bed."

She snorted a laugh. "God, I hope not. I was going to say sweet, sensitive, understanding and *so* fucking sexy."

He nodded. "Ah, yes, I am all those things too. I just wasn't sure where you were going."

Her lips twisted ruefully. "Maybe it's for the best that we just ... stay teacher and student." But the way she leaned in toward him spoke of the expulsion and termination of career kind of teacher-student relationship.

"Maybe," he said. "But *former* student. You are my *former* student. You're also all grown up."

Boy, was she ever.

"I am all grown up. I have a job. I have a house. I have a child."

"You do. You're very fortunate. Very successful."

"There are things that I don't have though ... things that I *want.*" She licked her lips at the same time her eyelids fell to half-mast. He could feel the heat from her body radiating off her like the surface of the sun. Combine that with her wild, spicy feminine scent and the angel on his shoulder was losing the battle to the devil.

"Don't leave yet," she whispered. "Not just yet." She tugged him toward her, eliminating the last few remaining inches that were between them, and drove her fingers into his hair. Her lips found his, and she pried them apart with her tongue, taking control of the kiss and tugging on the ends of his hair until a snap of pain jolted down to the base of his spine.

Growling, he lifted her up by her ass and plunked her on the counter. His hands roamed across her shoulders, down her sides. She didn't balk when he removed her coat. In fact, she released his hair and removed his coat from him as well, her fingers making quick work of the zipper. He noticed—boy did he notice—when the back of her fingers grazed the top of his erection. Then she did it again, and he thought he might come in his fucking pants.

It wasn't a frantic makeout. There was laughing and giggling, lots of heavy petting, and boy, did she like to bite. She also liked to be bitten. Celeste kept tilting her head to the side so he could go after her neck like a vampire. Each time he thought he'd taken it too far and bit her too hard, her whimper and moan of contentment would prove otherwise.

He'd wondered if she'd dressed for him when he spotted her sitting in the booth with her friends. Her top was a rich emerald green, billowy and soft, and the way it hugged her curves and cut low across her cleavage had him mentally drooling any time he glanced over at her.

And now those mounds were pressed up against his chest. He cupped one in his palm and kneaded it, enjoying the deep groan from the back of her throat that he caught with his kisses.

She is drunk. You cannot sleep with her. Ah, the angel on his shoulder must have found his strength. Or he was a cat and had multiple lives.

Max waited for the devil to pop up and encourage him to unhook her bra and draw a nipple into his mouth.

Nobody with horns or a pitchfork spoke up.

You'll regret it later if the two of you start this way. She deserves more. You deserve more.

Ah, that fucking angel.

Reluctantly, he pulled away. "I should get going."

Glassy-eyed and confused, she pouted and slid off the counter. Her lips were puffy and the skin around her mouth red from his stubble. He could also see several bite marks along her collarbone and neck. She'd probably have marks there tomorrow.

Bending down, she grabbed his jacket. "You're right. I'm sorry."

Feeling like a dick with a throbbing dick, he thanked her for his jacket, slouched into it and headed for her door. "Don't apologize, Celeste. You've done nothing wrong— neither of us have."

Inhaling deeply through her nose, she leaned against the wall. "That's what makes this suck all the more."

How freaking true.

"I'll see you tomorrow morning when I pick you up for our date." He opened the door.

She growled. "I'm going to be so freaking tired ... and probably hung over."

He grinned back at her as he stepped over the threshold and back out into the cool night. "Then I guess you best get to bed then."

She smirked and pushed off from the wall to grip the door. "You're a cunning one, Mr. Travis."

"It's Max," he called back.

"Yeah, and that's the speed my vibrator's about to be on," she murmured right before the door closed.

8

SATURDAY MORNING, Celeste woke up with the mother of all hangovers. Did she really have *that* much to drink? After the wine combined with all that sugary whatever from the sangria, her guts felt like she'd just ridden a roller coaster backward in the dark. Add in that her head pounded like her temples were made of bongos, and she literally crawled out of bed and across the floor to the shower, only to be startled at just who looked back at her in the vanity mirror.

She did not recognize that woman.

Not a lightweight by any stretch of the imagination, she'd really tied one on last night with the girls. Mason just kept sending over more pitchers, and Richelle or Bianca just kept topping her up. Lauren was encouraging it as well, saying Celeste had to drink her share because she wouldn't, otherwise her baby would be born a drunk.

She remembered most of last night, which was good. She remembered seeing Max. She remembered riding his motorcycle and holding onto him like a big, leather-clad sexy biker man—because he was. He just also taught math.

She also remembered making out with him on the side-

106 | WHITLEY COX

walk and then again in her kitchen. She also distinctly remembered brushing the back of her fingers over something incredibly long, hard and promising.

That had caused an ache so intense to form deep in her lower belly. Her pussy pulsed and her nipples beaded as they made out in her kitchen. And when he cupped her breast, she was worried she was going to come on the spot. It'd been a *loooong* while since she'd had a man, and a man like Max to break the dry spell was a good choice in thirst-quenchers.

Unable to look at herself any longer in the mirror out of fear it might crack, she went to peel out of her pajamas only to realize she was naked. She never slept naked.

Had she and Max ...?

No. She remembered seeing him leave. Hearing his bike roar down the road. Then she'd stumbled upstairs, grabbed her—she poked her head back into her room. Her vibrator sat on her nightstand. Ah, that's right. After he left, she'd taken care of business herself, then promptly passed out.

She stepped back into her bathroom and turned on the water for the shower. She should be punishing herself for her foolish behavior by stepping into the shower while it was still cold. That would not only wake her up but probably shock some sense into her too.

She had a somewhat clear head when she was away from him, but then the moment she was around him, her common sense fell asleep and her raging libido took over. She'd waited for him on his bike, for crying out loud, told him to have his way with her.

Cringing at her behavior last night, she hopped into the shower. It was still too cold. She deserved it.

She wasn't ready to tell Sabrina that she was in fact *dating* Max, but truth be told, she wasn't dating him—yet. She was going on *a* date with him to see if they had more than just animal attraction in common with each other. So she did what she did every Saturday morning when she had to drive Sabrina to work. She tossed on a pair of yoga pants and a tank top, threw her hair into a messy topknot and took her offspring to work, while a giant mug of coffee sat in a to-go mug in her SUV's cup holder. Only this time, since Sabrina was at a sleepover, she had to pick her kid up from Mallory's house, which was on the way to the Lavender and Lilac Bistro.

Thankfully, Paige's bistro was only a fifteen-minute drive, so Celeste had a good forty-five minutes to physically and mentally get herself ready for her date with Max once she got home.

After dropping off Sabrina at work, Celeste raced upstairs, peeled out of her yoga pants and tank top and stared at her semi-naked body in the mirror. Even after fifteen years, she still had faint, white stretch marks along her lower belly, and since her daughter started working for Paige and bringing home day-old baked goods, her hips and thighs had widened. She peeled her sports bra off over her head and cupped her breasts. Sabrina had been a boob-obsessed baby and nursed until she was two and a half. Celeste had wanted to quit nursing when Sabrina was eighteen months old, but the little beast would have none of it. She wasn't sure her breasts had ever recovered from her kid swinging on them the way she had.

Sighing, she opened her closet and reached for the sexiest bra she currently owned. It was still nothing fancy, just black satin with red lace on the tops of the cups and a tiny red satin bow on the front. There was red lace along the straps too. She couldn't remember when she bought the bra or the last time she wore it. She just hoped it still fit. Now if only she could find the matching underwear.

Twenty-five minutes later, she was dressed in what she hoped was a sexy yet casual ensemble of stretchy black skinny jeans, cute navy tennis shoes with little white anchors all over them and a dark green tank top that made her eyes pop. Of course, she'd have to wear more than just a tank top on the bike, so she dug out her old leather jacket from the depths of her closet and prayed it still fit. When forced to wear something outside her regular jeans, leggings, tank tops and boyfriend-style flannel shirts, she did a lot of praying that things still fit.

It fit. Thank God.

After applying minimal makeup, but enough to make her look like she was trying to be sexy on this date, she sat down at her desk, her knee bouncing uncontrollably as she began going through work emails.

She hadn't been on a lot of dates in her life and even fewer first dates. But somehow, this one had her on more pins and needles than any of the rest. Even her first date with Declan.

Because even though she knew Max, had kissed Max, she was still nervous to *get to know* him. They were sailing into uncharted territory. Dangerous waters with hidden, jagged rocks, white squalls and two-headed serpents lurking in the briny depths.

She was halfway through an email to a literary agent about an upcoming editing assignment when the doorbell bing-bonged and she leapt in her seat.

The clock on her computer said nine o'clock sharp. She liked a man who was on time.

Taking a deep, fortifying breath, she saved her email, closed her laptop and stood up. Her lips still held gloss, and a quick glance in the hallway mirror said her hair hadn't decided to go all frizzy. Her purse and jacket were already near the front door, so all she had to do was open it. She saw his body standing there through the mottled glass in the door. He was in his black jacket and had sunglasses pushed up into his hair. Other than that, she couldn't see his expression—until she swung the door open, that is.

Leaning against the post that led to a small porch overhang of her townhouse, like some 1950s greaser waiting to take his date to the sock hop, Max lifted his head and pinned her with those gray eyes she'd found herself dreaming about. His grip on the bouquet of flowers in his hand tightened.

"Hi," he said, taking a step forward and lifting the bouquet.

As if she'd had an injection of Tylenol and a tall glass of water, her headache vanished. She stepped back into the house, and he followed her.

"These are for you."

Her smile continuing to grow, she blinked a few times, thanked him and took the flowers with her into the house. "Thank you. Did you get these from Zara?" she asked, wandering into her kitchen and grabbing a vase from a cupboard above the fridge.

"Who's Zara?"

With a pair of scissors she grabbed from the cutlery drawer, she snipped open the gold paper Zara used to wrap the flowers. "A friend of mine owns Flowers on 5th."

"Well, that's where I got these, so I must have gotten them from Zara. She has the best selection in town, plus I like that she uses paper to wrap her flowers instead plastic. It's better for the environment." He leaned his elbows on the counter, and she could feel him watching her every move.

She glanced at him, making sure to add a brow lift. "Buy a lot of flowers, do you?" With a lopsided smile, she carried the full vase over to her breakfast nook.

His grin fell.

Uh-oh.

Was he caught?

"Uh, no, not really. I mean, I buy them for my mom and

my sister and my grandma. So that's like six bouquets a year there. Mother's Day for each of them, plus birthdays, plus my parents' anniversary. That makes seven."

With a chuckle, she lifted up onto her tiptoes as she fell in beside him, and her lips pressed against his cheek. "I'm kidding. It's fine. Men are allowed to like flowers too. You could have a subscription to her bouquet-of-the-month club, for all I know, and I wouldn't care. Flowers brighten up a space no matter who lives there." She reached for her phone off the counter and looped her arm through his. "Shall we go?"

He grinned down at her. "Let's roll, baby."

MAX SLOWED his bike down until they were at a full stop in front of Celeste's townhouse. It was closing in on four thirty, and she had to go and pick up Sabrina at five.

They'd spent the entire day together. Ate breakfast and lunch together, perused the used bookstore in Mukilteo, wandered along the water, rented fishing rods to try their luck on the dock with the rest of the reel jockeys and checked out the opening of a new brewery that was offering half-price tastings.

In his opinion, if he did say so himself, it was the perfect date. And even after nearly eight hours with Celeste, he hadn't had nearly enough of her. If anything, he wanted more. Her laugh, her smile, her whole attitude about life just made him want to bypass all the get-to-know-you stuff and jump right into the real-deal forever stuff.

But maybe that had been his problem in the past? He tended to jump in with both feet quickly. He fell hard. And he'd fallen hard for his ex. They met in September, were engaged by February and married by July. They were married for just shy of four years before things began to sour. Would they have turned, would his happily ever after have held an expiration date like a jug of milk if he'd taken it slower? Maybe he hadn't known Sharmaine as well as he thought he did. They certainly didn't want the same things or have the same philosophies about parenting, which was why they never became parents.

Mostly he was okay with the fact that he never reproduced, but once in a while he wondered if he would have felt differently if he'd been with someone else.

Celeste climbed off the back of his Bonneville and shook her red mane free of the helmet. He climbed off as well, unclipped his helmet and stored both his and hers on his seat.

Her green eyes twinkled like cut gems in the late-afternoon sun, and her cheeks held a rosy glow. It'd been a warm day, and they hadn't spent much of it in the shade. He probably had a bit of color on his arms and face too.

Smiling demurely, she dipped her head and made her way down the small path toward her front door, through the white picket fence and past the postage-stamp front lawn. He waited for her to unlock the door, and they were inside before he said anything, before he did anything.

But she didn't give him chance. Shutting the door behind him, she shoved his body into the wall and slammed herself into him, taking his mouth, her hands all over his body.

He'd kissed her a few times on their date, but those kisses had been chaste and quick, nothing like now. Now, she was fervent. Now she was demanding and wanton.

But they didn't have time to do what he wanted to do. To do what he knew she wanted to do. They were taking this slow, and they were sneaking around. Two things he wasn't opposed to but knew would be difficult for both of them.

With his cock now throbbing once again, and still pissed

off about the last time they were together, he regrettably, gently pushed her away. "I should go."

Her face fell and he instantly felt like a jerk. The color in her cheeks was no longer from the sun or excitement. She averted her eyes, toed off her shoes and made sure to show him her back as she hung up her purse and jacket.

Fuck. They'd had a perfect date and he'd gone and ruined it by pushing her away.

He needed to make things right. She was already sailing into unchartered waters here dating again, and he was her daughter's teacher to boot. She'd also shown him her insecurity and concern about his eye wandering to someone else like Mindy.

Celeste needed to know she was the only person he had eyes for. She was the only person he had anything for.

"I'm just going to grab a glass of water, then I have to go get Sabrina," she said, though it seemed like she was speaking more to herself and was acting as though he'd already left.

In half a stride he was in her space, grabbing her hand and whipping her around to face him. "What's going on?" He cupped her cheek, tilted her chin up so she was forced to look him directly in the eyes. "Do you think I *want* to leave?"

Confusion flashed behind her eyes.

"I don't *want* to go anywhere but upstairs to your bed, Celeste. But you have to go pick up your daughter and I want to do this right. I want to date you, woo you, earn the privilege of getting to go upstairs to your bed. I know you haven't been with many guys since Declan, I know this is a big deal, which is why I want to do this the proper way."

Celeste's breathing increased and her nostrils flared. The confusion in her eyes from earlier was replaced by a scorching gaze that made his own temperature spike.

Closing her eye, she leaned her cheek into his palm, and

placed her hand over the back of his. "I'm an idiot," she finally said on a sigh, opening her eyes and hitting him with another deep gaze filled with desire.

"You're the antithesis of an idiot."

Her smile was small.

"Trust me, Celeste, I don't *want* to leave." He pulled her forward and pressed his lips against hers. "Isn't there something about anticipation being an aphrodisiac? The longer the wait the greater the reward?" Now all he wanted to do was get her smiling again. Hear that laugh.

"Never been an overly patient person," she murmured, though he did notice one corner of her mouth lift. "Notice that I was married and a mother before my nineteenth birthday? Couldn't *wait* to grow up." The glint in her eyes turned rueful.

"More of an instant gratification person then, are you? Impulsive?"

"Rarely get out of the grocery store without buying a candy bar at the checkout. Not big on surprises."

"The surprise thing seems like more of a control issue to me."

Now they were both laughing. The unease in her eyes and the color in her cheeks had vanished.

"Go get your kid and call me later," he said, planting another kiss to her lips before reluctantly pulling away and heading to the door.

She was still holding his hand though and tugged him back by the fingers for one more kiss. "Thank you for a wonderful date, Max. I promise not to be so wishy-washy anymore. I want this and I want you."

Max's heart did a heavy *thump thump* in his chest and he rested his forehead against hers, intertwining their fingers. "I want this and I want you too."

LATER THAT NIGHT at Bianca's house, all the women gathered for wine night. Well, not *all* the women. Just Bianca, Celeste and Lauren. They'd talked several times about blending the two women's groups, the single moms and the women who were with the former single dads. After all, they all knew each other, all got along, and often went to other gatherings where everyone was there. But for some reason, Bianca, Celeste and Lauren didn't want to change what they had. They liked their nights with just the three of them. It also helped that they all lived in the same complex, so nobody had to worry about driving or cabbing home. But most of all, they were The Single Moms of Seattle. They had something in common with each other that not all the other woman did or understood. Eva, Zara, Paige and Richelle understood what it was like to be single moms, but they had men now, so it wasn't the same.

Thankfully, everyone understood and was cool with the arrangements as they were. Mallory and Sabrina were usually employed to babysit on Saturday night, which meant, once again, Celeste would be returning to an empty house, unless Sabrina decided to cab home and not spend the night at Eva's.

"I'm just doing sparkling water tonight," Bianca said, her complexion pale and her eyes appearing tired. "I woke up feeling as close to death as I've ever felt."

Celeste smiled, thankful that she wasn't the only one who'd overindulged. "Me too," she said in commiseration, cracking open a can of watermelon-flavored sparkling water and pouring it into a big glass over ice. "I drank *way* too much."

"Did Professor Washboard take you home?" Bianca asked.

Keeping her eyes down, she sipped her water and nodded. "Yeah."

"And then did you *ride* him?" Lauren asked, a handful of nuts in her hand.

No, but she wished she had.

She shook her head. "I did not. He was a gentleman, even though I threw myself at him." She glanced up at her friends. They were both grinning.

"Somebody is seriously hot for teacher," Lauren said with a snicker before she shoved the entire handful of nuts into her mouth. "Why didn't you ride that stallion?"

"Because I was drunk, and he was a gentleman." Though, at the time, she didn't want a gentleman. She wanted a he-man, caveman to grab her by the ponytail and haul her off to his cave. "I'm also still really distracted about this Sabrina thing and all the shit Eleanor is putting her through. I need to take it slow with Max so I can figure out how to balance a man and my child in my life. It's been a while since I've had to do that."

"Mallory might know," Bianca offered.

Richelle's daughter, Bianca's niece, was a year younger than Sabrina, so she still had another year left of junior high. The two had become close over the last year since Celeste and Richelle became friends. Most weekends the girls hung out together and often babysat the other kids in their extended family, which included all the former single dads and their children.

They all wandered into Bianca's living room, and each curled up in their normal corners of couches and loveseats. Quiet classic rock played from the television soundbar in the background, and the evening sun beat in through the windows.

"I think my biggest fear would be that little witch calling

child protective services," Lauren said. "All it takes is one person poking their nose where it doesn't belong ..."

"Yeah, but sometimes those nosy people save children and families from a dangerous situation," Bianca said. "But I agree here. Celeste having child services called on her would be ridiculous. I've never met a better mom."

Warmth bloomed in Celeste's heart from the kind words of her friend. But it competed with the frightening chill that raced the length of her spine at the thought of child protective services being called on her for something so ridiculous as a failed credit card and enforcing financial responsibility in her child. She also knew that people had CPS show up on their doorstep for less.

It wasn't like she'd lose Sabrina over any of it, but it still made fear ratchet up inside her at the sheer thought of it. Like she needed that added bit of stress in her life.

Lauren had a glass of sparkling water perched precariously on her belly, and she leaned back into the couch. "Look, no hands."

"That baby kicks, and your tits are going to be soaked," Bianca said with a laugh.

Lauren shrugged. "I'm always overheating as it is. It might be nice." She made a *gimme, gimme* motion with her hand to get Celeste to pass her the bowl of pretzels. "Thank you. Now, let's address the elephant in the room, shall we?"

Bianca and Celeste gave her quizzical looks.

Lauren rolled her eyes. "I want to hear *alllll* about Celeste's date with Professor Washboard. Did you get to see his washboard?"

9

MONDAY AFTERNOON after the school bell rang and the chaos in the hallways and outside the school ended, Max quickly collected his bag, bike helmet and notebook from his "office" and made to leave the school. No sense sticking around if he didn't have to. Besides, he had to be back later that night for the annual Parent, Student, Teacher Night. A night when parents joined their children and spent twenty minutes in each class, getting to know the teacher and hearing about all the things the teacher hoped to drill into the students' brains that year. Then there were tables set up in the gym with representatives from all the clubs available to join. It was mostly a night for the freshman or transfer students, but occasionally a sophomore or junior made an appearance.

He'd located a side door in the hallway just outside his classroom, and it took him directly to the parking lot. He didn't have to enter through the front doors and walk all the way through the school to get to his classroom. He could park down below and eliminate the likelihood of running into Mindy or seeing his students make out in the hallways. That had always weirded him out. Twenty-five or forty, there was something just so *pervy* about him being able to see a bunch of minors sucking face. It'd been particularly bad the year he'd been roped into chaperoning the prom. That dance floor had been nothing but a sea of face-sucking octopus-children. Limbs everywhere, lips everywhere. He'd even had to break up one couple that'd ducked behind a table and were half-naked.

Seriously, kids these days just didn't wait for a damn thing.

Why'd he choose to teach high school? Why not middle school or elementary school?

Probably because middle school kids were worse than high school kids with the puberty and attitude, and he'd never been a big fan of *little* kids. Sure, if he'd ended up having his own kids, he probably would have loved them, but other people's kids were another story.

He was a kick-ass uncle though. His sister had three kids, and they loved him and he loved them. He spoiled them all rotten and took them all often for a night or an entire weekend so his sister and brother-in-law could have some time alone. Though, since he'd been away in Vietnam, the kids had grown up a fair bit and gave their parents more space. They still liked hanging out with him for now, but how much longer would that last? Eventually, there would come a time when they wouldn't want to come hang out with their *cool* uncle Max for a weekend anymore.

Layla was eleven; Jaimie, nine, and little Booker had just turned seven. He'd probably love to come hang out with his uncle for a few more years. But the girls, maybe not for much longer.

However, as much as he loved his nieces and nephew, he also knew that a weekend with them was more than enough time for him. He couldn't imagine having to put up with thirty-plus little mouthy, jam-faced whiners five days a week, six hours a day. He'd lose his mind, particularly because they weren't his blood.

So teaching high school it was.

He knew he wanted to be a teacher. He'd always had a knack for explaining the unexplainable in a way that people seemed to understand, so he took his love of numbers and the ease with which he grasped math and got a degree in teaching.

"I thought I saw your motorcycle still in the parking lot," came a bird-like chirp from the doorway.

Max nearly dropped his bag and helmet. "Mindy!"

Damn it. He'd nearly escaped.

He backed up into his classroom and set his box and helmet down on at the table near the door. He needed to open some windows in the room before tonight anyway. The place had a tendency to get stuffy.

She entered the room, all smiles, oblivious to his plan to leave. She was dressed down in a pair of linen capris, flip-flops with gems on them and a dark purple tank top with a white cardigan over top. "I thought I was the only one left in the school. Nice to know I'm not alone."

Oh boy.

No way in hell was she the only person left in the school. Since it was Student, Parent, Teacher night, there would be staff milling about until the students and their parents showed up at seven. Pelton had been running around like a headless chicken all day.

She waltzed toward him, hunger in her eyes. She really was the epitome of a cougar. Even though she was probably only a few years older than he was, she stalked him, eyed him like he was a stag in the meadow and she hadn't eaten in nearly a month.

"It was so nice going out on Friday night, wasn't it? We should really do it again."

Nodding, he headed toward the window furthest from her. "Yeah, there were some pretty cool people there. A few other teachers I could definitely see myself becoming friends with. Sean McKidd, who teaches physics, he rides a motorcycle too. We talked about going for rides together."

Was that jealousy that flashed in her eyes? No, it couldn't be. She was quick like a puma and had followed him to the window, her hand landed on his arm before he could reach out and open the window. "Yes, very nice people. But I was thinking perhaps something a bit more *intimate*. It was oh so very loud on Friday. I could hardly hear myself think, let alone anything anybody else had to say. You can't really get to know people that way, you know?"

He shook himself free of her grasp as gently as he could and went about opening windows. Maybe he could crawl out one to escape the cougar. "I didn't think it was that loud, actually. I mean, yeah, it was a sports bar, but I had no problem hearing anybody."

Disappointment bloomed pink in her cheeks. She wasn't going down without a fight, though. "But as the newbies, we should really get together and chat, don't you think? Dinner maybe? I'd love to go for a ride on the back of your motorcycle. It's so sexy."

It's weird. When Celeste threw herself at him, he thought it was adorable, hilarious and sexy. When Mindy was doing it, it was the complete opposite. She seemed to almost be coming from a place of desperation. The way she looked at him, with so much hope in her eyes. There was more than just her being attracted to him there; it went deeper than that. A whole hell of a lot deeper.

"I would love to be friends with you, Mindy. But as far as dating goes, I have a strict no-dating-my-colleagues policy. I did it once, and it didn't end well."

Intrigue flashed in the pale blue of her eyes. "No. Who?"

"We met when we were both teaching at the same school. Fell in love, got married. But then we fell out of love and got divorced. The school and Seattle were both too small for the both of us, so I took off for a few years."

There went her hand back on his arm. "Oh, how tragic. So what made you come back?"

"She moved down to Santa Barbara with her new husband. And I missed my nieces and nephew. I don't want them to grow up without me being there to see it." It was like a warped game of cat and mouse. She'd touch him; he'd gently pull away. She'd chase, catch him again, then he'd discreetly escape.

The woman crooned. "Oh, that's so sweet. A man who loves children."

Well, kind of. He loved kids he was related to. Other kids he tolerated because that was part of his job.

All he did was nod. "Anyway, after that, I made a point of never dating anybody I worked with. It's just too messy. I hope you understand? I would love to be your friend, though."

Disappointment made her mouth dip into a deep pout. A pout that was almost too big to be real. He had a hard time believing she was ever genuine. Since the moment he met her briefly on the first day of school, to Friday night and now, she seemed incredibly fake. Insecure for sure and unwilling to put her true self forward. Celeste had mentioned that Mindy was recently divorced. Maybe she was struggling with a reinvention of her identity. Who knows? He wasn't a shrink.

"Heading home for a bit?" she asked, circling around him and peering into his stuffy office.

He nodded. "Yep. Grab some food. Come back for seven."

"I saw Celeste Howard at the bar on Friday. Do you know who she is? Did you see her?" Mindy spun around and faced him, her eyes now burning with a level of accusation and challenge he felt like a hot poker in his gut.

"I know who she is, yes." He owed Mindy zero explanation, and he wasn't going to give her one just to be nice.

She circled back around and behind him, her finger trailing along his back, sending a shiver straight down to his toes. And not the sexy kind of shiver—the someone-just-walked-over-your-grave-in-the-future kind of shiver. "You know, when I met her the other week, I had a hard time placing her at first. She looked so familiar to me. Or at least reminded me of someone."

Oh shit, now he had to bite. The last thing he wanted to do was discuss Celeste with Mindy, but here she was flogging that decaying, rotten horse. "Yeah, who does she remind you of?"

"The woman my husband cheated on me with. A redhead. Younger. I had to go and find her profile on social media to make sure the two women weren't the same person. They are not. Alastair left me for a woman with no brain and no children. I'm not sure Gia is even thirty. And Celeste is thirty-three." She clucked her tongue. "I could not even *imagine* being thirty-three with a teenager. With age comes wisdom. You *do* know she was a teenage mother, right? Such a shame. To throw your life away like that."

Did he give off the vibe that he liked the mean-girl type? Because that could not be further from the truth. If anything, it made an attractive person like Mindy turn downright ugly. Ugly bred ugly, though, and her daughter was as hideous a person as they came.

He took a step back and made sure to steel his expression. She wasn't getting an inch from him, not even a smile, not after a comment like that. "I'm not sure Celeste would look at it that way. That she threw her life away to have her daughter." Now, all he wanted was for this woman to leave him in peace.

Mindy's stare became fierce, and her nostrils flared. "Yes. Perhaps you're right. Though I'm sure she wishes she'd waited a few years before she started a family."

"Sometimes we don't always get that luxury and we're forced to play the hand we're dealt." No way was he letting Mindy speak so cruelly about Celeste. The woman had no idea what Celeste and Sabrina had gone through, the mud they'd had to slog through, only to come out on the other side shiny and vibrant, if not for a little dirt under their nails.

She didn't deserve to know.

Taking a deep breath, he pushed down his building frustration and rattled his keys in his hand to hopefully send the message that he wanted to leave. "I'm sorry you were cheated on, Mindy. That was unfair. My ex-wife cheated on me as well. Though we were having problems long before then, so I'm not sure it's the same thing. Either way, I understand what you're going through, and I'm very sorry. However, I *do* have to get going." As he spoke, he carefully backed her up toward the door leading out to the hallway.

Before she'd even realized it, he had her over the threshold between his classroom and the hallway. He locked his classroom door, balancing his box and helmet on one hand. She blinked as she took in her sudden new surroundings. "I ... thank you. I feel like we're even more bonded now than before. Both being new here, both burnt and jaded from failed marriages."

That was a stretch if he'd ever heard one.

If that was all it took to be bonded to someone, he was also soul mates with Gerald Palmer the English lit teacher, who was also new to Lakeview, divorced and jaded. Then there was Frank Kramer, the computer science teacher— though he wasn't new, but he was divorced, old, cranky and ready to retire. And he couldn't forget his motorcycle buddy, Sean McKidd. He wasn't new either, but he was divorced and an angry SOB. Rightfully so, though—the guy found his wife in bed with his brother—and his cousin! Yuck.

But he neither wanted to make a friend nor an enemy of Mindy, so all he could do was keep her as an acquaintance and hope she never found his home address. He smiled grimly and lied through his Dr. Gallagher-straightened teeth. "The makings of a friendship for sure. Now, I'm sure you have things to do before tonight as well. Don't let me keep you, please."

The woman still looked like she couldn't remember how she got into the hallway. "I ... uh, yeah. Sure."

He gripped the doorknob to the outside. "I look forward to it." Then before she could pounce on him and embed her cougar claws in his chest, he opened the door to the parking lot, stepped out and shut it.

10

MAX HATED PARENT, Student, Teacher Night. Hated it.

The only thing about that night that he was looking forward to was a certain freshman student of his showing up with her mother. Even though they'd had a wonderful date on Saturday, it still already felt like too long since he'd seen Celeste.

After a quick dinner and shower at home, he took his Bonneville back to the school, made sure his classroom didn't smell like half-dead old man and waited for the parents and students to file in.

They rotated the students and their parents through according to the student's class schedule. Twenty-minute intervals in each classroom. And, of course, Sabrina took math in the afternoon, the last class of the day, so he had to wait eighty minutes. Eighty long freaking minutes, the same spiel spewed from his lips four previous fucking times before she finally walked through his door.

His heart stuttered in his chest as Celeste flicked her gaze toward him, and a small, barely discernible smile lifted on her lips. She was quick to avert her eyes and stow her smile before anybody was the wiser—most of all Sabrina. They sat at the back of the classroom, which worked well for him, because he could easily speak just to her while the rest of the crowd thought he was speaking to all of them. The entire time he gave his memorized monologue, she refused to look at him. Rather, she appeared bored and let her eyes wander aimlessly around the classroom and faces. Then she flipped through a few of his handouts that the principal insisted he provide—information on how to help your kid succeed at math. They usually all got left behind when the room was empty. A waste of paper and photocopier ink.

By the time he was done, he was frustrated that she hadn't bothered to look at him once. Not once.

After what they'd done Friday night in her driveway and kitchen, and the last two dates they had—which he thought went great—why couldn't she give him a bit of eye contact? Was she still upset he left on Saturday and didn't whisk her upstairs to her bed? By the time he left he thought they were in a better place—the *same* place.

They were going to take it slow, get to know each other and let the anticipation build.

Was he behaving like the teenagers he taught and tolerated, to think he deserved even a flirtatious side-eye?

Probably.

Was he over-thinking things?

Most definitely.

Both the devil and angel on his shoulders were shaking their heads and telling him to grow the fuck up.

After he gave his "talk," it was time for questions—which people rarely had. Then one by one, parents introduced themselves to him—usually it was only the overachievers who bore more overachievers that approached him at the front of the classroom. Other parents couldn't give two shits about him so long as their kid wasn't being a little dick in class and passed. He liked those parents. He didn't like the ones that breathed down his neck and called him up when their precious spawn got an A minus or something.

Eventually, his classroom was empty. Completely empty. He hadn't even seen her leave, he'd been so preoccupied with the other parents and students. She must have carefully ducked out. That ate at him even more than her not making eye contact with him. He was still a human being, still a person, and he deserved to be acknowledged, didn't he?

Was he reading too much into this?

Yeah, he probably was.

He needed a good smack across the face with a wet washcloth to sort himself out. And it seemed like the devil and angel were both getting ready to dish out that dose of reality.

She was with her kid. Her focus was her kid. She'd already made that abundantly clear, and he'd told her he understood.

He could be an idiot sometimes.

Principal Pelton had put on a big snack buffet in the gymnasium, where all the school clubs and sports teams had banners, tables and representatives for the students to check out. He was due upstairs to continue mingling, but first—he needed a drink.

Aside from smelling like mothballs, his office-closet proved to be a treasure trove of hidden compartments, educational relics and, of course, that impressive stash of booze. Did Pelton know about the stash? Surely, booze on campus, whether for teacher or student, was a fireable offense. Well, that just meant he needed to keep the classroom door locked when he imbibed.

Once he tidied up the tables and chairs, tossed all his handouts into the recycling bin and shut off the lights, he retreated to his office and poured himself a dram.

They wouldn't miss him upstairs if he gave himself five

minutes to enjoy the smooth drink left behind as a secret gift by his predecessor, would they? Shutting his eyes, he leaned back against the front of his office desk and brought the glass to his nose.

"Got any more?"

He opened his eyes and thrust the glass out toward her. "You know I do."

Celeste took the glass and with a flirtatious smile, brought it to her lips. "That rough of a night?" The sexy line of her throat bobbed as she swallowed. She sipped it again before handing it back to him. He topped it up and took a healthy sip himself. Fuck, that was good. Mental salute and thank you to Mr. Mothballs. The man knew his rye.

"Not so much a rough night, but I will admit my ego took a hit when you wouldn't even look at me." He was never one to play head games or not say what he meant or felt. That had been the downfall of his marriage. Way too many secrets. Way too much resentment and lack of communication.

"Sabrina still doesn't know about us. I'm here tonight for her. My focus had to be on her."

Fair enough.

Now he felt like a right prick.

But that didn't stop him from goading her. "Then why are you here with *me?*"

She took back the glass and sipped it again. "She's upstairs with some of her friends. They're interested in joining the model UN."

"That's a good club. I was Germany, back in the day."

Her smile made his dick jerk. "Slovakia."

"So you've come down here to my dungeon to ..."

"To see you. I'm here for her ... but I came down here for you."

Well, if that didn't make his dick jump.

She set the glass down on the table next to his hip and

moved toward him, resting her hands on his chest. "I need to find a better way to balance my life. I've spent the last fifteen years focusing solely on someone else's needs and wants while sacrificing my own. But I don't have to do that anymore. It's just taking a bit of time for me to realize it. Sabrina doesn't need me the way she used to. She has freedom. And in turn that allows me some freedom too."

"Freedom to ..."

"Explore. Give in to my wants, my desires, my *needs*."

Fuck, the way she said *needs* had him sporting a full stiffy in his jeans in record time.

She glanced up at him. The green in her eyes and the way it almost seemed to swirl around her dilating pupils made his cock throb and his hands itch to grab her just like he'd been wanting to since the last time she'd come into his classroom, wanting to toss her across his desk and *teach* her.

"Can you help me find the balance?" she asked, her mouth now less than an inch from his. Her breath, whiskey combined with minty freshness, fell across his lips in cool puffs. "Help me fulfill my *needs?*" One eyebrow lifted.

His nostrils flared, and he reached behind and fisted her ponytail, causing her eyes to widen in surprise. "You're playing with matches here, Celeste," he said, struggling to keep his libido in check.

Her throat undulated heavily before her mouth split into a wide grin. "Am I?"

Tilting her head back, he dipped his mouth to her neck and raked his teeth over the soft, thin, creamy skin of her throat. He wasn't quite sure what had come over him, but he could tell she liked his assertion. Her pulse picked up tempo along her neck, and her breathing had begun to escape her mouth in quick pants.

She licked her lips, her eyes bright and challenging. "Are you going to take the matches away from me, *Mr. Travis*? Or are you going to *teach* me how to start a fire? Stoke it so it gets good and *hot*."

She squawked as he flipped her around and pressed her back against his chest. One of his hands pressed against her neck, keeping her head on his shoulder, while the other one splayed across her flat abdomen. "Oh, I can *teach*," he whispered next to her ear. "I think the greater question here is: Are you willing to learn?"

Her sharp inhale was encouraging.

"Do I need to muzzle you?" he asked, nipping at her earlobe and trailing his tongue down her neck.

"All depends."

"Hmmm." His fingers against her belly pushed beneath the waistband of her pants until he met with lacy panties.

"I can be quiet if I have to be," she whispered, her chest lifting and dropping with each heavy breath.

"Are you normally?" He inched his fingers lower still over her panties until he found a damp patch. He tapped her clit with his middle finger, and she jerked in his arms.

"No. At least I didn't used to be."

Lifting his hand up, he pushed his fingers beneath the elastic of the lace where short, soft hair met his fingertips. He'd never been one who liked a bare pussy, and he could just imagine that the hair between her legs was the same as the hair on her head. The thought of pressing his nose there, inhaling her scent before he devoured her pussy, made his dick throb. He knew she could feel his erection against her ass. He wasn't hiding it, and the way she wiggled her bottom across his lap said she felt it and she didn't mind it at all.

His middle finger dipped down between her folds and gathered drops of her silky arousal before dragging it back up toward her clit, where he began to make small circles. Her hips gyrated, and she bucked up into his palm.

Chuckling, he released his grip on her neck. "Give me

your mouth," he demanded, relishing in the way she shivered in his arms from his words.

With fire in her eyes and a moan that made him worry he was going to blow his load in his jeans, she turned her head and parted her lips. He swallowed her groans as he added another finger, both of them now circling her clit while his tongue claimed her mouth. The way she was thrusting against his fingers, causing them to slip between her cleft, told him she wanted his fingers inside her. He obliged, of course. Down through her heat, he trailed his fingers, tickling her plump folds, loving how fucking wet she was, how wet *he* made her. He found her core and pushed inside. The moan that bubbled up from the back of her throat in his mouth was enough to make him almost lose it completely.

But he reined it back in and told his balls to calm down.

She was tight. Really fucking tight. The way her pussy gripped his fingers, her ridges contracting around him, made his dick grow furiously jealous. His thumb pressed against her clit, and she spasmed in his arms again.

He could tell she was getting close. Her hip movements were growing more erratic, and her clit had doubled in size against his thumb. And then everything tensed on her, inside and out. Her mouth opened and she broke the kiss, a silent cry squeaking out of her throat. He kissed her harder as her climax exploded around him and she cried out inside his mouth, her short, shallow breaths escaping through her nose.

A gush of warm liquid flowed out over his fingers as she came, coating his hand and filling her panties. He couldn't wait until she did that over his face, until he got to drink every drop of her honey, lick his fingers clean and then go back for seconds.

Just as she'd grown tense in his arms, her entire body relaxed and she slumped against him. For a moment, he was actually holding her upright. Had she passed out?

Little whimpers filled his mouth before she broke the kiss. Her head lolled backward, and she rested it on his shoulder. "Mr. Travis, you are a dirty bugger."

WHAT THE HELL JUST HAPPENED?

Had Mr. Travis—Max—just fingered her in his office?

Yes, yes he had. And it was fucking glorious.

He pulled his hand free from her pants, and she wondered if he was going to lick it clean. A part of her hoped he would, but another part of her wasn't sure she was ready to see that. She was still in a state of shock at not only her own behavior, but at his transformation. Sure, the man was hot as hell, but he didn't give off a blatant dominant vibe. The guy just seemed to relaxed for that. But the way he'd taken such control just then, with his fingers on her throat … she'd never felt herself get so wet so fast in all her life. A rush of liquid had fled her body when he spun her around and gripped her throat. Add in the rush of adrenaline, nerves and lust, and she was like a powder keg of orgasms. And then he struck the match when his thumb strummed her clit.

He opened up a small pouch of Lysol wipes and grabbed one, wiping his finger on it before looking at her. It was probably for the best. If he licked his fingers, she'd probably have another orgasm, then fall to her knees and take his pants down with her.

She eyed the whiskey on his desk and reached for it, finishing it. Not that she needed the buzz. She was lightheaded enough already.

He tossed the Lysol wipe into a trash bin and lifted his gaze to hers, a small, sexy smile forming on his lips. "I want to do more of that," he said, taking the glass from her. He didn't fill it again though.

She swallowed and nodded. "Me too."

It startled her how easily he was able to turn the tables. She'd come down to his classroom, stepped into his office, into his space, taken his drink and showed him what she wanted. But before she could blink, he'd taken over. She'd never been an overly dominant person when it came to sex, but she knew what she liked, and she wasn't afraid to ask for it. She did, however, love it when a man took over and she no longer *had* to ask. He just knew what to do, how to do it and how to do it right. And even though she'd only had a small taste of Max, something told her he knew how to do all of it right.

"We should probably get upstairs," he murmured, not hiding when he adjusted his pants. She'd felt his erection behind her and had even rubbed her butt up against it a few times.

Nodding, she tucked her hair behind her ear and made for the door.

Footsteps in the hallway outside the main door had them both pausing.

But the footsteps weren't coming toward them. They were retreating.

"Did you leave the door open?" he asked.

Celeste shook her head. "It was closed when I got here, and I closed it again when I came in. I swear."

Had someone been in the classroom when they were ...?

Had someone been watching them?

She realized now that the door to his office had never been completely closed. It'd remained open a crack, which was so incredibly stupid now that she thought of it, but she also didn't think they were going to do what they did. At most, she thought they might kiss a little more but that if they started doing that, she'd have the common sense to shut the door first.

She didn't.

Being around Max made her stupid.

In long, quick strides, Max heaved open the classroom door and called down the hallway, "Who's there? This is Mr. Travis. This is my classroom. Who's there?"

She was right behind him; her hand fell to his back. It was warm and solid beneath her fingertips. "Whoever it was, they're long gone now."

"Yeah, I just wonder how much they saw ... or heard," he muttered. The muscles beneath her fingertips tensed.

Her thoughts exactly.

He nodded, which also shook her hand free from his shoulder. "You head out of the classroom first, then I'll follow a few minutes later."

"Okay."

His nostrils flared at the same time he reached out and grabbed her by the waist, knocking the wind out of her with the titanium wall of his chest. "I'm glad you came down to see me," he whispered, his mouth hovering just a fraction of an inch over hers. "Sneaking around is fun." Then he sealed the deal with his lips over hers, showing her yet again that he wasn't just a man who knew his way around numbers, but he also knew his way around a woman's body, and she couldn't wait to let him teach her everything he knew.

11

BACK UP IN THE GYMNASIUM, Celeste entered the full, noisy space. She knew Max wasn't far behind her, so she searched for her daughter's flaming red hair among the crowd. When she spotted Sabrina, she made a beeline straight in her direction.

"Where'd you go, Mom?" Sabrina asked, standing with two of her friends from junior high.

Celeste's eyes snagged Max's as he entered the gym, but then she focused back on her kid. "I had to use the bathroom, and the lineup for the one here was too long, so I went to explore a bit. Did you know they have a creative writing class here? I was reading the list of special electives on one of the bulletin boards. Apparently, it's open to any grade, so you could have freshmen in with seniors in the same class. A weird concept, but also cool. I wish they'd had something like that back when I was in school."

"You mean when you were a teen mother?"

"Excuse me?" Celeste turned around to find Eleanor Shelby standing behind her, looking all proud of herself.

"Well, you were, weren't you?" Eleanor lifted a shoulder

before glancing to either side of her, where two girls who didn't necessarily appear on board with her cruelty stood beside her like silent minions.

What the fuck was going on?

Celeste was not going to let some fifteen-year-old little bully make her feel shitty about herself. She was not ashamed of her life or her daughter. She tilted her head and was about to say something when Sabrina spoke up.

"My mom had me after she graduated high school. She married my dad. They were happy and in love until he died. So what if she got pregnant young? She finished school and has a great job, and she's the best mom in the whole world."

Tears sprang into Sabrina's eyes, and her complexion became a mottled and concerning shade of red. Was there more going on here than Celeste was aware? Had Eleanor been bullying Sabrina more since last week? Had it escalated to more than the bathroom vandalism, rumors and online bullying?

"Why are you *so* mean to me?" Sabrina choked out; her fists bunched at her sides. "What is your problem?"

There was the fire spirit she was raising. Celeste had never needed to be feisty like that during school. She'd never needed to defend herself against predators like Eleanor. Maybe it was because she had her sister Eva, who had been popular in school and had sort of paved the way for Celeste. Or perhaps it was because she'd been with Declan since they were freshmen and he was also popular. She never worried about being bullied or manipulated the way Eleanor was treating her daughter, so she had never developed a fighting spirit. That's not to say she didn't have a temper—she did, after all, have red hair—but she'd never used it in school.

Maybe that was to her detriment. She hadn't dealt with people like Eleanor before, so she was ill-equipped to do so now.

Eleanor's lips curled up into a smile that made Celeste's skin crawl. She shrugged. "See you tomorrow, *Sabrina*." She and her lackeys turned to go, but before they left, Celeste caught a look in the other two girls' eyes. They were not a fan of how Eleanor was treating Sabrina. They had consciences; they were just afraid of the she-devil.

Perhaps if she could get one of those girls alone, she could figure out why Eleanor had such a hate-on for Sabrina.

With Eleanor gone, Sabrina's friends were now comforting her as Sabrina sniffled and tears dripped down her face, her head hung low.

"She's a bitch. Don't listen to her," Madeline said, rubbing Sabrina's back. "We all know your mom is cool."

"Cooler than my mom, for sure," Joanie added. "My mom is *so* old. She's like ... *forty*. You guys are like the Gilmore Girls only cooler."

Sabrina lifted her head, her green eyes red-rimmed and still brimming with new tears. "I'm sorry, Mom. She's just ..."

A total bitch?

"She's been bullying Sabrina a lot since school started," Joanie said. "We can't figure out why."

"I know," Celeste said. "The things written on the bathroom walls, it's completely unacceptable. Who does that kind of thing?"

Joanie and Madeline exchanged looks, like there was more to it than just the scrawling on the bathroom walls.

Anger ratcheted up her spine, and heat filled her gut. Her mama bear was coming out. Nobody messed with her cub, nobody. Not even another cub. She'd burn down the entire forest, wring the neck of every last bear, every last animal that threatened her family if it meant keeping her cub safe. Maybe she did have a fire spirit inside of her as well. It just came out when her cub was in danger.

"Girls." She turned to Madeline and Joanie. "Can you all

138 I WHITLEY COX

just go sit on the bleachers? Maybe find one of your parents and hang out by them? I need to go do something quick."

Sabrina's friends nodded and wrapped their arms around their upset friend, steering her toward the bleachers.

Celeste thanked them, then headed off in search of one of Eleanor's cronies. Or Eleanor herself, or Mindy. She didn't really care who she found, but she needed to find someone, and she needed to get a few things straightened out.

Her eyes darted around the full gymnasium, and that's when she saw remora number one break off from the blood-thirsty tiger shark and head toward the bathroom. Now was her chance.

Elbowing her way through the crowd, she made it to the bathroom, but the girl had already gone inside. She would wait.

Not five minutes later, remora number one, with her dark hair and big brown doe eyes, emerged from the bathroom. Celeste snagged her arm.

The girl yelped but then stifled her surprise when she saw who had grabbed her.

"I'm sorry," Celeste whispered, letting go of the kid's arm but also encouraging her to step back into what looked like a P.E. teacher's office. "Can I ask you something?"

She nodded.

"What's your name?"

"Phyllis."

She kept her voice low. "Phyllis, can you tell me why Eleanor is so mean to Sabrina? What has my daughter done to this girl to make her a target?"

Phyllis's eyes darted toward the open door, and she nibbled on her lip. "I really shouldn't be talking to you."

Because she would get in trouble from Eleanor? Where the hell were they? Communist Russia?

"Last time I checked, this was a free country, kiddo. And I

could see back there that you didn't like the way your friend was treating Sabrina. Unlike Eleanor, *you* seem to have a conscience and know when someone is being unnecessarily cruel."

Phyllis teetered back and forth on her shoes. "I don't like how Eleanor treats Sabrina. Sabrina is a nice person. She's always been nice to me. But that's *why* Eleanor hates her."

What? That didn't make any sense. Phyllis was right though. Sabrina was impossible not to like. All her teachers had said that over the years. Sabrina was not a cliquey person. She was a friends with everyone person. A social butterfly, although on the shier side like Celeste had been, but she was never without friends. Which was probably why this problem with Eleanor was so hard on both of them. Neither Celeste nor her kid knew how to navigate the bully territory because they'd never had to deal with it before.

"Can you help me understand why Eleanor hates her because she is so nice?" Celeste asked. "That just doesn't make sense to me. Shouldn't you want to be friends with and nice to someone who is also nice?"

Phyllis's mouth twisted, and she shook her head, an impatient look crossing her face, as if Celeste had *so* much to learn about the intricacies of high school hierarchy. She did have a lot to learn—albeit reluctantly.

"Eleanor is popular," Phyliss started, "but she's popular out of fear. Sabrina is popular because she is nice and because everyone likes her. Sabrina was voted *nicest person in the school* last year in the yearbook, and that made Eleanor furious. It also doesn't help that Eleanor's boyfriend broke up with her over the summer, and it's rumored he wants to ask out Sabrina."

Holy shit.

It all came down to a boy.

She should have known.

Celeste had read that bit about Sabrina in the yearbook, but she hadn't thought anything of it besides the fact that it was true.

"Eleanor feels like she's losing her power. Her status." Phyllis glanced back toward the open door. "Not that she says that, but my mom is a therapist, so I know stuff."

Of course, Celeste's father was a dentist, so obviously she could perform a root canal that very moment. Chip off the old block. No education needed.

"Has Eleanor's ex-boyfriend asked out Sabrina?" Celeste asked. Damn it, she wished her kid would talk to her more. She knew about the graffiti on the bathroom walls and the online bullying, but she had no idea there was a boy at the center of it all.

And judging by the tears that sprung from Sabrina's eyes a moment ago and the shifty way Madeline and Joanie were looking at each other, there was definitely more to this story.

It was starting to make sense why Eleanor was lashing out. If she thought for a second her boyfriend dumped her so that he could date Sabrina, she'd be on the warpath for sure.

Did Sabrina know all of this too? And if so, why hadn't she told Celeste? All this stuff was happening with her kid right under her nose, and she had no idea. She was failing as a mom. Damn it, mom guilt was a vile beast. Motherhood really was a mental illness.

Phyllis shook her head. "Noah hasn't asked Sabrina out that I know of. But our whole grade knows he likes her and wants to ask her out. He sits with her if they have classes together and seeks her out at lunch. Any time Eleanor sees them together talking she gets really angry." Worry clouded her face. "I should really go, though. Eleanor is going to be wondering where I went."

And if she didn't get back in time, Lady Eleanor would

dole out twenty lashes for Phyllis's insolence? Off with her head?

Since when did crotch goblins have so much power?

Since parents stopped ruling the roost and chose being their kids' friend over being their parent and discipline went out the window.

Glancing at the door in case Eleanor or another remora was lurking, she turned back to Phyllis. "Can I ask you one more question?"

Phyllis's head bobbed, but her eyes remained wary. "Sure."

"It's Eleanor spreading all the rumors and writing all the stuff on the bathroom walls, right?" They all knew it was, but she needed confirmation from someone inside Eleanor's inner circle.

The young girl's eyes darted to the floor, but Celeste couldn't mistake the nod. "I've gone back into the bathrooms and erased a few of them. The meanest ones. I can't get them all, but I think what Eleanor is writing is horrible. Sabrina doesn't deserve it. None of it's true."

No shit, Sabrina didn't deserve it. Sabrina didn't deserve any of it. And of-fucking-course none of it was true.

Tamping down the rage, Celeste nodded. "Okay, go back to your tiger shark. Thank you for your honesty."

Phyllis glanced at Celeste in confusion before retreating.

Celeste needed to go find her kid again and get home. They needed to get the hell away from that school, away from Eleanor Shelby, and formulate a plan.

She was almost to the bleachers when she bumped into a rock-solid wall of muscle.

"Oh, pardon me," came a deep, sexy rumble from the sky.

She took a step back and looked up. Way, way up. The guy was crazy tall. Like six-foot-six tall. Celeste's eyes went wide as she took in the handsome giant smiling down at her.

"I can usually spot obstacles a mile away," he said, his grin growing wider. "My apologies."

Shaking her head and feeling a bit flustered from how gorgeous this man's smile was, not to mention the rest of him, she tucked a strand of hair behind her ear and chuckled. "I was distracted. Totally my fault. I also thought you were a lamppost and wouldn't move."

His laugh was like whiskey wrapped in caramel wrapped in dark chocolate. Smooth, satisfying and something you wanted more of. He stuck his hand out. "Alastair Shelby. Nice to meet you."

Alastair Shelby.

Another Shelby.

She didn't take his hand but rather took a big step back. "Y-you're Eleanor's father? Mindy's ex?"

Curiosity drifted behind the soft brown of his eyes. "I am, yes. Why? Do you know them both?"

Her head wobbled on her neck in some shaky kind of nod. "I do. Your daughter—"

"Hi, Daddy!" Of course, at that moment, Eleanor bounced up looking like a princess and batted her lashes lovingly up at her father. Celeste knew better though. Beneath that tiara were horns, and she'd tucked her arrowhead tail beneath her dress, so those who thought the sun shone out of her ass were none the wiser to her nefarious deeds.

Alastair smiled down adoringly at his daughter. "Hello, angel."

Oh, barf. Angel, really? Didn't he know she kept a pitchfork in her locker and had hooved feet in those glass slippers?

"This is ..." He tilted his head at Celeste. "I'm sorry, I never caught your name."

"Celeste Howard," she said with a rattled breath, her eyes scanning the gymnasium for Sabrina. She was still on the bleachers with her friends. Now Joanie's mom was sitting with them. Good.

He nodded. "Celeste Howard." He turned back to Eleanor. "Are you ready to go?"

Eleanor's smile was sickly sweet as she continued to gaze up at her father like one-hundred-dollar bills were currently exploding from his ears. "I am, Daddy."

Alastair faced Celeste again. "It was nice *running in to you*. Perhaps we can do it again sometime." He smiled, rested his hand on Eleanor's back and steered them toward the exit.

Celeste's feet were made of concrete. Her heart felt like it was preparing to explode out of her chest. She watched them leave, and just as she was collecting her thoughts and ready to go to her child, Eleanor glanced back, sneered and flipped Celeste the bird.

What the fuck was wrong with kids today?

Steam rose up out of Celeste's ears as she stomped her foot, grateful that it was no longer glued to the floor, and she made her way through the crowd to her child.

She was nearly at the bleachers when a cool hand on her arm stopped her. "That's my ex-husband."

Oh, for Christ's sake.

Sabrina was literally within spitting distance now. She and her friends were chatting jovially and eating from small bags of potato chips they'd grabbed from the snack table.

"I gathered that when he said his name was Alastair Shelby," Celeste said to Mindy, shaking herself free from the woman's icy grip. "I then asked him if he was Eleanor's father, and he confirmed it."

"What were you talking about?"

None of your damn business.

Celeste shook her head. "Nothing. We bumped into each other, apologized, he introduced himself, and then Eleanor showed up."

Mindy's pale blue stare heated. She didn't believe Celeste. Well, too freaking bad. It wasn't Celeste's job to protect Mindy Shelby's feelings. It was her job to protect her child.

But the fates must have thrust the Shelby parents into her path for a reason. Only, why had Eleanor been thrown into her path as well? Twice, for that matter.

"Mindy, it's come to my attention that Eleanor is continuing to bully Sabrina. More graffiti on the bathroom walls. More rumors. It's escalating, and it's starting to worry me. She's also been very rude to me this evening. I understand that your daughter is going through a difficult time right now, with yours and Alastair's separation." At the mention of her ex-husband's name, Mindy's nostrils flared and her lips pressed together to form a thin, flat line. "But she is being unreasonably cruel to my daughter. I know her boyfriend also ended things over the summer, which has to be hard, but again, it's not Sabrina's fault."

Mindy looked like a bottle of shaken-up Coke, ready to explode. Her body vibrated. "Don't you dare tell me how to raise my daughter. For all we know, it's *your* kid who's the bully."

Celeste could only blink.

Apple. Tree.

No wonder Eleanor was the way she was. Look at who raised her.

Mindy's anger-filled stare wavered at the same time Celeste felt a heat at her back and a familiar scent as fresh and addictive as a forest after a spring rain filled her senses.

"Good evening, ladies," Max said, his tone cautious. He positioned himself beside them, keeping a decent amount of distance between him and Celeste but an even greater distance between him and Mindy. "Everything okay here?"

Celeste's gaze flicked up to his. "Everything is just peachy,

Mr. Travis." All that earned her was a lip twitch and a couple of dilated pupils.

He pivoted his foScus to Mindy. "How are you doing tonight, Mindy?"

The smile she gave him was so damn fake, it made Celeste's fake Gucci sunglasses look like the real deal. "I'm well, Max. Thank you for asking."

"Where are your kids?" he asked, his gaze sweeping the gym, which had started to empty out.

"Sabrina is on the bleachers with her friends. I was just heading to her now. And Eleanor left with her father," Celeste said, watching as Mindy's complexion turned a disturbing shade of red at the mention of Alastair again.

"I will be the one to talk about my child. Thank you, *Celeste*," Mindy hissed out. "Why don't you run along to your daughter. I'm sure it's nearing both your bedtimes anyway, seeing as you're both children."

Oh no, she didn't.

Those were fighting words.

Celeste's head reared back. "Excuse me?"

Just like her daughter's, Mindy's mouth slid into a smug smile of triumph, like she figured she'd won the battle.

Too bad Celeste was out to win the war.

"I can see where your daughter gets her unfavorable attitude," Celeste said. "I do hope, unlike you, she grows out of such childish behavior. Her father seemed like a reasonable, mature man. Perhaps his influence on her will help her grow up to be a tolerable human being." She smiled a closed-mouth smile at Mindy before turning her attention to Max. "Nice to see you again, Mr. Travis. Now, if you'll excuse me, it *is* past my bedtime. I must go collect my daughter." Then, before Mindy could sling any more barbs, arrows or insults, Celeste vacated their little triangle of lust, unrequited lust and contempt and finally went to go gather her kid.

"Mom, what happened?" Sabrina's eyes rivaled the size of dinner plates when Celeste finally approached her daughter and her friends on the bleachers.

"Ran into Eleanor's dad, Eleanor and Eleanor's mother. I feel like the Shelby family is hell-bent on making our lives difficult." She glanced at Joanie's mother, Heather. "Did you have to deal with bullies when you were in school?"

Heather's lips pinned together, and she nodded, but just barely. "I did. A lot. I went to a very cliquey school."

Joanie's eyes turned sad, and she glanced at her mother, wrapping a protective arm around her shoulder. "I didn't know that, Mom."

Heather smiled grimly. "It's okay. I'm okay. I lived." Her dark gaze became heated and avid as she focused back on Celeste. "You need to cut off the serpent's head. That's the only way."

Celeste already knew that. She was just having a tough time determining which of the Shelby women was the head of the serpent.

Sabrina stood up, and Celeste reached for her, drawing her into her side and looping her arm around her waist. She needed to keep her daughter close. It was the only way she knew she could keep her safe. But she wouldn't be able to do that forever. She couldn't bubble-wrap her daughter and homeschool her. So she needed to arm her child with the tools and mental weaponry to take down the serpent. To vanquish the enemy. Behead the snake.

They said goodbye to Sabrina's friends and Heather and turned to go. Nearly in the clear, Celeste stopped in her tracks when a ripple of unease started at the base of her spine and inched its way up to the nape of her neck. She tightened her grip around Sabrina and glanced around the now nearly empty gym. Mindy was standing on one side of the big space glaring at her, her icy-blue glower visible at nearly fifty yards.

Her arms crossed over her chest, pushing up her cleavage, and the pinched expression of her nose and mouth suggested she'd just smelled her own fart. Mindy's eyes flicked away from Celeste, and she pivoted to see where she was looking.

Max was on the other side of the gym, watching her with an intensity she felt between her thighs. The heat of his need swept through her entire body.

She glanced back at Mindy, and the woman's stare had turned downright evil.

What the hell was going on?

Shivering, Celeste pulled her daughter closer, swallowed down the unease that stuck in the back of her throat like a chunk of stale bread, and urged them to move on. They needed to get the hell out of there before Mindy decided to come at her again, this time for breathing.

She knew he had to cut off the serpent's head to end the torture. Her only fear was that this particular beast was two-headed, out for blood and possibly invincible.

12

"THAT'S WHY SHE HATES ME?" Sabrina asked as they drove home that night. "But those aren't things I have any control over. I can't control who votes for me as nicest person. What am I supposed to do, stop being *nice?*" She tossed her hands up into the air and let the backs of them slam down against her thighs. "And as for the Noah thing ..."

Celeste was driving, so it was tough to see her daughter's expression, but she could tell by her change in body language and the slouch of her shoulders that there was more to this *Noah thing* than Sabrina was letting on.

"Has he asked you out?" she asked.

Sabrina's head spun to face her mother. "No!"

"But you've heard the rumors?"

All that got her was a teenage shoulder lift. And those said a lot.

"Do you like him?"

Sabrina rolled her eyes and glanced back out the window. "I dunno. He's like *super* popular and whatever and I'm not. Rumor is he broke up with Eleanor because he wants to date me. But I don't believe it."

Celeste believed it.

Who wouldn't want to date her kind, smart, beautiful child?

"Have you spoken with this Noah?" she asked.

Sabrina nodded. "We have math together. He sits beside me. Comes to talk to me at lunch a few times a week."

So she'd more than just "spoken" to him.

"You mean Mr. Travis's class?" Shit, she spoke before thinking.

Sabrina's head nearly flew off her neck with how fast she whipped back around to face her mother again. "Yes. Is there anything going on between you and Mr. Travis?"

"Mr. Travis—Max—and I are friends. We've known each other for a long time. And now that he's at this school and is your teacher, he can keep an eye on you. Let me know if things with Eleanor get worse." She fixed her child with a stern look of her own. "Because apparently *you* don't feel like you can talk to me. I know there's more going on than just the rumors and the stuff being written on the bathroom walls. When I mentioned it earlier, Joanie and Madeline looked at each other like my head was in the sand and I had no idea. That's not cool, kiddo. Spill."

Twilight had settled in, making it tough to gauge the color of her daughter's complexion, but Sabrina was as fair-skinned as Celeste, so it was easy to tell when red filled her cheeks. "I ... I dunno. I didn't think the rumors about Noah liking me were true until he sat beside me in math. Now he sits beside me every day. He texts me after school and on the weekend. Waves at me in the hallway, talks to me at lunch."

"And you like him?"

Sabrina didn't have to say a word for Celeste to know the answer.

All her kid did was shrug again. "I thought maybe it

would all blow over. That Eleanor would get another boyfriend and she'd leave me alone."

"And has it? Has she?" They pulled into their complex and swung a left to go down to their garage.

Sabrina shook her head. "No. She's such a bully."

"And so is her mother. Her father ... I can't tell yet. But he seemed fine. Stares at his child like sunbeams are coming out of her ass, but I won't hold that against him, particularly if, like you, Eleanor keeps her parents in the dark." Celeste hit the button for the garage door and pulled inside. The light in the garage came on automatically. She shut off the ignition and turned to face Sabrina, unbuckling her belt at the same time. "You need to talk to me, kiddo. I mean it. This Eleanor and Mindy shit could get real, and we need to have open lines of communication between us if we're going to hack off this double-headed serpent."

Sabrina's lips twisted. "I'm sorry. I'll talk more."

Celeste crossed her arms over her chest. "Okay, so talk."

Sabrina rolled her eyes. "It's just that it looks like Eleanor has taken the rumors she wrote on the bathroom up a notch, and she has some of the football players saying that I give out hand jobs to two guys at once for two bucks and blowjobs for a dollar after school under the bleachers. She says that we're so poor, it's the only way I can buy my clothes."

Why that little ...

Celeste's body couldn't make up its mind. It wanted to puke, scream, kill and run. Fight and flight. There was no either-or here.

With her fists clenched tightly around the steering wheel, she squeezed her eyes shut and spoke slowly. "I need to know everything that is going on. Absolutely everything, Sabrina. This is getting dangerous. Eleanor is out for blood—yours."

"I know, Mom. I just ... I don't know what to do. I'm basically just keeping my head down and hoping this will all blow over. That she'll get tired of harassing me and move on to someone else."

"But then she's torturing someone else. She is a bully. She lives—*thrives*—on the misery of others. It is her fuel. So as long as she knows that you are even the least bit affected by this, she's not going to stop. She's just going to up the ante."

Fear flooded her daughter's face. "What does that mean?"

Celeste had no clue. She didn't even want to start guessing.

"I don't know, kiddo. But it worries me what this girl is capable of. She's hurting, and she's angry. She feels rejected, and rejection is a dangerous motivator." Should she hire her kid a bodyguard? Was Eleanor capable of physically harming Sabrina? After what he'd just heard of Eleanor and how far she was willing to go, there wasn't much Celeste wouldn't consider the girl capable of. "I gave Max my phone number so that he can call or text me to let me know if something in school has gone down. I'd rather hear it from you though, kiddo."

Sabrina's nostril's flared. "Is that the *only* reason you gave him your number?"

No.

"You like him, don't you?" her child probed.

If she wanted honesty from her kid, her kid deserved honesty. Letting out a deep breath, Celeste nodded. "I do. And he likes me. But we both agree that *you* are what is most important here. So we're taking things slow. I don't want to do anything to hurt you or jeopardize your school year."

Sabrina's nose turned up, and she made a disgruntled face. "I don't like the idea of my mom dating my teacher."

"You don't have a say, kiddo. But know that we're not going to do anything to embarrass you or put you further onto Eleanor's radar."

"Impossible at this point," Sabrina muttered. "I'm wandering around with a red laser beam pointed on my chest, she's gunning so hard for me."

Celeste gripped her daughter's arm. "God, don't say things like that."

"Have you been on dates with him already?"

She made sure she was looking her daughter directly in the eyes. She wanted honesty from Sabrina, so she needed to give it to her daughter in return. "I have. We've been out twice, and they were really nice dates."

Sabrina inhaled through her nose and unbuckled her belt, but Celeste wasn't ready to let her daughter out of the vehicle. She hauled her fifteen-year-old awkwardly across the center console of the SUV into a hug. She was all limbs and grunts until she settled on Celeste's lap. She appeared annoyed, but the smile on her face and the sigh of content-ment as she rested the side of her head against Celeste's fore-head said otherwise.

"You are my number one priority, kiddo. Always and forever. But you don't demand my attention twenty-four seven anymore, and it's time I start living a bit of my life for me."

"But with my math teacher?" Sabrina groaned.

"He won't be your math teacher forever, but he's kind, smart and"—*one hell of a kisser*—"he likes me. So we're going to see where this thing goes."

"But what if you dump him and he gives me a bad grade in retaliation?"

"Then I will personally come to the school and kick his ass."

Sabrina snorted and started to laugh, which shook them both. She pulled out of Celeste's arms but remained on her lap. "I want you to be happy, Mom."

"And your happiness means the world to me, kiddo.

Which is why we're going to figure this Eleanor Shelby mess out together, even if it means I accompany you to school every day all day for the next four years to keep you safe." At Sabrina's groan, grin and eyeroll, Celeste pulled her daughter in for another hug and squeezed her extra tight. "Because you're my cub, and this mama bear doesn't let anyone mess with her baby. Otherwise, I will spill blood."

TUCKED into bed with a cup of Sleepytime tea on her nightstand, her book in her hand and her hair freshly washed and dried, Celeste let out a long, deep sigh.

With everything going on with her kid, she hadn't had much of an opportunity to process what had gone down in Max's office. Particularly what had gone down her pants.

Oh boy.

Wow.

Like, seriously, W-O-W. Wow.

She could easily chalk it up to the fact that a man hadn't touched her like that in a ridiculously long time, and that nearly any man could have manhandled her the way Max had and she would have submitted and orgasmed. But she knew that wasn't true. The way Max touched her, the hidden power, the control, the way he smelled, looked, felt. It was all him. Not just any man could have pulled such a primal response from her. But Max did.

She glanced at her nightstand drawer where her tried and true, battery-operated boyfriend—Henry Cavill—lived, waiting patiently to please her. After one night of drinking way too much wine with her sister, Bianca, Richelle, Zara, Lauren and Paige, Celeste had ordered the *ultimate* vibrator. It had the unpleasing name of *Tracy's Dog*—which was why she renamed it to the sexiest man in the universe—but boy, was it a woman's best friend. The reviews alone had all of them doubled over laughing, some of them on the floor, all of them with tears in their eyes. But only Bianca, Lauren and Celeste had ordered them, as the rest of the women had men in their lives and didn't see the need for *Tracy's Dog*—that is, until Bianca, Lauren and Celeste got theirs and provided their friends with their own reviews. Celeste swore she could hear colors after her first night with Henry. It wasn't long until all the women had one.

But she needed to get a decent night's sleep. So it was either Henry or a couple of chapters from one of her new favorite books in The Breaking Series by author Ember Leigh. That was another reason she was so drawn to Max. The man did jujitsu. In the last week or so since finding out he liked to fight, she'd pictured him instead of the hero of the MMA romance book she was reading. Max, all sweaty, muscles rippling, veins popping. Max, with his hands wrapped in tape, pinning her up against the shower wall, fully clothed, and stripping her until she was wet, wanton and willing to drop to her knees and ...

She glanced again at her nightstand drawer, this time with a hell of a lot more longing.

Could she play with Henry and then read one chapter from her book? Could she ever stop at *just one more chapter?* No. She only had a third of the book to go. She'd probably finish it that night and then possibly even start the next one. She had very little willpower when it came to a good book. Sleep be damned. She'd sleep when she was dead. But there were so many books and so little time.

But Henry be damned? Not so much.

Taking a sip of her tea, she put the bookmark back in her book and reached for her nightstand drawer, jumping nearly clear out of her pajamas when her phone began to vibrate.

She glanced at it, her hand paused on the handle of her night table.

Mr. T.

What the ...

Did he know what she was about to do?

Masturbate with Henry to thoughts of Max all sweaty, rippling and with his hands—and other things—back down her pants?

Setting her tea back down so she didn't spill it all over herself, she pulled the phone from the charger, swallowed and answered it. "Hello?"

"I saw you enter my name and number into your phone. You know it's me. Why so surprised?"

Oh, damn, she was going to orgasm on the spot if she wasn't careful. That deep, silky rasp of his had her nipples peaking to tight, painful points beneath her loose tank top, and her pussy began to throb. Now she wasn't just staring at her nightstand drawer with longing, she was staring at it hoping Henry had a mind of his own and leapt clear out of the drawer and into her lap.

"Sorry," she squeaked, taking another sip of tea to clear her throat. "I just didn't expect you to call me."

"Yeah, well, after what went down tonight in the gym"—*and down in your office*—"I figured it was only right. I didn't wake you, did I?"

"N-no, I'm in bed."

Was. That. A. Purr?

Could men purr?

No.

That was the sound a male lion makes when he's hungry, and not necessarily for a limping gazelle on the Serengeti.

"Yeah, me too."

Well, now she had visions of Max in bed. Was he naked?

Or was he someone who wore sexy black boxer briefs that left little to the imagination?

She licked her lips and sipped more of her tea.

"About Mindy, she approached me after you left. Went on and on about how young and immature you are. How she spoke with her daughter and Eleanor has done nothing she's being accused of and that you and Sabrina are just out to make enemies."

Celeste shot up in her bed, her tea sloshing out of her mug onto her duvet. "She said *what?*"

"Yeah. I tried to be as gentle as I could, because I *do* have to work with the woman, and we're not even a month into the school year, but it was hard listening to her spout all these lies. Not only about you, but about Sabrina too. I teach both girls, and although I haven't taught them long, I'm not an idiot and can pick out the good apples from the bad pretty quickly."

"Eleanor isn't just a *bad* apple, she's fucking rotten. And so is her mother."

"No argument from me. Did you find out anything? I saw you doing a bit of snooping. You managed to separate Phyllis from Eleanor, and then was that Eleanor's dad you were talking to?" That last bit was said with just the subtlest bit of edge to it. Was Max jealous?

"I did speak with Phyllis. Turns out, Sabrina was voted nicest person last year in their yearbook, and that pissed Eleanor off. Sabrina is becoming more popular because she is a nice person, whereas Eleanor is popular because of the fear she instills in others. Phyllis also told me that Eleanor's boyfriend dumped her over the summer and he wants to ask out Sabrina. He's in your class, too."

"Noah?"

"Yeah, have you noticed anything?"

"Just that he's got a real thing for Sabrina. Even a chimp

could see that he likes her. Always flirting with her, sits next to her."

Uncertainty wormed its way into her belly. "Do you think his feelings for her are genuine?" The last thing she wanted was for her daughter—who obviously liked Noah in return—to get hurt because Noah and his she-devil ex had some big scheme going on to take down the nicest person in the school.

"I think he genuinely likes her, yes. He's a good kid. Smart —really smart with numbers. He's been helping Sabrina. Reminds me a lot of—"

"Declan?"

His voice grew quiet. "Yeah."

"And does she flirt back?"

"A little bit, but not as much as he flirts. She just smiles a lot when they're together."

Her daughter did have the best freaking smile in the entire world, so it would be hard for Noah not to be drawn to her.

"Mindy mentioned to me that you look an awful lot like the woman her husband cheated on her with," he said, switching gears. "She was a redhead and younger. That might be where a large portion of her ire stems from."

Celeste was busy staring at the small damp patch on her duvet from where her tea sloshed, and she nearly sloshed more from her reaction. She needed to finish her tea and set the mug down. So much for the brew making her sleepy though. She was just getting pissed off.

She finished her tea, took a deep breath and spoke. "When did Mindy tell you this?"

"Earlier today. She saw you at Prime Sports Bar and came down to my classroom after school today. Mentioned seeing you and how her husband cheated with a younger woman, a redhead …"

"So like her daughter, she takes her anger out on innocent people? Her kid can't handle that my kid is liked because she's nice, and Mindy thinks I slept with her husband?" Her head was beginning to hurt. Not even Henry Cavill and his third setting would be able to help her. She rubbed at her temples.

"She knows it wasn't *you* who slept with him. But she still has a mad hate-on for you."

Well, duh.

"I don't know how she thinks that makes me want her and not you."

Celeste drew in a sharp breath. He wanted her. She already knew that, but it still made her skin tingle—and other parts too—to hear him say it so candidly.

"But I don't want to talk any more about them. I want to talk about what happened in my office."

She released that breath and cupped one of her breasts, her thumb strumming over her puckered nipple through her tank top. "I want to too," she said, dragging her teeth over her bottom lip.

"I liked that side of you. Coming into my office, drinking my whiskey, getting into my *space*."

And she liked the new side she saw of him as well. The side where he gripped her throat, ordered her to kiss him and shoved his hand down her pants.

"Sabrina knows we're seeing each other," she said softly. "I told her tonight ... after she guessed, that is."

"And are you okay with her knowing?"

She was and she wasn't. She would have liked to have gone on a few more dates with Max, really gotten to know him and decided whether they were going to work, before she brought her daughter into the mix. But she also hated keeping Sabrina out of the loop. In some ways, this was easier. She didn't have to sneak around with Max anymore. At least not when it came to her daughter. She wouldn't be shouting it from the social media rooftops anytime soon, though.

"So, now that Sabrina knows, when's our next date?"

"Ummm ..." *Was right now too soon? Could he come over and finish what they started earlier that night?*

"I could come over right now and we could ..."

Oh, now, that was definitely a purr, and it came from her.

"Max," she breathed. "You're saying all the right things right now."

The smile in his voice was unmistakable. "Yeah? Want me to say all the *wrong* things?"

She couldn't stop the groan or the *"oh God"* that made its way across the phone.

And his deep, dark chuckle of response had her eyes darting to her nightstand and her fingers twitching to grab Henry. "I'm excited that we're starting something, that you're willing to take the leap and see where this attraction of ours goes."

Yeah, *how* excited? Was he stroking that excitement? She'd "accidentally" felt it enough times to know he wasn't sporting a Vienna sausage in his Levi's, oh no.

"Me too," she whispered.

"I'll let you go to bed." God, even the way he said *bed*. She'd never had this primal of a response to a man before. She felt out of control. She reached for her nightstand drawer and pulled out Henry.

Her book would have to wait another night.

She flicked off the lamp on her nightstand and sank down into the covers. "Good night, Max," she whispered, sliding Henry down her torso between her legs. She turned him on.

"Good night, Celeste. Sweet dreams. And I'll see you next Saturday."

He hung up, and Celeste slid Henry inside her, her eyes

shutting and her back arching as Henry did what he did best and thoughts of Max paraded through her mind.

Maybe Seattle would do what it did best and rain on Saturday so they could just spend their entire date upstairs in her bed?

One could only hope.

13

THE FOLLOWING SATURDAY, Max, with Celeste's arms wrapped around him from behind, pulled back up to the curb in front of Celeste's house and turned off his motorcycle. The warmth of her at his back and her arms wrapped around him, her fingers splayed across his chest had become such a comfort, he mourned her touch when she climbed off the back of the bike.

"Thank you again for a lovely afternoon," she said, unclipping her helmet and handing it to him. "You really know how to plan a date."

He unclipped his own helmet and stored both on his seat as he climbed off and faced her. "It's easy to plan a fun date when you like who you're with."

Color filled her cheeks. "You thirsty?"

He wasn't, but he had a few more minutes to spare before he needed to leave, so he'd follow her into the house just to spend more time with her.

She unlocked the door and they stepped inside. "I've been meaning to ask you," she started, continuing on through the house to the kitchen, "have you noticed or heard anything new regarding Eleanor and Sabrina this week? Sabrina says the graffiti has stopped. Some of the football players are still making jokes, but for the most part, things have died down." She reached into the fridge and pulled out two cans of sparkling lemon-flavored water. She handed one to him.

"I haven't heard anything," he said, cracking open the can and taking a sip. He hadn't been thirsty, but now that he was drinking, he realized how parched he actually was. That was one of the differences between the full-face helmet and the brain bucket. The wind in your face constantly dried your lungs and palate right out.

She sipped her water, and her brows furrowed. "I'm just worried this sudden lull means she's cooking up something big."

Yeah, he hadn't thought of that, but now that she mentioned it, it seemed more plausible than Eleanor simply growing a conscience and deciding to leave Sabrina alone.

They drank their beverages in silence, watching each other over the rim of the can. He lifted a brow in challenge.

Her eyes rolled and he fought the urge to grab her hair, tilt her head back and claim her mouth again. Take the control he craved and *teach* her a lesson about manners. It was impolite to roll your eyes. Didn't she know that?

"Come over tomorrow for breakfast," she blurted out, setting her can down on the counter. "Sabrina works tomorrow, too."

He finished his can and set it next to hers. "You sure that's a good idea?"

Her bottom lip got caught between her top and bottom teeth, and she shrugged. "It's *just* breakfast."

Would it be *just* breakfast though? Sure, they'd only gone on a total of three dates, but they'd been *seeing* each other for several weeks now. He'd had his hands down her pants. He'd kissed her face off countless times. Was it finally time to go that next step?

His cock sure as fuck hoped so.

"She works at eight again, so come by around nine-thirty or ten. It'll give me a chance to cook."

He definitely wanted to see her again. Their time together today wasn't enough, and he didn't want to wait until next Saturday to see her, but was two days in a row taking it slow?

She stepped into his space and her hand fell to his chest. "I make a mean seafood eggs benny." The sparkle in her eyes had gone from sweet to sassy, and the lopsided smile that joined it was giving him absolutely no room to say *no*.

"I have my nieces and nephew for the night tonight, so can we make it eleven instead? Do brunch?"

Curiosity filled her eyes, and her head tilted just slightly. "What do you mean you *have* them?"

"I take my sister's kids every now and then for a night or two so she and my brother-in-law can have some time alone. Only now that the kids are a bit older and in weekend sports and stuff, it makes it harder to take them for a full weekend. So this time I'm just taking them for dinner, one night and the morning. Enough for my sister and her hubby to breathe and sleep in."

"That's really sweet of you."

"They're part of the reason I came back to the States. I didn't want them growing up without knowing their uncle, and I also wanted to help my sister out."

Her fingers curled in the fabric of his shirt. "As if you couldn't get even more irresistible."

He twitched an eyebrow and grinned down at her. "What if I told you I rescued geriatric cats from being euthanized and gave them a home for their final days? Would that make you drag me upstairs this minute?"

Her eyes widened. "*Do* you?"

He snorted. "No, but now I wish I did."

Rolling her eyes again, she grinned up at him, pulled his shirt until he was forced to move so it didn't rip. His lips hovered just over hers. "So brunch tomorrow?"

When she smiled, her lips brushed his. "Brunch." Then she tugged him again until his lips crashed against hers, his tongue swept inside and his dick was really wishing he had a houseful of old cats at home.

MAX PARKED his Bonneville at home, hopped into his Toyota Tacoma and headed over to Bridget's house. His sister, her husband, Elliott, and their three kids lived in a swanky part of Seattle on Lake Washington. Elliott, a stockbroker, did well for himself, while Bridget worked part-time as a respiratory therapist at the hospital.

The kids wanted for nothing, and yet they didn't behave like spoiled brats. He was proud of his big sister and how she and Elliott were raising their children. Respectable, respectful and a joy to be around. If they'd been little shits like some of his students, he never would have offered to take them as often as he did. But he loved his nieces and nephew, and rarely was it ever Bridget calling to ask if he could take them. It was Max asking if he could have them or one of the kids calling and asking if he was free for the weekend. And since he'd arrived back in the states, all three kids had called at least once, begging for a sleepover.

He'd even splurged when he was looking for a new place to call home and went with a two-bedroom condo, rather than a one-bedroom. He put a bunk bed in it with a double bed on the bottom and a single on top. The girls shared on the bottom while Booker slept on top.

At first, he thought the kids—given their ages now—

wouldn't like sharing a room, since they each had their own rooms and the girls shared a bathroom at their own house, but they loved bunking together. They bickered like normal children, but for the most part, the kids got along, and you could see the love between them.

Just like Max would do anything for Bridget and he knew she would do anything for him, Layla, Jaimie and Booker loved each other the way brothers and sisters should.

About twenty minutes later, he pulled into his sister's long gravel driveway and up to the front of the house. All three kids were already outside waiting for him, backpacks on their backs and pillows under their arms. Matching hazel eyes—the same as his sister's—lit up when he shut off his truck and opened the door. Booker was the first to leave their spot on the front porch, and he launched himself at Max.

"Uncle Max! What took you so long?"

Lifting Booker up into a big bear hug, Max growled and laughed, squeezing his nephew tight. "Sorry, I had a busy afternoon."

His sister and Elliott joined the kids. "Jaimie has a cough, but she says it's not bothering her." Bridget said softly, a quaver of uncertainty to her voice. She'd always been a worrywart. Or was she just worried that Max wouldn't take the kids and she and Elliott would have to cancel whatever plans they'd made?

Max shrugged and put Booker back down on the ground. "I'm sure she's fine. Nothing that a little ice cream and chocolate syrup won't cure, right?" He ruffled Jaimie's blonde hair, which made her grin up at him.

"I dunno, Uncle Max." She fake-coughed. "I think we might need to up the dosage of ice cream, chocolate syrup *and* add some cookie chunks. You know what they say, a cookie a day keeps the doctor away."

Layla and Booker were already loading their stuff into the back of Max's truck.

"Do *they* say that?" he asked his niece. "You'll have to introduce me to this *they* you speak of." He nudged her playfully, and with a giggle, she joined her siblings, who had already climbed into his truck.

"Thank you," Bridget said, leaning in for a hug. "I was looking forward to school starting, but that just seems to have made our schedules even more chaotic than they were during the summer. We're stretched thin, and we're not even a month into this madness."

"Maybe don't enroll your kids in so many extracurriculars," Max suggested, which only earned him an eye roll from Elliott along with a smirk of agreement and a huff of derision from his sister.

"Each child gets to pick two things they want to do, and unfortunately each child picked something different and at opposite ends of the damn city." Bridget raked her fingers through her long, dark tresses. "Add in practicing their instruments, language lessons, homework and mandatory swimming lessons, and not one night during the week is empty. I eat on the run, and—"

"And I eat by myself when I get home from work," Elliott added. "I keep saying we should get a nanny, but Wonder Woman here won't have it." He looped an arm around his wife and pulled her close. "We need tonight, Max. Thank you." He bobbed blond brows. "I think we'll finally get eight hours or more of sleep."

Max tossed his head back and laughed. "You two are just reaffirming my decision not to procreate. When you value sleep over sex."

The horn in his truck blared.

"Come on, Uncle Max!" Booker hollered from inside the cab, sitting behind the steering wheel. "Let's get going."

Max winked at his sister and brother-in-law. "Your spawn has spoken. I'll be by about ten forty-five tomorrow to drop them off." He headed around to the driver's side door. "Don't go *too* crazy, you two. I don't want to get a call from the ER because you decided to get wild with some weird kitchen utensils." He focused on Elliott. "I'm speaking directly to you, brother. No lightbulbs or whisks up the *you know*."

Elliott snorted.

"You can keep them longer if you want," Bridget called back. "Booker doesn't have soccer until three."

"No can do," Max replied. "Got a hot date."

His sister's eyes widened, and intrigue filled them. "Since when?"

"Can't talk. Gotta go have ice cream," he teased. "Your children demand it."

"Do we need to stop and get ice cream supplies?" Layla asked, after they'd been on the road for no more than five minutes.

All three of the kids were too light to sit in the front seat with him, so they were crammed into the backseat.

He shook his head and glanced into the rearview mirror. "Nope. I grabbed everything we'd need last night. Ordered pizza on my way over here, just need to stop and pick it up."

"Even the cookie chunks?" Jaimie asked. She was the wild card of the bunch. You'd never guess she was only nine years old based on how she spoke or the questions she asked. She was also the funniest of the three.

"I bought cookies, figured we could make our own chunks," Max replied.

Jaimie's mouth dipped into a frown, but she nodded and seemed to accept his answer.

"Can we watch a *Fast and Furious* movie?" Booker asked. "I love anything Vin Diesel touches."

Max had to keep himself from laughing. For seven,

Booker was a worldly dude. He'd also recently developed a passion for cars, and his obsession with *The Fast and the Furious* franchise had his entire family exhausted with talk of Nitrous and Turbos.

"We'll see, bud," Max said with a chuckle. "I think it's Layla's turn to pick a movie. Lay, what were you thinking?"

The quiet, serious one of the three, Layla lifted a shoulder. "I dunno. Maybe an Avengers movie?"

Jaimie rolled her eyes and made a noise in her throat. "Only because you're like *obsessed* with Chris Evans. He's not even the best Chris. Hemsworth all the way."

He had a hard enough time digesting the idea of eleven-year-old Layla being interested in boys, let alone nine-year-old Jaimie.

"I could go for some *Guardians of the Galaxy,*" Booker suggested.

And so the comparison and arguments over which Chris was superior—Pratt, Evans or Hemsworth—continued on through pizza pickup and all the way home.

They were just getting to his ground-level walk-up condo when a *meow* from the bushes had everyone pausing.

"Did you get a cat, Uncle Max?" Jaimie asked, all excited.

He shook his head. "I did not."

"A neighbor's cat?"

He didn't really know his neighbors, as he'd only just moved in, but he hadn't seen a cat in the two months he'd lived there.

They all bent down to peer beneath the shrub, where lo and behold, an orange cat with glowing yellow eyes stared back at them, looking terrified.

"Aw," Jaimie crooned. "It looks so scared."

"Can we keep it?" Booker asked.

"Mom has already said no pets because we're too busy," Layla interjected, making Booker pout and hang his head.

"Well, maybe Uncle Max can keep it and we can visit it," Booker suggested, hope in his eyes once again.

Max shook his head. "It probably belongs to someone in the complex. Let's just leave it be, guys." He unlocked the door and ushered them all inside, but before he could close the door, the cat ran in as well. "Hey!"

It ran up to Layla and began to weave in and around her Jeggings-clad legs, meowing and purring like crazy.

"I think it's hungry," Jaimie said. "We should run out and get it some cat food."

"I'm not feeding a random cat," Max said, re-opening the door and attempting to shoo the cat out. All that prompted from the feline was for it to dart into the next room.

Ah, shit.

They spent the better portion of the next hour trying to not get clawed to death in an attempt to remove the cat from beneath his bed. Eventually, he just gave up, locked the cat in his bedroom and prayed it didn't destroy anything, piled the kids into his truck again, and they all went to go get cat food and a litter box.

How on Earth had he gotten roped into it? He had no clue.

But as he was setting out a saucer of milk and a plate of Fancy Feast, he kept asking himself the same damn question.

14

SUNDAY MORNING JAIMIE, Layla and Booker were climbing back into Max's truck when a round man on a moped whizzed up, stopped next to them on the sidewalk and flicked up his visor.

"You kids like snakes?" he asked.

Max paused where he stood loading up his truck box with the kids' bags and turned, ready to tell this guy to fuck off.

Was he planning to whip out his trouser snake or something?

Max's expression must have registered with the guy that his question was creepy, and the man's nose twitched and eyes darted back and forth between Max and the kids. "Sorry, meant no harm. Just wondering if the kids like snakes. Got a pet snake."

In your pants?

If he said *in his pants,* Max was going to haul the guy off his moped and knock some fucking sense into him. Then he'd call the cops and report him.

"What the fuck, dude?" Max asked, not caring at this point that he swore in front of his nieces and nephew. It didn't help that Max also hated snakes. Had a fear of them, in fact.

"I like snakes," Booker said, hanging his head out the front passenger door. "How big? Like an anaconda? Those things get *huge*." Excitement filled his hazel eyes as he smiled at the man on the moped.

Max remained wary of the exchange between his nephew and the moped snake man. Thankfully, Booker and the guy were a decent distance away from each other, and the man seemed to understand Max wasn't one to be fucked with.

The guy on the moped smiled. "No, a big python. Beautiful thing. You guys leaving?"

"Going home," Booker said, his smile dropping into a pout. "Our uncle lives here. We're just visiting. We live—"

"Book, that's enough," Max said.

For Christ's sake, this creep did not need to know where his nieces and nephews lived.

"If you're back and want to meet my snake, let me know. She loves kids." He nodded at Max before speeding away. Did the guy live in the neighborhood?

Or worse yet, the building?

Fighting back the shudder at the thought of a snake in the building, Max finished loading the kids' stuff and waited for them to get all buckled in before he turned on his truck and took off back to his sister's.

After dropping off the kids with Bridget, Max made his way over to Celeste's house. He'd had an extra *thorough* shower that morning, making sure he was freshly manscaped and tidying up his close-shaved beard. He'd hit the barber right before school started, so his hair was behaving, but that wouldn't last for more than a couple more weeks. He had a standing six-week appointment with his barber, always had.

It was just easier than trying to get Massimo to squeeze him in last-minute.

Thankfully, the cat hadn't destroyed his bedroom in the short time he and the kids were at the store, so he locked the feline back in his room with food, water and a litter box on a bunch of newspaper. He still couldn't understand how he'd landed himself a cat, but if the "Found Cat" posters he and the kids put up around the neighborhood and complex that morning yielded any results, he wouldn't have a cat for much longer.

Double-checking his breath, he locked his truck and headed to Celeste's front door. Should he have grabbed another bouquet of flowers? He was showing up empty-handed. That didn't feel right. He should have swung downtown to Wicked Sister Chocolates and grabbed her a mixed box of bonbons. Was it too late to go now?

He glanced at his watch, which said he was already five minutes late. Heading downtown to Wicked Sister and inevitably having to stand in line with the rest of the cocoa-bean fanatics would certainly have him arriving late.

He just needed to suck it up and hope she didn't mind that he showed up with just himself and his smile.

Lifting his fist to the door, he knocked and waited.

How quickly Celeste was turning into a drug and he an addict. She consumed his thoughts when they were apart and fueled his dreams while asleep. And her kisses and the little noises she made when she liked what he was doing drove him wild and made him want to press more of her happy buttons and get her making more of those noises—only louder.

Noise on the other side of the door had him shaking himself loose and casually pushing a hand into his pocket.

He tossed on a big, sexy smile when she opened the door. "Hey."

That smile. It got him every damn time, and they hadn't even been doing whatever they were doing for very long. But it still got to him in a way that excited him like a roller coaster at Six Flags.

"Hey," she said, stepping back so he could enter the house. "How was your evening with the nieces and nephew?"

"It was good. Lots of ice cream, pizza and debating over who the superior Chris is in the Avengers franchise."

She scoffed. "Hemsworth, obviously. Accent wins every time."

He followed her into the house toward the kitchen, where nineties pop music played and the scent of bacon filled the air. He lifted an eyebrow. "Backstreet Boys?"

She handed him a frothy mug from beneath a fancy cappuccino machine. "Loved 'em. Still do. You gonna judge me, you can hand me back the latte and head on home." She grinned over her mug as she took a sip.

He sipped his latte and felt his whole body relax as the caffeine filled his bloodstream. "No judgment. How was your evening?"

She set down her mug. "Wine night with the girls again. It was good."

"Which girls?"

"Bianca and Lauren. They live here in the complex, and they're also single moms. Or at least Lauren will be when she finally has that baby. We're The Single Moms of Seattle."

"Did you buy that domain name?" he teased.

"No, but we should. Get letterhead made up, business cards and fancy pens with our logo."

"You have a logo?"

"Yeah. It's just a big glass of wine though, nothing too creative. But we feel it appropriately conveys what we're all about." She turned to the stove and checked a couple of pots.

"And you're all about wine?"

"Damn straight. Wine, bitching about our kids and abolishing the patriarchy. We get a lot done in our meetings."

"Have you mentioned me?" He'd already "met" the women of her group a couple of weeks ago at Prime, but at the time, there had been more than just three of them. He also knew one of the women at the table was Celeste's sister, Eva.

"You already know the answer to that," she said with a lifted brow. "Remember?"

"Oh yeah, you were all ogling me in that fishing picture." He knew his smile was cocky, but he didn't care. It made her smile and that was the only thing he cared about at the moment.

"Exactly. Now, you're a very popular topic of conversation." She opened the fridge and drew out a plate of cut-up fruit, placing it in front of him. "Lauren calls you Professor Washboard because of *that* picture."

He snorted and hid his grin in his mug.

"I keep telling them you're not a professor, but *Teacher Washboard* doesn't have quite the same ring to it."

"I *do* have a name, you know. You could call me Max rather than treat me like a piece of meat and objectify me by my appearance." Of course this was all said in jest, and the twinkle in her eye said she wasn't about to quit objectifying him anytime soon.

He didn't give a damn what she did to him as long as it wasn't kick him out before he got to kiss her again.

"They are both very *onboard* with us sneaking around. So we have their support."

Well, that was good, he guessed. That her friends supported Celeste seeing her daughter's teacher and the fact that that they were sneaking around to date.

She bit into a big, juicy strawberry, causing a trickle of pink juice to dribble down her chin. "Lauren thinks that I should've tackled you when you walked in the door and hauled you upstairs to my bedroom, make you earn the calories of your brunch." One dark red brow lifted on her forehead, and her freckles seemed to darken and become more pronounced as she stood there staring at him with challenge swirling in her green eyes, her cheeks growing extra pink. "What do you think?"

"I think I want to lick the strawberry juice off your chin first," he said, setting his latte down on the counter before lifting her up by the hips and planting her butt next to his mug.

Her smile and the raspy giggle that accompanied it only galvanized his need for her, and he brought his lips to the corner of her mouth, tasting the sweet juice from the berry but the even sweeter, spicier flavor of Celeste.

"I don't want to mess this up by going too fast," he said, kissing a trail down her chin to her neck. "I'm going to let you control the speed."

"What if I want turbo?" she asked, digging her fingers into his hair and lifting his head up so he could look at her. "What if I want to crank it all the way to eleven?"

His brow wrinkled. "I think you're mixing your metaphors. Though, nice *Spinal Tap* reference. Makes me like you even more."

"*These go all the way to eleven,*" she said with a chuckle, looping her arms around his neck. "Brunch can wait, but I don't think I can. I want to go to eleven now."

He wanted to go to eleven now, too.

Growling, he lifted her up by her butt so she was perched on his hips and he held her there. "Upstairs?"

"Upstairs, bedroom on the right." She tightened her hold

on him and squeezed her thighs, which only made his cock jump and his legs move toward the stairs. He climbed them with a speed that surprised him and, he hoped, encouraged her.

Her door was open and her bed made. Her room smelled just like her—sweet and spicy—and her décor was pure Celeste. Feminine and tasteful, with just a touch of wild, given the leopard-print throw pillows that sat in the center of her bed.

He fell on top of her, dispersing the pillows and causing them to tumble to the floor.

"You're sure?" he asked, sweeping her hair off her face and cupping her chin and cheeks in his palms.

She arched her back and ground her hips into his. "I'm a big girl, Mr. Travis. I know what and *who* I want."

"And that's me?" he asked, genuinely baffled that a woman like Celeste wanted him. He knew he was no slouch, but Celeste was out of his league in every way. Smart, beautiful, kind, funny. She had her shit together. She had her life sorted and organized. She was successful editor, a wonderful mother. She was a widow. She was more of an adult that he was or could ever hope to be. And she wanted him.

She shrugged, but her grin was cunning. "My other boyfriend couldn't make it, so yeah, *today* it's you."

"I'm not sure I like your sass, Ms. Howard." He ground his erection against her hip. Her legs spread for him, and her lashes fluttered.

"Not sure you like it? Or not sure what to do with it?" Her hands left his neck and drifted down over his back, her nails chasing a tingle that landed firmly in his balls.

Growling, he released her and sprang up. "Oh, I *know* what to do with it. He slipped down her body until his mouth rested directly over her pussy. She was in a light and airy skirt the same shade as her eyes. It fell just above her knee and had already ridden up her creamy thighs enough to have him salivating.

He shoved his hands beneath her and palmed her ass, pulling her panties down and using his head to push her skirt up toward her navel.

"Max," she breathed, shifting her hips up so he could finish removing her panties.

He lifted his head.

"You don't have to be gentle with me. I'm a big girl. I want this. I want you."

She wasn't a girl at all, and that's why he wanted her so much.

Max had never understood the allure of jailbait. He'd heard a few of his fellow teachers back in the day talking about how they had to keep things "professional" with a few of their students, as much as they didn't want to. But Max had never been like that.

When Celeste was his student, she was just that—his student. She was a girl.

But now, she was a woman. A mother. She had endured heartbreak and childbirth, marriage and loss. In the time since he'd first met her, she'd lived a lifetime.

"Where'd you go?" she asked, lifting up onto her elbows to look down at him. "You okay?"

He finished drawing her panties down her legs before lifting back up and pinning her beneath him, his lips just hovering a hair's breadth from hers. "Better than fine, baby. Just ... taking it all in." He kissed her chaste-like and went to move back down her body, but she grappled at him with a need he felt right down to his marrow.

"Don't go yet. Kiss me. Kiss me like you mean it."

He did as he was told, taking her mouth with his, prying her lips apart with his tongue and exploring the recesses of her mouth with a curiosity he wasn't sure could ever be stemmed. She met each plunge of his tongue with her own, dueling with him, but at the same time not. They danced a dance that was a challenge but also perfectly in sync. She nipped at his bottom lip and sucked on his tongue, arched her back and wedged a hand between them to stroke what he knew was probably gouging her in the hip by now.

She went for the zipper of his jeans, and he stopped her. "Not yet," he said, lifting off her once more. "If we're going to take this to eleven, we have a few things to take care of first."

A hum of intrigue and approval rumbled in her chest as he slid back down her body.

"Hold still," he demanded, ruffling her skirt up so it reached her belly button and her pussy was now in full view of him.

He licked his lips and dipped his nose to the small, trimmed tuft of hair at the top of her mound.

"Eva's an esthetician, and she does my waxing, but I just can't bring myself to take it all off."

He tugged on the fair, short, soft hair. "Good. Keep it. I like it."

She grinned down her body at him.

He pressed his nose into her hair again and inhaled deep. Just like the rest of her, her scent was sweet and spicy. Was that her body wash, or was that just Celeste?

With two fingers, he spread her pussy lips to reveal glistening pink, wet and ready for him.

With a flick of his tongue to her clit, he had her hips leaping off the bed.

She melted back into the mattress with a sigh, so he did it again, and again.

Each flick had her body jolting, her clit swelling and her mouth sighing.

Hunkering down onto his belly, he shoved his face into

her cleft, sucking her folds into his mouth at the same time his thumb rubbed her clit. Two fingers explored her slippery slit, pushing into her channel, where she gripped him like a vice.

Her ridged walls contracted around him as he fucked her pussy with his fingers and ate at her swelling nub like he hadn't eaten in a week.

She was trembling beneath him and around him in moments. But instead of pushing her over the edge, he pulled her back, removed his fingers and his lips and did nothing but long, deep, slow sweeps of his tongue up her center.

"Jesus, Max," she moaned, her hips churning.

"Is this not eleven?" he asked, drawing one of her labia into his mouth and sucking at the same time he tugged.

"You turn it up to ten and a half, then crank it back down to six. It's hard to ..."

"Hard to?" he probed, flicking her clit with his tongue just to get her attention.

"Hard to focus. Hard to ... come."

"Do you want to come yet?"

"Yes ... no. I don't know."

Ah, he loved it when they were so out of their mind with bliss they couldn't think straight. Then he knew he was doing his job properly.

"It's called edging, baby. Not a fan?"

"Big fan," she said with a strained, raspy whisper. Her fingers made a *gimme, gimme* motion. "I want *you*. We can do that later ... or another time. But right now, I want you."

But he was so looking forward to tasting her as she came across his fingers. He loved the little noises she made when she came in his office the other day. He wanted to hear those amplified. He wanted to turn those noises up to eleven.

Her fingers dug into his hair and tugged. "Fuck me, Max ... please."

Well, now she was just begging. He couldn't give her what she wanted just yet.

With a smile he knew made her pussy gush even more, because he felt it, he dipped his head again, plunged two fingers back inside her and sucked hard on her clit.

"Max ... oh ... God." Her whimpers and moans fed his need for control, and he laved at her swelling nub until he knew she was teetering on that precipice, then he pressed up hard with his fingers on her G-spot and she exploded around him.

Her back bowed on the bed, eyes slammed shut and fingers curled in the duvet. She was quiet at first, her mouth open with no sound coming out, but then her body relaxed and the moans followed. She bucked up into his mouth and swirled her hips, forcing his fingers to go deeper and his tongue to continue. He did just that, and another orgasm he hadn't been anticipating had her stilling and stiffening again. Liquid silk poured over his fingers each time she came, coating them. When he knew she was spent, her chest lifting and dropping like she'd just finished a sprint, he sat up and licked his fingers clean, making sure she watched him as he tasted her flavor off each one of his digits.

Her mouth opened to form a fuckable little *O* as she watched him. Lust and fascination flashed behind the deep green of her eyes.

"Fuck, baby, you taste good." He wiped his hand over his mouth before standing up, shucking his jeans, T-shirt and socks to the floor.

"That was ..." she said, blinking a bunch of times and staring up at the ceiling before focusing her gaze back on him. "Wow."

"Yeah?"

She nodded. "Condoms are in the nightstand. I'd get them, but it would seem my limbs are in a blissfully fatigued state." Her head turned to show him where the nightstand was, not that he'd miss it.

Chuckling, and with his cock bobbing and leaking precum against his black boxer briefs, he opened the nightstand drawer. His eyes widened when he saw her colorful array of pleasure toys.

"I've been alone for a long time," she said breathily. "Needed to learn how to take care of myself." There was no shame in her tone, and when he looked at her, her eyes held no shame either.

And why should she feel shame? She was a grown woman who knew what she liked, how she liked it and wasn't afraid to find her pleasure her own way.

The condom box was sitting on top, but lying beside it was a very intriguing piece of equipment. Pink and in the shape of a slanted *L* or a compressed and not too curved *C*. He picked it up. "What's this one called?"

Her cheeks already held a gorgeous hue of pink to them, but when he held up her "friend," that pink quickly turned to red.

"It's *technically* called Tracy's Dog."

His nose wrinkled. That was a horrible name.

"Yeah, I agree. Terrible. But I've renamed it to ..." She bit her lip, and her eyes turned daring. "Henry Cavill."

His eyebrows shot up his forehead. "The guy who played Superman?"

She nodded. "Yeah. He's like *the* sexiest man alive. I'd have ten of his babies if he wanted me to."

He should feel jealous, but he didn't. If anything, all these new wonderful things he was learning about her made him like her even more. Everyone had a celebrity crush. For him, it was Katy Perry. He'd father all her babies if she asked him to.

He turned the gadget over in his hand and studied it. "So this part goes *in* ..."

She nodded and grinned. "It does."

"And this part goes *on* ..." He pressed the button, and the whole thing began to vibrate in his palm. The bit that was meant to hit her clit began to make a sucking sound. "And it does the trick?"

Her lashes fluttered, and her nostrils flared. "And then some."

Turning the contraption back off, he stowed it in her drawer once more and pulled out a strip of condoms, tearing one free from the bunch. "Well, here's hoping I can do the trick *and then some* too," he said, climbing back onto the bed. "Does *Henry Cavill* go up to eleven?"

She shook her head, that plump bottom lip once again caught between her teeth. "He does not. Do you?"

Pressing her body into the mattress with his, he lowered down until his weight was on her, his lips hovering just over hers. "Baby, I go up to twelve."

———————

CELESTE DREW her nails down Max's back until she reached the taut, muscular globes of his ass. He still wore his boxer briefs, and she was still fully dressed—minus her panties—but he'd already made her come twice.

His lips on her neck and the way his teeth raked along her sensitive throat had her bucking against him, eager to feel him inside her, to feel him in her hand, in her mouth.

"Naked," he murmured against her collarbone. "Need you naked."

She needed him naked too.

"Goes both ways," said, digging her nails into his butt.

"Show me yours, I'll show you mine."

Giggling, she waited for him to lift off her, though she really did like the feel of his weight on her, and then she pulled her tank top up and over her head.

His eyelids dropped to half-mast as he raked her torso with his heated gray gaze. He zeroed back in on her breasts, which ached to be touched. Her nipples had puckered to tight points and were visible beneath the thin fabric of her bra. Since she and Max hadn't taken their clothes off yesterday, she washed her matching red and black panties and bra last night so that she could wear them again today. They were the sexiest thing she owned, and she needed to go into this whole sneaking-around-sex thing with her best skivvies forward.

His fingers curled into the fabric at the elastic of her skirt, and slowly, making sure to torture her fully with his knuckles against the skin of her legs, he pulled down her skirt.

Now they were even. Both in nothing more than their underwear.

A giddy thrill jolted through her like she'd just stuck a fork in a toaster. She was going to see Mr. Travis naked.

But he wasn't Mr. Travis. Not really.

He was Max.

And she was Celeste.

And he wanted her.

And she wanted him.

Taking a deep breath, she hinged up on her elbows and then sat up completely. He was kneeling between her legs, his cock standing up and making an impressive tent in his boxers. A darker black patch of fabric in the shape of a heart sat over the crown, and she licked her lips and reached for the waist of his shorts, pulling them down until his length sprung free.

Max's fingers spread through her hair on one side and he

cupped her cheek, urging her to look at up him. She tilted her eyes to his face and he guided her head forward. She opened her mouth and took him inside.

She already knew from the few times her hand had brushed against him that he wasn't puny between the legs, but now that she finally got to see him, see *it*, she knew he was blessed.

Slowly, he slid to the back of her throat, a moan bubbling up from deep in his chest, growing deeper and more feral the farther in she took him. His hand still cupped her face, and his thumb slid over her cheek as she began moving him in and out between her lips.

She circled the base of him with her thumb and index finger and followed the motion with her mouth, but he was quick to gently pry her hand from him. "Just your mouth, Celeste," he said, his voice seeming darker, smoother and more commanding than normal.

She did as she was told and used only her mouth, swirling her tongue around the head, twiddling it against and into the hole at the top. She lapped up the precum that leaked.

Was he watching her?

Did she dare check?

Opening her eyes, she glanced up at him. What stared back at her was frightening. But in the most exquisite kind of way. The hunger. The craving. The possession. It frightened and excited her, made her pussy gush and her core clench. She was about to deep throat him again when his grip on her jaw tightened and he pulled out of her mouth with a wet *pop*.

"Bra off," he ordered, tearing open the condom and rolling it on.

With fingers that trembled in anticipation, she did as she was told, chucking the black and red number to the floor.

He spread himself back over her, forcing her to recline on

the bed once again, his arms, ripped with muscles, bulging, veins popping as he bracketed her in. She shimmied down the bed a touch until she felt him notch between her legs. Another thrill chased its way through her, causing gooseflesh to ripple along her arms and her nipples to pebble even harder. He dipped his head and took one of the pearled points into his mouth and sucked.

Celeste could not stop or control the moan that burst forth from her parted lips. Sure, Henry did a top-notch job between her legs, but she hadn't had her nipples sucked the way Max was sucking them in far too long. And then he brought out the teeth. Oh, the teeth.

Her back arched, and she pushed more of her breast into his face at the same time she swiveled her hips to try to "catch" him and finally, at long last, take him inside her.

But he deliberately remained evasive. He toyed with her. Played her. Moved his pelvis in such a way that made her wonder if he'd once been a gymnast. Sexy flexi hips and then some. The man was certainly proving he could take it up to eleven.

But he'd promised her twelve. She didn't need twelve inches—dear God, she'd be walking like a cowboy for days—but she did need Max's twelve.

Growling but then inhaling abruptly when he scissored his teeth over her nipple, she dug her nails into his ass cheeks. "You're torturing me on purpose."

"Is this torture?" he asked, switching to the other breast and giving it the same, if not more thorough, attention as the first.

"You know it is." A hard huff of impatience fled between her parted lips when he clenched his butt cheeks so hard, she couldn't even dig her nails in any longer. "You're being a dick."

Lifting his head from her breast, he gazed down at her

with amusement in his eyes and a smile she wanted to equal parts smack and kiss off his handsome face. "I'm being a *dick?*"

"You know what I want, and you're deliberately not giving it to me," she said. "You're being a dick." Proper leverage was challenging given her position beneath him, but she lifted her hand, wound up and slapped him as hard as she could on his right ass cheek.

"You want dick from this dick?" he asked, moving one hand from the bed to cup and knead her breast to the edge of where it was almost painful but excruciatingly marvelous as well.

"I do," she said through gritted teeth. "So bad. Otherwise, I'll be forced to get it from Henry or my other boyfriend." She lunged forward and nipped at his chin. "Don't make me beg ... *Mr. Travis.*"

Max's nostrils flared, and the smile on his face disappeared. Fire, storm cloud gray and tipped with licking flames of bright white, danced in his eyes. "Again."

Huh?

Her brow wrinkled.

"Again. And this time beg."

Jesus, the man had a lot of sides to him. Sweet and sensitive one minute, and then the next he was this alpha, gripping her throat, cupping her cheek, pulling her hair and demanding she beg for his cock. And yet, through it all, she knew he would never push her too far or order her beyond her limits.

Smiling, she bit her lip. "*Mr. Travis* ... It's been *so* long. Give it to me, *please.*" She closed her eyes for good measure, bit her lip again, arched her back and removed her hands from his ass so she could cup her own breasts. "Show me twelve, Mr. Travis. Teach me."

It was a challenge not to giggle, but she did her best. After a moment, she pried one eye open and glanced up at him. A smile normally seen on the devil or a wily fox who'd just outwitted the farmer and broken into the chicken coop beamed down at her.

"You want me to *teach* you, Celeste?" he asked, trailing his hand down her arm, her side and finally her leg. His touch sent tendrils of need coursing through her, all of them landing and intertwining firmly between her legs.

She nodded. "It's all I've *ever* wanted."

Hooking one hand gruffly behind her thigh, he lifted it toward her belly. "Bend your knee," he ordered.

"Yes, sir." She did as she was told. He looped his arm around her knee, angled up on one arm and finally, at long, torturous last, he slid home.

Every cell of Celeste's body sighed all at once.

The anticipation, the longing, the orgasms from earlier—her body had been screaming for him, for Max. And now that he was finally inside her, no way was she going to let him go.

With her leg up, he was able to drive deep. And drive deep he did.

Those hips moved with a rhythm that beguiled her, had her seeing stars and smelling colors in moments. The angle drove her to the brink of madness. And he knew it. He hit her clit but not enough. Just the right amount to give her a taste but not enough to get her there. Not enough pressure, not the precise spot.

It was the best kind of torment, and she understood now more than ever why there was such an allure to the mix of pain and pleasure. Why delayed gratification was more than just practiced by the whip and flogger community. Because she knew when he finally gave her what she wanted, it would shatter her entire fucking world.

She hadn't even realized it, but she'd shut her eyes, so when he ordered her to look at him, she was at first startled.

"I want to see *you*," he said. "All of you. Don't hide from me, Celeste."

Blinking up at Max, she watched as his expression softened at the same time his cadence faltered. He was getting close. Thank God, because so was she.

But just when she thought he was going to let go so she could too, he stopped, dropped her leg, pulled out and rolled over to sit up against her headboard. "Climb on. I want to finish with you on top, your tits in my mouth. I want you to coat my balls when you come."

Celeste's bottom lip dropped open, and all she could do was stare at him.

Never in all her life, in her wildest imagination, most bizarre fantasies would she have ever pictured Max Travis —*Mr. Travis*—to be this dirty-talking, alpha sex god. And yet he totally fucking was.

He leaned over and pulled on her nipple. "More fatigue?"

And even though he was a sex god, he still knew how to make her laugh.

She scrambled up to her knees and straddled him, resting her arms on his shoulders for stability.

"Slow," he ordered. "Go slow."

"Yeah, slow," she whispered, sinking down onto his length, squeezing each inch she took him in further.

"Jesus, fuck," he murmured, cupping a breast and bringing the nipple to his mouth.

"Yeah."

Once he'd hit the end of her, she began to bob up and down, first slowly and then quicker. The new angle and the fact that he'd wedged a hand between them and was now playing with her clit had the orgasm creeping up on her at an alarming speed.

"Close," she breathed. "Really close."

"Me too, baby," he said around her nipple, tugging hard with his teeth. "You first."

He switched to her other breast, sucked her nipple hard into his mouth, and she detonated.

Starbursts, explosions, powder kegs covered in dynamite. She felt everything. All synapses fired at once. All neurons engaged.

She shook against him, uncontrollably, her words and sounds muffled as she tucked her face into his shoulder, inhaling his scent.

She wasn't even completely through her orgasm when she felt him still beneath her. His fingers on her clit paused, and he let out a long, slow exhale mixed with a deep, masculine groan.

When she collected roughly half of her senses, she contracted around him as he came, feeling him pulsing inside her, his cock throbbing against the walls of her channel as he filled the condom.

His lips were still wrapped around her nipple, but he released it on a loud exhale at the same time he pulled his hand from between them.

Celeste wasn't quite ready to lift her head yet. She kept her eyes shut and simply breathed him in, that forest after a fresh rain scent, mixed with sweat and sex. It was a heady combination that drove her senses wild.

They'd only just started *whatever* this was, but Max made her feel things. And she certainly hadn't expected to ever feel that incredible ever again, especially not the first time with a new man. And yet, Max made her feel safe. He excited her, challenged her, made her laugh and knew all the right buttons to push.

He'd burrowed deep beneath her skin in a short amount of time, and now that they'd finally taken the plunge, that flying, soaring leap from the cliff and ended up in bed together, she knew now more than ever that Max Travis was going to be a hard man not to fall in love with.

Dozy from the orgasm, she flinched when he patted her butt. "All right, well, that was nice. Thanks for the fuck, but I should really be on my way. Got a lot of papers to grade and such. We should do this again sometime. I'll call you."

15

MAX WORRIED the woman was going to get whiplash, she snapped her head back so damn fast. He was glad he'd gathered all his wits about him before he spoke and that he'd opened his eyes, because the fire—surprise mixed with fury —that shone back in her brilliant green had him laughing.

He tossed on a grin. "Just kidding."

Her expression softened.

"You didn't think I'd leave without lunch first, did you?"

With a scrunched nose, she reached for a pillow and swatted him in the head as he chuckled and tried to fend her off. "You're a dick," she said, swinging one leg over him and then the other before he slid out.

"Yeah, but I'm a dick you like. And judging by your reaction a couple of minutes ago, I've *got* a dick you like too." Still laughing, he stood up from the bed and went to dispose of the condom in her bathroom. Returning a moment later with a warm washcloth, he tidied her up and wiped down any wet spots on the bed. His balls were also coated, but he waited until the end to wash up those.

"I can easily put the eggs benny stuff away and serve you hot dogs," she said sassily, having snuggled under the covers of her bed.

He climbed back into the bed with her and tugged her against him. "Mmm, tube steak. A childhood staple and favorite. Can you cut them up and toss them into some mac 'n' cheese?"

She lifted an eyebrow at him. "I'm having a hard time figuring you out, Max Travis."

Yeah, he'd struggled with that for a while too. He never felt like he truly fit in anywhere.

He settled on his back, tucked one arm behind his head and drew her against him with the other. She began to play with his nipple, flicking it with her finger, raking it with her nail.

"You're an enigma," she said, pressing her lips to his ribs.

Exhaling, he closed his eyes. "Yeah? Why's that? Don't you like puzzles?"

"Sometimes, but you're more than just a puzzle. You're like four different people all rolled into one guy. Nerdy math teacher, motorcycle riding badass, sweet brunch date, antique book lover, and super-alpha dom who essentially force-fed me his cock."

He snorted. "I did not *force*-feed you anything. Let's clear that up first."

She rolled those pretty green eyes. "Fine. You didn't *force*-feed me your cock. But you're very bossy in the bedroom."

"And you like it." It wasn't a question. He knew she did, based on how she responded to him. "Did I deliver twelve like I promised?"

She switched her attention to the other nipple. "Well, when you promised me twelve, I thought you meant twelve *inches*, so I was a little disappointed there."

He pinched her butt beneath the covers, making her yelp. "Smart-ass."

She beamed up at him. "But yes, I'd say you brought your A game and took it up to twelve."

"I set the bar pretty damn high for the next round, didn't I?"

Her eyes flared. "The next round?"

Pulling his arm free from beneath his head, he rolled on top of her. "Brunch can wait a bit longer. I'm suddenly hungry for something else."

AFTER ROUND TWO, Max and Celeste got dressed and headed downstairs for brunch. He loved watching her in the kitchen. And not because a woman's place was in the kitchen—fuck that patriarchy bullshit—but because of how happy she seemed to be while she cooked. She hummed as she stirred the hollandaise, smiled while she poached the eggs, and didn't seem to get frazzled or stressed out about anything.

She also wouldn't let him help her. She remade them lattes, claiming that re-heating them would have been sacrilege, turned up the nineties pop music and hummed or sang along to Brittney Spears, 'N Sync and Jessica Simpson.

"You're sure I can't help you with anything?" he asked for what felt like the millionth time. He popped a strawberry into his mouth. They'd both worked up quite the appetite in her bedroom, so at the scent of her hollandaise, his stomach grumbled.

She turned around, a plate in each hand. "Nope, all done." He slid off the barstool and followed her over to the kitchen breakfast nook, where cutlery was already laid out, along with glasses of orange juice and the bouquet of flowers he'd brought her yesterday.

"Did Sabrina ask where the flowers came from?" he asked, taking a seat, his stomach making another noisy demand when she set the plate of deliciousness down in front of him.

"She did. I told her they were from you. I need my kid to be honest, so she deserves the same from me." She took a seat across from him and grinned. "Thank you for ..." She dipped her head, and color bloomed in her cheeks. "Coming over for brunch," she finished. But he knew what she really meant.

"I should be thanking you," he said before reaching over the table and tucking a knuckle beneath her chin. "I'm in this, Celeste. All in. Okay?"

A demure smile tilted her lips on one side. "Me too."

"Good." He picked up his knife and fork. "Now, let's eat this incredible-looking meal because I'm starving. Need to calorie-load for rounds three, four and five."

She choked on her orange juice. "*Five?*" She coughed, her eyes wide in what almost looked like terror.

He cut into his eggs benny and brought it to his lips. "Ah, maybe we'll hold off on the marathons for now, huh?"

She swallowed more orange juice and blinked away what looked like tears. "Yeah, something to aspire to, perhaps. Haven't done any of those in ..."

She didn't finish that sentence.

He knew she'd been with two other men since Declan had passed, but she'd already confessed that neither of those men had been memorable or had stuck around. So he could only imagine the thoughts that were bombarding her after what they'd done upstairs, particularly since he told her flat-out that he was in this. Because he was. They had a connection. He had feelings for her, and he wanted to see where those feelings, where their mutual attraction, could go if given the chance.

"You never did answer me upstairs," she said, nibbling on a strawberry.

"Hmm?" He fought the urge not to close his eyes and let the seafood eggs benny sweep him into a coma of decadence. This was how kings ate.

"When I said you were this puzzle I couldn't figure out. That you have like four different men all living inside you. The math teacher, the biker, the antique book lover and the crazy sex god. Do you have multiple personalities or something?" She began to cut into her brunch, but the expression on her face was that of caution.

He'd thrown her for a loop, he knew that. But he also knew she didn't necessarily dislike that loop. Celeste had fire inside her. She spoke her mind. If she didn't like how he was in the bedroom, she would have said something, right?

That had been the demise of his marriage. His wife refused to communicate to him that she didn't like his need for control in the bedroom. She didn't like it rough, and she grew to resent him for it. But had she brought her concerns to him, talked to him, communicated with him like a partner should, perhaps they could have worked it out. Instead, she turned to another man.

He set his knife and fork down and reached for his latte. "First, let me ask you something."

She didn't say anything, but the dip of her head said he had the floor.

"Did it bother you?"

"You mean the controlling bit?"

He nodded. "Yeah, the controlling bit, the hair-grabbing ..."

"You grabbed my throat in your office."

Yeah, he had. And that'd been fucking hot. Did she think it was hot though?

Warily, he nodded. "I did, yes. Did that bother you?"

She shook her head and nibbled her lip before replying, "No. I liked it. I know that if I didn't like something and I told you to stop, you would. I trust you."

He let out a deep exhale though his nose and slumped back in the booth. Thank fuck.

"But it still throws me for a loop, all these different sides to you. I like all of them, but you're unlike anybody I've ever met before. I mean ... I knew you first as my teacher. And even though I wasn't a virgin in high school, I was still naïve. I didn't even know about rough sex. But you're—" Glancing out the window, she blushed. "You're the last guy I would have expected to be *that* way. The motorcycle was a surprise too." She pivoted her gaze back to him. "I don't mean to offend you. I'm sorry if I have."

He smiled, and a small chuckle rattled in his throat. "You thought I drove a Subaru wagon with a roof rack for my kayak?"

That got him the side-eye.

He snorted. Yeah, she'd totally assumed that about him.

Chuckling, he shook his head and sipped his orange juice. "You wouldn't be the first. I do give off a *vibe,* I suppose. A nerdy vibe, if we're not pulling any punches. And you didn't offend me."

"I like that side of you," she was quick to say. "But I also like the other sides." She glanced away again, this time into the kitchen. "I don't know what I'm saying or what I'm trying to say. It's just that you have a lot of sides to you, and none of them make any sense combined into one guy." Filling her cheeks with air, she exhaled dramatically. "It's all coming out wrong."

He understood where she was coming from. It'd taken him nearly forty years to figure out who he was and be okay with that person. He didn't think he made sense for a long time either. Particularly after his wife left, he wasn't sure who he was at all.

"I don't have multiple personalities, if that's what you're worried about," he said with a forced laugh. "I'm one guy, one personality. I just have very *varied* interests. I like books, I like math, I like bikes, I like jujitsu, I like to travel, but I also like to fuck hard." Lifting a shoulder, he picked up his fork and knife again. "I just need to make sure you're okay with that last part. Not everybody is."

"Is that what caused your divorce?"

"Yes."

"She wasn't into it?"

"No."

"I didn't think it was that rough," she said plainly, seeming to have relaxed. She sat back against her seat and casually tucked into her meal. "I mean, I don't really have anything to compare it to. I've never been with anybody who liked it rough, but ... I dunno, I liked what we did do."

Thank fuck. "I'm not into the bondage and whips and stuff. I just like—"

"Control."

"Control," he repeated. "Yes. Control and—"

"Rough."

"Yes, rough."

"I'm okay with that, so long as if I say *no*, you listen. Do we need a safe word or something?"

"We shouldn't. Just say stop, and I'll stop."

Her head bobbed, causing her hair to break free from behind her ear and drift across her face. "I can say stop. But I don't want to."

His dick pulsed in his jeans. Fuck, he could definitely go for a round three now. Reaching across the table again, he tucked the strand of hair back behind her ear, but he kept his hand there and cupped her cheek like he had earlier when her mouth was wrapped so perfectly around his cock. He held it there a moment before releasing her. "Eat. You're going to need your strength."

BACK UPSTAIRS FOR ROUND THREE, Max rolled off a panting and sweaty Celeste. She was exhausted, but she was also damn happy.

Without saying a word, he slipped out of her bed and went to the bathroom to dispose of the condom. He was back beside her moments later.

He took her hand. His lips landed on each knuckle, his breath warm, his cheeks flushed.

"That wasn't too rough?" he asked, kissing her last knuckle but not releasing her.

She shook her head. "I like the hair-pulling. I like it a lot." Her bottom lip tucked between her teeth.

The fingers from his free hand wove into her hair on the side of her head. "It's long enough for a nice thick braid. That's always fun."

Celeste's heart galloped in her chest. "Yeah, sounds like it."

Releasing her hair, he trailed his fingers down her throat. "You're not hurt here either?"

Hurt? No.

Wanting more? Hell, yes.

Celeste hadn't felt this alive, this incredible in God only knows how long.

With her lip still rolled inward, she shook her head. "Not at all."

Their intertwined fingers untangled, but he didn't pull his hand away. He pressed it up against hers, comparing hand sizes, running his fingers against hers. It was oddly intimate, and she enjoyed it more than if they'd simply been holding hands.

"Is this going to become a weekend *thing* for us, Saturday and Sunday?" he asked, letting go of her throat but continuing to touch her elsewhere: her arm, her hips, her thigh.

"You mean I have to wait until next Saturday for another—"

"Isn't that what Henry is for?" he asked, laughing.

"He doesn't take it to thirteen like you just did," she said with a groan. "Henry can do many things and do them well, but he can't do everything. At least not *my* version of Henry. The man himself, I'm sure, is very talented."

"He's on your laminated list then, is he?"

Yes! Another person she could binge-watch television shows with. The episode where Ross created a list of celebrities he could sleep with even though he was with Rachel and then went and laminated that list, was one of her favorites. Though laminating the list had come back to bite Ross in the ass, so she would never laminate her list. "I love that episode of *Friends*. And yes, he would absolutely be on my laminated list. If I was dumb enough to laminate my list. Who's on yours?"

He laughed. "Katy Perry. Scarlett Johansson. Oh, and that actress from *Mama Mia*."

"Amanda Seyfried?"

"No, the other one. But yeah, her too."

"Lily James?"

"That's the one."

"That's a long list."

He rolled her to her back, their hands still together. "I'll toss that list in the incinerator right now if you want me to."

Spreading her legs so he could settle between them, she sighed in utter contentment. "Naw, keep your list. If one of those hotties propositions you, you have my blessing."

"Wednesday," he said, changing the subject and then kissing her. "I can't wait an entire week either. Come over Wednesday night. I'll cook you dinner. We can ... compare laminated and unlaminated lists, because I'm sure yours isn't just HENRY CAVILL in size fifty font."

She opened her mouth, about to say that Wednesday wouldn't work, when the sound of the basement door opening and shutting had them both freezing.

"Mom?"

Celeste's eyes damn near popped out of her head. She shoved Max off her so fast, he fell clear out of bed and onto the floor with a loud but manly *oof*.

"Shit!" Celeste leapt out of bed herself, tripping over a stunned and prone Max. "What the hell is she doing home early?"

"Mom?" Sabrina called again.

"Upstairs, honey. Why are you home early?"

"Aunt Eva, Scott and the boys all showed up to the bistro. They offered me a ride home. Paige said I could leave early, as the place was quiet." Her voice was already louder. It was only a matter of time until she was on the middle floor in the kitchen. Thank God, they'd cleaned up all their brunch dishes. Not even two coffee mugs remained out to cause suspicion.

However, Max's truck was parked right out front. But Sabrina only knew about his motorcycle, not his truck. And that truck could belong to anybody visiting any of the other townhouses. Right? She also knew about Celeste and Max, but Celeste wasn't ready for her daughter to find Max upstairs in her bedroom.

"I'll be right down," Celeste called, searching high, low and everywhere in between for her bra and underwear. She found everything scattered across her bedroom floor. Max had stripped her in a frenzy.

She was dressed but no less stressed in three deep breaths.

"I'm going to take a shower," Sabrina said, her voice even closer now. She sounded like she was ascending the stairs to their bedrooms.

Celeste glanced at Max. He had quietly started to gather and don his clothes. He was nearly dressed now, nervousness having replaced the happiness on his face from moments ago as he finished buttoning his shirt. "Where?" he asked, lifting his hands up.

She pointed at her bathroom. "In there until you hear her turn on the shower in her bathroom."

He nodded and headed into Celeste's bathroom, shutting the door behind him.

Celeste opened the window as wide as it would go and was just pulling the sheets off her bed when Sabrina poked her head through the door. "I thought you changed your sheets on Saturdays."

Celeste's heart hammered violently against her ribs. "I forgot to yesterday."

Sabrina shrugged. "Paige sent home churros. They're on the counter."

"Thanks."

Pausing, Sabrina wrinkled her nose. "It smells different in here."

Oh shit. It probably smelled like sex. Because a hell of a lot of it had occurred in there over the last few hours. Hence the open window. But not even the breeze could pull that from the air fast enough.

Celeste shook her head. "Like a *bad* smell? Like wet towel?"

"No. It's not a bad smell. Like ... woodsy or something. I can't put my finger on it, but it's familiar." She shook her head and blinked a bunch. "I'm gonna shower."

Celeste finished tearing the linens from her bed. "Okay, honey."

Sabrina gave her mother one last confused, almost suspicious glance. She turned to go but then whipped back around. "Was Mr. Travis here?"

Celeste's mouth opened, and the rest of her body froze in place.

"Is he *still* here? Is *that* why you're changing the sheets?" She made a look of disgust before her eyes drifted to the bathroom door. "Is he in the bathroom?"

Celeste closed her eyes. "We've been made," she said blandly. "You can come out of hiding."

The doorknob to the bathroom turned, and out came a sheepish-looking Max. He offered Sabrina a half-hearted wave. "Hey, Sabrina."

Sabrina's eyes flitted back and forth between her mother and Max, the look of disdain never leaving her face. She shook her head and muttered "Gross" before turning around and disappearing down the hallway.

Five *long* minutes later, the water in Sabrina's bathroom began to run.

"Well, that could have gone a hell of a lot worse," Celeste breathed out, dropping the sheets in her hands to the floor. "Didn't go *great*, but she didn't throw a fit. I'm going to call this progress."

Max stepped deeper into the room. "Tomorrow in class will be interesting. I wonder if she'll be able to look me in the eye now that she has a vague idea of what I just did to her mother in this room."

Celeste snorted. "She needs to get over it."

Exhaling, he nodded. "I should go. Maybe we should do this at my place so we don't get caught again?"

That wasn't a bad idea.

She followed him down the stairs.

"So Wednesday?" he asked, glancing at her over his shoulder but not stopping on his way to the front door.

She shook her head. "Not for dinner, I can't. Sabrina and I go to the gym on Monday, Tuesday and Wednesday together anyway."

"Aw, mother-daughter workout buddies?" His grin eased the nerves that had taken hold of her when she was forced to turn down his request for another date.

"Yeah. We started going together last year. Helps us both."

He opened the door. "Can you leave later? Come by *after* she's in bed?"

Her lips twisted in thought.

He must have understood her reluctance. "How about *I* come over after you text me, and even if we just sit outside on your porch or in my truck and talk, then that's all we do? Or if you *and* Sabrina are comfortable with it, we could sit on your couch and watch a movie or something. I don't want to cramp her style or yours. I mean that. I'm a patient man. Just because we now had sex doesn't mean it has to be all about sex. I'm not a teenage boy."

Grinning, she stepped into his space and pressed her hand to the center of his chest. "You sure know how to fuck like one though."

He tossed his head back and laughed. "That's the ultimate compliment."

She'd lucked out finding a man as multifaceted as Max. Kind where it counted but a man who also knew how to play dirty.

"Can you pull my hair even if we just sit and talk?" she asked.

The grin he gave her back and those damn dimples had her entire body clenching, particularly the parts he'd given extra special attention to earlier. "Absolutely."

The water upstairs shut off, and they both glanced at the ceiling for some dumb reason.

"But I need to go. I'll call you, okay? We'll plan for Wednesday." He kissed her quick, but it still made her body react.

Celeste closed the door and leaned her back against it, the stupid smile on her face so big it hurt her cheeks.

16

WITH A FULLY BELLY and empty balls, Max parked his truck in the underground parking garage of his building next to his bike. Since leaving Celeste's place, he hadn't been able to stop smiling. He'd even earned himself a few weird looks from drivers in vehicles next to him. When they all did the habitual turn and glance at the person beside them at a red light, he'd turned, as he always did, but he was smiling like a moron.

But who the fuck cared?

He was happy.

He'd double-checked a few times that his smile wasn't a serial-killer smile but just a guy who'd eaten good food and even better pussy only an hour ago.

If he saw somebody smiling like he was smiling, he'd probably assume that guy had a full belly and empty balls too.

Locking his truck, he made his way toward the front of the building when a "hey" behind him gave him pause.

He glanced around for the voice.

The *slap-slap* of shoes accompanied a man in probably his

mid- to late forties jogging toward Max. It was the guy from the moped earlier.

"You the guy putting up the posters about the lost cat?" the man asked. Even though he'd only jogged thirty feet from his vehicle, he seemed out of breath. He paused when he recognized Max. "Uh, hey." His wave was awkward, and his eyes became wary and shifty.

Max nodded. "Yeah. Found it under the hedge near my front door. Is it yours?"

The man's jowls wobbled when he shook his head. "Dear God, no. Can't stand cats. I like snakes."

Right. Fuck. The snake. Did that mean this guy lived in the building with a snake? If he was in the parking garage, he must.

An uncontrollable shiver sprinted up his spine. There wasn't much Max hated or was fearful of in life, but snakes were one of them. He'd had a fear of them since childhood. He couldn't pinpoint what instigated the fear, but from the age of about eight-years-old on he'd been fearful of anything that slithered.

And ending up on a tourist bus in Vietnam that was secretly smuggling enormous pythons beneath the seats had just set his fear to eleven for eternity. It wasn't until one of the smaller snakes got free and wrapped around his ankle as he slept against the window that anyone (besides the driver and his co-conspirator) even knew they shared their transportation vessel with almost two dozen serpents. But when he jumped and hollered, everyone on the bus became well aware.

It gave him the absolute willies to know that there was a snake just feet from where he lived. Where he slept. Where his nieces and nephew slept. Where his foster cat slept.

He knew what this guy's tombstone would say: *Eaten by a snake in his sleep.* Why did people feel the need to keep exotic creatures as pets? Were there tigers and llamas in the complex too?

"Do you know who the cat belongs to?" he asked, suddenly picking up on an odd smell that was wafting off the man. Did snakes have a smell? Did snake people have a certain smell?

Snake guy bobbed his head. "Yeah. She died."

"Did your snake eat her?"

Oh fuck. He'd said that before he put on his filter.

The man looked horrified, and he took a step back. "Fluffy would never."

"Your snake's name is *Fluffy?*"

"Yes. She's a Burmese albino python, and she's beautiful and loving and wouldn't hurt a soul."

Well, he didn't believe that for a damn second. If *Fluffy* was denied food long enough, she'd eat her master without a second thought and then come haunting the hallways for dessert.

Max held up his hands in surrender. "I apologize for the assumption. I'm not a snake guy myself—actually rather fearful of them, if I'm being honest. How did the woman die, and why is her cat out wandering around?"

The man's tongue flicked out between blood-red lips, and he wiggled his nose, reminding Max of a snake catching the scent of a field mouse nearby. "She lived a couple doors down from you in another walk-up. You're the new guy, right? One-zero-six?"

Max nodded. "Yeah."

"Sadie, I think her name was. Old lady. Only really saw her at the Homeowners Association meetings. But she died about a month ago. Right before you moved in. I never saw her cat out before. Must have been an indoor pet but escaped."

That explained the slender feel of the cat when Max

picked it up. Poor thing was practically skin and bones. It also refused to go anywhere near his front door.

"Do you know where I can contact Sadie's next of kin so I can get them her cat?"

Mr. Snake shook his head. "She didn't have any, I don't think. That's the rumor anyway. Place is still full of her stuff. Nobody to come and deal with it."

"So the cat has nobody?"

"If it dies, will you let me know?"

Why, so he could feed the cat to Fluffy? Max thought he might be sick. A snake in the building was something that should be disclosed to Realtors when they're showing units. It certainly would have made a difference in his decision to buy the place.

"I like to keep tabs on all the pets in the building, just ... in case, you know?"

No, Max sure as fuck didn't know. Just in case of what? In case Fluffy got lose and decided to make a meal out of the Cocker Spaniel on the second floor?

The guy's eyes were eager and buggy. "Taking an online class in taxidermy, always looking for more opportunity to practice."

What the actual fuck?

Shuddering, he made a mental note to double-check his vents and put some more heavy-duty screens on his windows. "Thanks for letting me know." He turned to go. Mr. Snake was giving him the creeps, and the fact that they were in a cold, poorly lit parking garage just made it seem all the more ominous.

He was nearly out into the bright sunlight and heat when Mr. Snake called him again. "Name's Glycon. It's the name of a snake god, if you're wondering."

He wasn't.

"Glycon Smith."

Sure it was, buddy. And Max's real name was Zeus Thor Morpheus the Fifth. The ninth earl of his own ass.

Max shivered and the hair on his arms stood straight up when the sunlight and warmth hit him, he glanced back into the parking garage, but Glycon, if that was his real name, had already slithered away.

The idea of a big snake living in the same building as him was definitely going to fuck with his sleep—if he ever slept again. Glycon better keep Fluffy fed, otherwise ...

He wedged his leg against his front door as he unlocked it, just in case the cat decided to make a run for it. He'd take it to the local shelter and drop it off there. Maybe somebody had already put out an APB on the animal and the shelters would just be waiting for it to show up.

Could you put out an APB on a cat?

He had no clue. He did watch a lot of police dramas though.

The cat was nowhere near the front door when he got inside. It was, however, curled up on his bedroom pillow, snoring away in a beam of sun.

He scratched the top of its head, causing it to purr and stretch, then finally pop one eye open.

"How you feeling, buddy? Full belly? Well rested? Wanna go for a drive?"

"Based on the tattoo in his ear, this guy's name is Sebastian, and he's almost fifteen years old," the vet at the shelter said, scratching behind the cat's ears.

Sebastian.

It was better than Fluffy.

"So you guys'll take him then?" Max asked. Something that didn't feel at all like relief wormed its way up his spine.

"We'll contact the owner. But if nobody claims him, he'll be put up for adoption."

"The owner was my neighbor. She died, and apparently she has no next of kin."

"Then he'll be put up for adoption," the vet confirmed. He reached into a small jar for a cat treat and set it down on the stainless-steel table in front of Sebastian. The cat gobbled it up.

"But he's healthy, right? I mean, I've only had him for a little over a day, and he didn't destroy my house. He used the litter box. He seems to be a good cat. Somebody will adopt him quickly, right?"

Sebastian lifted his head, and his yellow eyes blinked at Max. When he first found the cat, he never would have thought it was that old. But now, the longer Sebastian stared at him, the more he saw all those lives he'd lived. Did he have very many left, or had he used up eight already?

The vet's mouth dipped into a frown. "I'll be honest with you, not a lot of geriatric pets get adopted. People want puppies and kittens. A pet who will become a part of the family and stay that way for years to come. The financial risk with a geriatric pet is also the deterrent. A lot of them need medications or surgeries the older they get."

"But Sebastian is healthy?" Max ran his hand down Sebastian's soft, orange back, the rumble of the cat's purr easing his mounting anxiety.

The vet shrugged. "For fifteen, he certainly is. Mrs. Donahue took great care of him. That's who was his registered owner. And from the sounds of it, he was an indoor cat, and that prolongs their life and health as well. Besides being a little underweight and in need of a bath, he's extremely healthy."

"If nobody adopts him ..."

He already knew the answer to this. There was no cat

farm upstate that took old, senior cats and gave them a house to roam and a yard to hunt in until their final days.

The vet's eyes turned sad, and he sighed. "We only have so many cages."

Max inhaled and scooped up Sebastian. "Never mind. I'll keep him."

Happiness filled the brown of the vet's eyes. "I was hoping you would. I'll have Sherri at the front print out all of Sebastian's information for you, so you can just contact his vet if you have any questions."

"Thanks," Max said, for some reason pissed off with the vet but not entirely sure why. The guy was just doing his job. He probably hated the part where he had to put innocent animals down, but it was all part of the process. Bob Barker was serious when he told people to spay and neuter their cats and dogs. Overpopulation was no joke. Another reason why he'd never bothered to reproduce himself.

Sebastian nuzzled the top of his head against Max's chin as they made their way out of the examination room to the front desk.

The vet followed them out. "Some cats have been known to live into their twenties. And something tells me Sebastian hasn't lived through all his nine lives yet. This might be the beginning of a very long and new life for both of you."

Max grunted and accepted the printout of Sebastian's information. He glanced at the vet one more time before nudging open the door and heading to his truck.

He plunked Sebastian on the pillow he'd brought for him and placed on the passenger seat of his truck. "So we need to go get more food and a carrier then, hey?" he asked the cat, sliding into the driver's seat. "More food, a carrier, maybe some toys and then we'll go home?"

Sebastian blinked at him.

"Yeah, buddy. Close call, but we're going home."

WEDNESDAY EVENING after an at-home workout that had him sweating buckets and being stared at peculiarly by the cat the whole time, Max wiped his face with a towel and glanced at his phone.

It was only seven thirty. Celeste and Sabrina could still be at the gym for all he knew. She did say that she'd call or text him later that night.

He'd tried to give her some space after Sunday, but it was damn near impossible. She was buried so deep beneath his skin, the woman had touched bone. He waited until Monday night to text her. But that text turned into a phone call that lasted past midnight.

They spoke Tuesday night as well. This time they only spoke until eleven thirty, but they'd video-chatted for a half hour and he'd had a hard-on the entire time. Even though he'd seen her naked, tasted every inch of her body, the view of her sitting in a skimpy tank top and pajama shorts all fresh-faced and ready for bed had him rock solid.

But he wanted to see her. He knew her life was busy, and he'd never ask for more of her than she could give, but he also needed her to know that he was interested, and in more than just hooking up.

It was a delicate balance. He'd never dated a single mom before, and even though Sabrina wasn't a little kid who demanded twenty-four-seven supervision, she still relied a lot on her one parent.

Squirting water into his mouth, he reclined down onto an exercise mat in the middle of his living room and began to do bicycle crunches. He was fifty-six in when his phone vibrated.

Just leaving the gym now. Is ten thirty too late for you to come by?

His cock tried to leap out of his basketball shorts and head over to Celeste's now.

He texted back. *Ten thirty isn't too late at all. Where do you want me to park?*

Park up the street a bit, then walk around to behind my town-house to my garage. I'll meet you down there.

He sent her a thumbs-up emoji, which was *not* the emoji his dick wanted to send her. But he was too mature for an eggplant. Or at least he wanted her to think he was.

Since he had three more hours to kill, he continued on with his workout, upping his weights and doing enough crunches and sit-ups to make his abs burn, scream and cry but also pop like the washboard he knew she liked.

By the time ten thirty rolled around, he was yawning a hell of a lot but also excited. He slowed his truck down when he approached the row of townhouses and parked a few doors up from Celeste's along the sidewalk.

Careful not to slam the door when he shut it, he kept his eyes peeled on the bedroom window that he knew was Sabrina's. The shades were drawn, and the room appeared dark. Hopefully that meant she was asleep and not on the roof stargazing or anything.

He brought out his phone and texted Celeste as he continued to make his way down around her unit to her garage. It was a double-long garage, rather than double-wide. The front portion of the garage was an open carport without a door, and that's where Celeste's SUV was parked. Behind that was the retractable white garage door with the windows along the top. He rapped his knuckles against the door gently.

Was she already inside? The light was on.

He nearly jumped clear out of his skin when the door clunked and began to lift up to reveal Celeste standing there, her hair still damp from her post-workout shower but in a long, single braid down her back.

Oh fuck, yes.

A loose-fitting T-shirt showed the rainbow and prism from Pink Floyd's *Dark Side of the Moon,* faded on the front. A pair of comfy-looking cotton shorts covered the tops of her thighs, and her cheeks were rosy and extra-freckly.

He'd never seen anything or anyone so fucking beautiful.

The garage was void of any other vehicles, but two of the three walls were lined with shelves and neatly labeled bins. *Christmas Crap. Beach Crap. Skiing Crap. Camping Crap. Scrapbooking Crap.*

Along the third wall was a couch—a pullout couch, to be exact. And it was already made up with linens and pillows.

His gaze slid to her, and she smiled a small, coy smile that got his engine running hot.

"We didn't need the pullout when we moved here. Our living room is smaller. But I didn't want to part with it, so we just put it down here." When she shrugged, her T-shirt slipped off one shoulder.

It was impossible for Max to stifle his groan.

"I just feel weird leaving Sabrina at home so late at night to go ..."

"I understand."

"Besides her going to sleepovers or staying with my parents, I've never spent a night away from her."

He stepped toward her, his hands finding her hips. "I understand. It's okay. I'm okay driving here, if that's what you'd prefer."

Her eyes tilted up to his. "Yeah?"

He bent his knees so they were more eye-to-eye. "Yeah."

Smiling, but this time with a glint of mischief in her eyes, she stepped out of his embrace and back toward the door leading into the house. She hit a button on the wall, and the garage door clunked and began to drop down. She hit another button, and the overhead light went out.

"I'm okay just talking if you want to just talk," he said, his eyes adjusting to the muted light of a bedside table lamp next to the pullout couch.

"We've talked for hours for the last two days," she said, approaching him slowly, that sexy, slender shoulder still peeking out from beneath her T-shirt. "I'd say we've done enough talking, wouldn't you?"

Oh, his cock would definitely have to agree.

She rested her wrists on his shoulders and blinked up at him all innocent-like. "You gonna teach me again, *Mr. Travis?*"

He groaned. "That depends. Have you been a bad girl, *Ms. Howard?*"

She nodded and pouted. "I have. I forgot to do my homework."

Roughly, he reached behind her and tugged on her braid. "Not good, Ms. Howard. I am *incredibly* disappointed in you."

With her head back and chin up, she was forced to look up at him. Nothing but challenge and excitement gazed back at him, deep green with flecks of gold flashing fire, as the pupils dilated and her cheeks filled with even more color.

"You're not the boss of me," she bit out. "You can't tell me what to do."

With his hand gripping her braid tight, he hauled her over to where the bed was made and grabbed a pillow, tossing it to the floor. He liked where they were headed, but he also wasn't an asshole. The garage floor was cold, hard concrete, and she had bare legs.

"On your knees," he said, jerking her braid again so she was forced to do as he said.

A sly grin lifted one corner of her mouth. A mouth he intended to fuck.

"Make me," she shot back, having dropped to her knees

but keeping her eyes on him, the look of challenge, of defiance growing.

With his free hand, he unbuttoned and unzipped his jeans. It took some finesse to wiggle them down his hips with one hand, but he managed. His cock, ready since before he jumped out of his truck, was already leaking precum.

Still holding on to her braid, he cupped her jaw with his other hand and squeezed. "Open up, Celeste."

She flexed her jaw and shook her head.

He squeezed tighter, forcing her lips to part. "Open. Up."

The little pout and opening was enough, and he pressed the head of his cock between her lips. She relaxed and accepted him.

"Good girl," he said, releasing her braid for a moment to pet her head. He let go of her mouth and angled the rest of his cock into her mouth. He grabbed her braid again and began to move her head back and forth over his length, maintaining a rhythm that seemed to suit them both. Her hot little mouth, the way she sucked him hard, and that skillful tongue had him bucking into her face and staring down the barrel of the gun before he was ready.

Tugging hard on her braid, he pulled her mouth off him with an audible *pop*. Continuing to use her hair, he helped her to her feet.

"Bed."

"Yes." Her eyes glittered, and she skipped toward the pull-out, only to spring back toward him because he still had ahold of her hair.

Chuckling, he released her hair so she could climb onto the bed.

She shucked her shorts, revealing that she wasn't wearing any underwear, and watched with anticipation, licking her lips, as he undressed.

He'd barely managed to ditch his last sock before she

grabbed him by the waistband of his boxers and tugged him onto the bed.

"I've learned my lesson, Mr. Travis. You're such a good teacher," she said, her voice high and breathy. "Teach me more."

"Fuck," he growled, rolling her over to her back and caging her in with his arms. "You're something else."

"I've missed you," she said, the amusement leaving her eyes.

His smile faltered. "I've missed you too." Then suddenly things weren't all fun and games anymore. He wasn't Mr. Travis and she his petulant student.

They were Max and Celeste, and there was something hauntingly real going on between them. Something that had hit them both like an out-of-control train, but neither one of them seemed willing to jump off the tracks.

He claimed her mouth with his, tasting her. Savoring her. Exploring and letting her scent and the feel of her body against his, beneath his, imprint on his memory for all eternity.

With frantic fingers, she grappled at him. Pulled him harder against her, scraped her nails down his back and to his ass, beneath his boxers.

"Inside me," she murmured, pulling her lips away to break their kiss and bite his shoulder. "Now. Please." Her breath warmed his skin.

Fuck, they'd only done this a few times, but boy oh boy did he like it when she begged.

She didn't have to ask him twice.

He shoved his boxers down, reached for the condom she had placed on the nightstand in preparation, ripped open the package and rolled that bad boy on. Sinking back down to her on the bed, they both groaned as he slipped inside.

How did it feel so right this soon? She fit him like a glove.

Her responsiveness, her reactions to his touch, it was all so easy, so meant to be with Celeste.

Lifting her hips, she locked her ankles around his back at the same time he began to move.

"What if I want you on top again?" he asked, driving in deep before pulling back out again nearly to the tip.

She shook her head. "Sorry, *teach*, I'm a bad girl who doesn't always listen. I want you on top this time."

Grinning, he took her mouth again and they moved in perfect tandem. As if they'd been doing this for years, not less than a week.

Like clockwork.

She fit him

He fit her.

She tilted her hips when he plunged in deep and squeezed as he withdrew, her body quivering beneath his each time he raked his pelvis over her clit.

Her sighs and whimpers encouraged his fervor.

He was hot for her.

Her name was like a tattoo on his brain. *Celeste*. She was a drug and he an addict, and he'd come over late at night for a much-needed fix.

But fuck if that fix didn't have him seeing stars. Right into his bloodstream, running hot and fast, was nothing but Celeste.

With his tongue mimicking the movement of his cock, he fucked her mouth as thoroughly as he fucked her pussy until she was forced to break the kiss to catch her breath. Only when she did, he dipped his head, drew a nipple into his mouth, and she detonated around him.

Her nails scraped down his back just beyond the point of pain and had him crying out, but he was a masochist that way, and when she dug those nails into the top of his ass, he came hard. Sucking her nipple deeper into his mouth, he drove home and let go. She'd arched her back and stilled her movements; so did he. They lay there, both of them groaning, moaning, panting and sweating as nothing moved but her hot, wet pussy, milking his cock for everything it was worth.

When she went lax beneath him, he gently rolled off her. Both of them still breathing heavily, they stared up at her skis in their racks fastened to the ceiling.

"So, I forgot to tell you," he started.

She turned her head to face him.

"I got a cat."

17

It was the beginning of October, and although Sabrina and Max had yet to spend any time together besides that in the classroom, Celeste's daughter had come to accept that her mother was dating her teacher.

It probably had something to do with another guy.

One that went by the name of *Noah*. Since things with Eleanor seemed to have died down—for now—Sabrina had become awfully starry-eyed over the last few weeks, and although she hadn't mentioned whether Noah had actually asked her out, Celeste could tell her daughter was smitten and seriously crushing.

It was Friday afternoon and she was just finishing up work for the week when the front door slammed hard enough to shake the entire house.

That did not bode well.

Hitting *save* on her document, Celeste stood up from her desk and cautiously approached the thundercloud that vaguely resembled her fifteen-year-old daughter. "Care to share what that was all about?"

Sabrina's nostrils flared and her green eyes burned. "You promised!"

Oh, shit.

What the hell happened? What did she know?

Before she spilled any beans she didn't have to, she carefully chose her words. "I promised what?"

Shaking her head, disappointment all over her face, Sabrina let out an impatient huff. "Noah asked me to the homecoming dance."

And this upset her?

Had Celeste been this fickle of a child? She'd have to call her mom and ask.

"And that's a bad thing? I thought you liked him?"

"I *do*. And he likes me. But then Eleanor found out that he asked me to the dance and she said if I went with him, she was going to send *this* out to every email address on the school's database. She also said she'd post it to social media." She held up her phone, which had a video of Max and Celeste in his office doing ... what they'd done the last time they were in his office on parent-teacher night. His hand was on her throat, his other hand was down her pants, and they were kissing and moving and ...

Oh. Fuck.

"You promised!"

"Honey, I—"

"I didn't like that you were dating my teacher, but I got over it, because I saw how happy you were. But you promised you dating my teacher wouldn't make things more difficult for me at school. And now look!" Tears welled up in Sabrina's eyes, but her face was anything but sad. The girl was furious. "Eleanor is threatening to show this to the world if I don't leave Noah alone."

Celeste let out a deep breath and gently, slowly pried the phone out of her daughter's death grip. She immediately sent the video to herself and then sent the video to Max with the caption: *We've been found out by more than just Sabrina. Eleanor is out for blood.*

She set her daughter's phone down on the kitchen counter, steered Sabrina into the living room and encouraged her to sit on the couch.

"I'm sorry," she started. "I know what I promised, but—"

"But what? You just couldn't keep your hands to yourself outside the house? You had to hook up in my *classroom*. You were so desperate—"

Celeste held up her hand. "I'm going to stop you right there. I understand you are upset, and you have some right to be. However, I am still your mother, so watch your tone, young lady. Watch what you say to me. Now you, my darling child, are fifteen years old. I am thirty-three. I am single. I am allowed and free to see, date and sleep with whomever I so choose. I will not let you or anybody else dictate how I live my life. I am not desperate. I have barely dated at all since your father died because I am picky and I have made you my number one priority. However, Max—"

Sabrina went to open her mouth in protest, but Celeste lifted her brows in warning.

"Max and I are a good thing. We like each other. He treats me well. What we did in that classroom was irresponsible, but it was between two consenting adults. I know it cramps your style, but I have nothing to be ashamed of."

"Do you love him?"

"It's too soon to say. I really like him. I like spending time with him. He makes me happy."

"While in turn making me miserable," Sabrina muttered.

Celeste inhaled deeply through her nose before reaching over and tucking a strand of hair behind her daughter's ear. "Does Max—Mr. Travis make you miserable?"

Sabrina rolled her eyes. "No. But you know what I mean?"

She did, but she also needed her daughter to understand that what was happening to her was neither Max nor Celeste's fault.

"Has Max treated you any differently in class these past few weeks?"

Sabrina slowly shook her head. Her gaze was focused on a small tear in those godawful jeans she'd purchased a month ago. "No. He treats me like any other student."

"So it's not he or *I* who make you miserable. It's Eleanor. I need to hear that you understand the difference."

Sabrina sighed but didn't lift her head. "But why my teacher, Mom? You're hot. You're young. You could have any guy you wanted." She finally lifted her head and pinned a confused, sad, angry and tired look on her mother.

Celeste's heart ached for her daughter. The teenage years were so overwhelming. She didn't wish to go back to that time in her life for anything. But in an odd way, she was forced to relive them anyway. Through her daughter. Because every joy, every fear, every heartache Sabrina felt, Celeste felt them too. Her daughter was her heart, and when her heart hurt, Celeste felt it all.

She cupped her daughter's cheek. It was warm beneath her palm and she ran her thumb over Sabrina's soft, porcelain skin. "Because the heart wants what the heart wants, honey. Don't you wish you liked a different guy than Noah? Wouldn't it be easier if a different guy than Eleanor's ex-boyfriend asked you to the homecoming dance?" She took Sabrina's hand in hers, stopping her daughter from picking at the tear anymore. Even though that tear had been placed there by the manufacturer, there was no sense making it bigger.

"Two other guys *did* ask me to the homecoming dance," she whispered. "Finn and Wesley."

"But you don't want to go with them?"

She shook her head.

"Because you like Noah."

Sabrina nodded. "I really like him."

"And I like Max. I know it's not ideal, but it is what it is."

Sabrina squeezed her eyes shut. "But that video, Mom."

Yeah, the video.

That's when her phone started to vibrate. She already knew who it was.

The caller ID said *Mr. T* and it even had a picture of Mr. T himself—not Max, but the actual Mr. T. Then the ringtone started, but all it kept saying was *"I pity da fool."*

Sabrina snorted. "Seriously?"

Celeste laughed. "How could I not?" She answered the phone. "Hey, Sabrina's here."

He exhaled. "Fuck."

"I'm going to put you on speakerphone."

"You're sure?"

"Yes. Buck up, Buttercup. No more sneaking around." She hit the speaker option.

"Well, that's good. I'm tired of having to sneak over so late in the evening."

Sabrina's eyes grew to the size of saucers. "He's been coming over while I'm home?"

"Oh, shit, you already put me on speaker?" Max asked with a groan.

Celeste hung her head. "Sorry." She turned to Sabrina. "Yes. When you go to bed, Max has been coming over in the evenings a bit. We stay in the garage though so as to not disturb you."

Sabrina made a grossed-out face. "You don't—" She held up her hand. "Never mind. Don't tell me."

She wasn't about to.

"So Eleanor has the video," Max asked.

"She does," Sabrina confirmed. "She sent it to me after she found out Noah asked me to homecoming."

"And she threatened to send it to every email address in the school database—which I'm sure she can gain access to through Mindy," Celeste said.

"If I say *yes* to Noah," Sabrina added. She shrugged. "So I'll just tell him *no*. Then she won't leak it."

Oh, the naïveté of youth.

"Yeah, but she'll just continue to lord this information over you. Use it to blackmail you another way, another time," Celeste said. "We can't let the bullies win."

"I agree," Max said. "I double-checked and you can't see the drink glasses in the video. If they were full and noticeable, I could get fired for drinking on school property."

Silver lining? It was a barely visible one if it was.

"You two were *drunk?*" Sabrina asked, her tone a touch shrill.

Celeste's eyes rolled. "No. We had one drink between the two of us."

Sabrina didn't look convinced. Too fucking bad. They had bigger fish to fry.

They needed more heads in this game. They needed more shrewd minds who were used to dealing with manipulative fuckwads out for their own personal gain.

Leaving Max on the phone, she texted Richelle.

Within moments, the woman responded.

"You free tonight?" Celeste asked Max.

"Yeah, what did you have in mind?"

"Not a family dinner," Sabrina groaned. "I'm not sure I'm ready for that."

Chuckling, Celeste looped her arm around her daughter. "Not quite. But we are going to go visit Mallory."

MAX HAD BEEN GIVEN explicit instructions on what to pick up and where to be. He was nervous as fuck pulling up to the enormous Lake Washington home at seven o'clock, hoping he got the right pizza and the right ice cream. Liam and Richelle didn't live too far from Max's sister's place, but the house itself was a hell of a lot bigger.

Balancing all the pizza boxes and the ice cream in his arms, he slammed the door of his truck with his hip and carefully approached the front door. He was barely there when another Toyota Tacoma pulled into the driveway and three boys between the ages of eight and ten piled out of the backseat.

"Who are you?" one of them asked.

"I'm Max," he said, watching as a man roughly Max's age with dark brown hair, brown eyes and a slightly crooked nose came up behind the boys.

"Scott," the guy said. "I'm Liam's brother."

Ah.

Max nodded a hello. "I'd shake your hand but ..."

Scott chuckled. "No worries."

Another truck door slammed, and the gravel crunched to reveal Eva.

"Mr. Travis!" she said, unable to hide the surprise in her voice.

"Max," he said, tilting his head, as he couldn't exactly wave.

"Right, Max. I didn't know you were going to be here." She rested her hand on the tallest boy's shoulder. "Lucas, Kellen, Freddie, run along inside and go find Jordie."

"Do we get pizza, though?" Lucas asked.

"I have enough here for a football team," Max confirmed. "I promise there's enough to go around."

"What about the ice cream?" the middle-size boy asked. "There doesn't look to be much there."

"I believe Celeste and Sabrina were grabbing the majority of that. They just asked me to grab your Uncle Liam's favorite —peanut butter chocolate swirl—as their grocery store was out of it."

All three boys seemed to relax.

"Okay. That's good then," the middle boy said. "I'd hate for you to run out."

"Me too." Max chuckled.

The boys took off toward the front door and opened it without bothering to knock.

Just as they disappeared inside the house, more gravel crunched on the driveway to reveal Celeste and Sabrina in Celeste's SUV.

Thank God.

"Gang's all here," came a male voice from the house.

Max spun around to find the man he could only assume was Liam standing on the threshold. He looked an awful lot like Scott, only a bit older and with more gray at his temples.

Celeste and Sabrina piled out of the vehicle and joined them all on the walkway, bags of ice cream cartons in their hands.

"Well, come in," a woman encouraged from inside the house. "Liam, move out of the way so they can come inside. Max is probably sweating his ass off holding all those hot pizzas."

Everyone headed inside, and the woman who'd sympathized with Max's sweating ass introduced herself as Richelle. No more than five feet tall, Richelle had the personality of a person twice her size and instantly commanded the attention of everyone in the room. But it wasn't like she was an attention hog. No, she just had that kind of presence about her. When she spoke, people listened.

"Set the pizzas down on the dining room table," she directed. "I made room in the freezer in the garage for the ice cream, though I didn't know you were going to bring all thirty-one flavors."

"Couldn't make up our minds," Celeste said, glancing at Max as she and Sabrina headed toward the garage.

A hard hand landed on Max's shoulder and squeezed. "So you're Professor Washboard?" Liam asked.

Max groaned and rolled his eyes. "I guess that's what you could call me. Though Max works too."

Liam laughed. "Drink, professor? What's your poison?"

"Not picky. Beer's good if you've got it." He followed Liam over to a fancy leather-top bar tucked into a corner of his dining room.

"I've got everything, dude. So literally, pick your poison." He swept his hand in front of the impressive glass shelves that housed bottles and bottles of expensive liquor.

"I'll have a whiskey," Scott said, joining them. "No ice. I've got a bit of a chill."

"Coming up," Liam said, unscrewing the cap off a bottle of Maker's Mark. He glanced up at Max. "You a gin man?"

Max nodded. His eyes followed Celeste as she emerged from the direction of the garage, Sabrina behind her. The young girl's eyes darted to the top of the staircase, where another teenage girl waved and smiled. Sabrina took off up the stairs, and both girls disappeared.

"A lot of small-batch distilleries have opened up in Washington," Liam said, "making some real nice gin. Richelle and I went to a gin tasting event last month. Dropped over five hundred bucks on booze, and I'm not even a gin man. I mean, I'll drink it, but I prefer scotch."

"That's what happens when you make too much damn money," Scott chided.

"You want to try this one?" Liam lifted up a sexy opaque glass bottle that said Orca and Oak Distillery and Spirits,

234 | WHITLEY COX

Pear and Cardamom Gin. "I can drink this shit straight, it's so damn smooth."

Shrugging, Max nodded. "Sure."

"Ice?"

"Sure."

Liam cracked two ice cubes into a short square glass tumbler before pouring the aromatic liquor overtop. He handed it to Max.

Max brought it to his nose. It certainly smelled as described. Pear and cardamom. He took a sip. Holy shit, Liam was right. It went down like water, it was so smooth.

"So, shall we head out to the deck with pizza and booze to discuss the scandal?" Richelle asked, joining the men at the bar. She tapped the leather with one finger. "Pinot, barkeep."

Grinning, Liam did as requested and poured his woman a deep, dark pinot.

Eva looped her arm around Scott. "I'll have whatever Mr. Tr—I mean *Max* has. Richelle was telling me about your gin adventures, and it sounds amazing."

Liam obliged. "Celeste? Poison?"

"Wine," she replied. "Red."

Once they all had their alcohol—or liquid courage, as Max preferred to call it, given the circumstances and his current company—they took their pizza and headed out to Liam's enormous sundeck, complete with heaters, blankets, outdoor couches and a small stone firepit.

"So you mentioned a scandal?" Scott said though bites of pizza. "Whose scandal? What scandal? My company is getting into PR, not just marketing. You need a scandal dealt with? A secret baby covered up? A bit of insider trading you don't want Uncle Sam to hear about?"

Liam snorted. "Have you had to cover up a secret baby? Some politician's, perhaps?"

Scott shook his head. "Naw, not yet. Not sure I'd do it,

either. Philandering buggers deserve the scandal if they can't keep it in their damn pants."

Liam and Richelle were snuggled up on one couch, Eva and Scott another, while Max and Celeste sat in chairs next to each other. They'd hardly looked at each other since arriving and certainly hadn't spoken a word.

Since finding out about the video and knowing that Sabrina knew and had seen the video, Max's heart had not stopped hammering against his ribs, to the point where he thought he might be going into cardiac arrest. It was bad enough that she now knew her teacher was dating her mother, but she'd seen a video of them doing ...

He cringed at the thought of poor Sabrina having to endure the wrath of Eleanor and what it must have been like to see that video for the first time.

He'd completely forgotten that the door to his office had been left slightly ajar or that they'd heard footsteps in the hallway. But that had all been true. And those footsteps had been Eleanor. She'd snuck into his classroom and filmed Max and Celeste in his office.

Surely, there had to be some kind of criminal culpability there. Invasion of privacy?

Alas, his penchant for police dramas offered him little insight.

Richelle sipped her wine and leveled her gaze at Celeste and Max, one eyebrow lifting on her tanned complexion. "Spill. You texted me *911*, asking to rally the troops because you were on the wrong side of a scandal. Now you can't just leave me—leave *us* hanging. I've rallied the troops. Now tell us the scandal."

Celeste turned to look at Max and nibbled her lip.

Max reached for her hand and squeezed. "I'm behind you one hundred percent. However you decide to handle this."

Grimly, she smiled before turning to face the rest of them.

"We were caught by the girl bullying Sabrina. She filmed us in Max's office in a ..."

"PG-13 situation," Max finished.

She side-eyed him. "More like Rated R."

"Nudity?" Eva asked, inching forward on her seat, her mouth hanging open as she gaped at her sister.

Celeste shook her head. "No. But ..."

"Sexual activity," Richelle finished.

Celeste nodded before breathing out, "His hand was down my pants."

"But you can't see that," Max clarified. "You can't see what we're doing besides kissing."

"And gyrating ..." Celeste said in a low tone not quite under her breath.

"And she's planning to do what with this video?" Liam asked. "Go public with it?"

Celeste and Max nodded at the same time.

"Send it out to the entire school's email database—which is every student, parent and teacher. As well as post it to social media," Max confirmed. "Her mother is a guidance counselor at the school, so I doubt it would be that difficult for Eleanor to get into the portal."

"And Eleanor is the videographer?" Scott asked.

Celeste nodded. "Yes, and her ex-boyfriend likes Sabrina, and she likes him. He asked Sabrina to the homecoming dance, but Eleanor showed Sabrina this video and said if she goes to the dance with him, she'll post this video all over social media." Celeste took a long sip of her wine.

"Oh, for fuck's sake." Scott growled. "A teenager. That's who the fucking blackmailer is? That's what happens when every little snot-nosed winning sperm gets a phone." He turned to Eva. "The boys are getting flip phones with no data until they're smart enough to not send dick pics. If I ever see an unsolicited dick pic in their outboxes, so help me God."

Eva patted his knee. "Yes, dear."

"It goes deeper than that though," Celeste went on. "Sabrina was voted nicest person in the school last year, and that pissed off Eleanor. The girl has an ax to grind. Add in, her parents are going through a nasty divorce."

"Her father cheated on her mother with a woman who looks a hell of a lot like Celeste," Max added.

"And her mother wants Max," Celeste pointed out. "So we've got a real shit show on our hands. I've already gone to Eleanor's mother, Mindy, with regards to how her daughter treats my daughter, and she's of no help."

Liam pushed his fingers through his hair. "Christ almighty."

That was putting it mildly.

They were all quiet for a moment. Nothing but chewing of pizza and the sipping of alcohol filled the cool autumn breeze.

"You guys are together though?" Scott asked slowly. "That *tryst* on the video wasn't just a one-time thing?"

"It was one time in the office," Max clarified. "But yes, we are together." He squeezed Celeste's hand again and glanced at her with a smile he hoped conveyed how much he was truly *in this*, shit storm and all.

She glanced at him, her smile grim, but the understanding and appreciation in her eyes was unmistakable which eased his hammering heart.

Richelle finished her wine and stood up. "Okay, do either of you have a copy of this video?"

Max and Celeste exchanged nervous glances before nodding.

"Well, if there's no nudity and your hand is just down her pants, I'd like to see it. I'd like to see what kind of *scandal* we're dealing with." Richelle hit them both hard with a look that said her request was not up for negotiation.

Max's stomach hit his feet.

"I'm thinking we need to get ahead of this video," Richelle went on. "You guys go *public* with your relationship. No billboards or press conferences, but just don't hide. Make it social-media official. So if she does leak it, it will have less of an impact because it won't be *so* scandalous." She disappeared into the house. Celeste was up and out of her seat, chasing after her. Eva followed.

Which left Max, Scott and Liam on the deck in increasingly awkward silence.

"You could just walk away from this, you know?" Liam said casually, sipping his scotch. "Just end it now. Do you really want the headache?"

Max narrowed his brows at the guy sitting across from him. He knew of Liam's reputation in town, had actually Googled him as a potential lawyer to represent him during his divorce, but the guy's fees had been beyond Max's bank account at the time. Liam was shrewd. He was cunning. He was a baller in the business world. So for him to say that Max could just walk away had to have a deeper meaning.

"You have kids?" Scott asked.

"No. I'm divorced, but we never had children."

"You want 'em?" Liam asked.

Max shook his head. "Not now. Not at forty. Maybe five, ten years ago if you'd asked me that, I would have said yes. But I'm glad I didn't have them with my ex."

"You prepared to take on a teenager?" Liam asked, jerking his head toward the inside of the house. "I did it myself, and it's not easy. Love Mallory like she's my own, but the girl's got some attitude. Teenage girls are a mentally draining beast."

Max shifted his gaze between the two brothers with matching brown eyes and crooked smirks. He felt like a bug under a microscope.

"I don't want kids. But I want Celeste, and with Celeste

comes Sabrina, and I'm okay with that. She's one of my students and"—he glanced toward the house—"she's one of the few I like."

"That's not just because you're banging her mother?" Liam asked, refusing to pull any punches.

Max cleared his throat and leveled the man with his own challenging gaze. He knew what Liam was doing—vetting Max and looking out for Celeste and Sabrina's best interests —but he didn't appreciate the man's lack of diplomacy. He wasn't just *banging* Celeste. "No, that's not it at all. Sabrina is smart. She's kind. She's funny. She's all the very best qualities of *both* her parents. Because I knew her father too. I taught Declan, and just like Sabrina, he was smart, kind and popular for all the *right* reasons."

Scott and Liam exchanged looks but didn't say anything.

"I'm all in this with Celeste, and that means I'm all in this with Sabrina too. I've already told Celeste I would never make her choose between me and her daughter. That would be ridiculous. I just want Celeste and as much of herself she's willing to give me." He made sure he hit the brothers with a look that said this conversation was now over. He had nothing to prove to anybody, but he did appreciate that Celeste had so many people who had her back.

His words and look seemed to suffice. Liam and Scott both grunted, nodded and sipped their drinks.

"Then we wish you the best of luck," Liam said, lifting his glass into the air. "You're gonna need it."

Max grunted a response and brought his gin to his mouth for a sip.

To be honest, as far as potential stepdaughters went (was he really thinking that seriously into the future?) Sabrina wouldn't be a bad one to have. She was, as everyone at school could attest to, a very nice person. But why wouldn't she be, given the woman who'd raised her?

Unfortunately, since they'd all arrived at Liam and Richelle's house, Sabrina hadn't so much as glanced his way. She'd done everything she could to avoid looking at him. He'd thought there was something weird about her behavior in class earlier that day but had chalked it up to teenage angst. Had she already seen the video of Max and her mother by the time she had math with him in the afternoon?

If things between him and Celeste did progress, would Sabrina ever be able to look at him, to speak with him without either turning red in the face or glaring at him like laser beams shot from her eyes?

"Even though we didn't really see anything, that was still hot as hell," Eva said, the first to return to the deck. Richelle and Celeste were in her wake.

The look Richelle and Eva gave Max had the hair on his arms prickling up. He felt like a piece of meat and both women were starved hyenas cackling as they cornered him.

"Professor Washboard," Richelle said with a purr, sitting back down next to Liam and crossing her legs. "Well done."

Heat flooded his face, and he turned to Celeste. "You showed them?"

It looked like Celeste's whole body blushed. Even her ears changed color. "Richelle wanted to know what we were dealing with."

"And I was just really curious," Eva chimed in with a big grin.

"Now I want to see it," Liam interjected.

"Me too," Scott agreed. "I feel left out. Like the only guy to miss the Super Bowl because my cable went out. But everybody at the water cooler won't shut the fuck up about *that epic pass*."

"You still have a water cooler?" Liam asked.

"No, we have a break room with a Brita filter," Scott replied. "But you know what I mean."

"Gentlemen, can we return to the topic of Max and Celeste's first attempt at a successful Pornhub video?" Richelle said, winking at Celeste and then giving Max a coy grin.

Celeste groaned. Max muttered, "Fuck."

"It honestly wasn't that bad," Eva said. "It just looks like a really sexy kiss. You can't see your faces very well because you're kissing and it's far away."

"It's not a sex video that I think could get Max fired or either of you in big trouble," Richelle added.

"There is some definite gyrating going on, though," Eva said. "You can see his hand disappearing beneath her pants."

"But as far as graphic pornography goes," Richelle continued, "what you're doing is all *implied*. It could be simulated for all we know. Like movie sex. You're moving like he's got his hand down your pants. His hand *is* down your pants, but because we can't *see* anything, your faces are covered by each other's faces and it's taken from a distance it's a pretty tame video all things considered."

"We can't sue her for invasion of privacy?" Max asked, still worried about this "tame" video getting out and jeopardizing his job and ruining Sabrina's world as she knew it.

"If Eleanor had a video of Sabrina doing something, then we could, since she's a minor," Liam said. "But since you're both adults, we don't have much leverage."

"What's this little videographer's full name?" Scott asked.

"Eleanor Shelby," Max said, finishing his gin.

Liam frowned, his brows dipping into a deep V. "What's her father's name?"

Celeste finished her wine. "Alastair Shelby."

Liam pushed his fingers into his hair for the umpteenth time and breathed out a frustrated "Fuck."

"Guy's a defense attorney here in town," Richelle said, appearing equally irritated as her husband. "And a good one,

I'll admit. We have to be careful how we handle this. How we handle his daughter. We don't go after Eleanor unless we absolutely have to."

"Otherwise, Alastair will come for our throats," Liam finished.

"We should go to Alastair *first*. I've never worked with him, as he's a defense attorney and both Liam and I practice family law, but he's well-known in town. He's a partner at his firm and well-respected in the community. Hopefully he's a reasonable man and can see the error of his daughter's ways." Richelle reached for her plate that still held a slice of pizza.

"Sabrina and I actually ran into him at the grocery store earlier when we were grabbing ice cream. I agree, he seems like a reasonable guy. Was friendly, chatty. I got the impression that although he thinks his daughter shits rainbows and can do no wrong, if I went to him with the problem, he might be able to talk to some sense into Eleanor."

Max didn't like the idea of Celeste going to see Alastair, but he also knew she was getting to the point of desperation and would do anything to help her child.

Maybe he needed to go and speak with Mindy one-on-one. See if she would be willing to help with the Eleanor problem. Maybe if the plea came from Max instead of Celeste, Mindy would be more receptive.

Then again, if Mindy got a bee in her bonnet about Max being with Celeste, that could make the whole situation worse.

He had to try though. He needed to help.

"Not a bad idea talking to Alastair. If you think he'll help." Liam squeezed his wife's thigh and smiled lovingly at her before nodding toward Max's empty glass. "Refill?"

Max nodded, kissed Celeste on the top of the head and followed Liam inside to the bar. Scott joined them.

"Don't you dare show them that video," Richelle called after them.

"Fair's fair," Liam replied, craning his neck around to grin at Max and whispering, "We don't actually have to see it. As curious as we are, that's Celeste and your privacy." He poured them all another drink. "I will say though, kudos." He lifted his glass in a toast toward Max. "For Eva and Richelle to come back looking as hot and bothered as they did ..." He clinked his glass with Max. Scott did the same. "Good on you."

"You're in deep now, man. Not much of a chance to climb your way back out." Scott tossed back half his drink.

Max grinned as he sipped his drink. "Then it's a good thing I don't want to, huh?"

18

"You ready?" Celeste asked Max as they sat on her couch the next afternoon, her laptop in front of them.

"For what?" He gave her a confused look. "Does something huge happen when you change your relationship status? Balloons drop from the ceiling? A parade goes by outside?"

She side-eyed him. "You know what I mean."

Sipping his coffee, he shrugged. "I honestly don't. Seriously, Celeste, what changes besides the fact that it will be more than just our inner circle knowing that we're dating? You're changing your status, I'm changing mine, and we're going to post a few pictures we've taken together. It's not like we're famous or from feuding families. I hardly think this is a scandal."

"It affects my child, so therefore it is a scandal. It's not Brangelina level, but it's enough to devastate Sabrina."

Fair enough.

Exhaling through his nose, he set his coffee mug down, brought out his phone and nodded. "Ready."

She hit the cursor on her laptop to change her relationship status, and just like that, the world—or at least Celeste and Max's world—knew they were together. She then posted pictures of them together to the rest of her social media platforms with cute captions. He didn't go nearly as far. He changed his status and posted a couple of pictures. He rarely waxed poetic in real life. He wasn't about to fake it for the masses he didn't give a damn about.

Once it was done, he sat back against the couch. "Now what?"

"Now, we wait." She reached for her own coffee. "Feels a little anti-climactic, doesn't it?"

That was an understatement.

"I'm willing to do whatever you need to do to protect Sabrina," he said, setting his phone down on the arm of the couch and then looping his arm around her. "But this is all a bit weird to me. I work in the teenager realm, but I guess I'm still out of the loop in how this all works."

"You and me both, and I have a teenager." She huffed out a puff of air that made the hair around her face move. She turned to face him. "I really appreciate you doing this. We can't let Eleanor win. And Mindy has been zero help, so we need to do this on our own."

"What about going to Eleanor's father like Richelle suggested?" he asked, not liking the frisson of jealousy tickling the base of his neck. Celeste wanted him. He wanted her. He needed to trust. Just because Sharmaine cheated didn't mean every woman was a cheater.

And they needed to focus on the current problem, which was Eleanor and that video. And if Mr. Shelby was the solution to all of that, then they needed to try. Maybe the man was like Max and had no patience for this bullshit. Maybe he could ground Eleanor or cut off his daughter's cellphone plan or credit card until she wised up. That's what Max would do.

Hit 'em where it hurts the most—and that's their social life and their freedom.

Celeste hummed, tapping her finger to her lips. "I thought of that, and it's still an option. I just remember Sabrina saying that if I went to either of Eleanor's parents and Eleanor found out about it, she'd make Sabrina's life miserable."

"Mindy already knows, and that hasn't changed anything. Can it really get any worse?"

She slapped a hand over his mouth. "Don't say that. You'll jinx us all."

Max rolled his eyes and pried her hand from his mouth, kissing her fingertips. "Please don't tell me you're superstitious."

"I'm not superstitious; I'm wary. There's a difference." She made to pull her hand away, but he held on tight.

"I've been asked to chaperone the homecoming dance," he said. "I'll be able to keep an eye on things. Hopefully Eleanor hasn't watched *Carrie* and has access to pig's blood."

This time Celeste really did manage to wrench her hand from him. She stood up. "Why would you even say such a thing? This is my child we're talking about."

He fought the urge to roll his eyes and instead nodded, joining her where she stood in front of him in the center of her living room. "You're right. I'm sorry." He went to place his hands on her hips, but she stepped out of his reach.

"I know you think this is all ridiculous and a joke, but it's not. High school these days is a monster pit. My job is to help my daughter get through the next four years relatively unscathed. You joking about pig's blood doesn't help things. Kids bring guns to school because they feel rejected or bullied. Who knows how unstable Eleanor is or what she has access to? She videotaped us and is using it against my daughter. How low is she willing to go?

This may seem *funny* to you, but I can assure you, to Sabrina, it's her whole damn world right now." Her fists bunched, and she slammed them on her hips. The red in her cheeks slowly crept up her forehead and into her hairline, and the flare of her nostrils reminded him of a mother bear preparing to rip out the jugular of the person who stood between her and her cub.

Holding up his hands in surrender, Max stepped toward her cautiously. "You're right. You're right, and I'm sorry. I just ..."

"Don't understand," she whispered, crossing her arms in front of her.

He slapped his hands against his sides and shrugged. "You're right. I don't."

"And I don't either, to an extent. But I'm doing what I can for my kid. Sabrina still won't tell me everything that Eleanor is doing to her at school, but something tells me the kid is hell-bent on making my child's life a nightmare."

And that made Max see red.

Why were kids so damn cruel?

"Okay, so according to Facebook and Instagram land, we are now together. What else can I do to help?"

"You can friend and follow Mindy Shelby on social media so that she can see we're together. That should expedite her daughter finding out. Sabrina has already told her friends, and they're working on spreading the news as well."

Goddamn grapevine. That's how he'd found out about his wife's infidelity. And with a fellow teacher no less. The grapevine was another wretched beast that took on a life of its own if it wasn't pruned back and kept tidy.

He cringed as he brought up his phone. Mindy had already sent him a friend request, which he'd ignored for weeks. Wouldn't it look suspicious if he now all of a sudden accepted her request? Did he care? Fuck, he hated social media.

He accepted her request as per Celeste's instructions. Now what?

Celeste wandered into the kitchen. He followed her, though for the first time since they started seeing each other, he didn't feel welcome in her home. It wasn't just the change in the season or the cool air that accompanied the falling leaves. Celeste was giving him a full-on cold shoulder.

"You said you're chaperoning the homecoming dance?" she asked, leaning against her oven and tilting her head to look at him, arms still crossed over her chest—a clear message for him to back the fuck off.

He nodded. "Yeah. Not that I want to, of course. But I also don't have much of a choice, seeing as I'm the new guy. Figure it'll be a good excuse to keep tabs on things."

"I've been asked to chaperone as well," she said. "Sabrina's not too happy about it, but I told her I'd do coat check or something stupid like that so I didn't cramp her style."

Why didn't she tell him this sooner?

"I only received the email last night after we arrived home from Liam and Richelle's. Apparently, when I registered Sabrina for school, I also ticked some box that said *Yes, please contact me about parent volunteer opportunities.*" She rolled her eyes. "The woman practically begged me in her email. Looks like nobody wants to chaperone a bunch of sex-crazed puberty monsters."

He snorted and inched forward, hoping he could thaw her cold shoulder and their afternoon together wouldn't be completely ruined. "I'm sorry for making light of the situation earlier. I don't have kids, so I don't really understand, but I'm trying to understand."

Her gaze softened. "I know you are, and I appreciate it." She unfolded her arms and glanced away. "I mean, I think this is all completely ridiculous as well. Do I like that that video of us is in the hands of a teenager with bloodlust? Of course not. But neither of us were naked. It just looks like we're kissing—big whoop. But it's a big deal to Sabrina, so I need to take it seriously. She already feels like I betrayed her once. I can't let her feel that way again."

He reached for her, caging her against the stove. This time she didn't pull away. "I'll take my cues from you. And I will never make you choose between me or your daughter. I know who'd be the loser in that outcome, and it would say a lot about you as a mother and a person if the loser wasn't me."

Turning back to face him, her smile was grim. "Thank you for that." Her eyes still held a look that made his body turn icy. "She's still really upset. Can hardly look me in the eye because of that video. And who can blame her? If I found a video like that of my parents, I'd be pretty traumatized."

Much like her daughter couldn't look Celeste in the eyes, Celeste seemed to be struggling to look Max in the eye. She glanced away from him again, focusing on a section of her kitchen counter. Was she having second thoughts about them? Was dating him too much of a strain on her relationship with her daughter?

He'd always had a great relationship with his parents, but he could remember a time when Bridget was roughly Sabrina's age and she and Max's mom had not gotten along. Bridget, for all her pros, had been a moody, emotional teenager, and neither Max's dad or mom knew what to do with her. They'd braced themselves for the second coming when Max turned fifteen, but he didn't remember having the kind of rip-roaring fights with his parents that his sister did.

Had Celeste had a rocky relationship with her parents when she was her daughter's age? Was she trying to keep history from repeating itself?

He could help her. He could be her rock in the tumultuous sea that was parenthood to teenagers. He could be her life raft, her bailing bucket and her island of refuge when she felt like she was in over her head. Sure, she had her single mom friends and her sister, but she could have him to lean on too.

Celeste was a woman worth fighting for. She deserved to be happy. And up until yesterday when the shit hit the fan and they knew that video existed, he thought he did make her happy. She certainly made him happy.

Taking her chin between his thumb and finger, her turned her to face him again. "Where'd you go?" he asked softly, feeling like if he acted too aggressively or said the wrong thing, he might spook her. She already wasn't acting like herself, and it was worrisome.

She shook her head, but not enough to disengage his touch. "I just keep thinking about that night in your office. I was so stupid to go down there to you. Of course, Eleanor saw me leave and probably followed me. For all the girl's evil faults, she's not stupid. She knows how to hurt people."

He'd thought a lot about that night too since finding out about the video. But he didn't think she was stupid for coming to see him. They'd been foolish not to close the closet door completely, but the rest came as naturally to the both of them as breathing. At least that's how he felt. Celeste Howard could not be further from stupid. Celeste Howard could not be further from a bad idea or a poor choice.

"Look at me," he said, keeping the edge to his voice at bay.

Her gaze had drifted to the side again, but at his order, she focused back on him.

"You're not stupid. You're the antithesis of stupid. We both are, however, foolish for not having closed my office door. But you're not stupid. I don't want you to beat yourself up over this. We'll figure it out." Leaning forward, he pressed his lips to hers.

She didn't flinch or pull away, but he could tell her heart wasn't in the kiss.

Was he losing her before he felt like he truly had her?

Taking a deep breath, Celeste moved out of his embrace. "If you don't mind, I think I'd like to be by myself for the rest of the day. I have a lot on my mind and a lot of work to do. I'm behind on an edit."

Max's heart dropped clean to his feet. Nodding, he released her chin and backed away. "Of course. I have somewhere I need to be as well."

Curiosity piqued in her eyes but not enough for her to ask him where he had to go.

Truth be told, he'd only just thought of where he needed to go, and he wasn't looking forward to it, but he also knew that it needed to happen.

She saw him to the door, having remained quiet, her mind a million miles away, her eyes still unwilling to focus on him.

Opening the door, he braced himself for the chilly wind. He was grateful he'd brought his truck instead of his bike. He usually rode his motorcycle until the first week of November, but days like today made him happy he had a vehicle with a roof, sides and a heater.

"I'll call you," he said, standing on her threshold. "Tonight. And you can let me know if you want to see me tomorrow or not."

One side of her mouth tilted up, but it dropped just as quick. She leaned against the doorjamb and hugged her gray cardigan around her body. "I appreciate you understanding my need for space. This has just been a lot to process, and I think it's best if I do it alone."

He dipped his head in front of hers. "I get it. Just don't shut me out, okay?" He kissed her quick, smiled, though it never reached his heart, let alone any other part of his body, and then he left her.

Once he was in his vehicle, he turned to face her at the door, intending to wave, but she had already gone back inside and shut the door, shut him out.

He only hoped it wasn't for very long.

CELESTE PLASTERED her back against her front door and waited until she knew the coast was clear and Max was gone. She hated all of this. Hated how she felt, hated how she'd treated him, but something inside her told her to take a step back. She needed to do more to help her daughter and prevent Eleanor Shelby from hurting anybody else she saw as a threat.

Using her super sleuth skills, it didn't take long for Celeste to find the address she needed. With Sabrina at work and Max headed home, she was on her own.

But she had a feeling that was the way it should be. She alone had made the decision to go downstairs to Max's classroom that night at the school. She alone was responsible for not closing the door and letting things escalate the way they had. She could have said no and Max would have stopped. But she didn't say no. She didn't want to say no. And now they were all going to pay the price for her rash, selfish behavior.

With the address plugged into the GPS on her phone, she climbed into her SUV, checked her makeup in the rearview mirror, applied more lipstick and was on her way.

Not fifteen minutes later, Celeste pulled up to a big, brick house with a three-car garage, topiaries in the front yard and a Lexus parked in the driveway.

Taking a deep breath, she shut off the engine and opened her door.

She had no idea of the Shelbys' custody agreement or whether Eleanor would be with her mother or father, but she had to put one foot in front of the other and keep going forward toward that front door. Whether Eleanor was with her dad or not shouldn't matter. She needed to get Alastair Shelby on her side. She needed the man's help.

Lifting up her fist, she pounded on the solid wood door. The sound thundered in her ears and through the house on the other side.

With bated breath and sweaty palms, she waited.

Footsteps on the other side of the door had her tossing her shoulders back and focusing her gaze forward. It didn't matter that Alastair Shelby was incredibly tall, wealthy and handsome. She would not let herself be intimidated or distracted. She was a mama bear, and she was out to protect her cub.

The door opened, but it wasn't who she thought would be on the other side. A short, stocky woman of about fifty-five or so, with curly gray hair and almost violet eyes, blinked up at her. She wore a pale blue housekeeper's uniform. "May I help you?"

Swallowing, Celeste nodded. "I'd like to see Mr. Shelby, please. Is Alastair home?"

"Camilla? Who's there?" Alastair appeared around the corner, a tall tree dressed in a weekend casual getup of tan slacks, a yellow polo and brown loafers. The furrow in his brow disappeared the moment he saw Celeste, but the look that replaced it made her skin crawl. "Ms. Howard, what a pleasant but unexpected surprise." He thanked Camilla, and the woman disappeared silently. "Come in, come in. That breeze is a chilly one." He welcomed her inside and shut the door behind her.

The house, just like the outside, was gorgeous, with a vaulted entryway ceiling, a big contemporary light fixture hanging above them and a staircase to the right leading up to a series of doors on the second floor. Everything was modern, expensive and immaculate.

"Can I offer you a drink?" Alastair asked, wandering into a room just off the entryway. It appeared to be some kind of study slash games room. The furniture was dark wood, the tapestries a sandy color. A trolley of various spirits sat next to his desk, and he poured himself something amber from it. "Scotch? Vodka? Gin?" He took a sip from his tumbler.

She shook her head. "No, thank you. I have to drive and"—she glanced at the brass and mahogany mantel clock above his fireplace—"and it's not even noon."

Alastair shrugged and took another sip. "It's noon somewhere. That's one of the things that bothers me most about living where we do. In one of the last time zones. We're the last to get happy hour." His grin was enormous, just like his presence. He seemed different than the last two times she'd met him. He was more than just relaxed because he was in his own home and it was the weekend. Unlike the last time they met, something about Alastair Shelby gave her the willies, and she was instantly regretting her idea to come and ask for his help—particularly alone. The man was showing his true colors, and the vibe he was sending off with those colors had all the hair on the back of Celeste's neck standing straight up.

The look he continued to watch her with had ice cubes sliding up and down her spine until her legs felt numb and her fingers tingled. She made sure she had her back to the door and a clean getaway if need be.

"So, to what do I owe the pleasure?" he asked, sauntering toward her with a predatory glint in his eyes.

Celeste maneuvered herself so she was behind a chair but still close to the door. "Mr. Shelby—"

"Alastair, please."

She nodded. "Right. Alastair, I've come to ask you for your help."

"Anything. Name it," he said, far too quickly.

She gripped the back of the wingback chair and focused on her senses. She had to keep her wits about her around this guy. "Well, it's a bit of a sensitive nature, actually."

Intrigue filled his features, and he closed in the space between them, standing on the opposite side of the chair. "Ooh, what happened?" He finished his drink and held up a hand. "Wait, are you coming to me for legal advice? Do you need a lawyer?" They were close enough now she could smell the alcohol on his breath as well as his cologne. Neither were overkill, but the fact that she could smell them meant he was too close.

"I don't need a lawyer, no. I ... your daughter and my daughter seem to have some issues with each other."

Alastair's nostrils flared, and his posture changed from cavalier to high alert.

"I understand that this is a tough time for Eleanor, what with your and Mindy's separation. I also know that her boyfriend, Noah, ended things with her over the summer. However, her reactions to these incidents are affecting *my* daughter. Eleanor is lashing out at Sabrina. She is spreading false rumors about Sabrina, threatening to call child protective services on me because my credit card was declined and I made Sabrina pay for half of her own jeans. She spent the better portion of the last month writing offensive slander about my daughter on the bathroom walls of the school, and that has escalated now to several older football players taunting my daughter because of these messages."

It was impossible to get a read on the man. He hadn't so much as blinked.

So she continued. "Noah, Eleanor's ex, has asked Sabrina

to homecoming, and Eleanor is not happy about it. She has threatened Sabrina."

"Threatened *how?*" he asked slowly, his brows pinching.

Oh boy. She'd hoped she wouldn't have to go that far. "I have recently started dating a teacher at the school. He and I were ... *kissing,* and Eleanor recorded us on her phone. She is threatening to send the video to everyone in the school's email database as well as post it to social media if Sabrina doesn't turn Noah down."

She exhaled and shut her eyes for a moment. There, that wasn't so hard, was it?

"You're coming to me over a video of two people *kissing?*" he asked. The man's tone dripped with skepticism. She opened her eyes to find him appraising her with a look that matched his tone. "Either you're lying to me about what is on that video, or you're grasping at straws about my daughter."

Gnashing her molars until she thought she was for sure going to chip a tooth, she leveled him with a gaze she hoped conveyed the severity of the matter, as well as her displeasure with his doubt in her and what she told him. "What is on that video is irrelevant, and you know it. The fact that your daughter is threatening my child with anything is what is cause for concern. Her behavior toward Sabrina is borderline criminal. She's a bully."

At the use of the *B* word, Alastair's back snapped straight and his gaze turned molten.

Celeste swallowed and powered forward. "Now, I have spoken to Mindy about this, but she doesn't seem to be taking it seriously. She said she would speak with Eleanor about it, but that was weeks ago, and my daughter is still being bullied."

"Methinks the lady doth protest too much," he said with a smirk. "What's really on that video that you don't want out, hmm?" He stepped around the chair toward her.

She backed up.

He came closer.

She was now on the threshold of the door leading back to the entryway. "Mr. Shelby, I have come to you asking for your help in defusing this matter. The principal is aware of the situation, as is Mindy, and now you are as well. We all know how teenagers are, but we also know how fragile their hearts and egos can be. I implore you to please help your daughter and in turn help mine." Swallowing again, she was forced to lift her gaze along the long plane of his body until she reached his face.

A storm stared back at her.

But in that storm still lurked a letch. He reached out and twirled a tendril of her hair between his fingers. "I have a *thing* for redheads."

The man was a vile pig. He hid it well in public.

She casually stepped back into the foyer and fought the need to cringe from his touch. "I've heard that, yes."

Alastair rolled his eyes. "My ex tell you that? She always has had a penchant for the dramatic."

Her hand fell to the latch of the front door, and she gripped it like her life depended on it. "All I'm asking of you, Mr. Shelby, is that you speak with your daughter about the consequences of her actions. It's not too late for her to turn things around. I'm sure the last thing she wants to be remembered for in high school is that she was the mean girl."

"You mean the girl who leaked a sex tape of a teacher and another student's mother," he said with a derisive snort.

Heat percolated through her icy limbs, and she puffed out her chest. "It is not a sex tape. And even if it was, the fact that *your* daughter plans to leak it as a form of revenge against *my* daughter speaks volumes about what kind of a parent you are, and what kind of a person Eleanor is."

"And what does it say about you? The person *in* the

video?" he asked. He was close enough now she could smell his scotch-breath. And the longer she looked in his anger-filled eyes, the more she saw that he was struggling to keep them focused. He also swayed where he stood. The man was drunk. He'd been drinking before she arrived.

Now she knew there was no reasoning with him.

Mindy was no help. And now, neither was Alastair.

"What happened *after* my daughter left? Did you drop to your knees like I've heard your daughter is prone to doing?"

Her hand hit his face before her brain had time to register what happened. The man glaring at her, cupping his red cheek, looked equally stunned.

"The sooner you realize your daughter doesn't shit rainbows and piss lemonade, the better all our lives will be." Then, before she bypassed her brain and did something else that could be considered assault, she opened the door and fled the Shelby house as fast as her legs and Volvo SUV could carry her.

It wasn't until she was back in her own garage that the adrenaline finally started to leave her body and she began to shake.

What a colossally horrible idea that had been.

Why did she think going to Alastair Shelby would be a good idea?

Because you're desperate to help your daughter and hang on to Max, and you're floundering with ideas on how to do both.

Yeah, that was an accurate explanation. She was floundering.

And if she didn't figure out a way to get her head above water for good soon, she was going to drown and quite possibly take her child and the man she was falling for down with her.

19

"PROFESSOR WASHBOARD, YOU ARE A TALENTED MAN," Lauren purred, rubbing her belly as she sat on Bianca's couch that Saturday night and watched the video of Celeste and Max for what was probably the tenth time.

"All right, that's enough," Celeste said with a groan and an eye roll. "Give me back my phone."

"You honestly can't see anything, hardly even your faces," Bianca said reassuringly. "I mean, it's a hot video for sure. And you *know* where his hand is and what those fingers are doing, but you can't actually see anything. It's all assumption and filling in the blanks."

"Well, we know Max filled her blank," Lauren chided. "And then some." She bounced on the couch, setting her blonde ponytail swinging. "How's the sex? Is it amazing? I bet it's amazing. That video says a lot about what kind of a lover he is. Demanding but giving. Controlling but thorough. Like at any given moment he could just grab you by the ponytail, flip you around, throw your belly to the counter, lift up your skirt and suck your clit until you're speaking in tongues."

"Jesus," Bianca whispered, shaking her head. "You need help, woman."

"I need dick," Lauren corrected with a pained sigh. "A big, throbbing, veiny one."

"Don't you have like three different variations of Tracy's Dog?" Bianca asked, sipping her wine.

"Yeah, but I can't get to my cooch over my belly. A lot of good a vibrator does if you can't hold it in where it needs to be."

Celeste and Bianca exchanged amused glances across the living room.

"That Alastair fucker sounds so creepy," Bianca said, changing the subject. "I totally thought you were going to say he tried to feel you up or something."

He probably would have tried if she hadn't slapped him across the face and escaped when she did.

She glanced at her phone, where more notifications had already popped up since the last time she'd checked. The amount of people who *liked* her change in relationship status or had commented was disturbing. Did people not have anything better to do in their life than obsess over other people's relationship status?

"And how's Sabrina doing in all of this?" Bianca asked. "Richelle said Mallory and Sabrina have been texting a lot more than usual lately. Though the girls text all the time already, but the volume has increased."

"She's still hurt," Celeste said with a sigh. "Thinks I betrayed her trust. Which I kind of did."

Bianca and Lauren both shook their heads and said "Nuh-uh" at the same time.

"You are the best fucking mom ever," Lauren said. "And you didn't betray anything. The only betrayal would be you to your heart and clit if you didn't get with that man."

Bianca rolled her eyes. "I agree. The heart wants who the

heart wants. I learned that the hard way this year. My husband's heart—and dick—no longer want me. They want his twenty-six-year-old secretary, Opal. Hence why she's knocked up with his twins." Her brown eyes turned sad. "I just wish I'd known the last time we had sex was going to be the last time. I would have ..."

"Savored it?" Lauren asked. "I get that. Me too. I don't even remember the last time, so it couldn't have been that earth-shattering. Had I known it would be my last for a while, I would have sat on his face for like an hour."

Celeste snorted.

"You think this Alastair guy is going to be a problem?" Bianca asked. "I mean he obviously has no scruples if he cheated on his wife, laughed about it and is raising a demon like Eleanor."

That was Celeste's fear. That Alastair would get his hands on the video and use it against Celeste in some way because she'd slapped him and offended him. All three of the Shelbys had egos as fragile as a robin's egg.

"He could be," Celeste finally said.

Dread coiled its way around her body like a snake, slowly squeezing the life out of her until she struggled to breathe.

She was a fierce mama bear, but she was on her own parenting Sabrina. Eleanor had two parents who loved their cub and thought the sun shone out of her ass. What lengths would they go to to keep their precious spawn looking all shiny and innocent?

What yarns would they spin? What kind of havoc would they wreak?

Lauren reached across the couch and squeezed Celeste's hand. "Honestly, Celeste, I think the best thing you can do by your daughter and yourself is to just let the chips—or in this case the video—fall where they may. You're both adults, you were consenting, and you're in a relationship. It's not like you knowingly filmed yourselves having sex and put it up on some porn site and people found it. Sure, the location you chose wasn't completely private, but you can't *see* anything. Your intimate moment was filmed without your knowledge or consent, and you can see that on the video."

Celeste glanced at Bianca, who was nodding.

Lauren continued. "Show your daughter that her mother doesn't negotiate with terrorists and you're not going to let a little snot like Eleanor manipulate or embarrass you."

"The horny pregnant lady is right," Bianca said, earning a glare from Lauren. "It's harder for people to laugh at you if you're already laughing at yourself." She shrugged.

Celeste chewed on her nail for a moment and thought about it. They were right, and she knew *she* could do it, but whether her daughter could was another question altogether. Would Sabrina be able to shrug it off and stand up for herself, or would she play right into Eleanor's plan and turn Noah down for the dance?

SABRINA HAD CALLED LATER that evening and asked Celeste if she could stay overnight at her Aunt Eva's. She was already babysitting Freddie, Lucas and Kellan and had fallen asleep on the couch after the boys went to bed. Eva said she or Scott would drive Sabrina to work in the morning.

So that left Celeste home alone for the night. She thought about calling Max over as she stumbled up the sidewalk from Bianca's after wine night. But she wasn't sure what to say to him. The last time they'd spoken, she'd been distant with him, unsure where their relationship was headed after Eleanor had shown the video to Sabrina.

Her focus for the time being was her daughter and their relationship, and Max knew that. But she also didn't want to ignore him completely so that he broke things off with her. She did want him. She just came with baggage and responsibilities.

With enough wine to be properly pickled, Celeste staggered home from Bianca's house. She was almost to her front door when a hand landed on her arm.

"Where the hell do you get off talking to me like that? Hitting *me*."

The scent of his breath was enough to tell her that Alastair had been drinking—and a lot more since that morning. Her heart thumped against her ribcage. It fought for space in her chest with the air frozen in her lungs.

She whirled around and jerked free from his grasp. "I came to you for help. The two previous interactions we had made me think you were a reasonable, respectful and respectable man." God, she could not have been more wrong. "I came to you as one parent to another asking if we could work together and defuse the situation between our children, and instead you showed me exactly why Eleanor is the way she is. A product of her upbringing—or lack thereof."

"Why you—"

"Hey!"

Alastair's hand stopped in midair before he was able to bring it down on Celeste. She'd already turned away to protect herself.

Max came running down the path and shoved Alastair out of the way. "What the fuck?"

"Oh, well, if it isn't the finger-banging math teacher. Here to teach the slutty mom another lesson?" Alastair's gaze pivoted back and forth between Max and Celeste, but she could tell he was having a hard time focusing. The man was shit-faced.

Finger-banging math teacher. So he'd now seen the video.

Horror spun in Celeste's gut like a jagged-edged table saw blade, ripping up her insides to the point of agony.

Swallowing down the dread, she focused on the present and the immediate problem they faced. "Did you drive here?" she asked, scanning the car-lined street. She found his Lexus. It was parked in front of Max's truck. Had he been waiting for her?

"What the fuck is wrong with you, man?" Max muttered, shaking his head and staring at Alastair with not so much anger now as pity. "You don't even know us, and yet you're hell-bent on fucking with our lives. How sad your own life must be."

Alastair's face once again turned stormy. "Fuck you," he spat. "If you didn't want your little fingerfuck to get out, then you shouldn't have done it."

"I'm calling the police," Celeste said, reaching for her phone. "He drove here drunk, waited for me until I got to my front door and then he grabbed me." She dialed the non-emergency line and was just about to connect with dispatch when her phone was swatted from her hand.

"You stupid bitch," Alastair roared. "You're all stupid bitches. Stupid fucking red-haired cunts."

Now, Celeste couldn't tell the difference between tae kwon do, karate, jujitsu or kung fu, but she was pretty damn grateful that Max was well trained in one of them. He took down Alastair with nothing more than a punch to the ribs. Alastair buckled and crumpled at Max's feet, which was a long way to go for a tall guy like that. Max put him in a head-lock and squeezed until the man's eyes fluttered shut.

"You didn't kill him, did you?" Celeste asked on a hiss. Her heart kicked up a ruckus in her chest, mingling fear and excitement with her blood. Had she just witnessed a murder?

He shook his head. "No. Put him to sleep. Call the cops. He won't be out forever."

20

THE FOLLOWING Friday seemed to arrive upon them like a bolt of lightning. One minute it was Saturday night, and Max was taking down one of his student's fathers in the dark of night on Celeste's doorstep, and the next he was searching in the deep recesses of his closet for a tie.

After the cops had arrived at Celeste's house and carted Alastair away for driving impaired and attempted assault, Celeste invited Max in. They'd talked at length, mostly about what Lauren and Bianca had suggested earlier that night. But even so, things felt off between them. She didn't lean into him the way she once did, didn't look for excuses to touch him. They sat on the same couch, their knees touching, but the intimacy of that simple posture was no longer what it'd once been.

He felt like an intruder in her home and that touching her knee wasn't proper. She didn't know he was going to show up at her place, but after the way she'd been upset earlier when they'd "gone public" with their relationship on social media, he knew he had to see her, to make sure they were still on solid ground and she wasn't looking for an exit.

"I know Bianca and Lauren suggested we just roll with the punches and poke fun at ourselves, and I can do that if you can, but I'm wondering if then we should just *fade* out," she said, unable to keep her eyes locked with his. She fidgeted so damn much, her hands twisted in the fabric of her skirt. Her eyes darted everywhere but his face. Her knee bounced. He could smell the wine on her breath, and the heavy blush in her cheeks said she'd imbibed a fair bit earlier that night with her friends. The woman's fair complexion didn't allow her to hide a damn thing. Everything she felt changed her pigment, and right now she was not only drunk but terrified.

"What do you mean *fade* out?" he asked, hoping to God she didn't mean what he thought she meant. That she was indeed, looking for an exit.

"I mean ... end it," she whispered, finally bringing her eyes to his. "This has all been just a nightmare. I mean if we show Eleanor that she can't hurt us with this video, will she just do something more drastic to finally make us—my daughter—bleed? We've seen that her parents have absolutely no morals or scruples either, so we're dealing with a three-headed snake."

He cracked his neck side to side and shivered at her mention of the word *snake*. He'd already started looking for a new condo online in his spare time. He needed to get the hell out of that place if a big-ass snake lived there too. And now that he had a cat, he and Sebastian were appetizer and main course in one confined space.

Tears brimmed her mossy-green eyes, and she broke their gaze again. Her bottom lip trembled, and he itched to kiss it, to take her in his arms and absorb her frustration. Because besides fear, the other paramount emotion inside her was frustration. He knew so, because he felt it himself.

He was frustrated with how the two of them had become

pawns in one family's warped sense of entitlement, revenge and bruised egos.

Two people had fucked up their own marriage and, in turn, fucked up their child, and now that fucked-up child was fucking with Celeste's child and in turn fucking with Celeste and Max.

The Shelby family was fucked up, and they needed to learn that the world did not revolve around them.

He'd reached for her, and thankfully, she hadn't pulled away. "If we end this, then they win."

Her sigh made her entire body slump. "I know."

"I may have exacerbated things today myself by going to try to talk some sense into Mindy, just like you tried to talk some sense into Alastair."

Her lips twisted. "You can't squeeze blood from a stone. If there's no sense there in the first place, it's hard to talk any into them."

She had that right.

He cringed as he thought about his brief and fruitless meeting with Mindy. He'd shown up at her house around lunchtime. She was alone and had a glass of white wine on the go. In hindsight, he probably should have just turned around right then and there and not engaged with a person who was day-drinking, but his desperation to help Celeste and Sabrina pushed him to enter Mindy's house and watch as she closed—and locked—the front door.

"I'm seeing Celeste Howard," he'd said, believing the woman deserved honesty before any further conversation between them transpired. "I've been seeing her for about a month now."

Mindy's face turned stony, the hopeful glint in her eyes disappearing only to be replaced with a deep-seated look of betrayal.

"I wanted you to hear it from me," he went on. He didn't

owe her any kind of an explanation—they weren't ex-lovers —but he knew she had a thing for him, and if he wanted her help, he needed to show her respect and walk cautiously on the eggshells that clearly surrounded Mindy Shelby.

Her brow lifted. "Why are you telling me this?"

Max took a deep breath. "Because I—*we*—need your help. Eleanor is out of control. She's been spreading rumors, writing slander on the bathroom wall and terrorizing Sabrina. She has a video of Celeste and I … kissing, and she's threatening to email it to the entire school and post it to social media unless Sabrina declines Noah's offer to go to the homecoming dance."

Even when he said it in his head, the sheer ridiculousness of it all had his internal eyes rolling.

"You came to me over a video about *kissing*?" she asked with a sneer.

"It's more than just about the video, and you know it," he said. If he mentioned that his hand was down Celeste's pants, Mindy might very well start throwing things at his head. "Eleanor is writing horrible things about Sabrina on the bathroom walls."

Mindy lifted a shoulder. "Can you prove that?"

He really should have turned around the moment she answered the door with a wineglass in her hand. He was obviously going to get no cooperation from this woman.

Inhaling again through his nose, he let his shoulders lift and fall. "Listen, Mindy, I know you hoped something would happen between us. I'm sorry if I led you on in any way. That wasn't my intention. You're a beautiful woman, and I am truly sorry for how your husband treated you. Nobody deserves that. But I *do* have a policy against dating colleagues, and Celeste and I have a …" He couldn't say connection because that would just set the woman off more. "A history," he finally said.

Mindy's lip twitched, but he could see her hard shell beginning to soften.

"All I'm asking is that you talk to your daughter. She's terrorizing Sabrina. I don't care what happens to me. If I get fired over what happened, then that will suck, but I'll land on my feet. I always do. Celeste feels the same way. We're worried about Sabrina. Please, talk to Eleanor. Get her to stop."

Mindy's nostrils flared before she sipped her wine, her eyes boring holes into his face as she stared at him over the rim of her glass.

He cleared his throat and headed for the door, unlocking it and opening it so he had a quick getaway. "I'm sorry again for what Alastair did to you. You didn't deserve that."

Her expression softened a fraction.

With his hand on the doorknob and his body halfway across the threshold, he glanced back at her. "Please talk to Eleanor. If not for me or Celeste, then for Sabrina. She's innocent in all of this and I'd hate for either girl to wind up with a reputation at school that haunts them for the next four years." He left Mindy's house feeling like he'd only poked the hornets' nest rather than gone in with smoke and settled the hive.

Would Mindy lash out like her daughter because she felt rejected by Max?

Only time would tell.

He just hoped that if she did, it was only he who received her ire and she spared Celeste and, more importantly, Sabrina.

He told Celeste about his meeting with Mindy, but when he finished his tale, she didn't say much. Was she mad he went to Mindy?

He was only trying to help.

They sat there in her living room for a while just holding

272 | WHITLEY COX

each other and not speaking. Eventually, her breathing slowed down and her body became relaxed. She'd fallen asleep in his arms.

He stayed there a while longer and continued to hold her because even though she hadn't ended it, he somehow felt like the end of them might be near. She was struggling to find the balance, to not feel overloaded with mom guilt. And he knew that if she couldn't find a balance that worked, he would be the first thing to go.

They didn't see each other on Sunday like they normally did, and she texted him midweek to cancel their plans for Wednesday night. They'd only texted that entire week, and each exchange was brief and to the point. No matter how hard he tried to resurrect what little connection they had left and engage her in conversation, she refused to give an inch.

He thought about showing up on her doorstep during his lunch break one day, but he wasn't sure how that would be received, and he didn't want to push her away any further, so he gave her the space she requested. He fucking hated it though. He fucking hated all of it.

Now, in his closet, he found his tie—a thin dark gray thing he'd owned for as long as he could remember. Were thin ties still a thing? Would it only make him more of an outcast if he showed up to the dance wearing something from his college days? Did he care?

Not enough to go buy a new tie, he didn't.

With a black, button-down, long-sleeved shirt, his gray tie and dark wash jeans, he thought he looked formal enough that he wouldn't stick out like a sore thumb but casual enough nobody would mistake him for a student—as if the silver threads he'd found in his beard the other day wouldn't give him away. He'd found some in his downstairs hair too. Plucking those fuckers out hurt like a bitch, but he just wasn't ready to admit he was old enough for gray pubes.

Gray on his head? Fine.

Gray in his beard? Whatever.

Gray under his pits? Yeah, who cared?

But gray in his pubes? No fucking way. Not yet anyway. He'd be fine with it in ten years, but not while he was in his forties. Just no.

Sebastian wandered into the bathroom like a silent furry, orange ghost and weaved his body through Max's legs, meowing.

"Did I forget to feed you, buddy?" Taking one final glance at himself in his bathroom mirror, he ran his fingers through his hair and fiddled with it until it looked properly messy. "I'm still getting used to this having a cat thing."

He made sure there was cat food out for Sebastian, gave his new friend a thorough scratch behind the ears, kissed the top of his head, then headed outside to his truck. He would have liked to take the Bonneville, but it'd grown particularly cold in the evenings over the last week, and he didn't feel like freezing off his nads.

"Fluffy?" came a shout from around one side of the building. "Fluffy, where are you?"

Fluffy.

As in Fluffy the albino python?

Max froze in place, only his eyes moved as he scanned the property for a glistening, white, beady-eyed serpent.

Glycon emerged from the side of the building, still calling out for Fluffy. "Hey, have you seen Fluffy?" he asked, directing his question to Max.

No, Max had certainly not seen *Fluffy,* and he was fucking glad he hadn't.

He turned around slowly, arms in the air like someone held a gun to his back. "Your snake has escaped?"

Glycon managed to look offended. "She went exploring. She does it from time to time. I always find her. Found her curled up behind one of the building's hot water tanks last week."

Holy fucking God.

"Dude, I really don't like the idea of a snake being on the loose in the building I live in. I bring my nieces and nephew here."

Glycon's eyes perked up. "Oh, let me know when they're visiting next and they can come and meet Fluffy. She loves kids."

Because they're snack-size.

Max's eyes darted around the now dark property. It was getting chillier and chillier at night. A snake wouldn't survive outside for very long. Which meant it probably wasn't outside at all. It was inside the building, looking for warmth and a meal.

Sebastian.

Were any of his windows open? What about a vent?

Ignoring Glycon, he raced back to his house and double-checked that all the windows were closed and there was no way a snake could get into his apartment.

Sebastian didn't even acknowledge him as he ran around his condo.

When he locked the door behind him again, Glycon was standing on the stone path watching him. "My snake in there?"

Max gave the man a wide berth. "Fuck no, man. I went to double-check on the cat and make sure all my windows were closed and that there wasn't any way a snake could get in there."

"You took that old lady's cat?"

"I took him to the shelter and they said senior cats don't often get adopted, so I brought him home. A better fate than being euthanized simply because his owner died and he's old. Nothing wrong with him." Why the fuck was he telling Glycon any of this? He had to get to the homecoming dance.

Even saying that in his head, *he had to get to the homecoming dance*, made him want to gouge out his own eyes.

"I gotta go," he said, heading back toward his truck. "Stop losing your snake, Glycon. I'm sure I'm not the only person in the building who would be freaked out to know a big-ass python is on the loose."

"Fluffy wouldn't hurt anybody!" Glycon called after him. "She's misunderstood. People judge her by her size before they get to know her. But she's seven feet of pure love."

A chill ran rampant through Max as he climbed into his truck.

Seven feet of pure love.

Fuck, he was only six feet two, plenty small enough to be lunch for a snake.

He started his truck but rolled down the window. "Find your fucking snake, Glycon, or I'm telling the HOA she keeps escaping." Then he peeled away from the building, unable to shake the feeling of something slithering across the back of his neck or up his pants leg.

He had to move. Knowing that a snake was in the building was bad enough, but given the fact that she kept escaping, he was never going to have a good night's sleep again. And poor Sebastian. When he'd lived with the old lady a few doors down, she'd always been home to keep an eye on her cat. But Max worked. He had a life. He couldn't be home to keep Sebastian safe twenty-four seven. Snakes weren't stupid either. Fluffy could pick up Sebastian's scent and find a way into Max's apartment if she really wanted to.

Dread coiled around his stomach like a snake coiled around its prey, squeezing until it was devoid of oxygen, unable to scream for help . "Was that how Sebastian's owner died?" he whispered under his breath. Had Fluffy gotten into the apartment in search of Sebastian but found a bigger meal in the form of a sleeping old lady?

Fuck, his imagination could take a morbid turn.

Now he *really* had to move.

Maybe he should go live with his sister in the studio apartment over their garage until he could sell his place and buy a new one. Sebastian loved the kids, and they didn't have any pets, let alone a reptile that would consider Sebastian an amuse bouche and each of the children an afternoon snack.

He could already hear the music by the time he pulled up to the school. Kids filed out of vehicles from the student parking lot. All of the boys wore dress shirts and pants, some of them suits, while the girls sported everything from long, floor-length dresses to things he thought belonged on the runway for Victoria's Secret. Some of those hemlines were short. Like scary, jailbait short.

Celeste had texted him earlier that day to confirm a meetup time and location. Sabrina was going with Noah, and Noah's parents were driving them.

So far, no video had been leaked. Maybe, just maybe, Eleanor had had a change of heart or her parents had located an ounce of sense between them and bestowed it on their child?

Or shit would hit the fan later.

His money was on the latter.

Sabrina hadn't been able to even look at Max all week. She's avoided eye contact with him, never put her hand up once, and went so far as to get Noah to bring her assignments up to Max's desk.

He couldn't blame her though. Max and his attraction to Celeste's mother was the reason Sabrina was in the mess she was in. It was the reason she'd seen a video she never should have seen. If Max had been in her shoes, it would have taken him a hell of a long time to get over seeing his mother in a position like that.

He waited for her where Celeste asked him to wait, in the shadows like a lurking letch. But he did as she asked, because it was his fault they were in this mess. He and his damn libido.

She texted when she arrived, and he watched her approach. She looked incredible. She always looked fucking incredible.

Her hair was loose around her shoulders in thick, dark red, chunky waves, and she wore a sexy black leather fitted jacket, dark green skinny jeans and a billowy white silk top. But it was the shoes that had his jaw dropping and his cock jerking. Fucking tiger-stripe pumps. Bright red toenails peeked out from the tips, and the heel had to be at least four inches high. But she walked in them like she'd never walked in anything else, and he had to keep himself from growling when she smiled shyly at him and tucked a strand of hair behind her ear.

"Fuck," he breathed out, continuing to rake her body tip to toe with his eyes. "Fuck, Celeste, you look amazing."

"Had to look the part, right?" she said, her smile no longer shy but snide and sarcastic. "Do you think this is slutty enough, or should I ditch the pants and shirt and just go in in my underwear?"

Damn it. He fucking hated that she had to put herself through this at all.

What were they walking into?

He offered her his arm, and she took it. "Let's get this shit storm over with," she said with an exhale.

"Maybe it won't be a storm but just a heavy breeze," he offered. "A sprinkle of rain and northwesterly wind that's no stronger than a small-craft warning. No gale force or hurricanes. Just enough of a gust to move the sail."

She gave him a heavy dose of side-eye.

"I'm just trying to help."

The side-eye dissolved, and she faced him entirely. Her eyes were now sad, tired. "I know you are, and thank you. I'm sorry for everything. For this week, for last weekend. I just ... I needed time to focus on fixing my relationship with my daughter. She's a sensitive soul, and we've always gotten along well—for the most part. This took a toll on both of us. Her feeling betrayed by me is uncharted territory."

Pursing his lips together, he nodded. "She hasn't been able to look at me once."

"She will. Give her time."

They each took a deep breath and stepped into the gymnasium, both of their bodies stiff and on high alert as they braced themselves for whatever kind of a storm might be waiting for them.

Max spotted Sabrina and Noah before Celeste did. He pointed them out, and Celeste took stock of their location.

"I have to go to coat check," she said, pink flooding her cheeks. "Come find me if something happens." She slipped her arm from his and headed to the coat check station to start her job.

He watched her walk away, hoping to God that it wasn't from his life for good, before he finally turned around and went to go find Principal Pelton. He'd chaperoned dances before, but every school was different. Most of the time he didn't have to do much besides break up fights, stop people from taking drugs, and intercept kids from sneaking off to the locker rooms to go do drugs or have sex.

Max spied Sabrina and Noah on the dance floor. They were both laughing and smiling with a few friends. She caught him looking at her and immediately looked away. Would things ever get easier between them, or should he put in for a transfer to another school? Maybe then he could continue to date Celeste and Sabrina wouldn't mind.

They were two hours into the dance and nothing had happened. He was drinking a soda and chatting with Marge Babcock, a biology teacher who was preparing to retire in June. She was feisty and quick-witted, and he'd quickly made her an ally when the music abruptly stopped and the sounds of two people having sex burst forth over the speakers.

Moans and groans.

Followed by an "Oh, Max." And a "Fuck, Celeste."

Then a video on both the projector screens replaced the psychedelic images the DJ had put up. It was Max and Celeste in his office. Not that he knew much about videography, but whoever had done this had made the image clearer, and it was easier to tell that the two people in the video were Max and Celeste—if they weren't already saying each other's names.

Gasps floated around the gymnasium as students stopped dancing and everyone turned around to look at either Max or Celeste. Her red hair made it easy to find her over in her coat check corner.

Sabrina looked like she was going to puke. He glanced over at Celeste. She was staring at her daughter, her face a mottled red, chin trembling.

Whoops, whistles and hollers from students competed with the dubbed-over sounds of sex from the video.

"All right, Mr. Travis. You go, bro!"

He swung his gaze to Principal Pelton, who appeared scandalized. Though he seemed to be the only person in the gym who was.

He glanced back at Sabrina. She was looking at her mother, and he would have missed it if he wasn't watching. She nodded, but just barely.

Reaching into her purse, Sabrina pulled out her phone,

280 | WHITLEY COX

put on music, grabbed Noah by the hand and hauled him into the middle of the dance floor. She shrugged. "What are you gonna do? It's the downside to having a hot, young mom." Then she started to dance.

Holy fuck.

"That takes fucking guts," Marge said next to him.

It took more than just guts. It took strength. It took heart. It took kindness and forgiveness. Because even if Sabrina never forgave him, what mattered was that she forgave her mother.

He watched as other students began to shrug and start dancing as well. A few of the senior guys gave him thumbs up or head nods. Some called him "the man" while others simply said, "Yo, Mr. Travis!"

The DJ managed to commandeer his music and video again, and before too long, the video and sound were down and top forty was playing once again.

Crisis averted?

He glanced over at Celeste.

Eleanor and a few of her friends were crowding around the coat check.

Crisis not averted.

Not by a long shot.

"Did you and your widdle Sabweena rehearse that bit?" Eleanor asked with a sneer as she stood in front of Celeste in her white tube-top-style shorty dress.

She looked like she was heading to one of P. Diddy's rooftop parties rather than a freshman attending her first homecoming dance. The child's makeup was pretty heavy too. Dark smoky eyes, way too much contouring. It was like she was trying to hide beneath a veneer of being put together, when inside she was completely falling apart.

"No rehearsal, no script. That was all Sabrina."

Eleanor scoffed and glanced side to side at her cronies. One of them Celeste recognized as Phyllis.

Neither of her "friends" looked like they wanted to be there though. Nobody was smiling. Nobody was sneering either. The other girls just looked uncomfortable with everything coming out of Eleanor's mouth and standing next to her in "support" was the equivalent to standing barefoot on broken glass.

Celeste shrugged. "Look, Eleanor, you can hurt me as much as you want. Go after me with everything you have. But touch my daughter, hurt my daughter, and we will have a problem." She glanced at her nails. She needed a manicure.

"Was that a threat?" Eleanor asked. "Did you just threaten me?" She glanced around the area and raised her voice. "Did everyone else just hear Sabrina's mom threaten me? Threaten my *life*?" Turning back to Celeste, Eleanor's next words came out on a hiss. "You *do* know who my father is, right?"

Celeste nodded and leaned on hand bored-like on the table. "I do. I've met him. We've bumped into each other a few times. I also went to his house to ask him to help talk some reason into you, and he drove to my house drunk and tried to hit me."

Eleanor's cronies gasped, and the psychopath in white actually managed to look a bit uncomfortable. Her complexion darkened, and she shifted where she stood. "You're lying."

She was bored of this broken child. So utterly bored.

Celeste shrugged. "Fine, whatever, Eleanor. I'm lying. I'm a slut that makes out with her kid's math teacher in a closet and I'm a liar. Why not?" She made sure to raise her voice so people nearby could hear them. At the same time, she tossed her arms up into the air and slammed them down on the sides of her thighs. "I'm honestly bored of this. Bored of you. You tried to break my child, to hurt my child, and I will admit, that almost broke me. But Sabrina is a *good* person, she is a kind person, and she forgave me. And now that I know my kid isn't broken, how incredibly strong my daughter is, I couldn't give a flying fuck about you or what shit you have to sling at me. Everyone at this school who has half a brain knows what was on those bathroom walls about my daughter isn't true. And anyone with half a brain also knows that it was *you* who wrote them."

Eleanor shook with rage. "You're nothing but a teen mom who got knocked up in high school."

Celeste shrugged again. "Yep."

A crowd was beginning to gather around them.

"I'm going to call child protective services on you. You're a shitty mom."

Celeste grabbed her phone from her pocket and held it out toward Eleanor. "Go for it. You can use my phone."

Eleanor's head looked like it was about to fly clear off her neck. "You're just a big stupid fucking cunt-slut who likes to get fingerbanged in a closet."

"I am. Yep. Big ol' cunt-slut." *Deep breaths, girlie. Deep breaths. You're doing great.*

Eleanor was shaking even more. "You're ... you're a desperate, ugly old cunt, and your daughter is a desperate cunt who just wants my sloppy seconds!"

"Eleanor Hannah-Louise Shelby! That is *enough!*" A crimson-faced Mindy, whose head also looked like it was ready to fly off her neck, came barreling into the crowd and snatched her daughter by the arm. "How dare you speak to anybody like that, ever?"

"B-but ... Mom," Eleanor pleaded, her eyes wide, and face of contempt replaced with one of fear.

Mindy shook her head. The woman looked close to a coronary. "No. Do not say another word. We are leaving. Get in the car."

Eleanor's face turned even redder, and tears welled in her eyes. She went to run away, but the crowd closed in around her. Her eyes beseeched her peers for help, but nothing besides loathing and disgust stared back at her. Even Phyllis and the other girl had joined the wall of students standing around Eleanor, watching her fall from her throne. Her worker bees and drones had finally had enough of her toxicity. And when that happens, the hive turns on their queen to make room for a new one.

The queen bee had fallen.

As if she suddenly realized her fate, her slender shoulders collapsed and she hung her head. She was defeated, and she knew it.

Without another glance at anyone, Mindy marched her daughter out of the gymnasium. The crowd dispersed, and for the first time that night, Eleanor's cronies went off and did their own thing, and they were smiling.

21

EVEN THOUGH THE crowd had dissolved and the students were back dancing, Max stood there in place, completely dumbfounded. What the fuck just happened?

Was it honestly *Mindy to the rescue?* Were they in the fucking Twilight Zone or something?

Blinking a bunch of times to make sure he hadn't actually had a stroke and wasn't dreaming all of this as he rode in the back of a screaming ambulance to the hospital, he turned to Marge. "Did that just happen?"

"Sure did," she said. "Knew after the staff mixer at that Prime place that Mindy was a few bricks short of a load. Never expected to see her do that, though."

Neither did Max.

Particularly after what Mindy had said when he went to her for help last weekend. The woman seemed more inclined to let Max, Celeste and Sabrina burn rather than help put out the fire that would inevitably engulf her own child too.

Why the change of heart?

"You actually seeing that mom?" Marge asked, lifting a bushy salt-and-pepper brow at him. "Or was that just a biological thing? Itches to scratch and the like?" Her honey-colored eyes twinkled behind her cat's-eye glasses.

"We're seeing each other," he replied with a smile. "Though, you could say what happened in that video was pretty—"

"Primal? I'll say. I've been teaching biology for over thirty-five years. I've seen a lot. Seen a lot of animals make babies. That there was feral."

He was going to say impulsive. But yeah, primal, feral, those worked too.

His face was on fire, and he just stood there with his jaw slack and bottom lip slowly growing closer to the floor. "Marge, I—"

But she slapped him on the arm and started laughing. "I'm just messing with you, Max. I mean, don't get me wrong, that video was spicy. But if you two are happy, then that's great. Eleanor was in the wrong for filming you, and I hope she is disciplined appropriately for it. I also know she's been harassing Sabrina, spreading rumors and writing things on the bathroom wall. I know parents don't spank anymore, but that girl's ass needs a good paddling."

He relaxed—a bit—but his focus zeroed back in on Celeste, who was still in coat check.

"Go check on your girlfriend," Marge said, patting his arm. "I'm going to grab myself another soda." She took a couple of steps away from him before turning back. "You're in Seymour's old office, right?"

He made a face that said he didn't know.

"Downstairs, to the left of the bathrooms?"

He nodded.

"You find his *stash* yet?" There went that sparkle in her eye again. He wished he'd known her longer. Marge had probably been one hell of a fun colleague to work with over the years. She had a badass edge to her he could appreciate. Too bad she was planning to retire in June.

"You mean ..." With his thumb and pinky out, he discreetly tipped his fist up to imitate drinking a bottle.

She grinned and nodded. "Man had good taste, huh?"

"He sure did."

"I'll be round next Friday for a drink. Unless you've already finished it all?"

He shook his head, smiling. "Savoring it. I'll be sure to grab a second glass and pick up some pretzels too."

"I look forward to it," she said, before heading over to the refreshment table.

Chuckling, Max pried his feet from the floor and made his way toward Celeste but not before being stopped by Principal Pelton.

The short, slender bald man with big, wide eyes cleared his throat as he approached Max. "Quite the video, Mr. Travis."

Max's chest puffed on a deep inhale. "I'm sorry. We didn't have—"

Pelton held up a hand. "You were clothed and, from what I could tell, just kissing. Consenting adults. Just keep that shit off school property from now on, okay? I have enough of a problem keeping the students and their hormones from turning this place into spring break in Daytona. I don't need the staff acting like bunnies too." His brown gaze was scolding but also held a glimmer of humor.

As much as Pelton could be a neurotic headless chicken sometimes, the guy was pretty cool.

"Thanks," Max said sheepishly. "Won't happen again."

Pelton nodded. "See that it doesn't." He wandered off to the refreshment table, where he and Marge started chatting.

Phew. Crisis averted.

With wide eyes and hope, he sidled up next to Celeste's

table. "An evening of surprises," he said casually, keeping his eyes on the students.

"Yeah, you could say that."

"Did you know Sabrina was going to do what she did?" He peeled his gaze from the dance floor and hit her with it. The look she was giving him said Sabrina's response to the video hadn't been a surprise. "You knew."

Celeste pursed her lips together. "Eva was the one who helped Sabrina come around to forgiving me."

"But she doesn't forgive me yet," he murmured.

She fixed him with an impatient look. "You're not her mother. And it's not that she doesn't forgive you, it's that she's embarrassed about what she saw. If that was your mother in that video and your math teacher doing what we were doing, would you be able to act normal around the guy? Look him in the eye?"

Touché.

"Give her time. She's not angry. She's embarrassed, and she's hurt. This has taken a lot out of her, and if you ask me, she's handled this with a shit-ton more grace and poise than I think a lot of people would have."

She was right. Sabrina had handled things in a mature and graceful way. Particularly for a fifteen-year-old.

"Whose idea was it for her to say what she said?" he asked.

"We talked about what she could do *if* the video was shown tonight. We both had a feeling it would be. I gave her the option to do what she wanted but to know that no matter what, you and I would have her back and support her."

"So what she said came from her?"

"It did. It was all her, and I could not be more proud of my kid if I tried."

"You're raising one hell of a kid there, Ms. Howard," Marge said, coming up behind Max. "That girl's got a pair of ovaries on her the size of grapefruits." She chuckled, but then her face turned serious. "Not literally, though. That would be cause for concern. But you know what I mean. She's got cojones. Gumption."

Celeste's smile was carefree and her laugh like a song. "Thank you, Mrs. Babcock, that means a lot."

"And that video." Marge wiped her brow and fanned herself. "You two are quite the spicy couple."

Celeste groaned and turned her head, her complexion going pink. "Uh, thanks."

Continuing to laugh, Marge took her soda and what looked like a turkey sandwich (they didn't have turkey sandwiches on the refreshment table, so where did she get it?), and she went off to go mingle with other teachers.

"How are you after the things Eleanor said?" he asked. His parents had washed his mouth out with a bar of soap when he swore as a child. He wasn't sure if that was still a practice parents did, but if it was, Eleanor needed to chew on a whole bar of Ivory.

Celeste shrugged. "She's a troubled girl. A psychopath demon child created in the sweltering depths of Satan's hellfire, but she's a troubled child nonetheless."

He snorted. "I did not see it coming when Mindy intervened. Did you say something to her earlier this week to make her change her mind?"

She shook her head. "My focus has been on my daughter this week and rebuilding our relationship and our trust. I couldn't give two shits about Mindy Shelby. Though I am glad the woman finally came to her senses and was able to see her daughter for the corrupt monster that she is."

"You think it will amount to anything?"

She lifted a shoulder and sighed. Her whole body slumped, showing off a fatigue he hadn't see on her before. She'd been keeping it all together for so long for her daughter, and now that Sabrina was okay, Celeste was finally letting herself breathe, and the adrenaline she'd been surviving on was beginning to leave her body. "Who knows? I would like to say that it will, but the Shelbys have proven themselves to be an unpredictable three-headed serpent. I don't think we've hacked off any heads. We've simply wounded one of them and angered the other two."

Fuck, he hoped she was wrong.

WITH THE NIGHTMARE BEHIND THEM—AT least for the moment —Celeste was able to enjoy watching her daughter on her first date, at her first homecoming dance.

She had her own fond memories of homecoming. Declan had asked her to their first homecoming dance when they were freshmen, and from that night on, they were an item. He'd been her one and only, her first date, and for a long time, she thought he would be her last. It was after homecoming their sophomore year that they finally took the plunge and went beyond third base.

She hoped her daughter took things slow—slower than her mother—and enjoyed the fun and excitement of a new, young romance without jumping headfirst into a physical relationship. She was glad she and Declan had waited a year. And most of the time they were careful. They used condoms, and she went on birth control. But even so, nothing is one hundred percent effective—besides abstinence, but she was a realist and didn't preach that BS to her kid.

She and Sabrina had had the sex talk several times over the last few years. She laid it all out for her kid, the ins and outs (literally), how to be safe, and that Sabrina always had a choice. If Sabrina felt uncomfortable or had a change of heart, she could always say *no*.

The dance ended around eleven o'clock. Sabrina and Noah left when his parents came to pick them up, with Sabrina smiling and waving at her mother as she left, her hand in Noah's and a beautiful sparkle in her eyes.

Celeste stayed until all the coats were reclaimed. Then she went to find Max.

"How much longer do you have to stay?" she asked, finding him bent over and picking up some trash from the ground. "Are you on cleanup duty too?"

Standing straight up, he hit her with a look that made her toes curl in her pumps. "No. I'm going to head out in about ten minutes. Why?"

Celeste swallowed. "I—"

Max held up his hand. "I don't want to pressure you, Celeste. Tonight was rough. We had a feeling that it might be, and we came in wearing extra armor, but even so, I can see that you're scathed. Emotionally and mentally. You're tired. Take the weekend and give us some thought. I won't be the one to end this, because I want you. I want us. But if ending it is what you need, is what you and Sabrina need to remain whole, then I understand. I told you I would never make you choose between me and your child, and I meant that."

As if the man couldn't get any more perfect.

She wanted to tackle him to the floor and pepper his face with kisses, then mount him like a stallion and ride him until sunrise.

But they were in a high school gymnasium surrounded by his colleagues. People who had already seen too much of their relationship to begin with.

Also, his words held some truth.

Just because Eleanor was dragged out of the dance by her mother didn't mean the serpent was vanquished. Not by a long shot. Three heads still remained. And after tonight, she could only imagine that they were all out for blood.

Did she want to continue their relationship only to constantly be watching her back, watching her kid's back, worried about where and when the next strike from Alastair or Eleanor Shelby was going to come at them? Wouldn't it be easier for everyone—particularly Sabrina—if they just ended it? She could lead a normal high school life without having to worry about her mother and math teacher embarrassing her any further.

"Hey, Max, can you help us with this table?" called a male teacher from across the gym.

He lifted his chin in acknowledgment before turning back to face her. "Take the weekend, and then we'll talk, okay?" He rested his hand on the side of her arm, squeezed and was gone.

But the heat from his touch and the tingles it created lingered long after he was gone. She stood in place for a moment, shut her eyes and inhaled. His scent still hung in the air. Mingled with the smells of sweaty teenagers, pheromones and Axe body spray. But even through the fog, she could still pick out Max's scent. Uniquely fresh. Wonderfully masculine and all Max.

Taking a deep, fortifying breath, she left the gym and headed home.

Thank God tomorrow was Saturday. She needed her single moms to help her figure things out. To help her make a decision. But she already knew what they would both say. Lauren would tell her to ride him like a mechanical bull until the quarter ran out, and Bianca would tell her to follow her heart.

She was just pulling onto her street when a Lexus parked on the side of the road flashed its lights at her.

A Lexus.

Alastair?

But she quickly realized it was a different model and color, and she exhaled in relief.

Rather than pull into her garage, she parked in front of her house and got out. The person in the car got out as well. It was Mindy.

Bracing herself for anything—because the Shelbys had proven they were an unpredictable lot—she warily watched the woman approach her.

But the closer Mindy got, the more Celeste realized she had nothing to worry about. The woman was shattered. Completely wrecked. She wrung her hands in front of her, nibbled nervously on her lip and kept shutting her eyes for a few seconds before opening them and letting her gaze dart around the quiet, empty street.

"Mindy," Celeste said when they were finally close enough.

"Celeste."

Then silence fell.

Awkward silence.

Celeste fought back a yawn but didn't win and let it stretch her mouth out as if she were a lioness on the African savannah and she'd just devoured half a wildebeest. "It's late, Mindy. We've both been through a lot tonight. What can I do for you?"

Mindy lifted her head. "I owe you an apology."

About damn time.

But she didn't say that. The woman was there to eat crow. The least Celeste could do was remain quiet and receptive and not hand her a fork and tell her to "dig in."

"Alastair's infidelity and his drinking turned our whole family, our entire lives, upside down. I was angry that he left me for a younger woman—a woman who looks an awful lot like you. I was lost. Hurt. I was so lost, so hurt, that I was

294 | WHITLEY COX

unable to see that my daughter was lost and hurt too. I knew she was acting out because of the divorce. I just refused to admit how bad her behavior had gotten. We both started to spiral and act out in different ways. And then when Noah ended things with her, it only exacerbated her feelings of rejection and inadequacy. I know my daughter is a difficult person. I know she can be unkind, but she wasn't always like this. We used to be a happy family. She used to be a happy child with a good heart. I don't recognize her now, and that scares me."

It scared Celeste too.

But she also felt sorry for the woman standing in front of her. If Sabrina was acting out the way Eleanor was, Celeste would be terrified too.

Mindy licked her lips and sucked in a rattled breath.

"It wasn't until I realized Alastair helped her doctor and release that video that I knew my daughter was in serious trouble. I was in denial about it until then—and that is my fault. As a counselor and a mother, I should have recognized the signs sooner."

"But you were caught up in your own vortex of despair," Celeste said, looking at the woman before her with a new level of compassion and understanding.

Not that their situations were the same, but when Declan died, Celeste had been lost and hurt and angry for a long time. She became caught up in her own vortex of pain, and it was a tough one to climb out of. Thank God for her sister and parents, who stayed by her side and helped her get through a grief she thought would cripple her forever.

Mindy nodded. "I was. But when Eleanor put that video on the screen at the dance, and then came after you the way she did, said the things she said, I knew I'd failed her. Her father needs help. His girlfriend left him, and he's started to drink quite heavily. They staged a coup at his law firm and voted him out because of his erratic behavior. He's officially hit rock bottom, but at least now he seems to have finally realized it."

That explained his behavior last week and why he said the things he did to Celeste. It didn't excuse his behavior, but it certainly explained it.

"My sister is the superintendent of the school district in Spokane. They just had a vacancy for a guidance counselor come available at one of the high schools, and she offered me the job. She's wanted me to move back to Spokane—where I'm originally from—for a while. Eleanor can start school immediately at the same high school, and we can stay with my sister until we get sorted. We're going to leave Monday."

Celeste's eyes went wide. "You're leaving?"

Mindy nodded. "It's for the best. A fresh start for Eleanor and me. I need to focus on my daughter and help her get through this. It's like you said. I need to love her harder than ever right now, otherwise I'm really worried I might lose her completely."

"What about Alastair?"

"He's not allowed to see his daughter until he's been sober for at least sixty days. His toxicity poisoned all of us and I can't help my daughter if he's around and struggling with his own demons. I need to focus on *my* relationship with my child and help Eleanor rebuild her life. So she can start over. So we both can."

Celeste reached out and squeezed Mindy's upper arm. "Thank you for coming over here, Mindy. I know that it couldn't have been easy."

Mindy's lips twisted, and her eyes gleamed with unshed tears beneath the orange street light. "I'm sorry for the things I said, Celeste. For what my daughter has put you and Sabrina and Max through. You're a good mom, and Sabrina is a good kid."

"And you're a good mom for realizing your daughter

needs help and getting her that help. It's not too late. Kids are resilient and tough, and I have no doubt this move is the right thing for both of you. A fresh start, just like you said."

Mindy sniffled. "Thanks." She glanced toward Celeste's house. "You're raising one hell of a strong kid for her to say what she said tonight."

"I am. But I messed up too, and we're working on rebuilding our trust. I think it's a bit of a blow for both the parent and the child when the parent screws up. From day one, our kids think we're perfect, but when we finally show them that we're human, that we make mistakes, they're a little taken aback. How dare we screw up?"

Mindy snorted. "You got that right."

"But showing them understanding and forgiveness when they make mistakes softens the blow when we finally make ours."

"I don't know what you're talking about. I've never made a mistake in my life," Mindy said with a chuckle. "Unless you count marrying my husband. Only good thing to come out of that marriage was Eleanor, and right now I'm wondering if she'd have been better off raised by wolves."

Celeste smiled and squeezed Mindy's arm again. "You're going to be okay. You both will."

22

MAX PULLED into the parking garage of his building and shut off the ignition of his truck. He'd been invited to go out with Marge and a few of the other teachers for a drink, but he just wanted to get home. He hadn't had to deal with nearly as much as Sabrina or Celeste, but he was still mentally exhausted. And even though Mindy had come to the rescue and hauled her spawn out of the gym, Max still had to face Eleanor and teach her math on Monday.

He climbed out of his truck and locked it. He'd paid extra for a larger parking stall so that he could fit both his Bonneville and his truck in the space. Normally, he tossed the cover over his bike for extra protection and to hide it from prying eyes, but it appeared as though it'd somehow partially slipped off.

Making his way to the passenger side of the truck where his bike was parked, he went to adjust the cover when it moved on its own.

What the fuck?

And that's when he saw it.

Or *her,* he should say.

Fluffy.

The beast with her yellow and white scales was curled up on the seat of his bike in a tight coil. Part of her body drooped over the bike, including her tail, but she was well hidden by the cover.

Holy fuck.

Ice flooded his veins, and his feet became embedded in concrete. Fear like he hadn't felt in a long time gripped his chest like fists squeezing his lungs. He struggled to get out a full breath.

He couldn't see her head, but that didn't mean she didn't have one. It was just hidden, like the rest of her had been.

Jesus fucking Christ. There was a seven-foot python—which he realized was small for her size after he Googled albino pythons and learned they reached over sixteen feet in length—having a nap on his motorcycle.

Shaking as if he'd been thrown into an icy river, he dropped the motorcycle cover, blinked the spots from his eyes and pried his feet from the ground, running full tilt out of the garage to the grass at the front of the condo. The fresh air outside filled his chest until it burned, and he placed his hands on his knees and bent over, gasping.

He didn't even know which unit Glycon was in. Fuck. He couldn't just leave the snake there. But he also couldn't go back and get it.

What was he supposed to do now? Leave her there? Put her in a bag and take her to the lobby? No way was he touching that thing, no fucking way.

Animal control?

It was after eleven o'clock at night, but it was also the weekend. Surely his neighbors wouldn't hate him too much.

He hoped.

Walking out to the front of the building, he cupped his

hands around his mouth and called out, "Glycon! Glycon, come get your damn snake. She's on my motorcycle."

The building remained dark and quiet.

He did it again. "Glycon. I found Fluffy. Come get your fucking snake!"

A few lights in various units flicked on, and drapes were pulled back. One person opened their window. "Dude, what the fuck?"

"Do you know what unit Glycon is in? His snake is on my motorcycle, and I need him to come and get her."

"Did you say *snake?*"

More lights turned on in the building, and more windows opened. A few people stepped out onto their decks.

"Did he say snake?" a woman asked.

The first guy, with terror in his eyes, said, "Yeah."

"Do any of you know which unit Glycon is in? Guy, mid-forties." He made a motion with his hands to indicate that Glycon was on the rounder side. "Shortish. Like maybe five-five." Five-five, nothing more than an *hors d'oeuvre* for a seven-foot snake.

Heads shook, but then the woman on her deck spoke up. "You mean Greg? He lives two doors down, across the hall from me. Strange fellow. Unit has a weird smell."

Of course his name was Greg and not Glycon. Only a fucknut would change their name to something like *Glycon.*

"Can you go knock on his door and tell him I found his snake? She's on my motorcycle."

The woman nodded and disappeared back into her unit.

"How big is this snake?" the guy from earlier asked. "Like *big?*"

Max nodded. "Apparently she is seven feet of pure love."

"Holy fuck. And it's in our building?"

Max nodded again just as headlights from an SUV cast his shadow against his front door. But the vehicle didn't keep going. It pulled up to the curb behind him. That's when he noticed that it was a Volvo and who was behind the steering wheel.

At the same time Celeste got out of her vehicle, Glycon came bursting through the front door. "You found her?"

Max glanced at Celeste, then back at Glycon. "She's down in the parking garage, curled up on my motorcycle."

Relief filled the man's face. He was wearing nothing more than a pair of plaid boxer shorts and a thin white T-shirt that had seen better days. He wasn't even wearing shoes. "Oh, thank God. My poor baby. She must be so scared."

Max knew scared. He was still fucking terrified, and Fluffy didn't even look fazed.

With a mumbled thanks, Glycon took off down toward the parking garage, his feet slap-slapping on the cold concrete.

He didn't understand it. The obsession with keeping exotic pets—particularly ones that could kill you. Or people's fascination with snakes. But he understood love. And as warped as it was, Glycon loved Fluffy, just like Max had come to love Sebastian.

Pets were never on his radar; he thought his life was too busy. But Sebastian had fit right in, and in less than a month, Max knew his home would feel emptier without the orange beast who slept in the sun ray that streaked across Max's bed every afternoon.

The heart was a peculiar thing, and Glycon's beat for a seven-foot snake named Fluffy. Max just hoped it was a pet-owner relationship and nothing creepier.

"What the hell is going on?" Celeste asked, joining him on the curb, her expression concerned and curious. His heart thumped hard in his chest.

Yes, he understood love. Not only the love for a pet, but

the love for the person who completed you. He'd been missing both in his life for much too long.

Grabbing her arm, he hauled her toward his front door. "Inside, before he comes back with that thing." He glanced up to the windows of the other units. Everyone had retreated back inside. He planned to do the same. He unlocked his front door and rushed them both inside. "I have got to fucking move." Once she was in, he closed the door and locked it. But even that didn't seem like enough.

Sebastian came wandering out to greet them but stopped short and did a big, lazy cat stretch.

Celeste bent down and scooped him up in her arms, and they nuzzled each other.

"You know," she started, pressing her forehead to Sebastian's forehead. Both of them had their eyes closed. "My neighbor four doors down just put his townhouse up for sale. Three bedrooms. Corner unit with a big two-car garage. Not two deep like mine, but two wide. Lots of light, lots of room."

What was she getting at?

She opened her eyes and cradled Sebastian in her arms.

"You sure you want me as your neighbor if you don't even know if you want me as your boyfriend?" he asked, trying to get a read on her expression. Why was she there? Had she decided not to take the weekend to just end things there and then?

"Mindy came by my place a little while ago."

"What the fuck for?"

"To apologize. She and Eleanor are moving. They need a fresh start, a clean slate, and the only way for them both to do that is to move. Her sister works for the Spokane school district and offered Mindy a job at a high school, so Eleanor can attend the school and Mindy can work there. They'll have family and each other."

"Holy shit."

She nodded. "Yeah. Shocked the crap out of me too. But we reached an understanding. Being a mother to a teenager is like trying to tame a beast of your own creation. And I understand the challenges she's facing. When Declan died, I started to spiral too. You can get caught up in your grief to the point where it's all you can see. The rest of your life becomes a big, noisy, confusing blur. And even though Alastair didn't die, her marriage did. Their family as she and Eleanor knew it did, and they both started to spiral."

She was a better person than he was. After the way Mindy had treated him last weekend and the things she'd said about Celeste over the past month, he wasn't sure he had forgiveness in him. He certainly wasn't sure he had forgiveness or compassion in him toward Eleanor after the things she'd said to Celeste or the way she'd treated Sabrina. It was a blessing for sure the girl wasn't going to be in his classroom any longer.

"So the three-headed snake is no more," he said quietly. Even a one-headed snake was too much for him.

"The three-headed serpent never was. Alastair has a drinking problem and is apparently seeking help, and Eleanor and Mindy are going to go start a new life together. The three-headed serpent was really just three broken people spiraling out of control—but all of them on separate warpaths." She kissed Sebastian again before putting him down on the floor. But he didn't wander away like he normally did after a quick snuggle. He sat at her feet and rubbed his head against her shin.

"Does Sabrina know?" he asked, bending down to scoop up Sebastian. He headed into his kitchen and pulled out a bag of cat treats. Sebastian's yellow eyes followed his every move. He put about eight treats in a small toy and set both Sebastian and the toy down on the ground. The cat started to go nuts on the toy in an attempt to release the goods.

"Sabrina knows, yes. After Mindy showed up, I went inside, and Sabrina was just getting ready for bed. I told her that Eleanor won't be a problem anymore."

"Must have been a huge relief for her." Not even bothering to ask, he opened up his fridge and poured them both a glass of water. She thanked him and took a sip.

"Huge relief, yes. I'm not sure about you, but knowing that they'll be over four hours away lifts a significant load from my shoulders and mind."

A huge relief and then some.

"I was not looking forward to Monday and having to figure out a way to be in the same room as Eleanor, let alone teach her. So, yeah, a *significant* load for sure."

He still wanted to know why she was there. She could have called or texted him the Mindy info. Not that he was complaining. He hadn't spent any real alone time with Celeste in a while, and he'd missed her. He just hoped she wasn't there to end it.

Finishing his water, he set his glass down. "I have to ask, Celeste, why are you here?"

"Sabrina," she said plainly, her lip lifting up into a small, coy, sexy smile.

He shook his head. He didn't understand.

"You told me you'd never make me choose, and she told me I didn't have to."

He was around the kitchen counter and lifting her up onto his lips in one breath. "Thank fuck," he murmured into her hair, cupping the back of her neck and burying his face in along her collarbone. "I thought you'd come here to end it."

She angled her head to the side, and he raked his teeth down her throat. "Naw, if I planned to end things, I would have just done it in a text."

With a half laugh, half growl, he propelled them into the living room. "Like hell, woman." He fell back into the couch, sitting up so Celeste straddled him. Releasing her ass, her wrapped her hair around his fist and yanked her head back. "You came here to tell me—"

"That this isn't over. That *we're* not over. Not by a long shot."

She smiled, and his heart swelled in his chest to the point of a beautiful ache.

She shut her eyes and jerked her head. "You and those dimples. They're like a weapon. Put 'em away, put 'em away." Her laugh settled every nerve inside him, and he let a long, slow breath escape through his nose from deep inside his lungs. Since that video had been leaked, he'd struggled to fully breathe. Each inhale felt like he was fighting against an anvil perched on his ribs as he fought to draw in enough air to live.

But now that anvil was lifted. The weight from their shoulders had sloughed off too, and they were free. Free of the Shelbys. Free to be together.

"And you want me to move in four doors down?" he asked, lifting an eyebrow and releasing her hair. "Seems like a big step. We haven't even said the *L* word." And he wouldn't, not yet. He knew he was falling in love with Celeste, but things were still new, still fresh, and after the last few weeks, they needed to find a new normal before they busted out big words with big meaning.

But he held zero doubt that this woman was going to make him fall madly in love with her. He was already well on his way.

She nodded. "We haven't. You're right. And let's wait a bit to do that. But I also don't want to be here if there is a snake in the building. So maybe you should buy elsewhere. I'm just saying it'd be awfully convenient if we were neighbors."

Max's brows bobbed. "Yeah, convenient how?"

She dipped her head and brought her mouth next to his

ear. "*Really*, really convenient." Her tongue slid around the shell of his ear before she nipped the lobe. "You'd be like Henry in my nightstand drawer, only *so* much better."

"If I buy that townhouse, will you throw Henry away?"

She shook her head and wedged a hand between them. "Absolutely not. *But* if you buy the townhouse, I'll let you and Henry have a go at me at the same time." Crushing her lip between her teeth, she unzipped his jeans and fished around until she found him hot, hard and dripping for her. Her thumb swirled around the crown, the precum making his cockhead shine.

She brought her thumb to her mouth and sucked.

Max groaned and thrust up into her hand and the tight fist she made around his length. "You don't mind being here while Sabrina's at home by herself?"

She released his dick and slouched out of her leather jacket. He helped relieve her of her shirt next. "She told me to come talk to you. She said that after such a wonderful night with Noah, she now understands why you and I couldn't stay away from each other. That the heart wants what the heart wants."

He cupped her breasts in his hands and tucked his face into her cleavage. She smelled fucking incredible. He wanted that scent on him all day, every day. He wanted to wake up to it, go to bed beside it and have it drifting around him like a warm summer breeze while awake.

"And my heart wants you," she whispered, cupping his face between her hands and letting her lips coast across his.

"And my heart wants only you," he said, taking her mouth with his and flipping her to her back. Then he claimed Celeste as his all over again, because she was his. His heart wanted only her, and no scandal or secrets could ever keep them apart.

EPILOGUE

Eighteen months later ...

"Okay, are you ready?" Max asked Sabrina as he climbed into the passenger side of the Honda Accord and Sabrina bounced in the driver's seat.

She grinned at him. "So freaking ready. Thank you, Max."

He smiled at the girl who'd quickly become like a daughter to him. After their initial awkwardness surrounding the video, it'd taken her a few months to loosen up, but once she did, she and Max got along well. And it had been easier to separate their teacher-student relationship and their personal relationship than they thought. She called him Max at home but usually remembered to call him Mr. Travis at school.

Continuing to bounce in her seat, with happiness radiating off her like a star, she adjusted the rearview mirror. "Where to?"

"You're the driver. You decide."

She took a deep breath. Even though she'd been driving for a year, this was the first time she was going to drive a stick shift. Both his truck and Celeste's SUV were automatic, so Sabrina hadn't had the opportunity to learn a manual. But she'd finally saved up enough money for the car of her dreams, and it was a standard, so she needed to learn how to drive one.

Max borrowed his friend's older Honda, which was a stick shift, and promised to help Sabrina "master the ways of the clutch," as she put it.

So there they were.

Ready for their first lesson.

Squealing, she put her indicator on.

"Whoa, whoa," he said, reaching over and resting her hand on her arm. "Clutch all the way in, ease up on the brake and then give it some gas."

"But I only have two feet and there are three pedals." She glanced at him with fear in her eyes. "Who has three feet?"

"You'll figure it out. You'll get the feel for it. Just keep the clutch in and slowly pull your foot off the brake until you feel it *engage*, then take your foot off the brake and pump the gas."

She did as he instructed, and they bunny-hopped forward and stalled.

"Did I break the car?" she asked.

He shook his head. "No. You stalled it. Now, start over."

She followed orders again, and he made sure to remain patient, even though he knew he'd feel those jerks and jolts in his neck later.

Eventually, they were on the road.

"Gear down and go slow. We're coming up to a school zone."

She did as he instructed and came to a full, if not abrupt, stop at a stop sign.

"It's a four-way, and nobody else is here. You can go."

She tried to start in second gear and the engine revved, then the whole thing stalled.

"Oh my God, I can't do this." Her red ponytail whipping around midair, she spun to unbuckle her belt, but he stopped her.

"Sabrina, you've got this. Just put it back in first, turn on the ignition and try again. You. Can. Do. This."

With a rattled breath and tears in her eyes, she nodded and pushed on.

Before they knew it, they were back on the road. She glanced over at him with the smile on her face the biggest he'd ever seen.

"So, are you going to propose to my mom or what?" Sabrina asked, having stuck to the back roads in quiet, pleasant suburbia and not ventured onto any main thorough-fare that held traffic lights. He was grateful for that because as much as he loved her and was trying his damnedest to be patient, his nerves were running thin, and he wasn't sure he could take the interstate with her in the driver's seat.

Max whirled in his seat. "Um ..."

She glanced at him with some serious side-eye. "Well, are you?"

"I ... uh, I'd like to, yes. I just ..."

"What's the holdup?"

"Did you mother put you up to this?"

She rolled her eyes, and at that moment, she looked so much like her mother, it was spooky. "No. Mom hasn't said a word. But I *do* have a mind of my own. And I want to know why you haven't proposed. Don't you love her? I mean we all live together now, so I figured it was only a matter of time, but we've been in the same house for two months. What's the holdup?" She put her blinker on and turned right, entering busier traffic.

Max gripped the handle on the door. "I love your mother more than anything. I love you, too. I just ..."

He had no answer. He didn't know what the holdup was.

He loved Celeste, wanted to marry her. Wanted to spend his life with her. He just hadn't gotten around to asking her yet.

"You have my blessing, if you're wondering. If that was what was keeping you from doing it," Sabrina said. "Let's head downtown. There's a jewelry store near Pike Place that has a ring that is perfect for my mom. I spotted it last week when Noah took me birthday-gift shopping." Her fingers spun the white gold heart pendant that hung around her neck. "I saw it, and I knew it was perfect."

"Uh, I'm not sure if we're ready to go downtown yet. It can be a little hairy driving in all that traffic with all the lanes and lights and idiot pedestrians." His fingers tightened around the handle until his knuckles hurt as she took a hard turn on an advanced left green light. She knew the rules, and she knew how to drive. It was just jarring for him not to be the one in control, the one behind the wheel making the decisions. His fate, his life was at the whimsy of a seventeen-year-old.

"No, let's go. You need to at least *see* the ring in person."

"Are you going to propose to her for me too?" he asked, slamming his foot down where ordinarily a brake pedal would be when she gunned it to run a yellow. "Jesus, Sabrina."

"Sorry." She smiled back. "I just really want to show you this ring."

"And I just really want to be alive to still see it."

THEY'D BEEN GONE a lot longer than Max thought they'd be, and Celeste would have been worried if he hadn't texted her half an hour ago to say they were stopping to grab sushi for dinner.

Thank God, because she did not feel like cooking.

She'd been up most of the night finishing the first draft of her first novel and was now in the re-reading and editing mode. It was true what they say: We really are our own worst critic.

At times she found herself laughing out loud, utterly in awe of her own writing abilities, only to call herself a two-bit hack in the next breath when what she'd written belonged in the trash.

She'd never had to deal with this as a ghostwriter. Writing for someone else had been fun and easy. She was given the plot, the outline and tone of the book; she simply had to give it life. But when she wrote her own stuff, she had to do all the backbreaking creative stuff as well as breathe life into the story and characters. She had to do it all.

Bless Max and his support, though. Sabrina had been champing at the bit to learn how to drive manual when she found her dream car on a lot last week. But Celeste was on an editing deadline, and for some crazy reason, a literary agent actually liked the pitch of her own book, and they wanted the first draft to them by the end of the next week. Now she had another deadline to make as well. So Max said he'd take Sabrina driving. It was probably better he taught her stick shift anyway. Celeste would undoubtedly be a nervous wreck the whole time, slamming her foot to the floor, pretending there was a brake pedal there.

Her neck was sore and her eyes tired, so she saved her work, closed her laptop and moved to the living room to do some much-needed stretching. She needed to power down for the rest of the night, if not the rest of the weekend. No more screens. Unless, of course, Max wanted to curl up in front of the television and watch a movie. She could handle that. They rarely got through a movie before his hand was down her shirt or pants though. Eighteen months into their relationship, and they were still in that glorious stage where they couldn't keep their hands off each other.

Thankfully, they managed to keep that behavior to when Sabrina was out of the room. It was the least they could do, considering ...

It hadn't taken Max long to sell his old condo and snap up the townhouse a few doors down from her. Knowing that a snake was in his building lit a fire under his ass like Celeste had never seen. So by Christmastime, he was her new neighbor. But she and Sabrina didn't move in with him right away. They waited a year before Celeste put her house on the market and bought into Max's townhouse for half.

She wanted to make sure their relationship was solid and things between Max and Sabrina were going to work. Thankfully, they did.

Noise at the front door had her twisting out of a deep stretch and craning her neck around. Sabrina skipped—yes, *skipped*—toward her.

Love really was a miraculous thing. Sabrina and Noah were in love, and that love had transformed her moody, hormonal daughter into this happy, friendly person she enjoyed being around. She was still her kind self—that was as intrinsic as the nose on her face—but her mood was better. And Noah was a good kid. The two reminded Celeste of herself and Declan, in love and ready to take on the world.

"How was driving?" she asked, cracking her neck side to side. "Max have more gray hairs than when he left?"

Sabrina's smile was enormous but also devious. She giggled. "Driving was awesome. I'm a natural. Right, Max?"

Max emerged behind her, a big paper bag in his hand. "I have a few more gray hairs, but she is very good. A little lead-footed though. We need to work on gentler stops. I think I got whiplash."

Sabrina was still all smiles, and the way she was looking

at Celeste made curiosity meander its way up her sore back. "Why are you looking at me like that?"

"Like what?" Sabrina blinked her bright green eyes. "I'm not doing anything. I'm just happy I'm driving now. I'm going to go call Noah." She took off, her *stomp, stomp* on the stairs echoing through the house.

"How was it *really*?" she asked, sliding down into downward dog. Her hips were aching from all the sitting she'd been doing recently. She needed to get up and move. Maybe Max would want to go for a run tomorrow.

"She has some finesse to learn and needs to focus more on the traffic and not her excitement and who is in the car, but she's a good driver. We were all there at one point, so I'm trying to be patient and encouraging." He slid down to the floor beside her, placing the sushi bag out of the way. Sebastian was there in seconds, sniffing and peering into the bag. "I got you something too, bud, just wait."

Celeste arched her back into a delicious cat stretch. "Now I know why you do this all the time, Sebastian. It feels amazing." She tucked her chin to her chest and shut her eyes. "Thank you for taking Sabrina. I really appreciate it. And I appreciate you getting dinner. I'm bagged."

When she lifted her head, what glistened back had her falling flat on her stomach with a pained *oof*.

"You okay?" Max asked, helping her to her knees.

"What the hell is that?" She scrambled up with his help and pointed at the blinding ring on a velvet bed in a navy-blue box that he held in his hand.

"It's a Siberian husky puppy. I thought we should adopt a dog. What do you think it is?" He snorted at the same time his gray eyes rolled.

"I think it's an engagement ring."

He glanced at the box and then back at her with a look of

shock. "Ah, fuck. Wrong box. Now I'm wondering who got my puppy."

She shoved him in the shoulder, but he didn't budge. He only started to laugh.

"I don't know why I haven't done it sooner," he said. "I want to marry you. Have wanted to marry you since I found out my ringtone on your phone is: *I pity da fool*. But your daughter called me out, took me to see this ring, and just like when she saw it, she knew ... when I saw it, I knew too. This is *your* ring. You are meant to wear it, and we are meant to get married. The heart wants what the hearts wants, and my heart wants you. My heart wants this life, this family and every crazy driver and hormonal beast that comes with it."

A hot, fat tear slid down Celeste's cheek. She hadn't been expecting this at all. But she wanted to marry him too. She wanted to marry Max so damn much it hurt.

"The heart wants what the heart wants," she said, nodding through more tears and smiling. "And my heart wants you. For now, forever and for always."

He took the ring from the box and slid it onto her finger. "So that's a yes?"

She nodded. "That's a yes."

Smiling, he tipped his head back. "She said *yes!*" he hollered up the stairs.

A celebratory scream crashed through the house as Sabrina whooped and cheered.

With both of them on their knees, Max took Celeste in his arms. "The heart wants what the heart wants, and my heart wants this forever." Then he kissed her, because he could today, tomorrow and for the rest of their lives.

HOT FOR A COP - SNEAK PEEK

THE SINGLE MOMS OF SEATTLE, BOOK 2

Chapter 1

Soaked to the bone, pissed right the fuck off, and sweating like a pig in the sun—even though it was the beginning of December, dark, stormy and wet as hell— Lauren Green grunted at the same time the driver's seat of her Nissan Pathfinder squealed. She was attempting to wedge herself behind the steering wheel and was doing a shit job accomplishing it.

Her phone started to ring and she let out a loud, "MOTHER FUCKER" at the same time she wrestled with the wind to shut her door.

She finally managed to slam it closed, snatched her phone from her purse, put it on speaker on the cellphone holder attached to her dash and yelled, "What the fuck do you want?" as she attempted to fasten her seatbelt around her enormous baby-filled belly.

"To see if you wanted me to brew you some raspberry leaf tea," Bianca said quietly. "Get that Booty Call Baby moving on out of that belly."

"Fuck," Lauren muttered. "Sorry."

"How was your doctor's appointment?" Celeste asked. They were on a three-way call, as they often were. Her two best friends. Her fellow single moms. Well, Lauren wasn't a single mom yet, but she would be soon. She needed to be soon, otherwise she was going to lose her fucking mind.

Besides hearing that steady heartbeat and being reassured that the baby was healthy and in the right position, her doctor's appointment had been rather unpleasant.

"Did they do a stretch and sweep?" Bianca asked. "I always hated those. Painful as hell."

Lauren shifted in her seat. She was told after the invasive and painful procedure used by doctors to induce labor she might have cramping, bleeding and be a little uncomfortable. She was. More than a little.

Grimacing, she buckled her seatbelt under her belly. "Yep. Not my preferred way to have a man's fingers inside me, but at this point in the game the doctor could have stuck his dick in me if it induced labor."

Both her friends snorted in laughter.

It'd also sucked that it hadn't been *her* doctor. She was on-call at the hospital delivering other lucky women's babies, while Lauren got stuck with a locum; a man old enough to be judging her for her "condition" because it was unseemly and Lauren was a harlot. You know, being without a man and all. Getting knocked up by a booty call and choosing to do it all on her own. Not that he said these things to her, of course, but she could feel Dr. Judgey McJudgerson judging the shit out of her as he pushed two fingers into her cooch and scissored them around like her cervix had challenged him to a game of rock, paper, scissors, and kept throwing up rock.

She turned on the ignition, flipped on the defrost and let her vehicle warm up for a moment. The rain was coming in sideways because of the wind and hitting her windshield with a disturbing amount of force.

Starved, because she was always hungry these days, being forty weeks pregnant plus five days, she opened up a bag of dill pickle flavored mini rice cakes and started shoving them into her mouth three at a time.

"Did the doctor mention your dilation or anything?" Celeste asked.

The rice cakes had formed a gelatinous glob in the back of her throat and Lauren struggled to swallow it down without the aid of a big gulp of water. She chugged water from her bottle before answering. "Yeah, still tight as fuck. Like two centimeters maybe. Cervix was hard as a raw carrot too."

"Damn it," Celeste said. "I'll bring over some spicy chicken wings."

"I'll bring raspberry leaf tea and dates."

Lauren wrinkled her nose. "Why dates?"

"They help ripen the cervix and decrease the need for Pitocin. I ate dates like a fiend my last week of pregnancy with Charlie and he came so quickly with no need for drugs or anything. Barely made it to the hospital."

"And that wasn't because you had twins before him and they stretched the door as wide as a combine so he could just slide on out?" Lauren said, flipping on her windshield wipers and pulling out of the clinic parking lot. It was already dark out because well, duh, it was five o'clock on a Saturday (thank God her doctor's office was open on the weekends). Add in the storm that had come in off the Pacific earlier that day and she struggled to see ten feet in front of her headlights.

"Har-har," Bianca laughed forcibly. "Orgasms also help. You could just stay home and masturbate all night and not bring your crappy attitude over to my house."

Lauren turned off the side road and onto the on ramp for

the interstate. "Sorry. You know I'm not usually this big of a bitch. I just want this baby out of me so damn bad."

"I know, sweetie," Bianca said. "I'm just teasing you. We love you, bitchy, bloated and all."

She was just about to accelerate to the cruising interstate speed, when a blur of red brake lights in front of her had her slamming on her own brakes hard enough to engage the locking mechanism of her seat belt and make her lurch forward. "What the hell?"

"You okay?" Celeste and Bianca asked at the same time.

"Traffic jam," she muttered. She tried to see around the vehicle in front of her, but it was a futile endeavor. They were in four lanes of traffic and it was a gridlock. Not to mention the sideways rain.

"I just brought up Google maps on my phone and yeah, major traffic jam on the I-5," Celeste said. "Any way you can take an off ramp and do the side roads?"

"We're at a complete stand-still."

Warm liquid pooled between her legs. What the hell? She unbuckled her belt and shoved her hand down her pants.

Please don't let it be blood. Please don't be blood.

It wasn't blood.

She brought her fingers to her nose to make sure it wasn't urine. She'd started peeing herself a little at the slightest sudden movement. A lurch forward like she'd done when she slammed on the brakes easily could have made her empty her bladder.

It wasn't pee.

"Guys ..."

"You okay?" Celeste asked, panic in her voice.

"I think my water just broke."

"Fuck," both of her friends said at the same time.

"What do I do?" Lauren asked, craning around awkwardly into the backseat of her Pathfinder to reach for a towel.

"Don't panic," Celeste said. "Sabrina didn't come for another twelve hours after my water broke. So, this may not mean anything more than the start of labor. And that's what you went to the doctor for, right? To *start* labor. So, at least we know it worked."

"They had to break my water with the girls," Bianca added. "First babies usually take a long time to come. Hannah and Hayley were like thirty hours."

"Jesus fuck," Lauren muttered.

Attempting to breathe deep and stay calm, she put her vehicle in park and went to push her seat back further when the mother of all cramps pierced through her abdomen and lower back like she'd just run belly first into a hot poker.

She sucked in a deep breath. She rode out the pain, gritting her teeth and white knuckling the steering wheel. "I think that was a contraction."

"I'm going to time them," Bianca said. "Let me know when the next one comes."

Lauren nodded. "Guys, I can't have my baby in my car in the middle of a traffic jam in the middle of a storm. I just can't."

"It'll be okay," Celeste said, her voice not the least reassuring.

"If you can talk through the contractions, they're not that strong. The baby isn't coming just yet," Bianca said soothingly. "Remember the breathing from your pre-natal class."

"You mean the one I went to alone because I'm about to be a single mother?" Lauren blurted out, half laughing, half crying. "Because the guy I was seeing for three months, the guy who knocked me up, ran the moment I told him I was pregnant."

"We offered to come to the classes with you," Celeste said softly.

"You both have kids and lives. I need to be able to do

things on my own. I'm on my own with this ki—" She squeezed her eyes shut and arched her back in her seat as another wave of nauseating pain hit her harder than the last. "Another—"

She wasn't able to speak through it. Did that mean the baby was coming *now?*

"They're five minutes apart," Bianca said, sounding worried.

Lauren slumped back in her seat, panting. "What's the protocol before you need to start panicking??"

"Four-one-one," Celeste said quietly. "Four minutes apart, lasting one minute each, for one hour."

"That lasted just shy of a minute," Bianca added.

"Yeah, but they need to last an hour at that length and interval," Celeste said. "Her water *just* broke. Her contractions *just* started. She has time."

Lauren didn't feel like she had time. She'd been itching for this baby to make its debut for the last three weeks, and now that it was finally gearing up to do so she didn't feel prepared at all.

"Do you have the car seat installed?" Bianca asked.

Lauren nodded. "Yeah. Took it to the fire station and one of the fire fighters did it for me." And that man had fueled her rampant fantasies for a good two weeks afterward. Not that she could see her crotch anymore, or get her fingers or a vibrator there. She'd resorted to shower-head and it wasn't nearly as effective as some of her toys.

"What about your hospital bag?" Celeste asked.

"In the back."

"And towels or a blanket?"

"A few, yeah." She always had at least one blanket in the back of her car, and usually kept one or two towels in case she got caught in a rain storm or a spontaneous bug bit her and she decided to go for a swim in some random river or lake when she was out for a Sunday drive.

Having grown up in Nebraska and Utah, now that she lived on the west coast in gorgeous Seattle, she loved going for Sunday drives through the mountains. All the twists and turns to the road. The beauty of nature and the sound of birds chirping and water burbling. She loved her family back home in Utah, but she'd never move back, not when she had the Pacific Northwest to call home.

About to open her mouth and ask if she needed to find boiling water—obviously a joke—another contraction ripped through her. Each one was worse than the last. Each one lasted longer and seemed to be hitting her harder and more concentrated in her back and between her legs.

"Was that another one?" Bianca asked.

"Uh-huh." She reached for her water bottle and took a long sip. Wasn't she supposed to be chewing ice chips or something? Wasn't that what women in labor on TV were always chomping on?

"Has traffic moved at all?" Celeste asked.

Not an inch. "No," she whined.

"I think you need to move into the backseat," Bianca suggested. "Recline the seat to give yourself some space. You'll be more comfortable that way too."

"I ... I can't give birth in my car. I just can't." She'd always considered herself a strong person, an independent person, and yet right now, she felt helpless and weak and terrified of being alone.

"You might have to, honey," Bianca whispered. "I'm really sorry. But those contractions are strong, close and long. That baby is coming."

Tears sprung into Lauren's eyes and she shook her head violently. "No! No! No!" She poked her stomach. "You stay the fuck in there, you hear me? You are not coming into this world in the back of a Pathfinder in the middle of a storm. That's not your story. That's not *our* story."

"Get into the backseat," Celeste said gently. "You'll be more comfortable there."

With tears of fear, pain and utter frustration burning tracks down her cheeks, Lauren braced herself for the onslaught of rain, wind and another contraction.

She opened her door, but the wind caught it, flung it open and took Lauren with it.

———

Every fucking year. The closer to Christmas it got, the crazier people started to act. The more desperate they started to behave. Isaac Fox squeezed his eyes shut as he sat in his truck in the middle of the gridlocked bumper to bumper traffic in the plummeting rain and window rattling wind. He was glad he'd decided to drive his truck today and not his motorcycle.

Even though his father had drilled into his brain since the day he was born that any other bike besides a Harley was for pussies, he loved his Ducati Enduro Pro, and rode it to work whenever he could.

Fuck his old man.

Isaac was nothing like him, and determined to keep it that way.

Right down to what rumbled between his legs.

Only now that winter had officially hooked her frigid claws into each and every day, he was grateful he had a vehicle to tuck into. He couldn't even imagine being trapped in this fucking mess of a traffic jam on his bike.

Goodbye nuts and any chance of having children.

And because he was a cop—but off duty for the next two days—he couldn't very well weave in between the cars on his bike. That was setting a bad example and showing his privilege. Though he knew countless of other motorcycle riding cops who would have. Swerved between the vehicles or rode the shoulder to bypass the chaos.

But Isaac liked to stay above board. He went into law enforcement for a reason. So he could uphold the law, not break it when it suited him.

Opening his eyes again, he checked to see if the traffic in front of him had moved.

Nope. Not an inch.

Good thing he didn't have a wife and kids to get home to.

Not even a damn cat.

Normally, he liked his life. He had nobody to answer to, nobody to give him grief or a hard time for working late, or staying three hours at the gym and then going out for a beer after with his buddy. Nobody to pick up after. He could leave the toilet seat up without having to worry about being bitched out for it, or some kid throwing his keys and watch down into piss and paper.

Yeah, he liked his life.

Except, sometimes.

Like Christmas.

Like now.

He hadn't been home in … fuck, nearly ten years. Because there wasn't really anything for him there anymore. He wasn't sure he had a *home* per se. Certainly not a childhood home he could return to with memories carved out in every corner. A treehouse in the backyard and height measurements in the doorjamb. He'd never had a home like that. The only reason he knew those homes existed was because of television.

Originally from Nebraska, he, his mom and sister fled his abusive father and moved to Phoenix when Isaac was eight and his sister, Natalie, only five. But now that he and Natalie were grown, neither of them lived in Arizona. His mother remarried a man from Ecuador two years ago and moved down there to be with him. Natalie was studying abroad in Germany, getting her PhD in something sciency, and Isaac couldn't give two shits where his old man was. Six-feet under would be ideal.

So he really had no one.

Sure, he had friends. And he would call his mother and sister on Christmas, and he ordered them gifts online to be delivered directly, gift-wrapped and everything. But besides a few other cops—who had families of their own—he didn't have anybody who he could turn to in Seattle, who he could call *family*. At least not anybody he could spend Christmas with without feeling like a big interloper and outsider.

Which was why he volunteered to work Christmas Eve and Christmas Day. He took the long, ugly shifts because he could. So other cops with families and children could be with those they loved, while Isaac raked in the overtime and kept the crazies from looting empty houses like those two crooks from *Home Alone.*

His stomach grumbled and he went to reach for a granola bar from his bag on the passenger side of his truck when he noticed the person in the SUV next to him had opened their door.

What the hell? It was windy as fuck and raining like he'd never seen in his ten years living in Seattle. Who would leave their door just wide open? The wind was going to whip it clean off its hinges. That's when he saw the hand gripping the handle.

White knuckles.

The hand slipped, then scrambled to grab the handle again before finally failing and disappearing completely.

What the ...

Abandoning his granola bar, he unbuckled his belt and leaned over his bench seat to see what was going on. That's when he saw the woman on the ground, her face a mask of pure agony as she held one hand protectively over an enormous belly and struggled to make purchase somewhere on her vehicle with the other hand.

Holy fuck.

Before he could think twice about what he was doing, he was out of his truck and in the rain, running to the woman.

"I gotcha, I gotcha," he said, though he wasn't sure she heard him. The wind had probably carried his voice down to Oregon by now. With his hands beneath her arms, he helped her up. "Back in you go."

He made to place her back behind the wheel, but she screamed out, "No! I'm in labor. The baby is coming *now*. I need to get into the back seat."

What the fuck?

"Now?"

She nodded, her whole body soaked, blonde hair plastered to the side of her face. With cornflower blue eyes, full of more fear than he'd ever seen in his life and brimming with tears, she dug her nails into arm. "Help me, please."

He was a cop. Not a paramedic, he didn't know how to deliver a baby. He knew basic first aid, that was it. He'd hardly even held a baby, let alone caught one shooting out of a person like a football.

But, he was a first responder. And this woman needed his help. He would do what he could, even if it wasn't much.

"Okay, okay," he said gently, shutting the door to the driver's side and opening up the back passenger door. He folded the seat down so she could lay down through to the back hatch. The other seat already had a car seat installed. "You need me to call your husband or something?"

She climbed into the back on all fours, groaning and pausing as what was obviously another contraction hit her. He waited in the rain and wind until the contraction subsided and she climbed in the rest of the way.

"No husband. Doing this ... alone." She grunted as she flopped to her back.

Isaac climbed in, folded the driver's seat forward and sat on it. "What do you need from me?"

"Who's there?" came a female voice from inside the truck.

"Lauren, did you find a doctor?" asked another woman.

Isaac wasn't an idiot, there was no other person in the vehicle, so those voices had to be coming from her phone. "I'm not a doctor, I'm a cop," he said. "Who am I speaking to?"

"A cop? Well, it's better than nothing. We're Lauren's friends. Celeste and Bianca. Have you ever delivered a baby before?"

"No."

"Do you have your own kids?"

"No."

"A lot of good he's going to be," one woman muttered.

"Well, at least she's not alone now," the other replied.

"You need to help her get her pants off and place some towels beneath her. There is going to be a lot of blood. Her water already broke in the front seat."

"I should call 911. They can talk me through delivering the baby," he said, dreading the idea of being the first person a baby saw when he or she entered the world.

"You're not catching this baby," she said to him, her eyes wide in panic. "He's not catching this baby," Lauren cried out to her friends, her face twisting in more pain. "He's too hot to see me, to see *it* in such a godawful state. I watched those birthing videos. Everything swells and goes flat and nasty. No fucking way. I'll catch this baby myself. I think I've got a mirror on the compact in my purse."

"She's being ridiculous," one of the women murmured. He had no clue who was Celeste and who was Bianca, and at this point in the chaos, he didn't care.

"What's your name, officer?" the other woman asked.

"Isaac," he replied.

"Okay, Isaac, call 911, let them know a woman is in labor on the interstate, then maybe go knock on some car windows to see if there is a nurse or doctor or paramedic in the jam. Somebody to help you."

"Should I leave her, though?" He was a cop he should have known to call 911 first. This pregnant woman in such pain was making him forget all his training.

Lauren's face was once again scrunched up as she braved her way through another contraction. Her eyes were shut, her teeth gnashed and bared as she squirmed where she laid. "Go!" she finally yelled. "Go find me someone who can catch this baby. But then you come back." Her eyes flashed open. "Please, don't leave me."

He nodded and opened the door again. "I'll be back as soon as I can."

Isaac had been through war, he'd been through shootouts and armed robberies, hostage negotiations and talking people off bridges. But none of that compared to the helplessness he felt right now as he wandered up and down the rows of vehicles knocking on windows.

After graduating college, he enlisted in the marines and was deployed to Iraq where he served two back-to-back tours before returning to the U.S. and enrolling in the police academy. He'd never been to Seattle before, but a buddy in the marines had grown up in the Pacific Northwest and said there wasn't a better place to live. Stuart died before he was able to return home, but Isaac took his words to heart and decided to see what all the hype was about. Stuart had not led him astray.

The moment Isaac saw the sunset, the mountains and the trees, the ocean and the ferry boats, he knew he'd found his forever home. He found an apartment within a week and enrolled in the police academy a day later. And he hadn't looked back since.

Fighting the wind and rain, he attempted to shield his eyes and the droplets that felt more like shards of glass. It was to little avail. He should have grabbed his jacket from his truck, but he wasn't thinking about anything besides helping Lauren. Now, a ways away from her Pathfinder he worried she and the baby would be in distress if he didn't return. He needed to get back to her, but he hadn't found anybody that could help her yet. And he needed to help her.

A woman in a blue Corolla saw him approach her vehicle and she rolled down her window slightly. "Is someone hurt?" she asked.

"A woman is in labor. She needs help delivering the baby. It's coming now. Are you a doctor?"

She shook her head. "Midwife. I can help."

"Oh thank fuck. This way."

Nodding, she shut the lights off her vehicle, reached for a bag from the back seat of her car and followed him back through the cars, the wind and rain now at their backs, propelling them forward.

"Here, here," he said, pointing to her gray Nissan. "She's in the backseat."

The midwife nodded. "Is she alone?"

"Yeah."

"Are you comfortable staying to support her?"

No. But he'd do it anyway.

She didn't wait for him to respond and opened the door. "Hi there, I'm a midwife and I hear you're having a baby in this storm."

"Where's Isaac?" Lauren shouted.

"I'm here, I'm here," he said, poking his head around the midwife to see her.

"Can you climb into the backseat through the hatch and

go support her?" the midwife asked. "Maybe let her sit up between your legs. Rub her shoulders and hips. Let her squeeze your hand."

He nodded as the midwife climbed into the truck and shut the door.

Soaked through to his marrow and freezing, he knew he needed to get out of the rain, but he knocked back on the door before opening it. "I need to pull her vehicle off to the berm. Put her hazards on. Do the same for my truck. It's not safe the way we are now." Thank fuck his cop-sense was coming back, he was beginning to worry it might be gone for good.

Nodding, the midwife dropped the passenger seat the same way the driver's seat was and Isaac shut the door, popped the driver's seat back up and climbed behind the wheel. It took some finesse to pull over as all vehicles were bumper-to-bumper, but eventually he managed, tossed on her hazard lights and shut off the Pathfinder. Then he went to do the same to his truck finally calling 911 as he did so. They were dispatching an ambulance to the scene, but given the gridlock they would be severely delayed.

It felt like forever until he was climbing into Lauren's vehicle through the back. He was glad to finally be out of the rain, but terrified about what was going to happen next. Closing the back hatch door behind him, he helped Lauren up to a sitting position and scooted in behind her.

She was wet too, but that was probably from rain and sweat. Her forehead felt warm and she was limp like a noodle as he maneuvered his body around hers.

The midwife perched on the folded down driver's seat and dug around in her bag. "All right, those were some big contractions. Do you think you can talk now?"

Lauren nodded.

"Good. My name is Nicki. What's yours?" She snapped on some purple latex gloves.

"Lauren."

"Hi Lauren, nice to meet you. Now, while we're between contractions, I'm going to ask you a few questions. Are you okay answering them?"

Lauren nodded.

"Great. How old are you, Lauren?"

"Thirty-two."

"And how far a long are you?"

"Forty weeks, five days."

"Oh, so this little one is overdue. Your first?"

Lauren nodded again.

"And the father?"

"A guy I dated for a few months. He ran when I told him I was pregnant."

"That fucker," Isaac blurted out.

Nicki's eyes turned sad. "I'm sorry about that."

Lauren opened her mouth to say something, but another contraction came on first and she wailed and groaned in Isaac's arms, her body twisting, face contorting in pain. The midwife was staring at her watch.

When Lauren finally relaxed the midwife lifted her gaze. "And they've been like that for a while now?"

Lauren nodded. "My water only just broke like thirty minutes ago. Contractions started right after that. But they've been long and intense."

"We've been timing them," said either Bianca or Celeste from the phone. "They're three minutes a part and lasting for a minute."

Nicki put a stethoscope into her ears and placed it on Lauren's belly. "Friends?"

Lauren's head bobbed.

"How has your pregnancy been? Any concerns throughout?"

Lauren shook her head. "No. Doctor's say I'm healthy. Baby is healthy. I was GBS negative."

What the fuck was GBS? Was it a good thing she was negative?

"Good. No need for penicillin." Nicki went quiet and stoic for a moment as she listened to the baby in Lauren's belly. "Heartbeat sounds good. I have my doppler too if this didn't work, but I can hear the heartbeat just fine."

Nicki pulled a blood pressure cuff from her bag, wrapped it around Lauren's arm, inflated it, pressed the stethoscope to the inside of Lauren's elbow and then stared at her watch again as the cuff deflated.

Nodding, the midwife removed the cuff and stowed it back in her bag. "Blood pressure is normal. That's good."

"I had a stretch and sweep earlier today," Lauren said, her hands rubbing over the top of her belly. "Doctor said I was only two centimeters and hard as a carrot."

"Yes, well, that can change at the drop of a hat. And since you had the procedure that probably got things moving."

What the fuck was a *stretch and sweep*? *Hard as a carrot*? Did he want to know what that meant? Probably not. He could only imagine, and that image did not sit well in his brain.

"We need to remove your pants so I can take a look," the midwife said. "Are you okay with that?"

Lauren nodded. "Whatever. I ..." but just like before, she couldn't get the words out before the contraction hit her hard.

Isaac had no clue what to do. He placed his hands on her shoulder and massaged, but like hell if he knew if he was doing any good.

When the contraction ended, Nicki helped Lauren remove her pants and underwear. She was wearing a long gray tunic, dress thing, so at least she was able to keep her modesty.

Not bothering to look between Lauren's legs, Nicki put her hand beneath her dress.

"You're nine centimeters, Lauren. I can feel the head. This baby is coming now. How do you feel?"

"Like my body is going to be split two," Lauren whimpered, her head slumping to the side and against Isaac's shoulder. "I'm already so tired."

Removing his hand from her shoulder, he wiped the hair off her face. "You've got this, Lauren. You can do this." His encouragement sounded hollow to his own ears, but he had no idea what else to say. "What a story for you and this baby. Born in a storm."

God, had he really just said that? Fuck, he was lame.

"Do you feel like you need to push?" Nicki asked.

Lauren barely nodded, but she did.

Nicki smiled. "All right. Let's bend your knees and when that feeling comes again, let me know and we'll go for it, okay?"

"Okay."

Nicki glanced up at Isaac. "You ready?"

No. But he hadn't been ready for very much in his life, and that hadn't stopped him.

IF YOU'VE ENJOYED THIS BOOK

If you've enjoyed this book, please consider leaving a review.
It really does make a difference.
Thank you again.
Xoxo
Whitley Cox

ACKNOWLEDGMENTS

There are so many people to thank who help along the way. Publishing a book is definitely not a solo mission, that's for sure. First and foremost, my friend and editor Chris Kridler, you are a blessing, a gem and an all-around terrific person. Thank you for your honesty and hard work.

Thank you, to my critique groups gals, Danielle and Jillian. I love our meetups where we give honest feedback. You two are my bitch-sisters and I wouldn't give you up for anything.

Kathleen Lawless, for just being you and wonderful and always there for me.

Author Jeanne St. James, my alpha reader and sister from another mister, what would I do without you?

Megan J. Parker-Squiers from EmCat Designs, your covers are awesome. Thank you.

My street team, Whitley Cox's Curiously Kinky Reviewers, you are all awesome and I feel so blessed to have found such wonderful fans.

The ladies of Vancouver Island Romance Authors, your

support and insight have been incredibly helpful, and I'm so honored to be a part of a group of such talented writers.

Author Cora Seton, I love our walks, talks and heart-to-hearts, they mean so much to me.

Author Ember Leigh, my newest author bestie, I love our bitchfests—they keep me sane.

Ana Rita Clemente, the first "fan" I ever met in person. Thank you for beta-reading this one.

Andi Babcock, thank you for your beta-read.

My parents, in-laws and brother, thank you for your unwavering support.

The Small Human and the Tiny Human, you are the beats and beasts of my heart, the reason I breathe and the reason I drink. I love you both to infinity and beyond.

And lastly, of course, the husband. You are my forever, my other half, the one who keeps me grounded and the only person I have honestly never grown sick of even when we did that six-month backpacking trip and spent every single day together. I never tired of you. Never needed a break. You are my person. I love you.

ALSO BY WHITLEY COX

Love, Passion and Power: Part 1

mybook.to/LPPPart1

The Dark and Damaged Hearts Series Book 1

Love, Passion and Power: Part 2

mybook.to/LPPPart2

The Dark and Damaged Hearts Series Book 2

Sex, Heat and Hunger: Part 1

mybook.to/SHHPart1

The Dark and Damaged Hearts Book 3

Sex, Heat and Hunger: Part 2

mybook.to/SHHPart2

The Dark and Damaged Hearts Book 4

Hot and Filthy: The Honeymoon

mybook.to/HotandFilthy

The Dark and Damaged Hearts Book 4.5

True, Deep and Forever: Part 1

mybook.to/TDFPart1

The Dark and Damaged Hearts Book 5

True, Deep and Forever: Part 2

mybook.to/TDFPart2

The Dark and Damaged Hearts Book 6

Hard, Fast and Madly: Part 1

mybook.to/HFMPart1

The Dark and Damaged Hearts Series Book 7

Hard, Fast and Madly: Part 2

mybook.to/HFMPart2

The Dark and Damaged Hearts Series Book 8

Quick & Dirty

mybook.to/quickandirty

Book 1, A Quick Billionaires Novel

Quick & Easy

mybook.to/quickeasy

Book 2, A Quick Billionaires Novella

Quick & Reckless

mybook.to/quickandreckless

Book 3, A Quick Billionaires Novel

Quick & Dangerous

mybook.to/quickanddangerous

Book 4, A Quick Billionaires Novel

Hot Dad

mybook.to/hotdad

Lust Abroad

mybook.to/lustabroad

Snowed In & Set Up

mybook.to/snowedinandsetup

Hard Hart

mybook.to/hard_hart

The Harty Boys, Book 1

Hired by the Single Dad

mybook.to/hiredbythesingledad

The Single Dads of Seattle, Book 1

Dancing with the Single Dad

mybook.to/dancingsingledad

The Single Dads of Seattle, Book 2

Saved by the Single Dad

mybook.to/savedsingledad

The Single Dads of Seattle, Book 3

Living with the Single Dad

mybook.to/livingsingledad

The Single Dads of Seattle, Book 4

Christmas with the Single Dad

mybook.to/christmassingledad

The Single Dads of Seattle, Book 5

New Years with the Single Dad

mybook.to/newyearssingledad

The Single Dads of Seattle, Book 6

The Harty Boys, Book 2

Torn Hart
The Harty Boys, Book 3

Dark Hart
The Harty Boys, Book 4

Quick & Snowy
The Quick Billionaires, Book 5

Incompatible

Raw, Fierce and Awakened: Part 1
The Dark and Damaged Hearts Series, Book 9

Raw, Fierce and Awakened: Part 2
The Dark and Damaged Hearts Series, Book 10

ABOUT THE AUTHOR

A Canadian West Coast baby born and raised, Whitley is married to her high school sweetheart, and together they have two beautiful daughters and a fluffy dog. She spends her days making food that gets thrown on the floor, vacuuming Cheerios out from under the couch and making sure that the dog food doesn't end up in the air conditioner. But when nap time comes, and it's not quite wine o'clock, Whitley sits down, avoids the pile of laundry on the couch, and writes.

A lover of all things decadent; wine, cheese, chocolate and spicy erotic romance, Whitley brings the humorous side of sex, the ridiculous side of relationships and the suspense of everyday life into her stories. With single dads, firefighters, Navy SEALs, mommy wars, body issues, threesomes, bondage and role-playing, Whitley's books have all the funny and fabulously filthy words you could hope for.

YOU CAN ALSO FIND ME HERE

Website: WhitleyCox.com
Twitter: @WhitleyCoxBooks
Instagram: @CoxWhitley
Facebook Page: https://www.facebook.com/CoxWhitley/
Blog: https://whitleycox.blogspot.ca/
Multi-Author Blog: https://romancewritersbehavingbadly.blogspot.com
Exclusive Facebook Reader Group: https://www.facebook.com/groups/234716323653592/
Booksprout: https://booksprout.co/author/994/whitley-cox
Bookbub: https://www.bookbub.com/authors/whitley-cox

JOIN MY STREET TEAM

WHITLEY COX'S CURIOUSLY KINKY REVIEWERS
Hear about giveaways, games, ARC opportunities, new releases, teasers, author news, character and plot development and more!

Facebook Street Team
Join NOW!

DON'T FORGET TO SUBSCRIBE TO MY NEWSLETTER

Be the first to hear about pre-orders, new releases, giveaways, 99 cent deals, and freebies!

Click here to Subscribe
http://eepurl.com/ckh5yT

Made in the USA
Las Vegas, NV
06 December 2021

36192896R00208